Clara

Clara's Legacy

by

Katherine Hook

METHUEN

Published by Methuen 2013

1 3 5 7 9 10 8 6 4 2

This edition first published in 2013 by

Methuen
35 Hospital Fields Road
York, YO10 4DZ

www.methuen.co.uk

Methuen Publishing Ltd. Reg. No.

ISBN: 978 0 413 77703 4

A CIP catalogue for this title is
available from the British Library

Printed and bound in the UK by
CPI Group (UK) Ltd, Croydon CR0 4YY

For my father

Acknowledgements

Numerous people have been kind enough to help me with the research I undertook while writing this novel in my efforts to ensure authenticity. Justyna Majewska, Gallery Coordinator at the Museum of the History of Polish Jews in Warsaw guided me wisely as did both Rebekka Geitner at the BallinStadt Museum of Emigration in Hamburg and Grzegorz Hanula at the Warsaw Uprising Museum. Dr. Heinrich Schwendemann, who is based at the History Department at the University of Freiburg, also offered kind assistance. The Polish Cultural Institute in London was a valuable resource and Jeffrey S. Dosik and Barry Moreno of the Ellis Island Immigration Museum in New York offered clarification on a number of points which was much appreciated. I am grateful to these and many others for their help and guidance. Any errors or omissions which remain are my own.

Prologue

The single shot rang out and echoed through the wood. Startled birds flapped and took flight as the man crumpled at the knees and then fell to the ground at the feet of the German soldier.

The soldier waited for a moment. The rippling echo of the gunshot had evaporated and the wood was now eerily silent. He looked down at the body but could see no signs of movement.

He suddenly felt exhausted. He pulled his heavy coat close around him, placed his gun in the pocket and began to walk back towards the mansion. He did not see the gardener across the lake and had not realised he had been observed.

Reaching the mansion, two of his officers approached.

'Get rid of the body,' he barked.

He walked up the steps, opened the door and was gone.

New York
2008

New York is not the best place to be during a heat wave, unless you're the type who thrives in oppressive temperatures and stifling humidity. I am not one of them. In fact, breaking into a sweat the moment you step outside your apartment and walking about with your shirt clinging to your back like adhesive tape is my idea of hell. Anyone who says otherwise is frankly, to my way of thinking, some kind of a masochist.

The summer that year was brutal. The elderly and very young were cocooned inside their houses and everywhere conversations were punctuated by the rhythmic clicking and whirring of fans. Despite the best efforts of the city's park keepers, the vegetation shrivelled, turning to a brownish-orange colour, and the soil had become compacted, making a crunching noise underfoot. Just when it felt as though all the moisture had been sucked out of the city, the weather broke unexpectedly. The onset of rain brought with it much cooler air which was greeted with something close to rapture.

I was born and raised in Greenwich Village. It has a bohemian flavour all of its own. Its streets do not follow the city's main grid system, but maintain a haphazard order rather like a maze. With its many stalls, the village is an Aladdin's cave, a shopper's paradise. There are liquor and clothing stores nestling between hundreds of cafés, bars and restaurants. Creativity throbs everywhere: painters and artists dominate the area, exhibit in galleries and along the sidewalks, writers lecture and music floats through the underpasses.

To the south of Washington Square Park is Macdougal Street which, like others in the neighbourhood, is characterised by its narrowness. With its fascinating history and colourful architecture it draws many a visitor. One of the restaurants down there is *La Felicita*. Flanked by a genteel coffee house on one side and an expensive boutique on the other, it is noted for the exuberance of both its staff and its clientele and is always brimming with good-natured characters. For the past eight years I have rented the apartment above.

The Rossis treated me like a member of their family from the start. After weeks trawling through real estate listings I had spotted their advertisement for a one bedroom apartment pinned to the restaurant door one evening and instinctively knew it would be perfect for me. Over the years I grew accustomed to the sounds and aromas which floated up from their kitchen. There was the clattering of china as it was tossed down on a worktop, and occasionally, more alarming, the noise of crockery shattering on the unforgiving floor tiles. Then there were the raised voices usually punctuated by shrill laughter, periodically developing into heated exchanges more characteristic of the feisty Latin temperament. On a balmy evening delicious odours wafted in through my open window and on nights like these I welcomed being entertained to dinner, fussed over by Maria, and later Lena, a pretty young waitress who Stefano Rossi, the ebullient owner of *La Felicita*, always suspected was keen on me.

'Hey, Jon. Your star pupil is here,' Stefano hollered. The teasing was routine. 'His mama, she drop him off on her way to one of her cocktail parties,' he added.

'I do wish she wouldn't do that,' I snapped, getting irritated. 'How long ago?'

'Oh, maybe thirty minutes or so. Maria has given him a soda and cookies and he's as happy as a . . .' he hesitated for a moment, trying to think of the word he wanted, '. . . as a clam.'

'Thanks for helping me out again Stefano. I owe you.'

'No trouble, Jon. I only wish the boy could play a little better,' he chuckled.

'Me too, believe me. Will you send him up?'

Stefano was not only my landlord but had become a good friend. With his dark expressive eyes, trim figure and coal-black hair lightly peppered with flecks of grey, he had the look of a man still in his prime. Maria, his elegant wife, was just as striking, and together they made a handsome couple.

I unlocked the door to my apartment and flung open the shutters to release the oppressive heat. There were three rooms. One, larger than the rest, served as my kitchen diner and living room. Beyond were my bedroom and a small bathroom. Despite its size it was perfectly adequate for one person, and since I lived alone, I didn't need any more space. The décor was exactly as it was when I had moved in. Garish patterns in tomato red, burnt sienna and tangerine jostled along the walls and, although Maria's efforts had initially proved rather overpowering, I had grown accustomed to them.

Henry was a chubby, not especially prepossessing child of nine years of age and was, without doubt, the least talented of all my private students. He was the product of two (despite appearances, not *so* wealthy) New York socialites who somehow conspired to be on the guest list of every smart party going. As a result of all this extensive hobnobbing they frequently dumped their only child wherever they could. Learning a musical instrument – the cello in Henry's case – was fashionable amongst the pseudo-rich and so, regardless of his obvious lack of improvement, he was deposited without fail at my door every Tuesday evening. For all this I was fond of the boy, although his tuneless renditions could become so excruciating that Stefano and his staff would often strike up with some Neapolitan ballad in an attempt to drown out the aural assault.

My own decision to pursue a career in music had surprised my family. Clara, my grandmother, had sung and played the piano in her youth and when it became clear that I had some musical ability it was she who encouraged me to pursue my interest. She had suggested I study the cello because of my large hands and long fingers. My father, William, was proud of my achievements, but I sometimes felt he would have preferred it had I followed in his footsteps and entered the world of publishing, or, better still, become a banker or a lawyer and made my fortune. My mother, Elizabeth, however, had enjoyed considerable success as a painter, and encouraged my career choice. For me the path ahead was clear, and after graduation I took up a position as lecturer in composition at the Brooklyn College Conservatory of Music.

The lesson over, I eased Henry and his bulky instrument into the back of a cab. Then I made my way downstairs to eat. I pushed open the kitchen door and was met by a blast of steam from the numerous pans bubbling away on the large stove.

'Hi there, Marco. You the boss tonight?'

The young assistant chef was red-faced and clearly harassed. I watched in admiration as he stirred the largest of the containers.

'So it would seem,' he replied, wiping the sweat off his brow, before reaching for some seasoning.

'Looks like you've got everything under control,' I remarked trying to offer reassurance.

'Sure. Everything's OK but could you ask Lena to come and help?' Marco asked.

'Will do,' I said, patting him on the shoulder as I headed out into the restaurant.

Covering the walls were murals of the Adriatic coastline, the sea a glistening turquoise blue reflecting golden sunlight. Paintings of Sorrento, the terraces of Positano and the Islands of Amalfi and Capri hung in the alcoves, whilst scattered near the door were photographs of Sophia Loren and other young actors in their heyday. Three nights a week Paolo entertained diners with rousing performances on his mandolin. I enjoyed studying the paintings. My favourite depicted an olive grove through which a goatherd was leading his animals. It always had the effect of making me want to travel, and in particular to visit Europe, a long held ambition.

'How's everything Jonathan?' Maria asked, as I sat down at my usual table.

'Fine thanks. How are you?'

'Busy preparing for Stefano's birthday party on Saturday. It must be kept secret,' she said anxiously. 'Do you think he knows?'

'No. Not at all. He'll never suspect a thing,' I replied, hoping to put her mind at ease. I hadn't the heart to tell her about the conversation I'd had with her husband a couple of nights ago on this very subject.

A middle-aged couple entered the restaurant and Maria rushed over to greet them. A few minutes later a young woman approached my table. She was wearing a rather fetching outfit which emphasised her ample curves. It could not be denied that she was an attractive girl.

'My usual, please, Lena,' I said, hurriedly focusing on my menu. 'Oh, and Marco says he needs your help.'

She gave me a sweet yet knowing smile before heading towards the kitchen.

'You'll be bringing your *Nonna* with you, won't you, Jonathan? We couldn't possibly have Stefano's birthday celebration without your grandmother,' Maria called across to me, whilst scribbling down an order.

'Sure, you don't have to worry,' I replied, laughing. 'Grandma's coming. She's very much looking forward to it. Mom is taking her shopping for a new dress.'

❖   ❖   ❖

In comparison to everyone at *La Felicita*, my own family were more emotionally reserved. My paternal grandfather, Timothy Gray, whose family had emigrated from England in the 1700s, was a respected member of the community in his day, having established a reputation as an author of historical fiction. Timothy was not in the same league as Edgar Allan Poe and Henry James – at one time residents in the same neighbourhood – but he was nonetheless modestly successful in his trade. His bachelor years were spent roving from continent to continent, and it was not until he reached the age of forty that he decided to marry. On returning home in the winter of 1938, he met the becoming and well-educated, yet rather conventional, daughter of a prosperous businessman. Won over by his eloquence and charm, she accepted his proposal, and soon after the couple were hitched. Sadly for her – and despite promises to change his ways – Timothy could not tame his wandering spirit. I do not remember much about my grandfather – he died when I was still a young boy – but I do remember sitting transfixed on his knee as he recounted another adventure. One particular day came to mind when – as I roamed about the house trying to find something to do – I ended up in his study.

'Are you bored, young Jonathan?' he boomed, as he spotted me hovering in the doorway. 'Come to check up on what your old Grandpa is doing?'

'Yes,' I replied nervously, inching closer. I loved him dearly, yet at the same time was always very much in awe of this larger-than-life character.

'Come here then and I'll tell you a story.'

I nodded, and moments later I was perched on his lap, staring at the model sailing ship he had been working on. Then he proceeded to tell me one of his most blood-curdling yarns, concerning a hapless band of sailors who, having set sail in a vessel similar to the one he was carving, had encountered a ferocious storm. Often – perhaps in a deliberate ploy to cultivate my own imagination – he would break off from his narrative and ask me questions.

'And do you know what happened next, Jonathan?'

'They all drowned, Grandpa?' I would reply confidently.

'Not at first, my boy. Battered by the most terrible storms, and with the ship weighed down by the treasures they had stolen, they were soon blown off course and onto jagged rocks.'

'And then they all drowned?' I would suggest eagerly.

'Not all of them. Some, as you quite rightly say, came to a sad end, sinking to the bottom of the ocean. But there were those who clung on for dear life to whatever they could find – barrels, chests, pieces of the broken ship – and they were the lucky ones who made it to shore. Or so they thought . . .' he added ominously.

He proceeded to tell me the gruesome adventures of these poor men and I would listen with my mouth wide open. Later that night, tucked up in my bed, I couldn't sleep for thinking about those unlucky sailors descending to the depths of the sea or being gobbled up by hungry beasts or roasted over an open fire by ravenous natives.

I was thinking about my long-suffering grandmother, Louise, who was, in contrast, a gentle and quietly spoken woman, when I remembered to check the time. It was late and I had to get an early start. That was the trouble with living above a restaurant: too much good food and drink.

❖   ❖   ❖

'Hey, Jon,' David hailed me down the corridor. 'Wanna come to the Yankees game on Sunday? I've got a spare ticket.'

'Sure,' I said, without hesitation. 'They're playing the Blue Jays, aren't they? Ought to be first-rate.'

'Great! Catch you later.'

I watched as David, late for his lecture as usual, rushed off down the hallway and smiled to myself. The two of us had landed jobs at the Conservatory within weeks of each other and although we were from very different backgrounds we soon discovered that we had numerous things in common. Both the same age, we shared passions for music and baseball. Handsome and charismatic, David Rosen had had a string of glamorous girlfriends over the years but much to his mother's dismay he remained resolutely single. As for me, I'd not yet met a girl I wanted to settle down with.

I reached my classroom and started my preparations. Today I was setting my students a challenging assignment based on the principles of Serialism. As I scribbled instructions on the board I reflected on my own days as a student and recalled when I had first encountered this musical concept. My fascination with Arnold Schoenberg's invention had been a critical factor in my choice of specialism. Several of my compositions had been published, and I had gradually established a reputation within New York's music circles. However, I had yet to create something which I would consider my masterpiece. My recent efforts had been uninspired, and I was beginning to believe that I had developed a sort of composer's block. The strange thing was that this had never happened to me before. Once I had an idea in my head I could usually develop it rapidly, and it would soon mature into a substantial piece of writing. Paradoxically, being surrounded by gifted and creative people nearly every minute of the waking day seemed to compound the problem rather than help me resolve it. Suddenly I was jolted back to the business in hand. The teeth-jarring scraping of chairs on the hardwood floor together with the sound of chattering voices heralded the arrival of the young scholars.

The bell rang and my students dashed off to their next class, hurriedly filling their backpacks as they left. I gathered my things together and prepared to head home. As I stepped outside I was bathed in bright evening sunshine. Deciding to walk part of the way I strolled along the sidewalk. The trees lining each side of the street offered dappled shade and I was struck by the beauty of the plants and shrubs which adorned peoples' homes. I must have passed them hundreds of times before, yet tonight they were particularly eye-catching in the changing light. My attention was drawn to the splendid detached red brick and white-painted houses which were arranged in neat rows. Despite sharing a common feature of an overhanging lower room, there were subtle differences: some had brown-tiled roofs, wooden frontages, fewer or more steps leading up to the porch and one or two had a colonial feel.

Crossing Brooklyn Bridge on foot was always an exhilarating experience, especially with the wind whipping through your hair. Nevertheless, it was well worth the effort, for the views of the iconic buildings of Lower Manhattan were some of the best in the city. I paused to gaze into the blue expanse below. The Circle Line ferry was just emerging, having completed its brief passage under Roebling's magnificent bridge. It was full to bursting with smiling tourists, some of whom waved up at me. One of the happy faces reminded me of my maternal grandmother and I suddenly felt the urge to pay my family a visit. Back on terra firma I walked the short distance south to Fulton Street. Here I picked up the A train, getting out at West 4th. It was just after six o'clock by the time I reached my parents' house, clutching a bouquet of flowers and a box of crystallized ginger. The family home, originally a rambling old carriage house, was three storeys high. When my paternal grandparents had been alive my parents and I lived in a self-contained apartment on the second floor. After they had passed away it seemed the natural thing to stay put.

'Hello, Jon. Good to see you,' my father William said opening the door. 'You've come just at the right time. I'm setting the table for dinner.' I followed my father through the hall and into the dining room.

'Where's Mom?' I asked.

'Your mother's in the kitchen,' he said reaching across the table to place a napkin at the side of a dinner plate.

'OK. I'll go say hello.'

'Oh, by the way, how's that head of yours?' he called after me, brandishing a fork in one hand and laughing.

I grinned. 'It's much better now, thanks. You never forget a thing, do you, Pop?'

'You were invited to Stefano's wine-tasting night, as I recall and you suffered for it the next day.'

'I certainly did.'

My mother, Elizabeth, was checking the roast and did not hear me enter.

'Hmm, that smells good,' I said, laughing. I hugged her. Her hair had a faint smell of baking. 'Do you need any help?'

'No thank you, Jon. What brings you over this way then? We haven't seen you in a while. Everything OK with you?'

'Yes, great, thanks. Busy day at work as usual.'

'Oh, she'll love those,' my mother said as she spotted the candy.

'The flowers are for you. Where's Grandma?' I asked looking around.

'She's up in her room. You could go fetch her if you like. I'll put these in water. You're staying for dinner aren't you?'

'Sure. That would be great.'

Five years ago my grandmother, Clara, came to live with my parents, and despite her age she insisted upon occupying the third storey of the building. Reaching the second, I paid a quick visit to my old room, something I hadn't done in a long while. Sticking my head around the door, everything was just as it always had been, with the bed pushed snugly against one of the walls, and on it the multi-coloured patchwork quilt my mother had sewn on a quilting weekend in the mountains. Along the other wall stood the chest of drawers and, displayed proudly on top, the sailing boat my grandfather Timothy had given to me. I sank down in the chair for a moment or two, recalling the occasion shortly after his death when I had helped to pack away his amazing collection of objects. My grandmother, Louise, having so often remonstrated with him for being obliged to dust them all, lovingly wrapped each item in tissue paper as if it was the most precious thing in the world. One by one, they were tenderly lowered into the trunk and I half-imagined their owner appearing, lighting his pipe and beckoning me to him. Smiling at the memories I hoisted myself up again, dashed up the last flight of stairs and tapped gently on the door. Hearing a soft voice, I went in.

'Hello, Grandma. How are you?' I bent over to kiss her, and in return she gave me a hug.

'Darling Jonathan. It's lovely to see you,' she said.

Clara was at her dressing table trying to pin a brooch onto her blouse, but because of the onset of arthritis, was finding it tricky.

'I've got something for you, Grandma.'

She smiled as she saw the box of her favourite candies.

'Thank you, darling. How thoughtful!'

'Here. Let me help.'

I picked up her brooch and examined it closely. Its design was that of a golden snowflake, and when I held it up to the light its amber-coloured stones twinkled and flickered. Carefully, I attached it to her cream blouse and then stood back to admire my handiwork. Clara smiled and her face lit up.

'Grandma, you are beautiful.'

Clara Reinecke was an exceptional lady. Of all my relatives she remained my closest confidante. In her eighty-seventh year, she was still very attractive with a fine bone structure, blue eyes and soft, light-coloured hair. My mother and I knew very little about our German ancestry. Clara's mother had died when she was a young girl and Clara had been raised by her father. Apart from happy and amusing recollections of what must have been a very enjoyable childhood spent in Freiburg in Southern Germany, where she later studied, she told us very little about her early life. I had never met my maternal grandfather and Clara would only intimate that he was a good man who had not, despite endless speculation, abandoned them. My grandmother was unwilling however, for whatever reason, to discuss this episode. My mother and I never pressed her on the subject. Although she was highly selective in what she told people about her early years, Clara always talked freely about her life in this country, and the account she gave of the consequent struggles she encountered demonstrated the immense courage and inner strength she possessed.

Cast adrift, she wandered from place to place, whilst war raged, finding shelter where she could. When the time came for the birth of her child she sought the help of nuns at a convent in the mountains. Like other women before her, in a similar predicament, Clara was greeted warmly and cared for with great tenderness. Soon after, she resumed her rootless existence. It was as though she could no longer connect with her homeland and its people, whether through grief or perhaps because of the horrors she may have seen. When the war came to an end, and after more than a year spent living from hand to mouth, mother and daughter found themselves in Germany's British zone. News had spread of the establishment of refugee camps and assistance offered by the Hebrew Immigration Aid Society, who were prepared to help non-Jews. Clara saw an opportunity to make a fresh start. She and her daughter presented themselves as refugees. As she was weary and had a fragile appearance, her plight was not questioned. Further confirmation of her misfortune was a lack of identity papers; typically for many displaced individuals such documents would have been lost or destroyed and replacing them could present a huge challenge. Schools and libraries were set up in the camps, and books which had for so long been unavailable to Jews were now in abundance. Clara was put in charge of cataloguing. When at last visas had been obtained and, with the society's intervention, the opportunity of work, my mother and grandmother boarded a former troopship leaving Bremerhaven destined for New York. Built to carry smaller loads the vessel was heaving with human cargo. The cramped conditions and poor hygiene blighted the journey. However, companionship and regular square meals more than made up for their discomfort.

Clara and her young daughter, Elizabeth, had arrived in America on a wintry day in early February 1946 after six days at sea. Cold, hungry, alone and fearful of what the future might hold for them they had expected to disembark at the Manhattan waterfront together with other Europeans hoping to be admitted to America. For most of the passengers this would be the case. When it was Clara's turn the customs officer questioned the validity of her papers and she and her daughter were taken by a harbour tugboat to Ellis Island. Clara often described what greeted them on entering the arrival hall. It was pandemonium, with dozens of people – officials, doctors, immigrants – milling about everywhere. Families huddled together on benches, in corners and in doorways. Husbands placed protective arms around their wives and most clutched little bundles containing the only possessions they now had to their name. Elsewhere mothers cradled hungry, fractious infants, while toddlers tugged at their skirts, needing comfort and reassurance amid all the mayhem. For Clara and Elizabeth, the voyage from Bremerhaven had been a lonely one. They had kept mainly to the confines of the cabin, which had been allocated to women with young children, emerging only to take a turn with tasks, at meal times, or to walk along the deck when the weather permitted. For many passengers the crossing had been unendurable: the roughness of the sea had rendered them incapacitated. Now, once again on dry land, a number of these unfortunate individuals found themselves herded like cattle towards a maelstrom of confusion and uncertainty. There was a long period of waiting before finally those who had been detained through sickness were sent to the island's hospital for examination by a physician, presumably to check for evidence of any contagious diseases. My grandmother recalled seeing one Jewish family in particular who were clearly distressed at the prospect of undergoing tests. For these immigrants, fortunate to be alive after the horrors of the holocaust, the alarming experience must have reawakened the traumas of their recent past. The situation was further hampered by their inability to communicate, for most of them did not speak English. Some, like my grandmother, had a good command of the language, and complied swiftly with the demand to proceed toward the overcrowded dormitories which would serve as their home whilst their paperwork was straightened out and applications were processed.

Three days later Clara and young Elizabeth, together with

another family, were granted permission to leave Ellis Island and begin their new life in New York. Clara and her daughter were directed to the Great Hall and from there to the 'Staircase of Separation'. Here they were shunted down to the ferry terminus. On reaching Manhattan, the first port of call for all foreigners seeking new citizenship was the Lower East Side. Already tired and overwhelmed, my grandmother's spirits sank when she and her companions were deposited on the lengthy Canal Street. The tenement block they had been directed to was most unwelcoming. Wails and cries emanated from within, and out of every window makeshift lines of washing flapped like brightly coloured bunting in the weak winter sunshine. On entering the hallway, the women and children recoiled: nibbling on some food scraps beneath the stairwell was a pair of rats, who were oblivious to the new gaggle of interlopers. Climbing up to the rooms was a precarious business, and every so often one of the party lurched dangerously on a rickety tread-board. When they eventually reached the fifth floor a member of the group called Nathaniel tentatively pushed the door ajar to reveal a dismal-looking room with a sink in one corner and a small stove in the other. Leading off this was a slightly larger living space, with three small beds − upon which were piled a collection of dirty blankets − which would serve as cots for the youngest children. Across the hall was a communal lavatory and shower room which was shared by about sixty or so other residents on the floor. Conditions were appalling, but at least they had a roof over their heads.

The relief at having reached America safely was overwhelming and now Clara made the most of the opportunity she had been given. Aided by her grasp of English and with the help of the Hebrew Immigration Aid Society she found employment as a librarian at the city's New York Public Library and, shortly after that, she and her daughter moved to an affordable apartment over to the north east of Manhattan in the East Village where she would live, contentedly, for the next sixty years.

'How is your work at the Conservatory, Jonathan?' she asked. Clara looked in the mirror. Satisfied that all her preparations were complete she got up from her chair.

'Fine thank you,' I replied. 'The semester has gotten off to a good start.'

'I'm glad you're here. There is something I would like to give you. I fetched it out the other day hoping you'd call by.'

Intrigued, I watched as she walked purposefully towards the old closet and pulled out a rolled-up bundle of manuscript paper.

'When you have time I would value your opinion about this, Jonathan.'

She held it out to me and I accepted it with mild curiosity. From time to time she would produce items from her fascinating collection for my perusal, and here was another example. Flipping through the first few pages I could see it was a piece of music.

'I'll let you know what I think as soon as I've got a moment,' I replied, but as I said this I noticed a fleeting change in Clara's expression. It was not one of sadness but neither was it joyful. I pretended not to notice and she soon rallied.

'And how is that young student of yours coming along, these days? What's his name?' She thought for a moment. 'Henry is it?'

'Ah, yes, Henry! We soldier on together and very occasionally he produces something less offensive to the ear. I feel a little sorry for him what with the parents he has.'

'From what you've told me they don't seem to devote much time to him.'

'No they don't, and in all the months I've been teaching him I've never once seen them all together.'

She took my hand and we began to descend the stairs together.

'It's a great pity,' she sighed. 'Henry must enjoy your lessons however or he wouldn't come. You should consider that a compliment.'

'You're probably right, but I wish he would practise more. I doubt very much his cello sees the light of day all week.'

Having reached the ground floor we wandered into the living room. My father had finished all his preparation in the dining room and was sitting in his armchair, reading *The New York Times*. He peered over the top of his reading glasses when he heard us come in. The room felt cool which on hot summer days was desirable. Cosy and warm in winter it formed the heart of the home.

'Elizabeth's just finishing off in the kitchen. Supper won't be much longer.'

'Does she need any help, William?' my grandmother asked.

'No. Everything's fine, thanks, Clara.'

A few minutes later my mother appeared in the doorway to say that supper was ready.

'Your mother has had an interesting commission,' my father said, scooping up a couple of crisply roasted potatoes from the serving bowl.

Gatherings like these provided an opportunity to exchange news.

'It's an unusual one too,' my grandmother added.

'I've been asked to paint cats,' she announced.

'Cats! But you draw people,' I exclaimed. 'Who owns these cats?'

'Some old bachelor who lives Uptown with more money than sense,' my father said grinning broadly.

'How many?' I was eager to have details.

'Twelve,' Clara declared.

'Twelve!' I gulped. 'Will they sit for you individually? I hope they're well-behaved,' I said trying not to laugh and wondering how on earth so many cats could be persuaded to sit sedately while being painted.

'That has yet to be resolved,' my mother said chuckling. 'I told him it wasn't my usual choice of subject but he'd seen some of my portraits and was adamant I should do it.'

By now we had moved on to the cherry pie and whipped cream.

'How's the publishing world?' I asked my father.

'I'm working on a couple of interesting projects. A book about early pioneers and a new novel.' My father loved his work and his face lit up whenever he talked about it. 'What about you?'

'Things are going well,' I replied, choosing not to mention the little hiccup with my composition.

'That's good to hear. Shall we have our coffee in the living room?' my mother suggested, leading the way.

A little before ten, I reached for my jacket, grabbed the music which Clara had given me, and headed home.

The remainder of the week flew by. David and I finalised our plans for the game and, on Saturday afternoon, with only hours to spare before Stefano's party celebrations were due to get underway, I trekked Downtown to find a gift. Unless you were in the sun, New York could feel pretty cold in the fall. The skyscrapers acted as a form of wind tunnel, and as I walked along that afternoon there was a particularly strong breeze which made me regret that I hadn't put on an extra layer of clothing. The combination of local residents, commuters and tourists made for a crowded environment at the best of times, but since it was a weekend the city was teeming and progress along the sidewalk involved a careful game of dodging the stream of human contraflow, but I was weaving rather successfully, I thought. Shutting out the noise of the traffic and other extraneous sounds, I tried hard to think of a new theme for my composition but it was no good. My composer's block was starting to demoralise me, and I came to the conclusion that either I had been overworking lately and this was the way stress had decided to manifest itself or, just plain and simple, I had lost my powers of creativity.

Stefano's children and their families had returned to *La Felicita* for the evening, which pleased their Papa greatly. It had been a while since such a gathering of beloved family and friends had assembled at Stefano's restaurant and the atmosphere of warmth and affection was palpable. Guests arrived in dribs and drabs, and my family and I arrived at around eight. The first thing you noticed were the decorations: they were impossible to miss. My mother struggled to suppress a fit of the giggles, for it was obvious who had been overseeing the arrangements. Instead of a complementary collage, Maria's predilection for colour ensured the whole of one side of the room was swathed in a vivid purple, and, as if in competition, the other half was awash in a sea of sickly lime.

We tagged on to a long receiving line of high-spirited people and were affectionately welcomed by Stefano and Maria. Offering our congratulations, we each handed over a variety of presents. After a somewhat lengthy and arduous search, I had come across a watercolour of a Neapolitan fisherman, and thought it would neatly fill up the remaining space on the restaurant walls. As soon as he had unwrapped it my dear friend made loud protestations of delight – *grazie, grazie, è magnifico* – and promptly dashed off and fetched his hammer and some nails and enthusiastically positioned it in the spot I had anticipated.

A little while later Stefano gestured for quiet. He thanked us all for our kind gifts and for our continuing love and friendship. As he spoke, he gradually became more emotional and by the end of the speech tears were rolling down his cheeks. His little grandson, Marcello, wandered over, caught hold of his hand and led him back to their table.

The general level of chatter rose, punctuated with squeals of delight from some quarters and earthy chuckles elsewhere. Just when anticipation was mounting Carlos burst out of the kitchen, followed by Marco carrying heavily laden trays of appetizers. There was *insalata verde* and garlic bread, from which a glistening stream of butter oozed out and trickled down one's chin.

I noticed, in the flickering candlelight, that my grandmother had a far-away look in her eyes. The first course consumed, we were served a special Italian dish of beef cooked in red wine and herbs with pasta.

'How is work going, son?' my father asked between mouthfuls.

'Fine,' I replied. 'The new intake this year is very promising. Some good composers in the making.'

'And how's David?' my mother enquired.

'Very well. Same as always.'

'You should bring him over for supper. We always like to see him, don't we Mama?'

'Yes,' Clara nodded.

'Did I tell you, Pop, we're all going to the game tomorrow? Peter managed to get tickets. You should join us sometime?'

'Thanks, son. It's good of you to ask, but it would be a shame to waste a ticket on me. Take your mother instead. I'm sure she would enjoy it,' and he winked at me.

'William,' my mother said, in mock exasperation. 'Now what would be the point of that? You know I don't have a clue about baseball.'

24

Their amusing exchange was cut short, for just then a most intriguing creation was carried into the room by a proud Carlos. Everyone caught their breath, and then spontaneous applause erupted, which the chef acknowledged with a neat little bow. The large cake had been skilfully sculpted into the shape of a fishing boat, complete with masts and billowing white sails. The model of a sailor – bearing a remarkable resemblance to Stefano – was leaning over the edge casting his net into the blue, glistening surround, illuminated by flickering candles.

Marcello Senior toasted his father's good health, and this was followed by a chorus of glasses striking one another. The remainder of the evening was spent in drinking, chatting and dancing to the mellifluous tones of Paolo's mandolin. Never the most agile or graceful of movers, and not familiar with the intricate steps of Southern Italian dances, I was unexpectedly in great demand as a partner for some of the younger women at the party but I suspected this was due more to the fact that the ratio of younger males to females was significantly low, than for any other reason, although I rather fancied my chances with one or two of them.

At one point during the revelries – and when I had almost collapsed in a heap from over-exertion – I happened to catch sight of Stefano and Clara talking animatedly in a corner. No doubt they would be reminiscing about old times as they so often did. Thoughts drifted into my mind of a war-torn Europe, and my grandmother's early life about which I knew so little. These ruminations, helped by an over-indulgence of full-bodied Italian wine, were causing my head to spin. When I looked again, I could see that Stefano had been dragged back onto the dance floor by Maria and Clara was sitting alone again. She was no longer smiling. Our eyes met briefly and I was sure she was crying. I was just about to walk over to her when my mother beat me to it. She must have noticed Clara's change in mood. A comforting arm was placed around her shoulders and it wasn't long before both women were chatting and smiling.

Later that evening as I was checking my messages back at the apartment, I caught sight of the manuscript my grandmother had asked me to look at balancing on the edge of my desk. I had left it there days ago and had clean forgotten about it. I picked it up and slumped into a chair. The first thing I noticed was that the composer's name was missing and that the quality of the printing, though good, was not what I would have expected. My initial impression when Clara had first given it to me was that it was the work of some obscure German composer. However, now I was not so sure. I went over to my piano and played the first few bars. The opening theme was remarkably poignant, capable of plumbing the very depths of the soul, and exemplified what I had been discussing with my students at the Conservatory earlier that very day: the power of music and how it can define a personality and sometimes a whole nation. I continued to play and was soon wrapped up in the phrasing and adventurous harmonic texture, not to mention the evocative word painting.

Many hours later, I crawled into bed. My grandmother's unhappiness must have affected me more intensely than I had realised, and my dreams were dominated by images of Clara together with the sound of the music I had been playing. Because of this I was relieved when it grew light and, after a quick shower, I dashed to the drugstore to pick up some pills for my hangover. The game wasn't starting until after one and David and I had arranged to meet there. I sat down with a strong cup of coffee and began to sift through the morning newspapers but soon fell asleep again, waking at noon.

'Hey, Joanne. Great to see you.'

I hugged her, and gave her a peck on both cheeks. She was with Peter, her partner and both were good friends of mine.

'There's David,' Peter shouted, pointing towards the stadium entrance.

I followed the line of his finger and spotted a familiar figure zigzagging his way through the crowds. I had started to wonder whether David would make it in time. As I watched he was suddenly swallowed up by the crowd surging its way towards the stands, and then, quite unceremoniously, he was spat out.

'Sorry I'm late. You'll never guess what happened,' he started to explain, as he tried to catch his breath.

'Fall asleep on the subway?' I chipped in mischievously.

'How did you know that?' he asked, looking at me in disbelief.

'You have form,' I laughed. 'Had an exhausting evening did you?'

A smile crossed his lips and for a fleeting moment he had the look of someone reflecting upon something pleasurable. He swiftly changed the subject.

'Good to see you, Joanne.' He hugged her and then, turning to Peter, smacked him good humouredly on his shoulder.

Peter and Joanne had been together for years. I had met Peter at university. He was an archaeology student and we lived in the same halls. With a rucksack slung across one shoulder and his trademark beard and shaggy hair still intact, he had hardly changed. Whenever we met up, my mind recalled those endless conversations late into the night about ancient civilisations, and Peter's plans to travel to as many historic sites as he could. Over the years he chalked up a substantial number, usually accompanied by Joanne during her school vacations.

The Yankees game proved to be a thriller, and we all became quite wrapped up in it. Sadly the home team lost, and all four of us joined a dispirited band of Yankee supporters trudging away from the stadium.

'That's the second game we've lost in a row,' Peter said despondently, breaking our gloomy silence.

'Let's hope we'll have better luck next time, eh?' I tried to sound positive.

'I'm starving. Let's go eat,' Joanne said.

It had long become an established custom to eat at one of the local diners and, over a leisurely meal, we caught up on each other's news. Tucking into his steak and fries, Peter enlightened us about his latest research. David, on the other hand, provided some judiciously sanitised accounts of his most recent romantic encounters.

Several bottles of wine later, we said our farewells and Peter and Joanne headed for their home in the north of the city. David and I hopped on the subway that would take us south.

'You're pretty quiet tonight, Jon. Everything OK?' David asked.

'Sure, I'm fine. I was just thinking,' I smiled back at him. My head was preoccupied with thoughts about music. My grandmother's manuscript had taken a strange hold on me and I felt as though I was becoming slowly obsessed with it.

'What's on your mind? Wait, I bet I know,' David ventured, laughing. 'You met a girl at Stefano's party last night – a dark haired Italian goddess I expect – and you can't stop thinking about her. Am I right?'

'Sadly, no. It would have made my mother's day if I had.' I hesitated for a second or two. 'Have you ever dried up?'

'*Dried up*? What do you mean?' David sounded surprised.

'You know. Can't think of anything new to write. No inspiration.'

'Sure. Occasionally. But remember, Jon, it's not my greatest skill. You're the maestro when it comes to composition,' David acknowledged.

'That's what I mean. Well, no. I don't mean I'm *that* good at it, but I should be able to write something. The other night my grandmother gave me an old manuscript, and I can't get the tune out of my head. My mind's plagued by someone else's music and I can't get any of my own stuff down on paper at all.'

By now we had stopped walking and were both leaning against the wall of an old building.

'You've just been working too hard. Maybe Henry's played one too many notes off pitch,' David suggested.

His words cheered me up. He was right. I had just been overdoing it lately.

'Sounds like you had a great time at the party though. Drank large quantities of Italian vino, perhaps? And all those beautiful women. I envy you.'

'Actually there was one girl there who would have suited you.'

'You should have got in there yourself, Jon.'

'I gave it my best shot, but sadly she was more interested in Paolo.'

'Too bad,' David grinned broadly as he offered his commiserations.

We boarded the subway train and then went our separate ways at Bleeker Street.

The final days of September slipped by quietly without much excitement. In the wake of his party Stefano was in good spirits for days. My private students came and went and Henry, to his credit, learned to play one of his pieces more effectively. All of the assignments I had set my students at the Conservatory had been duly handed in, and despite it being a complex task, the standard of their work was high. I was considering the prospect of how many of them might end up composing for a living, when David joined me in the lunch line. At this time of day it was not uncommon for the two of us to be found standing shoulder to shoulder with a group of jostling students on the street outside. Having purchased our lunch from the cart we set off for a walk.

'How was your morning?' I asked him.

'Good, thanks. There's some real talent amongst my new students,' David explained.

'You're right. Some of their work is impressive.'

'Hey, I called in on my folks last night,' David suddenly said.

'How are they all?'

'Good thanks. While I was there my Dad and I got talking and he asked me to bring you over one evening.'

'Your father wants to see me? What for?' I was puzzled.

I pictured Ira Rosen in my mind. He was a distinguished looking man – tall, lean with a beard – in his early sixties who had been a very successful stockbroker in the city. He had decided to scale down his workload so he could spend more time with his wife and grandchildren. I was surprised to learn that Ira had requested a meeting in this way and I was intrigued.

We reached our usual bench and as we ate our burgers continued the conversation.

'Well. What's it all about?' I asked impatiently. Curiosity was beginning to get the better of me.

'He didn't say,' David said nonchalantly. 'Just mentioned you as I was heading off home. Could be it's because he likes your company pure and simple. You haven't seen them for a while.'

'I guess not,' I said.

'Oh, and he suggested a day. Next Thursday. For supper. Is that all right with you?'

'Yes, I should be free. You'll be there too I hope?'

'Sure. Mom keeps telling me I need fattening up. Doesn't think I'm doing a good job living by myself.' He grinned. 'Don't eat beforehand though. Remember how much we were forced fed last time?' David laughed.

I had not forgotten. On the day in question, feeling hungry after work, I had made the fatal mistake of purchasing something from the Conservatory snack bar. Later that evening Rebecca Rosen, concerned, in her caring, maternal way, that I was looking much leaner than usual, had plied me with so much food and drink that I could barely stagger home.

The Rosens lived in one of the most fashionable and charming of the city's suburbs, the Brooklyn Heights. Set in an area full of old New York character, and with views of the harbour, their smart, four-storey brownstone occupied an enviable position. It was no longer strictly a family residence – both their children lived elsewhere – but the house never felt empty. On the contrary, there was always a lively atmosphere since it served as a venue for meetings and community functions. Its owners, Ira and Rebecca Rosen, were philanthropists and pillars of the Reform Jewish community, and generously welcomed everyone into their home

A little before eight o'clock the following Thursday evening, I approached their house. The windows dazzled me with their reflection of the sun, which hung in a sky streaked with shades of purple, orange and blood red. I turned once more, as I had done several times on my walk from the subway, to observe the play of light on the water. Seconds before I knocked on the door, I remembered to pinch my cheeks so I wouldn't look too washed out.

'Come in, Jonathan. It's very good to see you.'

Ira let me in, shaking my hand vigorously as he did so.

'It's good to see you too, sir,' I replied.

'Are you keeping well?' he enquired.

'Yes. Pretty well.'

'What a wonderful sunset,' Ira exclaimed.

'Best I've seen in a while,' I agreed.

As I walked into the hall my senses were bombarded with a pungent aroma of scented candles and I was squeezed fondly by Rebecca. She had a rather gangling frame, which her daughter Judith had inherited, yet this didn't detract from her feminine appeal. I had visited their home many times over the years and on each occasion Rebecca and her husband had shown me considerable generosity.

'How are you, Jonathan?' she asked as her dark eyes scrutinized my features. 'You look well. Not quite as pale as before.'

'Thank you,' I said, smiling to myself.

'How are your family? We haven't seen them in a while.'

'They're well thanks. My father is considering retirement but I don't think he's ready yet. He would find it difficult to adjust, I expect.'

'Ira thought that at first, didn't you darling?' and she glanced at her husband, now sitting in one of the leather armchairs, 'but you've never regretted it, have you?'

'Gosh no! Haven't had the chance to become bored. Besides, I've still got my consultancy work. The beauty of it is, Jonathan, is that you can take time out when you want to,' Ira explained. 'I'll have to have a chat with your father sometime and try to convince him of the advantages.'

'David will be here in a minute,' Rebecca explained. 'He's

picking up Abigail on the way. She's a nice girl. About your age, perhaps a bit younger. She's the daughter of two of our oldest friends. Works as a consultant haematologist at the Brooklyn Hospital Center. Oh, and she happens to be very musical as well.'

'Is she?' I said, trying to sound enthusiastic.

'Indeed she is,' Ira interjected. 'She has a beautiful singing voice. As a matter of fact she's looking for an accompanist and David suggested you.'

My interest in her ceased abruptly and I became irrationally annoyed. It was obvious my friend, who had more spare time than me, was intending to palm this young woman off onto me, which meant that there had to be something wrong with her. It was rare for David to refuse a woman what she asked, and it would be very difficult for me to turn her down face to face.

'That'll be them now. Good. We can eat,' Rebecca said as she got up to answer the door. 'Ira dear, pour Jonathan a drink, will you?'

Whilst his father was fixing the drinks, David came in, followed by his guest. I could not stop myself from gazing mesmerised at the stunningly attractive woman. Her deep brown hair framed her oval-shaped face. Her eyes were large and dark. She had a small yet full ruby mouth. Her figure was sinuous and she was of medium height. Conscious that I was staring, I hastily diverted my gaze. David, who had missed nothing, flashed me a cheeky smile and introduced us.

'David tells me you work at the Conservatory,' Abigail mentioned as we sat down, clutching our glasses of wine.

My friend and his father were engrossed in an earnest discussion, and Rebecca had vanished into the kitchen, from where a delicious aroma wafted around the house.

'Yes. David and I started there within a matter of weeks of each

33

other and have been friends ever since. Have you known his family long?' I enquired, noticing the delicate line of her nose.

'We all used to play together – David, Judith, my brothers and I – when we were young. Our parents have been friends for about thirty years.'

'Rebecca tells me you're a haematologist. That must be very challenging.'

'It can be. A large part of my job is spent working with cancer patients and when you are able to help them or ease their suffering then it is very rewarding. There is the flip side, of course, and each time you lose a patient it can be traumatic.'

'I've been told you sing and need someone to accompany you,' I continued.

Abigail's cheeks flushed to a deep shade of pink and I sensed that she was embarrassed.

'When I was at high school I used to take music lessons and at one time couldn't make up my mind whether to study medicine or music.'

'Do you regret your choice?' I asked.

'Oh, no, I didn't mean to give that impression. I love my job and besides, I don't believe I'm that talented a musician,' Abigail explained.

'Ira has given a very different impression. He says that you are most accomplished.'

'The thing is, I've been asked to sing at a rather important function in the spring and I will need to rehearse with someone. David says he's too busy and he wondered if you might have some time.' She hesitated before continuing. 'It wouldn't have to be every week. Perhaps every fortnight would do. But you mustn't feel you've got to do it. I could find someone else.'

'Of course I'll do it,' I heard myself saying, perhaps a little too eagerly.

Just at that moment Rebecca reappeared carrying a dish of piping hot food.

'Thank you, Jonathan,' Abigail said, giving me a sweet smile before getting up to offer Rebecca assistance. 'Perhaps we could talk about it later.'

'Ira, will you carve the meat please?' Rebecca asked.

I was invited to sit next to Rebecca whilst her husband took his position at the head of the table. David sat opposite me, and Abigail was on his right. Rebecca was without question an excellent cook, and had prepared some of her favourite dishes for us. I always found eating at the Rosen household an interesting experience and tonight was no exception. We passed our plates to Ira, who handed each one back weighed down with several mouth-watering slices of beef. We were then invited to help ourselves from the serving dishes which were arranged on the ivory-coloured tablecloth. I spooned a portion of carrots and prunes next to my meat and then filled the remaining space with a potato pancake and a dollop of apple sauce. Rebecca handed me a basket of poppy seed bread and I thanked her before taking a piece and passing the rest to David. When each of us had been served and were poised to begin eating, we waited expectantly for Ira to begin to recite the blessing.

'How is work these days, Jonathan? Are you still enjoying it?' Rebecca asked.

'Yes, I like my job.' As I responded I sensed Abigail's eyes studying me.

'Have you ever thought of moving to teach somewhere else?' the young woman asked.

'Yes, if a better position comes along.'

'As long as you're happy in what you are doing that's the most important thing, surely?' Ira interjected. 'And how is little Henry?'

A smile crept over Rebecca's lips at the mention of the boy's name and, as everyone began to chuckle, I tried to explain to

Abigail about my long-suffering association with the boy, including the worsening intonation. She seemed highly amused.

Rebecca offered everyone second helpings. Abigail politely refused but David and I were obliged to accept despite fervent protestations that we were full.

'I wish David didn't work so hard. We rarely see him at all lately,' Rebecca said wistfully.

At the mention of his name, David, whose glass like mine, had been refilled several times during the meal and whose eyes had now taken on a glazed expression, started slightly in his chair.

'What's that, Mom?'

'I was just saying to Jon that you are so busy lately you hardly have any opportunities to socialise and meet new people.'

David raised his eyebrows. We both knew what was coming. It usually followed a set pattern.

'He needs to find a nice girl and settle down. It's time our eldest child gave us some grandchildren, don't you agree, Ira?'

It was said in good humour, but at the same time her words were intended to strike a chord. I began to wonder, as I always did at this stage, whether David's parents were really oblivious to their son's insatiable attraction to the opposite sex.

'I know plenty of eligible girls you'd get on with,' Abigail chimed in, evidently wanting to participate in the sport.

'Really, my dear?' Rebecca's voice had risen in pitch and I could tell that she was seriously contemplating the prospect. 'We should organize a party and you could invite them along.'

During this brief exchange between Rebecca and Abigail who were evidently enjoying themselves immensely, I observed my friend's reaction. He had begun to squirm in his chair – unmistakably ill-at-ease – and there was no sign of his naturally gregarious self. The topic of his single status had taken a new direction as never before, and quite out of the blue there materialised the worrying possibility of him being 'fixed up'. David relished his freedom and was not yet ready to yield to 'the shackles of matrimony' as he perceived it. Ira, who had been listening with amusement, sensed his son's discomfort and decided it was a good moment to join in.

'How would that suit you, son? Just think, you could take your pick. What more could a man desire?'

The ensuing laughter dissipated the tension and David, his sense of humour restored, added some light-hearted banter of his own.

The first course out of the way, Rebecca fetched dessert, which consisted of delicious melt in the mouth macaroons. It was now, that I began to feel woozy. Just then a faint voice in the background brought me hurtling to the present.

'Sorry sir?' Ira had spoken but I battled hard to focus my attention on what he was saying.

'I've something rather important to ask you, Jonathan. We'll discuss it over coffee, I think.'

That was the cue for Rebecca to go and put the kettle on, followed by Abigail who had offered to help tidy away the dishes. At Ira's request, I took the seat nearest the open French windows. I felt a cooling breeze on my face. David was balancing on the arm of the couch next to his father.

'Are you aware of *Yom Hashoah,* Jon? The day set aside in the Jewish calendar to commemorate the Holocaust?' Ira asked.

'Yes,' I replied. 'I'm not exactly sure when it is, but I've heard of it.'

'It takes place in April,' Ira continued. 'You are wondering why I've mentioned such an occasion?' he asked as he and David looked at each other.

'Well sir, I have to say that I am a little curious.'

Before Ira could elucidate further, the two women emerged from the kitchen carrying four fat cups and a heavy coffee pot.

'Have you asked him yet?' Rebecca enquired, handing Ira his coffee.

'I was just about to darling,' her husband said.

Rebecca and Abigail sat down. At that moment I began to feel rather self-consciousness, as all four of them had positioned themselves so that they faced me, and each pair of eyes was probing mine.

'For this special day the elders of our synagogue have decided to commission a piece of music to commemorate this tragic event in our history. Would you be willing to write it, Jonathan?'

With dulled senses it took a moment or two for me to digest exactly what had been said. When it had sunk in I gave my reply.

'But what about David? Surely he should do it?'

'The simple truth is, Jonathan . . .' David hesitated and there was an unfamiliar gravity to his tone, '. . . you are the best man for the job. It is an important work and you are more capable of its creation than me.'

'But you are Jewish and I am not,' I protested. 'Surely that makes you better qualified!'

'We would like you to do it, Jonathan, because you have such a rare talent,' Rebecca said.

I sat there considering her words. It was true that of the two of us I was the composer, but David had nevertheless produced some highly influential and moving works of his own.

'I assume it would be a choral work. What sort of scale did you have in mind?'

'We have a competent choir who are all eager to perform, and we were envisaging that the work would form the finale to the programme for the evening.' From his animated explanation, Ira was delighted at my initial show of interest.

The unrelenting humidity of the evening had not eased by the time

I clambered into bed, though a gentle wind had blown up from somewhere. Lying there listening to the shades rustling I reflected on the evening's discussions and, in particular, the assignment I had been cajoled into accepting. I slept peacefully, well into the small hours and then, quite without warning, I awoke cold and shivering. The memory of my dream had not evaporated and I could recall it vividly. Somewhere dark and dingy I had seen the hunched figure of a man. He was writing something, but because of the poor light it was not possible to make out what it was. Suddenly he began to score violently with his pen and then, scrunching up the piece of paper, he tossed it to the ground before burying his head in his arms. That image, and the feelings of frustration and utter despair associated with it, lingered in my head until I drifted back to sleep again.

❖ ❖ ❖

'Jon, are you there? Are you awake?'

I scrambled to pick up the receiver as I awoke to hear my mother's voice.

'Is everything all right, Mom,' I asked groggily. I rubbed my eyes and then glanced at the clock. It was still early.

'Yes, dear. There's no need to worry. It's just that your grandmother has caught a bit of a chill.'

'When did this happen?'

'Yesterday afternoon. We thought it best to call Dr Stewart.'

'You should have told me. I would have called round.'

'You were at the Rosens, and besides the doctor said that there was nothing seriously wrong. She just needs plenty of rest, that's all. How was your evening?'

'Fine thanks.'

'Do you think you could stop by tonight?'

'Sure Mom.'

'Thanks Jon. When I checked on Mama earlier she said she needed to see you.'

'Do you know what about?'

'No and I could tell she didn't want to be pressed further.'

'That sounds like Grandma. Tell her I'll be there about seven.'

At twenty past six that evening I emerged from the subway. I walked the couple of blocks to my parents' street, stopping off to purchase flowers from one of the markets. The sun had begun its descent, and all the indications pointed to it being another glorious sunset.

My grandmother's condition had not worsened according to my mother, and as I looked at her sitting propped up in bed she seemed under the weather but not seriously ill.

'What lovely flowers, Jonathan. There is an empty vase on that shelf over there. Could you see to it for me please, darling?'

I drew some water from the tap in the upstairs bathroom, and arranged the flowers as best I could before placing them on the centre table.

'How are you feeling, Grandma?' I asked, sitting down beside her.

'I feel better already with you here. Help me with these will you? They've slipped a little.'

I arranged two white pillows so they supported her back. She kissed me on the forehead, something she had done regularly since I was a small child.

'Mom said you wanted to see me,' I said.

'Yes, I need to speak to you, Jonathan,' she said, taking my hand. Her expression had altered suddenly and I was reminded of how she had looked on the evening of Stefano's birthday party. 'We've always been close, haven't we?' she continued, squeezing my hand harder.

'Yes we have, Grandma.'

'There is something I must show you, Jonathan. Go to my closet,' her voice began to falter, 'and take out the box you will find inside.'

I did as she asked. Carefully, I lifted out a long, narrow, battered wooden container.

'The key is in the second drawer of my bureau,' she explained.

I rummaged about until my fingers alighted upon a cold metal object. Despite the trembling of her hands, she inserted the key into the lock and turned it. There was a sharp click, and then slowly my grandmother raised the lid. After delving about in the box for several minutes she finally removed an old photograph and a small, neatly folded document. She handed both of them to me and I took them over to the window. The evening sun had begun to peep from behind a cloud and, as it did so, some of its rays fell directly onto the picture. For a moment I gazed incredulously at what I saw. The likeness to myself was uncanny. Then I unfolded the honey-coloured paper, discoloured by age, to reveal a handwritten letter.

Warsaw
1942

Dr Marek Ruzanski picked his way through the maze of bonfires which, despite the heavy downpour the night before, had begun to smoulder again. Wisps of smoke curled silently upwards as the strong breeze fanned the flames, re-igniting the charred remains of plundered clothes, shoes and books. The pavements had taken on a moist hue but the rain had done little to wash away the traces of blood splattered indiscriminately across the street and the ominous stains had merely grown fainter. In happier times the deluge would have freshened the air, and while a keen wind had since sprung up, the atmosphere was rank. As Dr Ruzanski approached Karmelicka Street the fetid smell overwhelmed him He reached for his scarf and covered his face. This area of the Warsaw Ghetto had become notorious for massacres and beatings. Dr Ruzanski looked around nervously as he neared the corner. Each day their peripheral existence was lived out on a knife-edge, and all those Jews confined within the Ghetto expected to face death. His emotions, like those of many others, had grown dull and were now irreparably numb. To survive the day-to-day inhumanity required desensitisation.

As Marek approached one of the gates, he reflected upon what life had been like before the Nazis had invaded Warsaw. He tried to recall the sights and sounds of the once vibrant city: the joyful shrieks of carefree children playing in the streets, neighbours chatting animatedly with each other over garden fences and in shops where food had been in plentiful supply. He recollected the spectacle of overcrowded tram cars with passengers hanging out of the windows and balancing perilously on the tread boards, waving cheerily as they passed their friends. He remembered elegant ladies in brightly-coloured gowns accompanied by smartly-dressed men making their way to the opera or to dine at one of Warsaw's fashionable restaurants. Now all the happy memories had been silenced, squashed by a malevolent force, to be replaced with haunting sounds of torment, anguish, loss, grief and bleak, unrelenting, deprivation.

For Marek, like many other Jews who had secured employment beyond the Ghetto boundaries, his journey at this hour of the day – a little after seven o'clock in the morning – had become part of his daily routine and as he approached the barrier he came upon a familiar scene. A gang of about forty children was clustered near the gate waiting for an opportunity to slip out of the Ghetto. The majority of them had been orphaned in the brutal, great deportation, and in desperation were now reduced to roaming the streets and begging. Their emaciated frames were inadequately clothed with filthy, dishevelled rags, and their harrowing cries were clearly audible. Each of these little children – and, tragically, a great number had been deported to the camps – had been remorselessly brutalised and their futures were highly precarious: while some guards showed a degree of compassion and allowed them a passage to freedom, others merely shot them in cold blood. Children or not they were enemies of the State.

Suddenly Marek was knocked off balance by a pair of these juveniles barging past as they made off down the street. Their curious appearance caught his eye and he turned around to look at them. The two boys had completed a successful scavenging mission and were now returning to the Ghetto with their spoils. Each was wearing a roomy outer coat under which they had concealed numerous items creating the illusion of an unusually ample belly. Suddenly, a single gunshot reverberated in the air and a shocked silence hung over the area. Marek's heart sank as he steeled himself to hear the sound of a body striking the ground. When nothing happened relief washed over him and he found he could breathe normally again. It seemed that the German soldier's purpose was only to disperse the noisy gathering. The children began to trudge away dejectedly and Marek hurriedly covered the remaining yards to the checkpoint where three guards – a German, a Pole and a Jew – were stationed. The latter was a member of the Ghetto's police force: the Jewish Order Service.

'Pass. Where is your pass?' the Jewish policeman demanded crisply, his expression cold and austere.

'Just a moment,' Marek responded, anxiously fumbling inside his jacket. He knew he had it with him, but the abject terror at not being able to produce the document was crippling, for now the penalty was summary execution. Once these papers had been simple enough to obtain with a modest sum; in addition, in those days, guards could be bribed. There had been a major clampdown however back in August following an attempt to assassinate Jozef Szerynski, chief of the Jewish police.

Marek handed his pass to one of the guards who snatched it from him. Whilst he checked it, Marek studied his face. The two of them had been on speaking terms before the war, but now Hersz treated him like a stranger. It was obvious Hersz enjoyed his work and within the community it was said that all the power, such as it was, had gone to his head and he was no longer to be trusted. His uniform suited him well. The blue cap – inscribed with *Jüdische Ordnungsdienst*, together with the hefty boots, wide belt and truncheon – gave him a swagger of authority. Hersz took great pride in his appearance, and those souls who were unlucky enough to find themselves crouching before him would have been able to see their own reflection in his highly-polished boots.

By now a long queue had formed. The lazy German guard leaning against the gatepost smoking, and Tomasz, the Pole, who had always struck Marek as being more normal and humane, were galvanised into action by the sheer volume of the Jewish work party.

'Move on,' Hersz ordered dismissively.

Marek walked through to the other side. Here, for the best part of the day, he and his fellow workers could enjoy freedom from the enclosure which until the most recent clear out had corralled half a million Jews like animals. With their blue and white stars of David – the *Magen David* – the Jews were instantly recognizable and as a consequence vulnerable; the reception they received at the hands of their Polish compatriots could be mixed. There were some amongst the Poles who afforded them pity and charity often at considerable risk to themselves. Other Poles were hostile however and regarded the Germans' intervention as proportionate. Jeering, finger-pointing and abuse such as 'filthy Jew' were all commonplace taunts flung at them by adults and children alike as they made their way to and from work.

The early morning silence was abruptly shattered by the wails of factory hooters heralding the start of the new shift, followed by the sound of footsteps sloshing in and out of puddles.

'Hey Marek! Wait up!'

Turning he saw Daniel Jankowski, his childhood friend, approaching. The two of them lived a couple of streets away from each other. Daniel and Marek had been inseparable until university when their interests had led them to pursue different career paths.

Now strangely, the two of them had been reunited, having suffered the same fate as many others – devaluation – when numerous occupations had been declared illegal by the occupying Nazis. As a musician, Marek was now regarded as dispensable, along with fellow artists, writers and teachers. Daniel, a noted physicist, who possessed one of the finest scientific minds of his generation, had suffered the same indignity.

For those Jews who had tricked their way into work by convincing the Germans that they had the relevant experience, conditions were severe. Rather than accept destitution for themselves and their families, Daniel and Marek had joined the workforce at a munitions factory which specialised in the manufacture of bullets. The transition was not an easy one. Daniel was familiar with the conductive capability of the metals used and would no doubt have been able to magnetise them, but the intricate job of casting and filing these objects, the task to which he had been assigned, did not hold much appeal. Without proper protection hands unfamiliar with physical labour soon chafed after hour upon hour of repetitive action. Marek's hands cracked and bled, sometimes profusely, and it proved difficult to conceal the injuries from the eager German guards as they patrolled the factory, but over time they had become conditioned to the work and now any smooth skin had been replaced by calluses.

'Have you heard about the Frizmans?' Daniel asked quietly as he joined Marek in the line of gaunt workers queuing for their midday meal of soup and bread.

'No, I haven't heard anything,' Marek whispered.

Izrael and Esther Friszman were an elderly couple who lived on Niska Street, not far from the Ghetto's boundary wall. They had no children and since the internment the Ruzanskis had watched out for them as best they could. Even before Daniel spoke, Marek knew the news would be distressing.

'According to Jakub's wife who witnessed everything, they were rounded up and taken away.'

Jakub shared a work bench with Daniel. His family had accommodation two doors away from them.

'Where were they taken?' Marek asked.

'Marched off to the collection point.'

Marek's heart sank. From there many of the Jews were deported to their deaths. The stories of cattle trucks crammed full with terrified people were no longer mere rumours. These passengers would be delivered to the death camp at Treblinka. At the mention of it, feelings of anger and frustration began to well up inside Marek.

'The whole apartment was cleaned out.'

Marek steadied himself against the work bench.

'Thank God they would have been spared the walk,' Marek said, thinking aloud, as he envisaged the pathetic, helpless souls as they trudged lifelessly toward their inescapable fate.

Izrael and Esther occupied rooms within a short distance of the collection point and, mercifully, would have had a better chance of avoiding the beatings normally endured by those herded together from farther afield in the Ghetto. To have finally reached the railway siding, however macabre it might seem, offered a form of relief for many Jews would have been beaten and shot indiscriminately en route.

Marek glanced at Daniel, but his friend was lost in thought. Daniel and his wife, Vera, had met when they were students and they had married soon after graduation. They had decided to delay having children while they both pursued successful careers, then, shortly before war was declared, Vera gave birth to a little girl. The first year of their daughter's life was spent in comfortable and secure surroundings, but then came the decree establishing the Ghetto which aimed to have the entire Warsaw Jewry contained within its walls by the end of October 1940. A strict form of rationing followed, consisting of a daily allowance of around 200 calories. This was a starvation allowance, so Daniel, like the rest of Warsaw's Jews, was forced to barter. Successful in obtaining food rations, his daughter continued to thrive.

Lunch at the factory did not improve in either quantity or nutritional value and the offering that day was cabbage soup. Marek watched his fellow workers huddle together in their respective groups as they ate. Some perched on wooden crates or bricks whilst others sat on the ground, each man with tilted head eager to pick up the muted conversation in progress. From time to time a new face would join the group. There was little shelter or shade to be found in the factory grounds, and so, depending upon the season, the workers either baked in the fierce, unrelenting heat or shivered in the bitter cold. The winter months would not be long arriving and it was then that they envied the factory guards who were well kitted out – muffled up in hats, scarves and sturdy boots – in stark contrast to the workers' inadequate clothing. Polish winters could be bitter and many who were frail and undernourished had perished in the previous year's freezing conditions.

Daniel and Marek made themselves as comfortable as they could on their makeshift seats and were soon joined by Edek, Adam and Mendel, a clean-shaven man in his early forties. Before the war he had been a master craftsman, a maker of fine crystal in the form of ornamental tableware and cut glass chandeliers. With his considerable dexterity and nimble fingers it was hard for his co-workers to compete with him, and he held the record for churning out the greatest number of bullets each week.

'The situation is becoming more critical by the day, don't you think?' Mendel said quietly. 'The Germans are at their worst. It is building up.' He bowed his head a little lower. 'The rat catchers and their vermin raids have doubled, even tripled.'

'They appear to have increased the head count, that much is true,' Adam weighed in.

Edek Malenka, who had been listening intently while eating, rubbed his spoon until it glinted clean in the sunlight before carefully placing it in the empty bowl beside him on the ground. This was a ritual he had not changed since his first day at the workshop. He surveyed his surroundings furtively, something they all did if they had any information of a controversial, or potentially hazardous, nature to impart. He knew there were Jews who could not be trusted, those Nazi informers who had trodden the Faustian path, eager to demonstrate allegiance to the Party.

Older than the others by several years, Edek, and his younger brother Adam, had owned a jewellery shop in a wealthy district of the city, which before the war had a reputation for supplying the rich and famous with glittering accessories to be worn at banquets, balls and state functions. Precisely what happened to all their highly-priced stock was uncertain. However, it was rumoured that Edek and Adam had had sufficient time to spirit most of it away, though naturally they were reluctant to reveal where. This once portly, self-satisfied and highly successful businessman, whose shrunken frame was evidence of the barbaric conditions in the Ghetto, beckoned everyone nearer.

'When this re-settlement operation ends there will soon be another with atrocities on a scale far greater than we have ever witnessed,' Edek observed.

As he spoke his breath rasped in his throat and he tried to stifle a cough which threatened to convulse him. With the physical deterioration had come a decline in health and his friends had long suspected that Edek had contracted tuberculosis. Despite their suspicions none of them dared to discuss their health publicly for fear of being overheard. To admit weakness or to be seen exhibiting signs of a disability would result in immediate deportation to the camps. Those who had managed to avoid the horrifying massacres which had begun in July were extremely fortunate. A staggering number – around three hundred thousand human beings – had so far been transported to the extermination camps. As Edek struggled to regain his composure Marek averted his eyes. The harshness of his words had the effect of concentrating his thoughts. He stood up, wandered over to a corner of the compound and squatted against the fence where he could think in private.

'Edek's right, you know,' Daniel said as he sat down beside Marek and, leaning against the heavy chain link fencing, began rolling a meagre amount of tobacco between two flimsy, thin pieces of paper. 'The Germans will settle for nothing less than total annihilation next time round,' he continued, scraping an almost completely spent match against the ground in an attempt to light it.

'Yes I know,' Marek responded. He looked across at Edek who was holding forth again. 'At least he will be spared it all.'

The two friends sat in silence for a moment.

'Has there been any news about your nephews?'

With the escalating troubles many Jewish families had decided, reluctantly, to trust the safety of their offspring to a network of sympathetic Gentile families. Children would be smuggled out to small outlying villages, often deep in the surrounding countryside. The process involved months of meticulous preparation. Each child had to be conditioned into adopting a way of life which was alien to them. All knowledge and practice of Judaism was supplanted with Christian rituals and customs. Perhaps even more distressing was the renunciation of family ties. Those children who had more 'Aryan' characteristics found the physical transition easier, whereas the typically dark Jewish child would be obliged to have his or her hair bleached in an attempt to conceal their identity.

'No, Marek, we've heard nothing,' Daniel replied, unable to hide his concern. 'Mama is beside herself with worry, but she tries hard not to show it.'

'I hope the children are safe. It takes time for news to filter through,' Marek said trying to sound optimistic. 'When were the boys handed over?'

'About two weeks ago. They're being looked after by a family out at Zakopane,' Daniel replied quietly.

'And will they stay with this family indefinitely?' Marek asked.

'No. The risks are too great. New arrivals in a community are bound to arouse suspicion. The boys will have to be split up and passed on to different families,' Daniel explained.

The piercing sound of a guard's whistle echoed across the yard signalling that the workers' all too brief rest period was at an end. Daniel and Marek returned to their work benches and the remaining hours of the shift passed uneventfully except that, to his surprise, Marek exceeded his personal record of bullet production by a quarter.

At six o'clock every evening the Jewish workers left the factories, warehouses and shops and swarmed back to the Ghetto. The listless columns of men passed through the checkpoint and as they ploughed on, flanked by the typically impassive, heavily-armed German soldiers, Marek spotted another procession heading towards them. It was clear from the way they marched, sluggishly and laboured, that these unfortunates were destined for the collection point. The Nazi sadists – or 'corpses' as they were nicknamed because of the skull insignia sown onto their caps – had swooped again, emptying homes with their imperatives – 'All down! All Jews down!' – and herded the frightened residents into huddles in the streets. As the distance between the two groups lessened Marek could hear a faint hum, then a recognizable chanting of prayers, accompanied by the unmistakable noise of the crop, a favourite tool of the German SS. As the formation passed it made a sharp turn northwards. It was a chilling sight. Frantically Marek scanned the faces of those sunken-eyed doomed beings, searching for loved ones who might have been snatched up in the fray. He didn't recognise anyone and the motley band passed on by, shoulders hunched and chests heaving in time with the heart-rending sobs. The experience had drained him of what little energy he had and his body felt leaden. Conflicting emotions – relief and guilt – welled up in his breast. He was safe – for the time being – whereas others were not.

An indication of all being harmonious in the rooms the Ruzanski family now occupied was the smell of cooking. Often potent, it tickled Marek's nostrils as he returned from work each evening. The general hubbub echoing along the building's corridors had long since been muffled, and now as he approached his family's apartment he increasingly heard the word 'shush' calling for silence. On nights like these Marek would find himself thinking about their old family home on Krucza Street. It had probably been plundered shortly after their departure, along with most other Jewish properties.

Izak and Eva Ruzanski were not ostentatious and had furnished the rooms on Krucza Street comfortably and modestly. Characteristic of the interior of these city apartments was a fondness for large pieces of furniture such as cabinets. Izak had equipped his study with a bureau where he would sit for many hours, and Marek had his piano. Their only treasures to speak of were some old paintings, handed down through the generations, and one or two luxurious rugs.

And then a little under two years ago, at Jewish New Year, the Germans had declared that all non-Jews residing within the confines of the newly designated Ghetto must relocate. They were given four weeks to prepare. At the same time Polish Jews, not already resident in the area, were ordered to move into the Ghetto. This sinister development had not come as a surprise to the Jewish community. Rumours had circulated for ages, suggesting that a major separation was likely, and, as soon as construction began on a series of walls it became inevitable. Rachel and Marek were still living at home. Lidia, their older sister was married, and she and my mother were extremely anxious at the prospect of being cramped together with strangers in unsuitable living quarters.

The often heated and lengthy discussions about what should be kept, should a Ghetto be established, had proved superfluous. The proclamation specified that only some bedding, a few sentimental items and a refugee bundle – a *flüchtlingsgepäck* – would be permitted. Such a feat of organisation proved an impossible task for the invading force and it was decided that the deadline for the securement of the Ghetto would be extended to the middle of November. Finally, after several weeks, and on a damp and gloomy day, the Ruzanskis and other Jewish families assembled on the slippery pavement outside their home. The rain dripped slowly off their coats as they bade farewell to friends and neighbours who wished them luck and assured them that all would be well. They were unaware of the inhumane conditions which would be imposed upon their Jewish friends. Twenty-seven thousand apartments covering an area of less than three square miles accommodated thirty per cent of the city's Jewish population. A typical apartment averaged two and a half rooms, and it was not uncommon to find six or more people forced to share each room. The Ruzanski family had been allocated rooms on Franciszkanska Street and for two years they, together with fifteen other Jews, endured the most appalling conditions. Gradually disease, illness, the brutal round-ups, and the Germans' mindless, savage butchery, took its toll and now there were just seven of them left.

Using the agreed signal, Marek tapped four times on the old brown varnished door. Shortly afterwards footsteps could be heard along the inside passage, followed by the sound of the key in the lock. A less obnoxious cooking aroma drifted out onto the landing as Rachel, Marek's sister, opened the door. She had not long returned from the Ghetto hospital where she worked as a volunteer.

'Horsemeat tonight instead of the usual clotted horse blood? That's a welcome change,' Marek said, making his way into the living room.

'Ruben managed to get hold of some that had been smuggled in early this morning,' Rachel explained.

'Is he here?'

'No but he should be home soon. He's meeting some of his people over at Zamenhofa Street.'

'I wonder why?' Marek asked.

'He wouldn't say. You know he's very secretive when it comes to telling us what he's up to.'

'He should be back by now. It's curfew,' Marek said, noting the time on his wristwatch.

Life in the Ghetto could be monotonous with all its restrictions. And yet each member of the family knew everything could change dramatically in a split second. No one was more aware of this than seventeen-year-old Ruben Kenigsberg. An only child, he had lost both parents in the winter of 1941 when they were savagely murdered in front of him during a random attack. Their throats had been cut and his father's tongue had been sliced clean from its base.

Izak Ruzanski sat in an armchair reading the latest issue of *Gazeta Zydowska* the official Ghetto newspaper. Hunched over his bureau, and unlikely to have realised Marek had returned because of advancing deafness, was Ezra Furzay. He was often to be found whiling away the hours scribbling on what bits of paper Ruben managed to scavenge for him. Professor Furzay had spent all of his working life in academia, and Marek particularly enjoyed the companionship of this rotund, balding little man whose absent-mindedness added to his eccentricity. Sometimes Izak and Marek would take a sneak peek at the papers which Ezra left scattered around the apartment. Theorems and calculations filled the pages, all totally beyond comprehension.

Ezra had been billeted at Franciszkanska Street with Mara, his wife of almost fifty years. She was the epitome of sweetness. Although possessed of a remarkably youthful and rosy complexion her stature and proportions were not dissimilar to those of her husband but, where Ezra was unconventional in his behaviour, Mara's habits were ordered and predictable. Each morning she would be the first up. She would set the table for breakfast with what limited provisions were in the larder. Ruben would join her, and Marek was always next. The two men would then depart: one for the factory and the other for a day of dangerous exploits. Then Mara would return to the space she shared with her husband and lay out his clothes ready for when he awoke. Plumping up the pillows on their makeshift bed and rearranging the pretty balls of wool in neat rows were important habits which reminded her of her former life. Her children had sensibly left Poland at the first sign of trouble – though not before begging their parents to join them – and Mara had a need to continue her role as the nurturing matriarch and doted on young Ruben. The remainder of her day would usually be spent writing her journal, and, together with Eva, making garments to sell from the material which Ruben acquired from one of the rag warehouses.

Izak Ruzanski had been unable to find work. Without a work permit an individual was easy prey during the early morning manhunt for labour. A lack of employment was a source of tension, worry, sadness and engendered a loss of self esteem. Before the war Izak had been a successful businessman and director of a company manufacturing and supplying surgical instruments for many of Warsaw's hospitals. For an influential and well respected member of the community, the requisition of his business, overnight, by the Germans was abominable. The proud bread winner and patrician had been reduced to dependent and pauper. The Jews were forbidden to earn any sum greater than five hundred *zlotys* and were obliged to deposit their money in blocked bank accounts.

Marek stood in the kitchen doorway and watched his mother and sister as they cooked. He had such admiration for these women with their warm brown eyes, both equally attractive, one a younger version of the other, and was in awe of what they achieved each night in these sparse conditions. On the stove, sited towards the centre of the kitchen, was a sizzling pan. Eva was in the process of turning over one of four browning steaks as Rachel lifted a heavy metal container filled with boiled potatoes.

'Let me take that. We cannot afford to drop it, can we?' Marek offered, taking hold of the handles and carrying it to the draining board.

'Thank you,' Rachel said. 'We're going to eat well tonight.'

'Thank God we will,' Eva agreed.

Once he had drained the vegetables and the potatoes, Marek set them down on the dining room table. Forming a centrepiece was a basket of bread rolls and a glass for each of them. Alcohol was still being distilled within the Ghetto, but for how much longer was uncertain.

'Has Ruben been out all day?' Marek enquired positioning his chair at an angle so he could watch his mother.

'Yes, and I'm concerned about him. Smuggling is so dangerous now.'

'It always has been, Mama,' Marek said casually.

'But one day he may not come home and what will Mara do then?' Rachel said as she lifted some plates down out of the cupboard. 'She's beside herself with worry every time he goes out and doesn't settle until he's back.'

'You must talk to the boy. Try to discourage him,' Eva implored.

Smugglers were the undisputed heroes of the Jewish Ghetto and the goods they secured could make the difference between life and death, and yet mortality rates amongst the smugglers were dangerously high.

Just as the family sat down for their supper there was a brisk knocking at the apartment door. Mara immediately scuttled off to welcome the returning 'prodigal grandson' but when she opened the door she gave an involuntary gasp.

'The boy must have been involved in another skirmish,' Izak said wearily.

These clashes were never serious and usually involved rival gangs of Jews.

'You mustn't worry so much about me Mara. I can take care of myself,' Ruben could be overheard as he tried to reassure her. It was obvious that his attempts to placate the tearful elderly lady were ineffective.

'Your face, Ruben, and just look at your arm!' Mara's trembling voice could be heard.

Eva and Rachel rushed out into the hallway to investigate, and now all of them traipsed back into the room behind the wounded party.

'They're only scratches and they don't even hurt,' Ruben insisted. Despite this bravado, the boy bit his lip in an attempt to quell the pain. 'See what I've brought you, Mara,' Ruben said digging into the hidden recesses of his jacket and pulling out several balls of brightly coloured wool. 'Perhaps you could make me something with it. Maybe a sweater for when it gets colder?'

Such was Mara's delight on receiving this rare commodity that all traces of her earlier anxiety disappeared. She smiled and, bending forward, kissed the boy's forehead. Then, eager to add these new items to her growing hoard, she bundled them up and hurried off to her room. As soon as Mara was out of earshot Izak turned to Ruben and addressed him sternly.

'How did this happen?' Izak demanded.

Ruben looked uncomfortable. His normally healthy complexion had paled, emphasising the shocking contrast between his fair skin and the trickle of blood which oozed from the cut on his cheek. Before answering, the boy flopped down on a nearby chair and as he did so the ripped cloth of his shirt exposed a deep jagged, gash to his forearm. At that moment Eva reappeared from the kitchen with water and bandages and gasped with horror when she saw the extent of his injuries.

'I had to move quickly. The Germans were closing in and a few of us dashed into one of the derelict buildings in an attempt to lose them.' Ruben paused for a moment, exclaiming briefly as he raised his arms to allow Eva to remove his shirt. 'I had to drag myself through a broken window to make it back out onto the street. I was lucky though,' he continued, trying not to wince as Rachel gently dabbed a few precious drops of iodine onto his cheek. 'The others weren't.'

On hearing this, Izak let out a heavy sigh and then fell silent.

Perhaps he thought better of rebuking the boy further. Rachel was eager to fetch Dr Bilinski in case stitches were needed but Ruben reassured her that his injuries would heal perfectly well by themselves.

❖   ❖   ❖

The family settled down to eat. There was a deliberate attempt during meal times to keep the mood cheerful and light-hearted and this was especially true this evening.

'There has been another transmission today and the news is good,' Izak declared from across the table. 'Rommel has suffered a significant defeat in North Africa.'

Despite the risks – owning a radio was a capital offence – the family still listened to BBC broadcasts in secret. They were a crucial link to the outside world.

'That's good to hear,' Marek responded enthusiastically, although deep down he suspected the Jews would now be subjected to vicious, avenging acts of brutality. As well as the wireless, news filtered through from various sources on the outside and, consequently, many in the Ghetto had been able to follow the key developments in the war, such as the invasion of the Soviet Union and America's recent entry into the conflict. Hopes ran high whenever they learnt of resistance to the Nazis. There were reports that this was happening throughout Poland.

Eva and Rachel returned from the kitchen with pudding. Everyone ate slowly, taking time to savour the egg custard and its meagre scraping of jam. Before the war puddings such as this would have been considered banal; now because of its rarity it had become a great delicacy. The family ate in almost reverential silence.

'I've received news from Lidia and Benjamin,' Eva said when she had finished.

'How are they?' Marek said.

'Safe and well,' she told them, 'but Benjamin gave Lidia a bit of a scare recently.'

'Why?'

'Apparently he caught a heavy cold which went straight to his chest, and for a day or so, Lidia thought he might be suffering from tuberculosis.'

'He's lucky he wasn't,' Ruben chipped in.

'Will we be seeing them again soon?' Mara asked.

'It's far too risky for them to venture any distance at the moment,' Izak interjected.

Lidia and her husband had been housed on the western outskirts of the Ghetto, where the situation was equally grave. In order to lower morale further, the Germans censored letters, and links between families and friends were tenuous. Occasionally, Marek got word to his brother-in-law via a network of trusted co-workers, and Benjamin sent information back vice versa.

The dinner things were tidied away and the family briefly retired to the living room to drink coffee. With little or no fuel, the temperature of the living space could drop dramatically. Typically, with only a cold and empty grate to stare at, the women would sit in the kitchen gossiping, their chairs forming an arc in front of the cooking stove where their bodies could absorb any residual heat. Games such as bridge and chess were favourite pastimes and even Ezra could be persuaded to participate.

'Have you got any cigarettes?' Marek asked.

Ruben rummaged in his pockets and then, grinning, handed one over.

'They were partly responsible for this,' he said, pointing to his cheek, 'but I suppose it was worth it.'

They wandered out onto the landing. It was gloomy at night – because of the bombing raids there could be no light – and it was now well into the hours of curfew. The whole Ghetto was enveloped in total darkness. Abandoned buildings – forlorn and cheerless by day – took on a sinister air by night. Ruben perched on the window ledge and Marek sat at the top of the staircase. Leaning forward to light a cigarette, Ruben was momentarily immersed in moonlight.

'Don't you think the stakes are getting too high?' Marek asked breaking their companionable silence.

Ruben turned his head towards the window, the warmth from his smoke-filled breath forming a patch of condensation on the glass.

'Don't you take risks, Marek?'

'Yes, of course. We all do, but they are not as dangerous as the gambles you take every day.'

He turned back to face Marek.

'Each morning when you leave this apartment you may not reach your destination. A German soldier could pick you off at any moment for no good reason, or you could just as easily find yourself herded onto a cattle truck. None of us know how much time we have left, but surely preservation of life is by far the greatest form of revenge. Your family need me to do what I do. We would all have starved months ago if I hadn't.'

What he said was true. Despite his daredevil escapades, the boy possessed a wisdom beyond his years.

'You are still young, Ruben, and shouldn't jeopardise your future. Besides what would Mara, Rachel and Mama do without you?'

He coloured slightly at the mention of Rachel. Just then, as they stubbed out their cigarettes, a piercing noise cut through the stillness. It came from the floor above and sounded like the scream of a young child in the grip of a nightmare. Although occasions such as these were very common, it had a disconcerting affect upon both men.

'Come on. Let's go in,' Marek said softly. It was cold and his limbs were beginning to feel stiff.

Back inside the apartment it was quiet. The rest of the family had retired for the night. Later, as he lay in bed surrounded by the eerie blackness, Marek could not stop himself from thinking about the unpredictability of death. He tried to imagine how he might feel when confronted with the actual moment, assuming his life was not snatched away without warning. Terrified maybe, or resigned to his fate, were the sentiments that came to mind. In the end he came to the conclusion that he would rather not know, and then he drifted off to sleep.

A chill north wind blew across the plains, bringing with it the first of the season's heavy frosts and snows. There had been flurries back in the autumn, but these had merely been an illusion created by a blizzard of tiny feathers whirling in the air having escaped from the bedding of those who had been massacred. As Marek stepped out of his family's apartment building, a blast of cold air stung his face. His eyes watered and his chest began to ache. He used to savour mornings like these and had once welcomed the clean, bracing air which could have an invigorating effect on his mind. Now, inadequately prepared for the bitterness which greeted him, he hunched his shoulders and began to walk quickly towards the factory. He knew the conditions would be much harsher once the hard winter had set in, and many of his fellow Jews would face illness and death as the temperatures plummeted further. The footpaths and streets were slippery underfoot, and Marek walked more slowly than usual. Ahead he noticed other workers, including Daniel, taking similarly hesitant steps. The dusting of snow reminded him of charming picture postcard images, and yet hidden beneath the fine coating were the bloody marks of mindless brutality. Whatever the conditions, the Nazi fetish for marching prevailed. Should a man slip, which happened frequently, he was subject to a stern glare, barked at, or prodded with the butt of a rifle. Interestingly, when it was the turn of a German soldier to lose his footing, he would curse, grit his teeth and, in typical German style, plough on as if nothing had happened. At these points in the journey and despite all the general disorder and grimness it provided a few moments of light relief.

The work parties never deviated from their usual route to and from the factory, and as they marched Marek began to feel increasingly vulnerable. Ruben's talk of untimely death had unnerved him and he thought of nothing else until the checkpoint became visible and he was suddenly distracted. The same group of pathetic waifs from the previous morning had congregated again. Their incessant wailing filled the air and Marek tried to focus his thoughts on other things in an attempt to block out the sound. However, in a matter of seconds everything changed. As if from nowhere, a vehicle screeched to a halt and half a dozen German SS soldiers spilled out. A deathly silence descended. The children were paralysed with fear and shock. Then they took flight like a startled flock of birds, fanning out in all directions, their screams echoing and ricocheting off the surrounding buildings. People shrunk back into doorways and pinned themselves against walls.

Marek shuddered involuntarily as he caught sight of the expressionless faces of the German soldiers. Instead of showing compassion and mercy towards these vulnerable youngsters it was evident from their icy stares that these monsters were immune to such rudimentary humane feeling. Marek could hear the familiar sounds of guns being primed for use, and then it began. Each child was mown down indiscriminately and not one was spared. Cascades of bright red blood sprayed across the ground, melting away the pure white. The children closest to the soldiers were despatched at point-blank range, their little bodies bouncing in the air with the bullets' impact and then falling to earth like rag dolls. Pools of congealed, dark red fluid and brain matter oozed from their shattered skulls.

The marksmen did not linger. Climbing back into the truck they were swiftly driven away towards another section of the Ghetto. An eerie silence descended. Despite resisting the urge to retch on numerous occasions, Marek could not do so this time, and he vomited violently in the gutter. Exhausted, he leant against the wall and steadied himself for a moment. As his breathing gradually became less laboured he tried to remove the bitter taste from his mouth. He then turned and steeled himself to pick his way amongst the sea of lifeless bodies.

Marek walked briskly as he approached the checkpoint. Along with a few other men he had become separated from the main work party in all the confusion and he was anxious to reach the other side of the gates, and to distance himself from the carnage. He wanted to avoid being press-ganged into taking part in the clean-up operation. Reaching the checkpoint he fumbled for his papers but was suddenly waved through. Looking up, Marek could see the German guard was equally appalled by the murderous spectacle. He soon regained his composure, however, for Marek overheard him bark some orders and when he looked back the stream of people passing through the gate had come to an abrupt halt. Marek thought of Daniel, whom he had lost sight of farther back, and hoped he would not be one of those forced to collect the bodies.

The mood at the factory was sober that morning. Men who had been press-ganged into clearing away the children's bodies were visibly shaken and subdued when they eventually arrived to start their shift. During the lunch break the tension eased a little, but the Jews' feelings of hatred and loathing for the Nazis had only intensified. After queuing for a helping of watery broth, Marek, Daniel and their friends gathered at their usual spot. They could see Edek was getting weaker with each passing day – his grey skin and visible red rings around his eyes were worrying signs – yet regardless of this Edek seemed to be in good spirits, and his cough had improved slightly. Always a great source of up-to-the minute information he could not wait to speak.

'Bunkers,' Edek whispered excitedly. 'Bunkers. Everybody is building one.'

They all knew what he referred to. 'Bunker' was Ghetto slang for a shelter or hideaway, which was regarded as something of a necessity as the threat from the Germans escalated.

'Several of us are joining forces to construct one,' Mendel, who had a tendency to gobble his food at a faster rate than the rest of them, reported.

'What are you two going to do?' Daniel asked the Malenka brothers.

'We have engaged the services of a very skilful engineer who is going to . . .' Adam paused to look around and then lowered his voice before continuing, '. . . fit one underneath our cellar.'

'His plans are quite ingenious,' Edek added. 'It will be very costly, but we have decided to be independent. It is safer that way. Fewer people to worry about.'

There were murmurs of approval from the group.

'It's devising something original. That's the secret,' Mendel said. 'It's got to be undetectable and yet easily accessible during round-ups.'

'I've heard of bunkers behind ovens and stoves,' Adam chipped in.

'Sounds a good idea just so long as the ovens and stoves haven't been used recently,' Marek said, injecting a touch of black humour.

'No need to worry about that with the shortage of fuel,' Daniel remarked derisively.

'There are, of course, the more unsavoury ideas.' All heads turned in Edek's direction. 'Beneath outdoor lavatories.'

There was a collective gasp of disgust from the men.

Depending on its size, a shelter could accommodate either several families, or just one, yet when the time came to use them it was often a free-for-all.

'And you?' Edek asked Daniel. 'If you haven't thought about it yet you really should.'

'We can't afford one of our own. We've arranged to share with our neighbours.'

Edek then fixed his paternal gaze on Marek, eager to hear his thoughts.

'You're right, Edek. I suppose we must organise the work quickly before materials run out and while there are still men able to do the job.'

The lunchtime discussions had a galvanising effect on Marek and for the remainder of the day he was preoccupied with the practicalities of where to position his family's bunker.

Daniel and Marek's journey home was not without incident. They made their way to the bottom of Nowolipki Street and were just about to turn the corner into Zamenhofa Street, when Daniel suddenly grabbed his friend's arm. A moment or two later they heard some all too familiar words.

'All downstairs! All Jews downstairs!'

The impatient German SS officer repeated the order loudly and with menace. The two friends flattened themselves against the wall, fully aware of the jeopardy they faced now that an operation was in full swing. The imperative traditionally heralded the start of a round-up but the deportations had ceased for the time being. A Nazi patrol had been checking apartments and had discovered Jews where they didn't belong. Not wanting to draw attention to themselves, they had no choice but to listen as their unfortunate kinsmen were herded out of the building. They could hear the sound of a door being flung open, followed by footsteps shuffling along the pavement. One in the group nearest to them – a woman – had begun to cry softly and shortly afterwards the howls of a terrified infant were heard. Marek's heart began to pound in his chest and beads of sweat quickly formed upon his brow.

'Shut your mouth, Jewish pig,' the order rang out, swiftly followed by sounds of heavy blows raining down in rapid succession upon the German SS officer's victims.

The club was one of a range of effective tools adopted by a regime obsessed with cruelty and terror, and after a few minutes of heart-rending whimpering, reminiscent of a wounded animal, an ominous hush descended. The assembled group was ordered to line up and place their hands above their heads. Daniel and Marek looked at each other, a mixture of apprehension and strain registering on their faces. Then six precision shots, delivered in perfect rhythm, reverberated across the street. This was followed by the dull sound of bodies hitting the ground. None would have been spared. Both men opened their mouths to speak, but before either one could manage a word they both vomited into a nearby drain. The sheer mental exhaustion brought on by their harrowing ordeal had sapped them of their ability to communicate and the two men walked back in silence.

Over supper that evening, and with Marek recovered from his traumatic experience, the Ruzanski family discussed the revelations about the bunkers. The conversation became very animated and soon turned to the serious matter of how they would construct one within the apartment.

'The attic is the obvious solution, especially since our apartment is situated on the top floor,' Izak suggested.

Others, however, could see the disadvantage in such a scheme, and swiftly disagreed.

'Darling, it's not such a good idea. We would be sitting ducks,' Eva said, stroking her husband's hand affectionately before adding, 'Surely the Germans would think of looking there first? I really don't fancy our chances of escaping over the roof tops, do you?'

'You are right, my dear,' her husband said smiling at his wife. 'Sadly you and I are not getting any younger.'

'I know. What about a secret room? We could surely outwit the Germans that way,' Rachel suggested.

'Where would we put it?' Ruben posed the obvious question.

'Behind the cabinet in the dining room,' Rachel explained, her face flushed with excitement.

'Dig a hole in the wall big enough for an adult to crawl through and then devise a system for pulling the cabinet back in place. It might work,' the young man said.

Izak glanced over at Mara and saw she was frowning. She was probably contemplating the worst for herself and Ezra. Scrabbling through tiny apertures between cavity walls or, even more perturbing, squeezing under floorboards, did not have much appeal for either of them. Nonetheless the apartment offered plenty of scope for development. The difficulty was deciding upon the most practical idea.

As Rachel's idea was discussed further, Ezra, who had been doodling away contently, suddenly put down his pen.

'I have devised a foolproof plan,' he announced, excitedly. 'I have just re-checked all the dimensions and it should work perfectly.'

'Tell us, Ezra,' Rachel asked curiously.

There was a momentary pause before his reply came.

'The laundry chute.'

'What laundry chute?' Izak asked.

'Ah! You didn't know there was one? I heard about it purely by chance,' Ezra said.

'Where is it?' Marek enquired impatiently.

Raising his right hand he pointed vaguely towards the kitchen wall.

'It has been sealed up for years, but it forms a passageway between this and other rooms in the house.'

'How did you find out about it, Ezra?' Eva asked from across the table.

'Shortly after Mara and I came to live with you, I became acquainted with an old gentleman who lived on the ground floor who knew the history of the property. It was owned by a wealthy Jewish merchant and where we are sitting now was once their linen room.'

'That makes sense,' Izak said excitedly. 'The dirty laundry would be propelled downwards and returned the same way once it was clean.'

'Ezra, you clever old thing. Your idea is brilliant,' Ruben declared.

'So the entrance is somewhere in this room?' Marek asked as he looked around.

'I have a good idea of where the shaft leads to – down in the basement – and it ought to be easy to calculate its position up here.' Ezra paused. 'If you would like to take a look, I've drawn a diagram with some measurements.'

The table was hastily cleared as Ezra diffidently slid his

diagrams into the centre. At first glance it just looked like an accurate representation of the kitchen, with the stove and sink unit, even table and chairs, outlined in pencil. However, upon closer scrutiny, they could see a vertical passageway running parallel with the cavity which divided the rooms from the neighbouring property.

'I can explain everything in more detail if it will help,' Ezra said, tilting his head to glance again at his calculations. His spectacles, normally safely perched on the bridge of his nose, slipped forward. As he pushed them back into position he continued. 'As soon as the chute has been located we'll need to make a platform which will hold our collective weight, with a trap door through which we can escape to the basement by ladder.'

'Just how wide is this chute?' Ruben wondered. 'I'd always assumed they were pretty narrow.'

'My calculations have allowed for a generous width. If my memory serves me correctly, it was used to convey other items as well, such as large packing cases and pieces of furniture,' Ezra explained.

'How would we hide the entrance?' Marek asked. 'The Germans are not easily fooled.'

'It's unlikely that a single width of wood would disguise the hollowness of the cavity when tapped. That would be a major flaw,' Izak said, yet it was obvious he was reluctant to cast doubt on the scheme.

'Ah! But my friends,' Ezra pressed on undeterred, 'there would be wooden panels around the entire room forming the dado with cover strips to make the joints invisible, and if each one is positioned on batons fixed to the wall, each should sound exactly the same if struck.'

Ezra was confident of his plans. Marek had never seen him in such an assertive mood. One final, and yet crucial, matter which needed resolving was how everyone would get into the shelter from the kitchen.

'Lift the panel and it will come away easily. As soon as the last person is inside it can be secured in position using two clamps,' Ezra explained, pointing to another diagram.

Mara, who had hung on every word her clever husband had uttered, now caught hold of his hand and kissed him proudly.

'It's a splendid idea, Ezra. And one that has every chance of working,' Izak remarked optimistically.

Marek had not seen his father so invigorated in a long time.

'I agree,' Eva said, her mood much improved.

'Mara and I can think about what to put in it,' Rachel said enthusiastically.

'I can make cushions if Ruben can find me some material,' Mara remarked patting him affectionately on the shoulder.

'I'll try my best. And I'll make sure we have plenty of food.'

'A carpenter should be engaged immediately,' Izak declared.

'I can ask the Malenkas. They're sure to know one,' Marek proposed.

'It's getting late. We can discuss everything further in the morning,' Eva said getting to her feet.

The following few days were suspiciously peaceful. Atrocities such as the ones Marek and Daniel had witnessed had become less frequent, and while a lull was welcome, it was strangely unnerving. Maybe the Germans were scheming and wanted to catch the Ghetto residents off guard. Progress had been made on the Ruzanski's bunker and a carpenter agreed to undertake the work in between his other jobs. With remarkable efficiency the cheery fellow had constructed the secret hideaway, complete with matching panels and access to the basement. Just how much protection it would offer the family in practice was uncertain; however, everyone felt more secure knowing they had 'a bolt hole', as Izak described it, to take refuge in.

◆ ◆ ◆

Despite the barbaric conditions the Jews endured they clung to a cultural and social life within the Ghetto. Covert underground schools flourished – often disguised as soup kitchens – and orphanages and secret libraries were set up. There were poetry evenings, visits to the theatre, as well as a host of other entertainments. Musical performances had been sanctioned by the Germans, such as those given by the Jewish Symphony Orchestra and chamber ensembles, but only on condition that the programme excluded works by German composers. Those who refused to restrict themselves to compositions by Jews would be punished if caught. Tragically, many of the Ghetto's musicians had been transported to Treblinka during the *Gross-Aktion* –which took the form of mass deportations – earlier in the summer. Despite the dangers, Marek was one such dissenter who had taken the decision to flout what he regarded as petty regulations designed to encourage a deeper spiritual decline. He had directed a number of musical activities prior to the outbreak of war, and was approached shortly after entering the Ghetto by friends and colleagues to form a choir. He had on occasion witnessed SS soldiers smashing a member of the stringed, wind or brass families into tiny pieces purely out of malice and spite. Marek found it increasingly difficult to comprehend how the Germans, members of a supposedly 'supreme race' which had over the centuries produced some of the finest exponents of the musical, artistic and literary worlds, could now behave like philistines.

'Barbarians with hearts of stone. How is it possible that the influence of one man can reduce a nation to this?' Daniel had said angrily as they walked home from the factory that evening.

They had just walked past a burning heap on top of which a charred violin was just visible. Daniel was himself a talented viola player and Marek could understand his friend's vehemence.

'What are you thinking about?' Marek asked him as they walked on.

'Nothing important. Are we practising as usual tomorrow night?'

For some time now they and a few of their co-workers met once a week, after the curfew, to sing in the basement of a disused warehouse. The risks involved were considerable so they had agreed to tell no one.

'Yes. Have you told Vera?'

'No. She would worry too much.' He paused. 'It's the only secret I've kept from her.'

'If you'd rather not attend we'll understand,' Marek reassured him

By now they had reached the point where their paths would diverge.

'No, I'll be there,' Daniel said. 'Besides I'd miss Amos' fiery concoction.'

The two friends laughed and said farewell for the evening.

As 1942 came to a relatively peaceful end, a number of workers from the factory congregated at Edek and Adam's apartment to toast the New Year, thankful to have survived the past twelve months and forever mindful of those who had perished. The Ghetto's residents had witnessed a systematic eradication of its people, leaving the streets covered with bodies and blood and excrement escaping from the failing sewers and a mere 60,000 Jews occupying a greatly reduced area. Their generous hosts had arranged for large amounts of alcohol to be smuggled into the Ghetto, and for the first time in a long while Marek got very, very drunk. Ringing in his ears as he staggered home that night were Edek's pessimistic words:

'Those bastard Germans. They're up to something, you wait and see.'

Edek was proved right. January began ominously. Without warning, and, not long after the *Reichsführer-SS*, Heinrich Himmler, had visited the city, there was a significant increase in the number of German guards stationed at the checkpoints and Jewish working parties were forbidden to leave the Ghetto. When the news reached the Ruzanski family, Ruben and Marek ventured out onto the streets near their apartment, curious to see what was happening. Arranging to meet at the corner of Wolynska Street in half an hour they split up.

On the surface everything appeared normal, but then Marek heard the sharp crack of distant gunfire. He froze. The noise began to amplify by the second until eventually he realised why. The sound was moving towards him rapidly and would reach him within minutes. Then suddenly, a vehicle pulled up a little way off, its brakes screeching, and Marek felt a fierce grip on his arm. Petrified he turned and to his relief saw it was Ruben.

'Let's get out of here,' the young man shouted over the cacophony of deafening gunfire. 'We've got to warn the others.'

Together they raced back, ducking as bullets whizzed past, before hurling themselves headlong into their apartment building and up the stairs. With the Germans hot on their heels there wasn't time to knock on each apartment door – the enemy had taken everyone by surprise – so the men yelled warnings as they raced up the stairs in the hope that some of the inhabitants would hear. By the time they reached the top floor they were both breathless and could hardly spit out the words coherently as they burst into the apartment.

'Quick! Into the shelter! Now! They're right behind us.'

The family reacted with disbelief but as the realisation sank in, it filled them with fear. Heavy footsteps could be heard on the stairs. Apartment doors were smashed open, followed by the echoing screams of victims who had, despite Marek and Ruben's best efforts, been taken unawares. A volley of shots silenced them all.

Ruben yanked the panel from the kitchen wall and Eva and Rachel clambered in. Mara and Ezra were next, but unexpectedly Ezra turned and ran back to the living room.

'My drawings. I've left them in the bureau. I must get them,' he said frantically.

'Ezra!' Ruben yelled lunging forward in an attempt to stop him, 'There isn't time.'

'I should have destroyed them. I'm a fool.'

'You next, Mara. Come on. You can do it,' Ruben said encouragingly, trying to control the anxiety in his voice. 'Ezra will be back in a moment.'

Mara did not move. She refused to climb into the bunker until her husband had returned. There was little time to plead with her. To physically force her through the gap carried too great a risk.

'You're next Papa, then Ruben. I'll wait for Ezra,' Marek said hurriedly.

At the very moment that Ezra returned, clutching the vital paperwork, the door burst open and they heard threatening shouts and the tread of military boots. Marek and Ezra knew that time had run out and embraced each other quickly. Mara stood devotedly at her husband's side, as she had done throughout their life together.

'*Shalom*, my friend, until we meet again,' Ezra said calmly.

Marek grabbed the documents and hurled himself through the opening. He crawled the short distance to where the others were huddled together in the candlelight while Ezra positioned the panel behind him. Ruben kept a protective arm around Rachel's shoulders. Izak cradled his wife.

At first they couldn't hear anything. The German intruders had not yet reached the kitchen. Like predatory beasts the soldiers moved from room to room, painstakingly searching each one for their prey. Then they found them.

'Where are they, old man?' one of them snarled.

There was no response. Ezra and his wife were sitting at the table.

'Where are the others? We know they are here somewhere,' the soldier demanded. There was a sinister edge to his enquiry. His face was full of menace. 'Let me see,' the soldier continued as he surveyed the kitchen. 'Where might they be? Perhaps hiding in the attic?'

Suddenly a rally of shots was fired into the ceiling. Mara let out a startled cry. Marek was concerned his mother and sister might react similarly but both women, with tremendous effort, controlled the urge to cry out.

'Ah! Perhaps here.'

Within seconds a rhythmic tapping began. The soldier slid an object over every panel, and each time the wood was struck it sounded identical. Holding their breath, Marek and Ruben exchanged frantic looks. The tension was unbearable. They had rehearsed this scenario many times and, as an extra precaution, a layer of cloth had been attached to the interior of the board to reduce the chance of detection. The moment passed and then nothing. It was broken by hurried footsteps and then the noise of a crop being brought down sharply upon the surface of the table.

'So you don't know where they're cowering like swine?' the soldier demanded.

He was now deeply frustrated. The Germans hated being cheated, and were at their most dangerous when undermined. Feelings of guilt were filling Marek's mind: it should have been him and not Ezra and Mara at the mercy of those monsters.

'I will ask you *one . . . more . . . time . . .*'

There was a scuffle of feet.

'If you don't give yourselves up you cowardly Jews, the deaths of your friends will be on your conscience.'

He spoke in an absurdly casual manner, so incongruent with the grim nature of the heinous crime he was about to commit. Ezra and Mara had somehow maintained an eerie composure but seconds later Marek's fears were realised. Chairs were dragged across the tiled floor and a scuffle followed.

'Perhaps this will encourage you to talk, you Jewish pig.'

Ezra was choking. Mara, powerless to do anything, called out her husband's name. She was becoming hysterical. The Nazi brute struck her with such force that she hit the floor with a heavy thud. Her moaning was soon overshadowed by the gurgling and spluttering noises of strangulation. In a futile attempt to block out the awful sounds Rachel and her mother covered their ears. A grief-stricken Eva had buried her head deeper into her husband's chest. Ruben cradled a quietly sobbing Rachel, as tears flowed down her cheeks. The inevitable was about to happen and the family steeled themselves against the agony of it. There was a single, loud rasp as Ezra desperately tried to draw breath, and then his body slumped to the floor.

'On your knees, idiot Jew,' the Nazi's voice boomed.

A muffled shot rang out. Then there was silence. The torment for their beloved friends was over. None of them dared move. A chair was roughly kicked aside, followed by heavy footsteps echoing down the hallway. The soldiers had deserted the apartment and were on their way to inflict misery, if not death, on the occupants of the next.

'Ruben, we'd better go down to the basement and check the coast is clear,' Marek whispered. 'Papa, you, Mama and Rachel, you must stay here until we know it's safe. We'll be as quick as we can.'

Ruben understood. It was imperative to ensure that the Germans had moved on and were not playing a cunning, sinister waiting game. They needed to buy some time, to clean up the carnage so that the family would be spared the sight of it.

The two men climbed down slowly, eventually emerging, apprehensively, from the laundry shaft. For a minute or two they scrabbled around in the murky basement, the only light coming from chinks in the masonry at street level. Much to the men's relief they appeared to be alone but just as they were about to walk back upstairs, Marek became aware of a pair of eyes peeping at them from a narrow recess between the floor and the bottom steps of the staircase. In one swift movement Ruben extracted a small boy who promptly began to whimper and wriggle. Marek signalled for the child to be silent, and Ruben clamped an unwelcome hand over his mouth. The struggling ceased and then the child pointed towards the door. Ruben removed his hand.

'The soldiers have gone. Dashed down the stairs and ran out into the street,' the child explained.

Marek recognised him as one of the children who lived on the ground floor. He was about ten years old.

'Are you certain of this? It's vital that what you say is correct,' Marek told him.

'The noise of the boots hurt my head,' he said raising his hands. Once again he pointed to the front of the building, then added, 'I heard the truck drive away.'

'What's your name?' Ruben asked.

'Moshe.'

'Why didn't you stay with your family?'

'I ran away. It's too dark in the shelter.'

The child had clearly been very brave throughout his ordeal, however, now his eyes had started to well up.

'Shall we go and find your family Moshe?' Marek said, taking hold of his little hand.

The boy led Marek back to his apartment where they found his family safe and unharmed. Ruben took a hasty look outside.

'The child's right. It's quiet out there. The soldiers must have moved on,' he explained as he caught up with Marek in the hallway.

'Are you going to be OK? If you'd rather leave me to get on with it I'll understand. I know Ezra and Mara were very dear to you.'

Ruben's lower lip began to tremble slightly. He bent his head low, perhaps embarrassed at this rare display of emotion. Without a word, slowly, but resolutely, he began to climb back up the stairs.

The sight which met their eyes as they entered the kitchen was horrifying. Mara had been shot in the head at point blank range. The gore had cascaded over walls, ceiling and floors and turned their stomachs. Overwhelmed by their loss it took a little while for them to steady themselves but they needed to work quickly. Having carried their friends' bodies to the basement – which would serve as a makeshift mortuary – they wiped away the gruesome detritus as best they could. Then Ruben and Marek crawled back into the bunker.

The Ruzanskis spent the next four days in hiding. None of them knew how long the brutal operation would continue and whether the SS would return. The element of surprise was another thing the Nazis prided themselves upon. At times the family could hear shooting, which was often heavy and prolonged. It was decided to mark the passing of Ezra and Mara in the traditional way with an improvised *shiva*. Prayers were lead by Izak and psalms were recited. In keeping with tradition sitting at a low level was easy to achieve given the confines of the bunker, as were the restrictions on bathing and the wearing of freshly laundered clothing. The old custom of friends and neighbours visiting with gifts of food was not a possibility.

After the fourth day the Germans withdrew and the Ruzanskis, like thousands of others, emerged from their shelter at sundown exhausted but relieved. Six thousand Jews had lost their lives, but not without a substantial number of German casualties. The Jews had retaliated bravely and proved to be a force to be contended with. To completely overthrow such a mighty enemy was not feasible, but what the Jews had achieved gave the Ghetto residents a glimmer of hope – at least for the present.

The Ruzanskis were not able to bury Ezra and Mara themselves. They had to entrust their friends' remains to others since the Jewish cemetery no longer fell within the Ghetto boundaries. Izak said a simple prayer and they sealed their farewells with a kiss. Just as their bodies were being lifted into the cart that would carry them away forever, Rachel, who had been clutching something, stepped forward. It was a single red rose Mara had once fashioned out of cloth and given to her as a gift. Placing it to her own lips she then laid it tenderly in one of Mara's hands. She was returning it with her love.

❖ ❖ ❖

Those Jews caught unawares during the recent barbaric raids were determined never to find themselves in such a vulnerable position again. Ingenious systems were devised to warn of imminent danger and a number of interlinking passages between the apartment buildings were designed. Mercifully, Lidia and her husband Benjamin had survived the latest round-up operation, as had Marek's close friends at the workshop, although the lunch queue was considerably shorter. In spite of this the mood was buoyant, one of solidarity and optimism. Over lunch Mendel filled them in with details of the counter-attacks, which had undermined the German resolve.

'Did you hear about the skirmishes on Niska and Zamenhofa Streets? Apparently our men put up a good fight with grenades and guns and several Germans were packed off to hell.'

'Ah, my dear friend,' Edek interrupted, 'it is good that the Jewish people have become more pugnacious, but we don't have the means to overthrow such force.'

'We know,' Daniel snapped, 'but it gives us all hope, however tenuous. None of us wants to die prematurely and yet we're all aware that, save for a miracle, we'll meet our end here or in the camps.'

He got up and paced about and was soon standing over by the fence smoking. Adam broke the awkward silence which had settled over the group.

'Will there be a rehearsal tonight, Marek?'

Marek had given little thought to the choir. Several of his work colleagues were regular attendees including, at one time, Edek. Sadly he could no longer take part. The effort of singing placed too much strain on his weak and wasted lungs.

'You're right. We should meet,' Marek agreed.

'Daniel's angry and resentful just at the moment. Let him be for a while,' Edek said, placing a reassuring hand on Marek's arm.

Despite being generally cheerful, Daniel possessed a darker, brooding side to his personality which often led to bouts of anger.

The wretchedness of their situation simply added to the blackness of his moods. The inability to improve their lot was a frustration every Jew shared; however, unfortunately for Daniel, he railed against the impossible.

Amos Fuswerk was the first to arrive for the evening's rehearsal. Rummaging inside his coat, he pulled out several brown bottles. Amos' home-brewed concoctions were always welcome. It raised the spirits and warmed the blood, which was something they would all welcome on a night such as this. The temperatures had plummeted recently and the snow which had fallen over a week ago had not yet thawed. Jakub, Eli and Adam were next to troop in, stamping their feet to regain some warmth.

'It's a good thing we're not playing instruments. Our hands would be too stiff to move,' Eli remarked with a smile as he tried to warm his white-tipped fingers.

Soon the little basement room, poorly lit and heated by a barely smouldering brazier, was full of low mumbling voices.

'What have you brought for us tonight, Marek?' Enoch, a bass, asked.

'I have a piece of my own we could try.'

It was the first composition Marek had written for months and the idea of performing something new was greeted with enthusiasm. Eli, the choir's secretary, worked at a printers' shop in the Ghetto, and had secretly produced copies, slipping them in amongst his regular work. The choir soon mastered the first page and they had moved on to tackling the second when Daniel entered quietly. Space was made for him amongst the tenor line, and as Marek handed him a copy of the music he smiled. The temptation for his friend to flout the Nazis' rules had proved too great. The choir persevered with some success, and were soon ready for Amos' beverage. Its quality could be variable, but a guaranteed constant was its potency and tonight's offering was no exception. They toasted the recent successes in routing the enemy. The fire began to burn a little brighter now and they crowded around and raised their battered mugs.

'To life,' Enoch exclaimed.

'To life,' the men cried in unison.

Marek looked around the room and smiled as the men downed the brew in a single swig, wiped their mouths and began to show signs of being more relaxed.

'This reminds me of life before the war,' Enoch remarked.

'What's that you say?' Adam asked, his eyes already showing signs of glazing over.

'Our rehearsals. Amos and his liquor.'

'Do you remember that one time? Just before a performance . . .' Eli chipped in.

'Yes,' Marek laughed. 'It was almost a disaster. Do you remember Amos?'

The little man was pouring from the third bottle. He looked up grinning broadly.

'I believe I do. Some of my finest.'

'Vintage '37 you called it unless I'm mistaken,' Marek added.

'Could strip paint off walls,' Daniel chuckled.

'And more,' Enoch exclaimed, chortling.

When all the bottles were empty it was time to resume the practice. Marek selected one of their favourite pieces and counted his friends in. Without the use of a piano the choir were obliged to perform a cappella. Though only few in number, they were a bunch of gifted individuals who could interpret a composer's intentions down to the most subtle nuances.

Without warning, the door burst open with such force that it came away from its hinges as two surly-looking Nazi soldiers, each clasping guns, rushed in. They stationed themselves silently on either side of the doorway. They were followed moments later by a tall, handsome man with a fair complexion, piercing blue eyes and light blond hair. His presence filled the room. With his distinctive collar patch and shoulder strap it was possible to discern his rank of General – *Oberst-gruppenführer* – the most senior rank in the SS. He looked around the room imperiously until his gaze came to rest on Marek.

'Singing Jews,' he sneered, raising his eyebrows. 'I take it you are in charge here?' His steely eyes tunnelled deep into Marek's.

'Yes,' Marek answered, as boldly as he could, trying hard to suppress the overwhelming anxiety rising within him.

'And your name?' he asked.

'Dr Marek Ruzanski.'

'A medical qualification,' he said looking impressed. Marek's response intrigued him and his expression altered.

'My doctorate is in music.'

'Ah! A cultured Jew . . .' he commented thoughtfully.

'There are a great many cultured Jews,' Marek exclaimed proudly.

'No doubt you are right,' he retorted.

The General's manners were impeccable but the interrogation ended quite abruptly when he caught sight of the music scores resting on an old wooden crate. As he rifled through them Marek held his breath for amongst them were works by well-known German composers. Then he alighted upon Marek's composition. Turning the pages, he began to hum the themes lightly under his breath. After what seemed an interminable amount of time he put the music down again.

'Your meeting has finished,' he declared to the assembled group, his words cutting through the silence like a knife.

No one moved. The members of the choir remained rooted to the spot with fear. Sensing this, the officer suddenly clapped his hands as if to break their trance-like state.

'Go! Go!' he reiterated, waving his hands dismissively. 'You have nothing to fear.'

Each member of the choir quickly gathered their things together and hurried towards the door.

'Please remain for a moment Dr Ruzanski.'

As soon as Marek's friends had disappeared the General signalled for the guards to depart as well.

'Please, Doctor, take a seat,' he said, gesturing towards the nearest bench.

'I will remain standing,' Marek told him.

'As you will, Doctor.'

He shrugged his shoulders then reached across and snatched up the music.

'I assume this is your composition?'

'Yes.'

'Simplicity and complexity combined. You are a fine craftsman.'

Marek said nothing.

'You must feel stifled here. A talent such as yours requires a larger arena,' he said thoughtfully as he began to stalk about the room.

Marek was unsettled by such perceptive remarks. Questions began to enter his mind as the pacing continued. What was this man thinking about and why had Marek been detained in this way? If he was going to be punished, even killed, why hadn't it happened yet and what had become of his friends? At last the General stopped pacing.

'I wish you to listen carefully. I have a proposition for you.'

Marek's heart began to race. Nazis were not renowned for their altruism, especially where Jews were concerned.

'I have been sent to organise operations in Warsaw,' he explained. He hesitated momentarily as if carefully considering his words. 'My skills are required by the Party.'

88

He did not elaborate further. He didn't need to. The reason for his summons was obvious. The Germans had experienced humiliation in the latest round of deportations and they would probably draw on their chief strategists for advice. The sheer arrogance this man exuded, together with his apparent fearlessness, explained his presence in the Ghetto at this hour. The Nazis made a point of avoiding the Ghetto after dusk for fear of attacks. No doubt he had come under heavy guard.

'As a man who, like yourself, appreciates culture, I intend to host certain events during my stay. Some theatrical performances and music, perhaps,' he continued.

'For the Jewish people?' Marek interjected.

'No. That won't be possible.' His answer was emphatic. 'There will be one occasion in particular which will surpass the rest, and to which I intend to invite some of the most powerful men of the Party. At this you will perform your masterpiece.'

It took a moment or two for the full impact of what he had said to sink in. No words came and then, in as composed a voice as he could muster, Marek replied.

'As much as I try I cannot possibly imagine how any work of mine could provide interest for the clientele you speak of.'

'Perhaps I should explain further. Richard Wagner was one of the greatest composers of all time, would you not agree, Doctor?'

'That is debatable,' Marek responded curtly. 'His music is, it has to be said, innately powerful, capable of arousing great passion in people. It is easy to see why a fascist government would adopt such a composer, exploiting and misappropriating his music for their own ends.' He was forgetting his situation.

'Ah! I see.' Clasping his hands tightly behind his back, he began to walk around the room again. At length he stopped. 'My proposal is this. You are to compose a choral work in the Wagnerian style. In it you will glorify neither Judaism nor make any reference to

God, but instead you must pay homage to the Führer and the Third Reich. You will complete the task in precisely two and a half months. That should give you more than enough time.'

Marek did not look him in the eye but instead stared straight ahead. The shock had been too keen.

'Do you have anything to say?' The Nazi general was impatient for Marek's response.

'And who would you ask to perform the work?'

'Your men will sing. You have trained them well. They are very talented.'

'What you ask is not possible. Such a work would represent the antithesis of my beliefs and a betrayal of my people.' Marek's voice was shaking, as the feelings of anger and intense hatred he felt for this man took hold.

'Your response does not surprise me,' he said without emotion. 'In fact I would have expected nothing less from a man of such integrity. However, I believe you will be inclined to change your mind when you are aware of the advantages of such an arrangement. As a reward for your services,' he said patronisingly, 'I will guarantee your personal safety and that of your family. You will not suffer anymore than what is natural. In the longer term none of us knows what will happen, however. I am sure you are well aware of this'.

He had made it abundantly clear. If Marek refused to do what was being asked of him his family would be snuffed out like candles. It was emotional blackmail.

'I doubt my friends will agree to it. Perhaps you forget that they have principles too,' Marek said

'They will receive the same assurances.'

Marek's cheeks felt flushed and his skin felt as though it was burning. He wanted to lash out physically but knew it would achieve nothing.

90

'You will need time to consider this opportunity. However, these will be the arrangements. At precisely eight o'clock each week day morning a car will be waiting for you on Gesia Street. You will be transported to my villa where you will work until evening. The same vehicle will take you back to the Ghetto. In two days' time a car will be waiting and if you have chosen wisely you will be there to meet it.'

Then, abruptly, he disappeared.

❖ ❖ ❖

Marek did not mention the unsettling encounter to his family. He knew it would distress them, especially so soon after Ezra and Mara's deaths. Later when Ruben returned, Marek took him aside on the pretext of needing a cigarette and explained what had happened. Ruben was dumbstruck.

'Do you believe you have a choice?' he asked once everything he had been told had sunk in.

'Do *you* think I have?'

'No.' Ruben's response was blunt.

'How can I possibly agree to it?' Marek asked in desperation.

'Maybe you won't have to.' The boy slipped off the ledge and extinguished the cigarette stub with the heel of his boot. 'I mean, anything could happen in the next two months. The war could end.'

The likelihood of this happening was slim, and his words of comfort rang hollow.

'What will you tell them?' Ruben asked, nodding in the direction of the apartment.

'I have no idea but I will have to mention something.'

'The truth?'

'Perhaps just some of it for the moment.' There was a pause.

'We had better go back or they'll think something's wrong. We have been out here long enough to smoke ourselves into a stupor.'

Two days later Marek was waiting a little way down Gesia Street. It was early – only a quarter to eight – and he had some time to think. He had assembled the choir, and explained the Nazi's demands. They were horrified at what was being asked of them, and, not surprisingly, tempers flared. The men knew they had little choice but to acquiesce. The threat to their loved ones' lives was too great, and something with which they could not take a chance.

At precisely eight o'clock, a black car rounded the corner of the street. An SS soldier got out and opened the rear door. Marek recognized him as one of the guards who had burst in on their rehearsal last week. He climbed in and they set off.

The car turned onto Al. Jerozolimskie, one of the main arterial roads which crossed the city. People were picking their way through the rubble and, despite the devastation, Marek envied them their freedom. An elderly woman – stick in hand and dressed in black from head to toe – was waiting patiently to cross the road. A mother whose children were lagging behind her urged them to hasten their steps. Etched on their faces were the grey, cheerless expressions Marek had become all too familiar with. Then it struck him that for each Pole he could see, there were as many, if not more, German soldiers. The once bustling Warsaw metropolis had all but lost its vitality, and in its place an oppressive atmosphere hung everywhere.

They continued to travel south. Back in 1939 Marek had

been dismayed by the bomb damage and plundering inflicted upon the once imposing Royal Castle which dominated the old town's square, and now he was appalled to see further widespread destruction. The day had begun brightly, although temperatures were still bitterly low and as they drove past Edwarda Park and then Lazienkowski Park the sun's rays reflecting off the blanket of snow was blinding. The feelings of exhilaration at experiencing such unspoilt beauty soon faded away when Marek spotted several large tanks and other armoured vehicles parked indiscriminately throughout the area.

Ahead Marek could see one of Warsaw's mansions. Constructed centuries ago, it was a fine example of the city's architectural craftsmanship and was mercifully intact. Its steeply pitched red tiled roof and cream stonework glistened in the bright light, and it was just the kind of property one could imagine a high-ranking Nazi officer commandeering as a residence. The car gradually came to a standstill at the entrance to the long drive, and four soldiers hurried to open the large wrought iron gates. The grounds of the house were magnificent. To the right, some way off, a shimmering expanse of blue caught Marek's eye. It was a lake, complete with an ornate stone bridge spanning the water at its far end. On the opposite side of the driveway was a well-maintained knot garden composed of evergreen shrubs.

The soldiers escorted Marek up the steps to the door and then vanished. He stood dwarfed beneath its portico-style entrance and, just as he was wondering whether to knock on one of the huge wooden panels, it opened to reveal the SS General waiting in the hallway.

'Good morning Doctor or, should I say, *Kapellmeister*? Did you enjoy your journey through the park?'

'Very much thank you,' Marek replied nervously.

'And how do you like my temporary home. Splendid, isn't it? It belonged to Count and Countess Liszinski who kindly donated it for the good of the Party,' he explained, laughing dryly.

'How very magnanimous of them,' Marek observed sarcastically.

The corners of Franz Reinecke's mouth creased into a smile as if the impudence had amused him.

'There is much to be done. Follow me,' he ordered brusquely.

The interior of *Dwór nad Jeziorem* (Mansion by the Lake) did not look as if it had been tampered with in any way, and from initial impressions it had the air of a family home rather than a military headquarters. Marek followed General Reinecke through one wood panelled room after another, each sumptuously decorated. There were heavy brocade curtains, richly-coloured tapestries, and rugs covering large areas of the polished wooden floors. A variety of ornamental clocks struck the half hour, and on numerous walls portraits of aristocratic men and women fixed the men with their gaze. Eventually they reached a room in the east wing which would be Marek's work place for the next two months. A great surge of warmth engulfed him as he entered the room. In the hearth a fire was burning fiercely. Then there was the smell, a subtle fragrance which, Marek discovered came from a large vase filled with iris blooms.

'The room is to your liking?'

'Yes,' Marek replied trying to hide his enthusiasm.

Nodding, the General left abruptly, closing the door firmly behind him.

The medium-sized room had a table at its centre and two expansive armchairs on either side of a pink marble fireplace. Decorating the walls were sketches of plump angels playing lyres and pipes in celestial settings. The grand piano was encased in polished mahogany. When Marek struck the keys he was rewarded by a light touch and his fingers glided over the notes with ease. Wandering over to the window, he looked outside. Trees and grass and flowers did not feature in the barren landscape of the Ghetto, and to be so close to nature had an intoxicating affect upon Marek. This part of the house overlooked the lake and he found himself staring dreamily at the expanse of water.

Returning to the fireplace, Marek noticed an oval-shaped mirror positioned above the mantelpiece. There was a looking glass in the Ghetto apartment, but he rarely used it because the quality of light in the bathroom was poor. Now in the bright daylight he was able to study his appearance, and was unprepared for what he saw. His brown eyes were discernibly blacker, emphasised no doubt by the dark circles under them, and his skin was dry and pallid. His shoulders looked slimmer beneath his jacket and shirt, and his arms had become less muscular. Though neither dishevelled nor unclean he decided his hair needed tidying. He passed his fingers through it and then checked himself. What was he thinking? There was no room for vanity. About to turn away from the mirror, he was startled when the door suddenly opened. A wave of embarrassment washed over him.

The eyes surveying him belonged to a matronly woman, probably a few years older than his mother. Her face appeared stern but her cheeks were rosy and dimpled. Her hair was pinned back into a chignon and she wore a tightly fitting pale blue dress and flat shoes. Marek decided she must be the housekeeper. He did not sense any hostility. The two continued their mutual sizing up of one another.

'The General asks whether you require anything? Have you eaten this morning? We can prepare breakfast for you.'

Marek declined the offer politely, having eaten some bread and one of the eggs his mother had managed to purchase. Satisfied with the response she scurried off. Besides, there was also the question of pride. Images of grotesquely bloated bodies covered in festering sores scavenging around the rubbish heaps for rotten potatoes swarmed into his mind. Marek wondered where the housekeeper's loyalties lay: was she a benevolent Pole who sympathised with the Jews' plight or was she impervious to their hardships? The Poles themselves were suffering under the German occupation: since invading the Nazis had shown them nothing but contempt, subjecting them to extreme forms of exploitation and humiliation.

Marek spotted a tall jug of water and some drinking glasses. Earlier nerves had left his throat dry. He had quite a thirst. As he raised a glass to his lips his hand trembled slightly. The situation he found himself in was unsettling. The beautiful surroundings belied the true reason for his presence. Feeling refreshed, Marek knew that he had to come to terms with the bald facts. As much as he detested the task he had accepted he could not procrastinate any more. Placing his fingers on the keys, he tried to remember when he had last sat at a piano. He started to perform a Bach Prelude and Fugue which he followed with some Beethoven and Schumann. When he finished, he stared at the still pristine page of manuscript. The words the Nazi officer had used at their initial encounter about how the work should 'glorify' Hitler and his evil henchmen echoed in his thoughts.

For several minutes Marek stared blankly at the clean music sheet then stretched his arms out in front of him. The first thing he needed to do was to consider the medium. It had to be choral, yet what form should it take? He visualised each of the vocal styles in his head and assessed them individually against a set of criteria. Having examined the options he decided that, with only eleven men available to perform it and no instrumentalists, he would have to adapt the form to fit the music.

A quarter of an hour later, and following an experience which could only be likened to pulling teeth, Marek had committed a few words to paper. 'Fatherland', 'glory' and 'conquest' were amongst them, but, suddenly overwhelmed by feelings of shame, he grabbed his pen and violently scored heavy, deep lines through the text. Scooping up the paper he tore it into several pieces before tossing it onto the fire. His frustration and anger expelled, Marek returned to the piano. He decided to concentrate on composing the music instead. He chose to play an extract from one of Wagner's music dramas and from the moment the sounds resonated in his ears he was reminded of how richly chromatic the harmonic language was and how brilliant was the use of dissonance. Strings of augmented sixths, dominant sevenths and ninths littered the compositions, often with delayed or no resolutions. As Marek played, his mind drifted to an earlier chapter in his life in which, as now, he was the main protagonist performing this same passage. It was at the Warsaw Conservatoire during his time spent there as a teacher.

The sound of a log falling in the grate disturbed Marek's reverie and brought him back to the present. It was not difficult to see why a despot such as Hitler should join the ranks of Wagnerian supporters. As well as being megalomaniacs, both composer and dictator shared similar backgrounds. Both believed they had suffered at the hands of a society which had nothing but total disregard for them. This acted as a catalyst for an overweening sense of persecution, almost paranoia, which manifested itself in a hatred of the Jews. The Nazis were quick to home in on the fascist qualities identified by many as inherent in the composer's works, and it was alleged that the Führer himself declared 'whoever wants to understand National Socialist Germany must know Wagner'.

Marek heard a faint knocking at the door. Hesitantly taking hold of the brass handle he opened it to find a young girl of about eighteen holding a tray. He peered at the clock and noted the hour: it was a little after one. He had completely lost track of time and hadn't realised the morning had slipped by so quickly. Marek beckoned her into the room and watched as she placed the tray onto the table. She wore a maid's uniform: a black dress, crisp white apron and neat polished dark shoes. Marek studied her pleasant, but not overly attractive, face and her light-coloured hair, pulled back rather severely at the crown. She did not seem like an avid follower of fashion. Marek sensed unease on her part. Perhaps she had never been in close proximity to a Jew before.

'Thank you,' Marek said, noticing a brief smile pass over her lips. 'Please will you pass on my appreciation to those who prepared it?'

She gave a slight nod and then disappeared.

Though conditioned through months of starvation to suppress the pangs of hunger, Marek was ravenous. The smell of the food stimulated his appetite. Impatiently he removed the lids to reveal a steaming plate of rich stew accompanied by a bright assortment of root vegetables and potatoes. Stacked to the side of this were slices of bread and a little container of oil, and on the other side a strudel of glazed apples and nuts encased in layers of pastry.

Not having eaten properly for many months, Marek was overcome by a strong urge to sleep. Back at the piano he picked up the pencil, intending to write the first few bars of the piece, but he felt his head loll gently downwards until it rested upon both his arms. He was awoken by the sound of knocking. To his amazement the hands on the clock now read six o'clock. He got up, trying to shrug off all signs of sleep, and dragged his feet to the door. It was the housekeeper again at whom he now peered, bleary-eyed. Marek thought he detected a look of amusement on her face then he realised why. If anyone had been listening they would have heard nothing but snoring.

'It is time for you to leave,' she said.

Marek hurriedly gathered up the blank sheet music and stuffed it into his case. No words were exchanged as they walked along the hall to the front door. It was dark and Warsaw had taken on a different appearance. There were no street lamps to guide the way because of the enforced blackout, only the vehicles' dimmed headlights. What remained of many ruined buildings destroyed in the Luftwaffe's bombing raids and, later those orchestrated by the Soviets, loomed into view with their jagged silhouettes against the night sky. It was as though all life had been sucked out of the city. Marek was deposited at the same spot where he had been met that morning. On the opposite side of the street he could make out a few figures in the shadows, but they showed little interest in the German soldiers or their passenger. He began to walk home. Some of the gutters were still full with blood from the shootings, and in one of them someone had tossed a half-eaten apple. Moments later, an urchin dashed out from nowhere, grabbed the bloodied fruit and crammed it into her mouth.

Climbing the stairs, Marek was surprised to encounter two men on their way down. He instantly recognised Yakov, the carpenter who had built the Ruzanski's new bunker a few weeks previously. They swapped some brief pleasantries before bidding each other goodnight. It was no surprise the men were in buoyant mood. With all the modifications and improvements to bunkers commissioned in the wake of the troubles, they were in great demand. Skilled workers in the Ghetto were enjoying a resurgence of their trades, bringing them financial rewards far in excess of what they might have earned before the war.

'How was your day, Marek?' Eva enquired as he entered the living room.

She was sitting, needle poised in hand, about to draw the thread through a tatty-looking garment belonging to her husband. The sight of her tending to a chore Mara would normally have done was touching. The Ruzanski family had tried to bear the loss of their beloved friends with stoicism, but there were so many poignant reminders which made it difficult to adjust.

'It went well, Mama.'

Eva was aware, as were Izak and Rachel, that there had been a change to her son's daily routine and he was now spending his working day at one of the requisitioned houses in the city, but, despite her concerns, she had not sought an explanation. Marek enquired about the bunker and the stranger he had bumped into with the carpenter.

'Yakov recommended him. He is an excellent plumber. Come . . .' she said leading him to the kitchen, '. . . see for yourself.'

Marek clambered inside the bunker and crawled around. An ingenious system of electric wires and pipes were in the process of being installed, to equip the shelter with electric light and proper sanitation. They had made considerable progress in just one day.

'They'll be back tomorrow. They had some spare time in their schedule and fitted us in,' Eva explained, as she popped her head through the entrance.

'Better than having to make do with a chamber pot, don't you think?' Rachel chirped up mischievously as she rinsed the turnips.

'That's true,' Marek agreed as he slid back out through the narrow passage.

Some families not only had the same amenities they would soon enjoy, but their bunkers could be stocked with enough food to see out the war. The Ruzanskis were unusually fortunate for Ruben had been able to provide a substantial number of non-perishable food items.

'I have some good news,' Eva blurted out suddenly.

'What's that Mama?' Marek asked curiously.

'Lidia and Benjamin will be spending the Sabbath with us.'

Eva's delight at the prospect of seeing her daughter and son-in-law again was tangible.

'Something to look forward to. How long is it since we've all been together?' Marek wondered.

'It's been several months now,' Izak said having joined them.

'We'll need some extra provisions,' Rachel said raising her voice as she spoke.

'I'll do my best,' came the response from the other room.

'Don't take any unnecessary risks, Ruben,' Izak urged the boy.

The timing of Lidia and Benjamin's visit was propitious since on the surface, at least, things did appear to be back to the way they were. Shops and, more importantly, the Ghetto's hospital had reopened and the *Judenrat* – an institution set up by the Nazis to act as a conduit or mouthpiece through which the Germans could issue their decrees to the Jewish people – was operating normally to all intents and purposes, despite having endured the heavy loss of many of its members. It was run by a Jewish council presided over by the *Obmann,* a position of some importance. The Judenrat might have appeared to have the welfare of its people at heart but Jews took little heed of its directives. Corruption was rife amongst its ranks and it had become distant from those whom it purported to represent.

Later that night when Ruben and Marek had retired to the space they shared the boy called across to Marek in a half whisper.

'Well, how did it go today?'

'The city is in a bad way.'

'From the raids?'

'There's more to it than that. It's as though a pall of misery has descended, choking everything it clings to. They've desecrated the parks with their tanks.'

'That's not surprising. The Germans have no respect for what doesn't belong to them. What about the villa? Is it as grand as it sounds?'

'It's very impressive but it's been neglected.'

'Gold and jewels.'

'I haven't seen any. Besides the Nazi would have quickly spirited anything like that away.'

'Who did you see today apart from the German?'

'A rather austere housekeeper and a timid maid who brought me a delicious meal.'

'Delicious! Eh! Not horsemeat and turnips then?' the young man said dryly.

'I believe there were turnips in it amongst other things.'

'What about something sweet?'

'Strudel.'

'Don't tell me it was scrumptious too,' Ruben said feigning envy.

'I'll bring whatever I can home next time,' Marek reassured his friend, beginning to feel decidedly guilty.

'Did you write anything?'

'Not a single note,' Marek told him.

Ruben leaned further across his eyes wide with expectation. 'What do you mean?'

'I fell asleep.'

'For how long?'

'Hours.'

Ruben smiled broadly.

'Well done, my friend! Keep up the good work.'

The wind was raw, and as Marek walked briskly to the pick-up point he looked forward to warming his hands in front of the roaring fire. On arriving at the house Marek was marched to the music room at a rapid pace by the housekeeper. The flames were leaping in the grate, and to one side of the hearth stood a scuttle full to the brim with coal. It made Marek's blood boil to think of how many people were dying in the Ghetto from cold. The freshly re-filled water jug stood proudly on the dresser and the scent wafting from the flowers was refreshing. The view from the window was breathtaking. Everything was shrouded in white. Icicles hung from the trees and shrubs in jagged points, and now the sun had penetrated the early morning mist. Her rays reflected off the icy waters and created the illusion that the lake was covered in gold. He stood and marvelled at the landscape and, for a moment or two, forgot his troubles.

Marek knew he would have to write something. It would not be long before his 'employer' would check on the progress he was making. He sat down at the piano and reached for a fresh piece of manuscript paper. Next to the pile was a row of sharpened pencils, which he found irksome. Nothing had been left to chance. He worked quickly, scratching away furiously for extended periods. Holding the pencil made him wince because of the injuries he had sustained at the factory. Gritting his teeth and trying his best to block out the pain it was not long before his natural flair for composition kicked in. He reviewed his scrawl. There it was: the opening theme which, with its added seventh and augmented sixth, had a distinctive discordant flavour. This would more than adequately meet the criteria for a triumphant beginning. Under normal circumstances Marek would have been pleased with his efforts but now he resented the talent he had been blessed with.

Towards the end of the morning, Marek's concentration was broken by the sound of clanking metal in the hallway. He jumped up nervously, not knowing what to expect, as a young man of about sixteen who was quite slim with tousled light-brown hair opened the door. There were traces of dirt smuts upon his cheeks, forehead and forearms, and he was carrying a metal bucket piled high with chopped wood. He hovered on the threshold just as the girl had done the previous day.

'Hello. Have you come to check the fire?' Marek asked as he set his load down in front of the grate.

'Yes, sir. My name's Dominik. I was told to bring some wood,' he explained.

'Thank you,' Marek said, and resumed his work.

As he dashed down a few more notes, Marek caught the boy squinting at him out of the corner of one eye. He smiled to himself. He was obviously a great source of curiosity.

His job done Dominik slipped away.

By lunchtime Marek had completed the whole of an eight-bar theme for high tenor. This would form part of a melodic chain, so idiosyncratic of Wagner. He had not, as yet, written a single word of the text.

Lunch was brought once again by the young woman. Still ill at ease, she did not linger for long. However, before she darted away, she managed a brief smile which Marek found encouraging. The food looked delicious and he tried to decide what could be smuggled home. After careful consideration he concluded that nothing but the bread could be transported successfully, for, without proper containers, his pockets would become flooded with a congealed, glutinous slop. Feeling guilty, he tucked in with gusto.

As Marek reached the steps to the family's apartment building later that evening, his ears were bombarded with the sound of heavy banging.

'What's that you're doing, friend?' He was curious to know what the stranger busy at work in the hallway was doing.

'I'm installing some alarm bells,' he replied, pointing proudly to a gadget he had just fixed to the wall. 'This button will warn everyone of danger.'

'It's a good idea,' Marek agreed, congratulating him on his workmanship.

'Systems like this are popping up all over the Ghetto,' he explained. 'We'll be ready when the Germans decide to strike again.'

Marek envied him his optimism and truly hoped he and his family and many others like them would be prepared for the next onslaught when it came. He had the uneasy feeling that they would not.

Days passed. There had been no further visits from General Reinecke. From within the music room Marek could sense little of what was happening elsewhere in the house. He could imagine the daily routines of the other members of the household including, to some extent, those of the Nazi. From time to time the sound of distant voices broke the silence, but essentially he was cut off. Despite this he was steadily gaining in confidence. One thing he was intent on doing was to encourage the maid to talk since her reserve, both embarrassing and irritating in equal measure, was beginning to unnerve him.

'Hello again. I'm Marek,' he announced just as she was about to scurry back to the kitchen.

'My name's Angelika,' she replied, startled, her cheeks flushed to a bright scarlet.

'How long have you worked here?'

'Nearly three years.'

'So you must have worked for the previous owners?' Marek was interested to learn something about them.

'Yes, we all did, until the Nazis arrived.'

'Were your employers forced to leave?'

'Yes,' she explained, more relaxed now and quite eager to talk. 'One day a group of Nazi officials turned up. We all kept out of their way, except for Mrs Dabrowski. She had to take them food.'

'Is she the housekeeper?'

'Yes. The Germans told the Liszinski family that they had to give up their home for the good of the Party and that they must leave straight away.'

'And what does everyone think of the new master?'

'He is not our master,' she declared indignantly. 'We work here because we have to, just like you.'

'Ah!' Marek muttered under his breath. So they had discussed his presence there. Thinking for a moment he then asked, 'Does he bother you?'

'No. He keeps to himself most of the time. He sometimes has meetings here with other Nazis and he often disappears at the beginning of the day and doesn't return until much later. We do as we're told. That's the best way, so Mrs Dabrowski says.'

'How long has she worked here?'

'Most of her life. She met her husband here when he was in charge of the stables.'

'The previous owners used to keep horses?'

'Yes, but that was a long time ago.'

'And does her husband still work here?'

'Yes, he's the gardener.'

'I haven't met him yet. What about your family?'

'They live in the city. My father has a small shoe repair business and my mother stays at home to care for us. My brother, Dominik, works here at the house as well.'

'Yes, I've met him. He attends to the fire.'

'They say you are a composer.'

'Yes that's right.'

'Is it true you have to write music for the Nazis?'

'Yes. I wish the circumstances were different.'

Suddenly the girl began to fidget. She looked towards the clock.

'I must go. I've stayed too long. Mrs Dabrowski will have jobs for me.'

❖   ❖   ❖

The afternoon light faded quickly, but Marek was so heavily absorbed with the workings of a particularly complex part of the composition he didn't notice. So engrossed was he that he did not hear someone steal into the room. He did not know how long he was observed, but glancing up he was startled at the sight of a figure hovering in the shadows. With the click of a switch the ghoulish apparition evaporated, and in the lamplight Marek recognized General Reinecke.

'I did not mean to alarm you, Doctor. You were immersed in your task. Now I have disturbed you. What you were composing was most intricate to the ear. Are you certain your choir will be capable of such a challenge?'

'They are excellent singers,' Marek retorted angrily.

His mouth curled into a half-smile and Marek cursed himself for having risen to the bait.

'Of course their performance will be splendid,' he said reassuringly as he moved closer. He was a foot or two away from Marek's shoulder and near enough to view the score. 'Your progress is impressive. I would very much like to hear all of what you have written, if you would oblige.'

Marek braced himself and then began.

At first the Nazi's inscrutable expression remained intact. Then something extraordinary happened. A few bars into the music there was a twitching at one corner of his mouth followed by the involuntary explosion of a smile. The officer's hand began to sway in time with the rhythm. Feelings of sheer joy and passion that the music evoked could not be suppressed even by those with an iron will.

'Magnificent, *mien Kapellmeiste*r, magnificent,' the German exclaimed, clapping his hands together. 'You are as talented as I judged you to be. I predict it will be your finest work. Truly, a masterpiece.'

Marek ought to have felt flattered by this fulsome praise. The General had ignored the Jew's aloof indifference and had instead launched into a detailed analysis of the work. The use of harmony, keys and melody were discussed at length and all his observations were disconcertingly accurate. When Marek thought he had finished, the General suddenly spoke again.

'The words? I did not notice any.'

'It is my method,' Marek said hoping that his rehearsed response would sound convincing. 'I prefer to compose the music first and then add the text later.'

'Ah! You take your inspiration from the music. I believe Wagner wrote the libretto first.' His demeanour altered as he added tersely, 'Words can be difficult to select.'

It was obvious he had seen through the excuse. This did not bother Marek quite as much as the fact that General Reinecke was extremely knowledgeable and intelligent and would not be easily outsmarted. He had no choice but to battle on.

Marek woke at dawn to hear the plaintive notes of a bird outside the window. It had been some time since he had heard birdsong. In winter many birds emigrated to warmer climates, but now even the robin, that most territorial of creatures, had abandoned the Ghetto and its residents. Animals can sense human pain and sorrow, and the little creature's song was soft and emotive. It did not settle long and moments later, with a fluttering of wings, had vanished. How he envied the little bird. Free to travel anywhere without the mortal fear of the Jewish race. Marek climbed out of bed and drew back the threadbare curtains.

'Is it late Marek?' Ruben asked, rubbing his eyes.

'No. Usual time. The sun's risen and there's no mist. It's going to be a lovely day.'

'Weather-wise,' the boy said brusquely, stifling a yawn.

He was right. It was impossible to predict exactly how each day would turn out and if everyone would still be safe at its end.

'It is Monday?' Ruben asked.

'Yes. Will you be seeing action today?' Marek asked knowing that for Ruben, and others like him, the stakes had been raised.

'Some Polish freedom fighters have secured intelligence about the location of an arms depot in the city.'

'What? You're surely not thinking about getting involved. A place like that is bound to be heavily protected.'

'It is, but there's another way in through the adjoining building. Some of our Polish supporters have dug a tunnel,' Ruben explained.

It came as no surprise to Marek that Ruben had been recruited to help. His reputation as the Ghetto's most successful smuggler was not for nothing. The consummate professional, he was also utterly fearless. There was a genuine need for more arms. The Jewish Military Union – the *ZZW* – had a cache of weapons and ammunition, but they needed more in preparation for the big battle which, according to their sources, lay ahead. The two friends shook hands before going their separate ways, and wished each other luck.

The drive to the Nazi's villa was not as monotonous as usual.

One of the soldiers, Ernst, had a filthy cold and was feeling sorry for himself. Blowing his nose at regular intervals, he had soon made as much use of his handkerchief as was hygienic. He asked his companion if he could borrow his. Then, after complaining bitterly about his posting to Warsaw, he launched into a tirade in which he cursed the harshness of the Polish weather. His colleague, Viktor, who also hailed from a milder climate, joined in, adding a few choice invectives of his own.

'Those Jews must freeze their balls off,' Ernst muttered.

'That is if they have any,' Viktor retorted before sniggering.

'We have balls. You can be sure of that,' Marek interrupted in fluent German.

The two of them were taken aback at hearing their passenger speaking their own language, despite it being customary for educated Jews to be multilingual, and Marek sensed they didn't know quite what to do next. Minutes passed and when the retaliation Marek had expected did not materialise, it dawned on him that, however frustrating for them, the soldiers were under strict orders to deliver their passenger back and forth in one piece. A little later the stricken soldier took out a packet of cigarettes from his jacket pocket and, after handing one to Viktor, leant across and offered another to Marek.

'Maybe this will warm you, Jew,' he sniffled with derision, his eyes bloodshot from the cold.

The sub-zero conditions made it difficult to get the iron door handle to budge, and Marek had to grip the lion's head with both hands. The cold metal made him wince and he was relieved to step inside and take shelter from the merciless elements. No one was there to meet him and he made his own way to the music room. The speedy pace which the General and his housekeeper had set previously meant that most of the portraits lining the passageways had registered as little more than a blur but he now had an opportunity to study them. It soon became obvious that the family descendants shared common characteristics: noble foreheads, strong noses and deep blue eyes, and handsome, rather than beautiful, faces. In most of the paintings the subject was astride a magnificent steed, which suggested a passion for the outdoors and equestrian pursuits. Marek was reminded of what Angelika had said about the stables somewhere in the grounds and wondered why they were no longer in use. Perhaps, as with many of these grand homes, funds had run short and there was the need for economies.

Entering the music room, which was no longer a place of foreboding, Marek noticed a number of changes: someone had placed a bowl of fruit on the table and a bottle of cordial next to the water. Perhaps they had been provided at the whim of a satisfied Nazi officer but Marek suspected it was an act more characteristic of the sympathetic Mrs Dabrowski. More significant was the fact that fruit could be easily concealed in deep pockets. Marek made good headway and began to look forward to lunch and eliciting further information from the now affable maid. Anticipating her arrival a little before one, he unfastened the door. After setting the food down in its regular spot she tugged at her apron and Marek noticed a twinkle in her eye.

'I have an important message from the General.' Angelika hesitated for a second or two as if trying hard to recall his exact words. 'He says you should look around the grounds after you've eaten your lunch. The, the . . . ,' she broke off again, '. . . the experience may provide you with the inspiration you need.'

Marek thanked her. When she had gone, however, anger got the better of him. Though couched in elegant terms, the Nazi's missive was unambiguous. The man was ordering his employee to begin work on the text. Well, he would have to wait.

His forecast of fine weather proved correct, though ice still carpeted the ground and it was bitterly cold. His threadbare coat and Mara's knitted scarf did not provide enough warmth. The air was fresh and clean – unlike the atmosphere in the Ghetto which had become stale and rancid, contaminated as it was by the smell of rotting foodstuffs and human detritus – and Marek inhaled slowly, savouring its purity. The thick ice crunched underfoot. Reaching the lake, Marek inspected the frozen water. Most of the ice had formed an opaque film on the surface but in other areas it was translucent. Following the bank for a few yards he crouched down, straining to make anything out in the murky depths. There was a fair amount of weed, but just as he was hoping to see a fish or two a fuzzy image spread over his area of focus. He toppled backwards and his heart began to pound.

'Frightened you, did I?' said a gruff voice laughing.

Standing over him was a tall, willowy man of advancing years. His skin was weather-beaten and wrinkled and he had a small nose and thin-lipped mouth, and his eyes retained a youthful sparkle. Offering him his hand, he pulled Marek up.

'Out for a saunter, are you?' he enquired, examining the stranger's inadequate clothing. 'You could do with some thicker boots you know.'

'What you say is true,' Marek responded. The longer he remained immobile the more certain he became of this fact.

'You must be the musical Jew I've been hearing about.'

'Yes, I suppose I am,' he said laughing. 'And yourself?'

'Dabrowski. Head Gardener. There's a fair bit of land worth exploring if you're keen,' he said pointing to an area a way off to the right. 'Straight ahead – see it – is a small copse and through it – out the other side or around it depending on which route you take – is a summerhouse. A pretty little building.'

Marek nodded. He was trying very hard to control his teeth

which had begun to chatter uncontrollably. Mr Dabrowski was now busy pointing to something else and didn't notice his new acquaintance's discomfort.

'See, there. Beyond the house. That is where I spend most of my time.' At this stage he became aware of Marek's forlorn state. 'You'd better go back inside and save your explorations for another day,' he said, sounding concerned.

With that he trudged off, heading for the spot he had shown Marek moments earlier.

Ensconced in the music room again, Marek stood watching the fire's amber flames race up the walls of the chimney breast, and gradually began to thaw out. When the numbness had worn off and he could once again flex his fingers, he continued without interruption until it was time to return to the Ghetto.

The factory choir was due to meet that evening. Marek arrived at the deserted building a little earlier than usual and was perturbed to see a light on. Much to his relief he discovered Amos inside, sitting on an old packing crate smoking a cigarette, his short legs dangling a few inches from the floor. His pockets were bulging and Marek reckoned that he had brought another couple of bottles with him.

'How is your work going?' Amos asked.

'Things could be worse,' Marek explained. 'How's life at the factory? Any news of Edek?'

'I'm afraid he's not too good,' Amos explained. 'He's had another fit.' The tenor of his voice was serious.

'Where was this?' Marek pressed him further. It was important to find out.

'At his machine. It's only a matter of time before one of the guards sees him,' Amos said, shaking his head.

'He should stay home now surely?' Marek suggested. 'What does Adam say?'

'Adam agrees, but Edek won't give up.'

'I suppose working gives him a purpose to go on living.'

'Exactly,' Amos agreed. 'But it won't be long now.'

Marek could feel the emotion welling up in his throat. He swallowed hard. Edek was a good man.

'Are they feeding you?' Amos asked.

'As a matter of fact they are, though I would swap it all for factory rations and my old job. There haven't been any improvements I presume?'

'Of course not. Still just watery soup and stale bread.'

Marek studied his friend carefully and suddenly felt compelled to say something.

'Amos, you don't have to do this, you know.'

Of all the choir members Amos had the least to lose. Tragically his wife had contacted typhus and had passed away a few months earlier, and his children and their families had been dragged off to the camps. He said nothing but slid off the box. He pulled out one of the bottles and passed it to his friend.

'Let's have a glass before the others get here,' Amos suggested.

'Why not?' Marek smiled gratefully.

He dashed over to where several packing cases had been stacked against the wall and rummaged about in one of them. He returned with two tin mugs, and his companion poured a liberal amount into each. Marek took a generous mouthful of the clear liquid, but was soon coughing violently. Amos, who had survived his swig unscathed, chuckled.

'Powerful stuff,' Marek croaked in between convulsions. 'What's in it?'

'Oh, this and that. I've been experimenting,' he chortled, unable to hide his amusement.

114

'Any more of this and I'll be conducting from under the table.'

The rest of the choir arrived soon afterwards, and crowded around Marek, eager for news of his work at the Nazi's mansion. They listened attentively and then Enoch asked to look at the new score. Marek handed it to him and the others scurried to his side to look.

'Such an arresting opening.'

'The harmony is bold and daring. A challenge to perform.'

'Very stirring.'

'Marek, what you have created here is the beginning of a masterpiece,' Daniel said with admiration.

There was almost a scrum as they each grabbed a drinking mug. On such a cold night everyone was eager to benefit from the warming alcohol coursing through their veins. In no time at all the room was echoing with the sound of gasping, coughing and spluttering. Amos and Marek laughed and exchanged a conspiratorial smile. Some time later, the men said goodbye to one another, fortified more than usual for the walk home.

'You didn't see Ruben while you were out did you?' Eva called from the living room.

'No Mama. Isn't he back yet?' Marek yelled loudly as he bolted the apartment door. Then he remembered what Ruben had said earlier that day. Danger was such a dominant element in their lives that it had almost become trivialised.

'Do you know where he is? Did he say anything?' Izak asked.

Usually nestled in his armchair at this time in the evening, he was staring out into the darkness.

'He had a job to do somewhere in the city. But he'll be back. It's still early for him.'

'On the other side of the wall?' Eva was horrified.

'Yes,' Marek hesitated, wondering whether to tell them everything he knew.

'What exactly is he involved in?' Rachel said, emerging from her room.

'The Germans have a stockpile of weapons in a warehouse and the Resistance wants to get its hands on them.'

'And they're using a boy to do the job for them,' Rachel exclaimed angrily.

'He's exceptionally skilled and they know it,' Marek said.

'You knew this and you did nothing to stop him?' There was sharp anger in her voice.

'What do you think I could have done?' Marek shouted in retaliation. 'There's nothing I can do to stop him when he's hell-bent on doing something. Ruben knows the risks, and besides we're all going to die soon anyway. So let him die a hero if he wants to.'

Rachel burst into tears, ran to her room and slammed the door behind her. Eva followed, leaving Izak and Marek alone together.

'We'll give him an hour and then we'll go and search for him,' Marek said.

Izak nodded, settled back in his chair and picked up his newspaper. Marek knew it was a ploy to kill time because his spectacles were still in their case. Marek searched for a cigarette. Unfortunately he had finished the last one the night before, and wished Ruben would hurry up and come home with his stash. The minutes passed slowly and the two men began to feel more and more unsettled. Eva came out of Rachel's room, declaring that she was going to make everyone a hot drink, but not before berating her son for upsetting his sister. The hour soon passed but still there was no sign of Ruben.

'Right, we'd better go and see what we can find out,' Izak said.

Nothing stirred out on the street. It was a little after ten, and well into the period of post-curfew. However, this was no longer such a perilous time. The majority of Germans refrained from patrolling the Ghetto after dark following the Jewish resistance in January. Izak and Marek edged their way along in the shadows. Fortunately the moon had temporarily hidden itself behind a scudding cloud. They were making their way to the headquarters of the *ZZW*. It was eerily quiet, and another night of heavy frost and arctic temperatures. They took care to tread softly on the crisp ice, hoping not to draw attention to themselves. It was foolhardy to become too complacent. The Germans were unpredictable at best and, because of this, some families had taken to sleeping in their bunkers indefinitely.

Suddenly the two men heard noises a yard or two ahead. They stopped in their tracks. Whatever the source, it did not sound human and yet they could not take any risks. Then the clouds shifted and illuminated the ghastly sight of three corpulent rats gorging themselves on a decomposing body. One of them had nibbled away the flesh from part of the face to reveal grey-coloured sinew and bone, and was trying to tear strips of skin from the other cheek. A second was trying to work an eye from its socket, making jerking, stabbing movements with its teeth. It was clearly most skilled at this, for the other orb had been tugged out successfully, had rolled and was now balanced on the nose tip. The fattest of the three rats, having discovered the carotid artery, was smeared with congealed discharge and it was the slurping noises as it feasted which could be heard. The Ghetto residents had become inured to spectacles such as this. When they saw the two men, the rats scampered across to the other side of the street. Marek signalled to his father and they quickened their pace, eager to pass through this dangerous and uninviting neighbourhood.

Soon the two men reached a building on Muranowska Street. Izak tapped gently twice on the door. He waited for a moment before knocking again. The door swung open to reveal a young man. In little more than a whisper he asked them politely what their business was.

'Can you tell Ludwik Pirovicz that Izak Ruzanski and his son would like to talk to him please?'

The stranger ushered them inside and asked them to remain in the hallway. The building – the same design as their own – had several storeys, with apartments on each level. Soon footsteps were heard along the passage, and in the darkness they could make out the shadow of a man in his early twenties – similar in age to Marek – approaching. Ludwik had been a popular individual in the community before the war, but his involvement with the Resistance required that he now kept a low profile.

'How is your father, Ludwik? I haven't seen him lately,' Izak enquired, as the two men embraced.

'Keeping as well as any of us can in the circumstances. And how are things with you, Marek?'

'I'm well thank you,' Marek replied, shaking his hand.

'Will you be joining us in the final battle?' he asked, staring him directly in the eye.

'I will do my bit when the time comes,' Marek answered emphatically, wondering if Ludwik's network knew of his association with General Reinecke.

The three men walked down some narrow steps to the cellar, Ludwik's tall, strong-built frame hurrying ahead. The air was thick with cigarette smoke and Marek could hear hushed murmurs. This part of the building served as the nerve centre for the resistance movement, and half a dozen men were huddled over what appeared at first glance to be a large document. As one member moved it was possible to make out a map of the city with red rings encircling particular areas. Ludwik introduced his guests to the assembled group. Then he led them to the other end of the cellar.

'How can I help you?' he asked earnestly, drawing up three chairs.

'Do you have any news of Ruben Kenigsberg?' Izak asked. 'We believe he took part in one of your missions today, but he hasn't returned.'

'Ruben. Yes. The great smuggler. A clever fellow indeed,' Ludwik said thoughtfully.

'Is he alive?' Marek came straight to the point.

'I'm sorry to say I don't know. There were quite a few casualties,' Ludwik explained.

'Did you secure the weapons?' Izak asked.

Silently, Ludwik dug inside his jacket pocket and took out some cigarettes, which he offered them. Marek took one.

'It was always going to be difficult to pull off but our men did well,' he continued. 'Got most of the stuff out, but then the Germans must have become suspicious.' He paused for a moment. 'Perhaps they'd been tipped off. According to initial reports we lost five men, two made it back and one is still unaccounted for.'

'Ruben,' Marek said quickly, looking at his father.

They stood up to go but as they approached the stairs Ludwik called out after them.

'Abraham was with Ruben. He made it back safely.'

'Where can we find him?' Marek asked.

'He lives a few streets south of here,' Ludwik explained, giving them directions.

'Will it be too late to speak with him now?' Izak said, checking his watch.

'Vladek can go along with you. He knows the code and is very reliable.'

The young man was still standing guard at the door. Ludwik spoke to him, and from his reaction it was easy to discern that he was glad to be relieved of his sentry duties and entrusted with an important errand to run.

Once again father and son were at the mercy of the climate. Sleet was streaking across the sky and pricking their eyes. Marek was wearing gloves but he knew that it wouldn't be long before his hands started to turn a deep shade of blue. Vladek shot off at a brisk pace and the Ruzanskis followed behind as quickly as they could. He had a thorough knowledge of this area of the city and it was not long before they were waiting in the courtyard which formed the hub of nearly all apartment blocks. Their guide explained that, because of the system, he would have to abandon them for a little while but before the energetic youth disappeared out of sight he reassured the Ruzanskis that he would be back. True to his word, he was.

Marek and Izak were directed up a flight of stairs to a first floor landing where, slouching against a door, his form half-obscured in the dimness, they found Abraham Leber. As he saw them approach he stepped out of the shadows. He had pulled a jacket on over his nightclothes, and appeared considerably strained and edgy. He apologised for having to conduct their discussion on the landing. His family were asleep inside and he didn't want to disturb them. The three men huddled together so the level of their voices could be kept to the minimum.

'So you're trying to find Ruben?' Abraham asked. He paused. 'Well, the truth is I don't know what's happened to him.' Becoming agitated he added, 'He may have got out alive or he might be dead. The Germans could have picked him up but I don't know for sure . . .'

120

'Weren't you with him?' Izak asked sympathetically, just as a parent would coax a young child.

'Yes I was, but it was more difficult than you may realise.' Abraham shivered and pulled his jacket tighter around him. 'There is a warehouse in the city where the Germans keep a huge stockpile of weapons. The plan was to steal them. At first I thought it was a crazy idea because the area is heavily patrolled, but we received some new intelligence which made it clear that each afternoon there is a change of guards, but the process takes a while.'

'And this would create a weakness you could exploit?' Marek suggested.

'Not quite enough time but yes,' he replied. 'The warehouse is situated in a busy section of the city where there are scores of people milling about. It was agreed the Polish underground would set up a decoy to distract the guards' attention, which, in theory, would give us enough time to grab what we had come for and get away safely.'

'How were you proposing to enter the building? Surely it would have been madness to attempt this in broad daylight, even with the decoy in place?' Izak asked in disbelief.

'They'd dug a tunnel through from the neighbouring building,' Marek explained.

'How do you know this?' Abraham was clearly vexed and started to fidget nervously.

'Ruben told me,' Marek said, eager to put the poor fellow at his ease.

'By midday we'd left the Ghetto. There's a hole in the wall on Leszno Street.' Abraham relaxed slightly. 'The Poles had smuggled clothes through for us.'

He had light-coloured hair like Ruben which would increase his chances of mingling with the crowds.

'At first everything went according to plan. The new guards

arrived, the diversion was in place – the Poles had booby-trapped a house on the opposite side of the street – and we advanced on the signal. We got as much out as we could, then it all started to go wrong.' He blew on his hands and then sank down and crouched against the wall.

'The Germans were taken in at first. Perhaps they found the explosives too easily, or perhaps someone tipped them off. Anyway, before we knew it guards from both shifts were piling into the warehouse. Ruben and I dragged ourselves back through the tunnel and out to where the truck should have been waiting.'

'The truck wasn't there?' Marek asked.

He nodded. 'The priority was to secure the weapons. That was agreed beforehand. When we got outside the truck was driving away without us. We had no other choice but to make a run for it. We ran like wildfire ducking their bullets, but five of our men were hit. Dead.'

'Ruben. He wasn't one of them?' Izak asked.

'No. We stuck together.'

'And then?'

'We kept running until we spotted an alleyway off the main street. There was a wall on one side and Ruben jumped clean over it. I didn't stop and that's the last time I saw him.'

Neither Izak nor Marek spoke as they walked back. They were too busy trying to make sense of it all. Ruben could normally extricate himself from the most perilous situation; however, maybe this time his luck had run out.

After a sleepless night, Marek wandered into the kitchen and was surprised to find his father sitting at the table nursing a mug of coffee.

122

'Would you like some?' Izak offered.

Marek picked up the pot and watched as the gloopy substance trickled out.

'I couldn't sleep for thinking about Ruben.'

'Me too.'

'It would be better to know, don't you think? At least with Ezra and Mara . . .' Izak's voice trailed away as he heard his wife approach.

'Any news?' Eva asked anxiously.

'Come and have some coffee, darling, and I'll tell you what we've found out.'

While his parents chatted Marek resolved to make his peace with Rachel. He filled a second cup with the steaming thick liquid. She was still sleeping so he placed it on the bedside table and perched on the edge of her bed. She began to stir.

'Ruben. Is he home?' She said hazily, rubbing her eyes.

'I brought you some coffee.'

'Is he dead?' She pulled herself up.

'You know what Ruben's like,' her brother said trying to sound light-hearted. 'He's got nine lives. What little we know is fairly inconclusive at the moment. He became separated from the rest of the group and they didn't see him again.' He hesitated and shifted awkwardly. 'I'm sorry I shouted at you last night Rachel. I shouldn't have done that.' They rarely had cross words, even as children, and he regretted his loss of temper.

'I'm sorry too, Marek,' she said grasping her brother's hand and drawing him closer. 'I've been thinking a lot about death. I can't get it out of my mind. My own and yours, and mother's and Papa's and Lidia's.' As she said this, her lip quivered and tears started to well up in her beautiful brown eyes.

'You mustn't think like this,' Marek implored her, trying to give some reassurance.

'I've been considering all the things I wanted to do with my life. I'm too young to die and so are you.'

Marek stroked her cheek lightly.

'Do you really believe Ruben's alive?'

'I hope he is.'

Rachel smiled faintly.

'I've got to go now, but I'll see you tonight.' Marek leaned forward and kissed her forehead. 'Drink your coffee before it gets cold.'

Despite his work, the day passed slowly, and Marek found himself thinking of little else but Ruben and his mysterious disappearance.

By evening the Ruzanskis still hadn't heard any news about Ruben. There was no trace of him. If he had been picked up by the Germans it wouldn't be long until news filtered through via the *Judenrat* – the Germans were fond of gloating – but they had little choice but to wait. Eva and Rachel busied themselves preparing for Lidia and Benjamin's visit, and the latest edition of *Gazeta Zydowska* had been delivered to occupy Izak.

For a second night Marek found he was unable to sleep. He unbolted the apartment door, just in case Ruben found his way home. Too many things were buzzing around in his mind: music, Ruben's disappearance, and Rachel's morbid thoughts. It must have been well after midnight when he heard a noise. His first thought was that it might be Izak who was struggling to settle. Marek was not at all frightened, merely curious. He slid out of bed, but before he could reach the door someone stepped inside.

'Ruben! Where have you been? We've been looking everywhere for you.'

'I thought you'd all be asleep by now. I didn't mean to wake you,' the boy whispered hoarsely.

124

'I haven't been able to sleep,' Marek said groping around for some matches.

In the candlelight he could make out a wad of cloth that had been wound around his head just above the temple.

'Ruben, you're hurt!'

'Is there any coffee?' Ruben asked.

Taking care not to wake anyone, they tiptoed to the kitchen. Ruben was limping badly. As he prepared the coffee, Marek told him what had transpired the night before and how much of the story they had managed to piece together.

'Papa and I went to see Ludwik,' Marek explained.

'You went to see him?' the boy said sitting down.

'We needed to know what had happened to you.'

'What did he say? How many men did we lose?'

'Five.'

The boy lowered his eyes.

'What about Abraham? Did he make it?'

'Yes.'

'Thank God!'

'He told us how the two of you became separated when you jumped over a wall.'

Marek drew up another chair.

Ruben took a breath and began his tale. Marek listened engrossed.

'At a little after three the sound of the explosion echoed in my ears. That was the signal and I hauled myself through the tunnel followed by Abraham. The sight which greeted us was like that of a treasure trove, although, instead of brightly coloured trinkets, it was stuffed full of weaponry. It was my job to pass guns through the tunnel where they would be taken to a wagon. There was no time to lose. Then I heard something which made my blood run cold: German voices and the heavy tread of boots heading in our direction. We heaved ourselves back inside the passage and scrabbled furiously on our hands and knees before making it out to the road. I scoured the empty street in disbelief; there was no sign of the truck. We, like the others who were keeping guard, had been thrown to the lions. There was nothing for it but to run and run as fast as our legs could carry us. The Germans would be after us in no time at all. The sound of gunfire reverberated through the air, followed by several bullets narrowly missing my head. One by one I heard the thud of friends falling to the ground. Only Abraham was still at my side. The bullets kept coming and my chest began to tighten. Just when I thought there was no way out I glimpsed an alleyway directly ahead. On one side there was dense undergrowth and on the other a wall. Mustering all my reserves of energy I jumped and cleared it in one go. I remembered landing hard and then nothing. The next thing I was aware of was a haze through which figures loomed muttering incoherently. At first I fancied I was dead. Suddenly there was a sharp pain in my head and the hovering shapes gradually took human form. Voices became louder and more distinct. I was lying in a bed and a woman was perched on its edge. She had compassionate eyes and a concerned expression on her face. Soon I drifted off to sleep. When I awoke the next day I was sore but felt refreshed. I spent the morning sitting in front of a roaring fire enjoying the best meat stew I've tasted in a long while.'

'So you landed in someone's garden.' A smile crossed Marek's lips.

'Yes, but it wasn't a soft landing as you can see. I'd ended up in the garden of a Polish couple and caught my head on a jagged stone.' He patted the dressing. 'It was quite a blow from that height and I knocked myself out. I'm not sure how long I lay there but, when I came to, it was dark and someone was shining a torch into my face. Their dog found me, which was a good thing too. I could have frozen to death. They helped me into their house and put me to bed. The woman must have washed my wounds and bandaged my head. That part of it is just a hazy picture. Someone else came to see me – a man, I think – who held up various objects and asked me to name them.'

'That might have been their doctor,' Marek suggested, 'checking for concussion probably.'

'I think he put some stitches in my head and gave me something for the pain. Here, I've still got some,' he said putting his hand in his pocket and taking out a small glass bottle of pills. 'When I woke the next day I was anxious to leave straight away, but the woman wouldn't let me, saying I would have to wait until nightfall when it would be safer. She explained the Germans might be hunting for me and with my injury I would be an easy target. So I was obliged to rest until evening, eat and keep myself warm. They wouldn't give me their names, and they didn't want to know mine nor how I had ended up amongst their shrubs. I had the feeling they'd probably helped others before me.'

Ruben was beginning to show signs of exhaustion. He was barely able to keep his eyes open. Marek helped him to bed and within seconds he had fallen asleep. The Gentiles who had helped him would have done so on pain of death. There were still some acts of kindness amongst all the abominations of the wicked world.

Marek's composition was developing well, and grew by several bars each day. The temperature had lifted a degree or two, and after lunch, he ventured outside. He had decided to follow Mr Dabrowski's advice and visit the summerhouse beyond the thicket. Trudging across the grass was not easy however. The ground was waterlogged and the inadequacy of his boots soon became apparent. In no time at all his trousers were spattered with flecks of mud, which was ankle-deep, and his socks were sodden. Eventually he arrived at a group of trees, tall and dense enough to obscure any view which lay ahead. He hesitated for a moment, wondering whether to beat a path through the middle or to skirt around. He thought the latter would probably be quicker. He squelched his way around the copse, following the line of the trees, and, as he emerged on the other side, caught sight of a charming little structure – fashioned in the same style as the mansion – a little way off. The winter sunshine reflected off the pale stonework, and he was struck by its neatness. Flanking the entrance were two fluted columns and as he approached his attention was drawn upwards to the entablature, upon which had been sculpted graceful sylphs with flowers in their hair and fawns at their feet. Marek peered through one of the windows, but could see little more than a number of chairs stacked in front of the glass. The door was not locked but its wooden handle was swollen and it took a hefty shove before he was in.

The house hadn't been aired for months and the smell of damp was overpowering. The plaster, a delicate shade of pink, was peeling off the walls, and there were drips of hardened candle wax dotted across surfaces and along the floor. Marek stood for a moment soaking up the ambience. It was easy to imagine how things might have been once, with elegantly-dressed people sipping from crystal glasses while engaged in lively conversation. There was, oddly he thought, a fireplace, but then it occurred to him one might be needed during late summer evenings prior to the onset of autumn.

Marek pulled the door to and set off to explore the gardener's domain. He found a path which seemed to lead towards the general area where the old man had pointed. At first it ran parallel to the side of the mansion, and then it forked left across a patch of open ground towards a cluster of outbuildings. Before reaching these, and in a westerly direction – protected on three sides by a stone wall – was what must have once been an old-fashioned kitchen garden. As he wandered through the garden Marek looked for Mr Dabrowski but couldn't see him anywhere. There was little to see in the way of plants apart from a patch of winter cabbages growing in the muddy earth. Next to them, still upright, were a variety of bare stalks. They had already yielded their crop and had started to rot. Other produce would have been harvested months ago and put into dry storage. He suspected he was enjoying a sample of this as part of his daily meal. In the bottom corner of the plot was a glasshouse where Mr Dabrowski did much of his work. From the outside it was difficult to ascertain what was going on inside, as every pane of glass was dripping with condensation. Keen to find out what sorts of plants were being propagated inside the hothouse, Marek slid the door across its runner and was hit with a dank, cloying blanket of moist air, no doubt ideal for the host of unusual flowers which were clearly thriving.

'Pretty aren't they? But you should take care to secure the door behind you. They don't take kindly to the cold.'

Marek spun around to find Mr Dabrowski quickly pulling it shut.

'Sorry,' he stuttered. 'Of course, yes, I should have realised.'

'Like flowers, do you?' he asked, grinning.

'The ones in the music room are very pleasant. Do they come from here?'

'Indeed. I grow them every year at this time. Always do well with the proper care. I see you've been out to the summerhouse,' he said glancing at my trousers and boots.

'You can tell,' Marek laughed as he peered down at his heavily soiled shoes.

'See you haven't acquired the proper footwear yet.'

'No, I haven't but it's difficult . . .' Hesitantly Marek started to explain it was hard to come by such things when he was suddenly interrupted.

'Follow me.'

They set off at quite a gallop, and soon came to a ramshackle shed almost entirely covered with ivy. The gardener wrenched the door open to reveal piles of clutter.

'What size are you?' he called out.

'Size?' Marek repeated, rather puzzled.

'Boot size.'

'Ten,' Marek replied, raising his voice.

Mr Dabrowski rummaged about for what seemed like an age before emerging with a pair of knee-high waterproof boots.

'Not very warm but with an extra pair of socks they'll do.'

'Thank you. These are just what I need,' Marek said gratefully as he yanked off his old boots.

'Would you like to see the stable block?' he asked.

'Yes, very much.'

'Do you like horses?' Mr Dabrowski enquired as they tramped through the remnants of snow which had turned to slush.

'I used to ride in my youth, usually when we took holidays in the country.'

'Fine beast, the horse.'

The stable block was long and narrow and, like the shed, showing signs of age. Several tiles were missing from its roof and more than one window was lacking a pane or two of glass. Inside, it was dark and gloomy and there was a distinct feeling of neglect.

'Had to get rid of them all. No money, see.'

'How many horses did they have?'

'At one time we had thirty.'

'As many as that. What breed were they?'

'Several varieties. Some were bred for racing. The Liszinskis were all very keen riders.'

Mr Dabrowski sat himself down on a nearby upturned metal pail and beckoned for his visitor to do the same.

'I first started working here when I was a young lad of fifteen, almost sixty years ago now. I was taken on as stable boy – mucking out the stalls, grooming the animals – and loved every minute of it. The best part, however, was exercising the horses. I'd take them round the estate and before long I knew every inch of it. Later when old Albert retired – he was in charge here – I took over until the horses were sold. He said this with a wistful look in his eyes. 'It was a bad day when the last one went.'

'It must be hard work being in charge of all this land. Do you have any help?'

'Dominik does all the heavy work specially in planting season. He also helps around the house at this time of year when there's not much to be done outside.'

'I've met him. He attends to the fire in the music room.'

'That's him. He's a quiet lad but not averse to hard work.'

'Did you enjoy working for the family?'

'Always treated me fairly. Never put on those airs and graces like a lot of gentry do. When my wife and I married they gave us the lodge as a wedding gift, to live in for as long as we need it.'

'That was very generous of them,' Marek remarked. He hesitated a little before asking, 'Do you have much to do with the German?'

'Not if I can help it. I try to keep out if his way,' he replied sharply. 'Does he pester you much?'

'He checks on my work. Do you know why I am here?'

'Yes, I believe I do.' He chose not to elaborate but cast me an understanding look.

'I ought to head back. Thank you again for the boots,' Marek said getting to his feet.

'Don't work too hard,' the gardener called after him.

As Marek had suspected from the start, this old gentleman was an honest sort. He dipped his boots into an old stone trough in the middle of the courtyard, cracking the ice first with his heel. The shock from the cold water took his breath away, but he needed to remove the large clods of mud stuck to the soles. Once back in the music room, Marek arranged the boots on a couple of sheets of manuscript paper, and tucked them away to one side of the dresser until their next outing.

'What have you done to your trousers, Marek? You look like you've waded through a muddy field,' Eva asked, in the same chiding voice her son remembered hearing as a child. His sister quickly joined in and, whilst Marek was being harangued by these formidable women, Ruben looked on and grinned from ear to ear.

'You'd better take them off and let me wash them for you. You can't be seen looking like that.' His mother was a very proud woman.

Ruben was significantly better, though he had a dark purple bruise over one of his eyes. The headaches had lessened, and he was not so dependent on pills to quell the pain. Dr Bilinski had recommended the boy rest for a few more days and to refrain from any excitement in the near future. This they all knew to be as impossible as holding back the tide. Perhaps the incident might make him take a bit more care. Later that evening Ruben had good news to report. A member of the *ZZW* had paid him a visit to say that all the weapons had successfully found their way into the Ghetto in readiness for the big event.

Friday arrived, marking the end of Marek's second week at the mansion. The morning had passed without interruption, but during the afternoon he was on his guard in case the Nazi might appear. When he did not Marek assumed he was occupied elsewhere. It was the Sabbath, and the eagerly-awaited visit of Lidia and her husband Benjamin. This holy day was observed by the family each week but tonight would be special. They would dine like kings on food scavenged by both Papa and Ruben. Marek's contributions had also been carefully stored for the occasion. Celebrations traditionally began at sunset; however, since the internment they had learned to be pragmatic.

The table had been set and Eva had changed into her best dress – the only other dress she possessed – and was stirring one of the saucepans on the stove. Marek leaned over and studied the viscous liquid, which was making some curious plopping noises. It reminded him of the bubbling mud pools he learned about at school. He took a piece of cake, wrapped in a leaf of music paper, from his pocket, and Eva squealed with delight. Izak was less relaxed, but then he had always worried about his children's safety and, naturally, even more so now. Crossing the Ghetto had always been a hazardous thing to do even in the so called 'safe hours', and anyone found in an undesignated building paid a harsh penalty. Benjamin had promised to bring some drink with him. Just as the tension of waiting had become unbearable, there was the sound of knocking. Moments later Lidia and her husband, led by Rachel, walked into the room.

'Lidia, my darling girl.'

Eva's joy at seeing her daughter was touching to witness and they clasped each other tightly. Grabbing hold of Benjamin she hugged him too. Even Ruben, who as a rule did not enjoy displays of emotion, was squeezed so hard by Lidia he winced with the pain of his recent injuries.

'Come on everyone. Take your seats,' Eva urged them.

Izak extinguished the lights and his wife, according to convention, lit the candles and said a short blessing. Izak delivered the *Kiddush*, usually recited whilst holding a glass of wine – in this case vodka – symbolising happiness and joy. The *Challah* or special bread was passed around next. Sadly it was neither freshly baked nor plaited, and instead consisted of scraps which Marek had saved from his lunches.

For a while Marek observed Lidia and was struck by her appearance. Equally as attractive as Rachel, with her big round eyes and jet-black hair, there was, nevertheless, something subtly different. She looked so healthy. Perhaps it was the brown sweater she was wearing which complemented her skin tone. Rachel had, it was true to say, become much thinner of late – not to the point of emaciation, more a heightened delicateness – but Lidia, by comparison, had neither gained nor lost weight, and there was an aura about her. Maybe being back in the bosom of her family was having a profound effect.

As the reunited family settled down to eat it wasn't long before the subject of the war and how it was progressing cropped up. Benjamin was an avid listener of the BBC radio transmissions and he had vital information for the family.

'Have you heard about what's happening in Russia?'

'The Sixth Army surrendering in Stalingrad. Won't do us much good,' Izak said cynically.

'Why not, Papa?' Lidia asked as she reached for another piece of bread.

'Who do the enemy take their anger out on when defeated? Us.'

'You're right, Izak,' Benjamin chipped in. 'It'll be doubly worse now, what with Rommel's defeats in Africa.'

'Apparently the Nazis are offering rewards to those prepared to betray Jews.' Ruben, who had said little so far, now joined in.

'Well there are plenty who would be willing to do that,' Rachel said bitterly.

'Enough,' Eva said. 'Less of this gloomy talk. We're together for the first time in months, thank God, so let us enjoy ourselves. How is life in your street, Lidia?'

'It is very much like Greek drama. One day tragedy, the next comedy.'

'Well, we'll hear the comedy first, I think,' said her father.

My sister shot her husband a look. It would be his job to relate the tale.

'There is this old gentleman who lives on our floor who is rather . . .' Benjamin hesitated for a moment, '. . . rather forgetful.'

'He's become terribly absent-minded lately,' Lidia said, with laughter in her voice.

'Does he have a wife?' Mama chimed up. It was typical of her interest in people to want to know every last detail.

'No,' Lidia said, 'I don't think he's ever been married. He often talks about a sister, but she's long dead, so they say. Sorry, darling. Do go on.'

Benjamin picked up the tale again.

'Because of his failing mind he is, as you might imagine, continually losing things, or so he believes. The other day he couldn't find his false teeth. At first we all humoured him, and tried to reassure him that they would crop up somewhere. After all, things like that don't tend to go unnoticed.'

'He seemed to be comforted by this,' Lidia butted in again.

'Do you want to carry on with the tale, darling?' Benjamin asked, feigning exasperation.

'No, Ben. You tell it better than I do,' Lidia laughed.

'I'm not sure I do. Anyway, if I am allowed?' Benjamin tugged on his ear before carrying on. 'Zachariah — that's his name — suddenly announced to everyone he'd remembered what had happened. The teeth had been placed overnight on the windowsill and they had been pilfered by a bird who was now wearing them.'

'What! It would have to have been a pretty large bird, I should say. The old boy must be mad.' Ruben's comments sparked off a series of spontaneous laughs and giggles around the table.

'Don't mock the elderly, young man. You might end up like him one day,' Izak teased.

'Perhaps it's a good thing I won't live that long,' the boy fired back.

'Did he really believe that he had seen the bird?' Rachel asked.

'Apparently so,' Benjamin replied. 'This huge magpie was following him about everywhere he went, jeering at him and mocking him with those clacking teeth. He'd been spotted wagging his finger at the imaginary creature and accusing it of running off with his belongings.'

'So what happened? Was it all fantasy?' Izak was impatient to hear more of the tale.

'Lidia.' Benjamin glanced across at his wife and smiled broadly.

'I was the person who found them,' Lidia announced with a pleased expression.

'How did you manage it?' Rachel asked, propping her head on her elbow.

'All his neighbours were drafted in to help find the teeth and clear up the mystery which was driving everyone to the point of madness. Zachariah was so adamant he could hear those clacking teeth and nothing we could say or do would persuade him otherwise. It made me wonder if there might be some plausible explanation after all. So I sat him down one day and got him to check his pockets, though he assured me he had done this already without any luck. Then by chance I noticed something peeping out from under his shirt collar. I asked if he would let me take a look and do you know what it was? He had a little leather pouch around his neck and guess what was inside? The teeth, of course. He would slip everything he valued into the pouch for safe-keeping, but he would soon forget he had done this. Oh! And remember the noise? Whenever he moved so did his teeth.'

'Clever, darling,' Eva said proudly as she passed the fruit around. Marek felt satisfied with his week's pilfering.

'Unfortunately Benjamin and I have learnt of something horrific which we think you should all know about.' Lidia hesitated before continuing. 'It concerns those who get taken to the *Umschlagplatz* and what happens to them afterwards.'

'They get transported to the labour camps, or rather death camps, don't they? It's common knowledge,' Rachel declared.

'Yes it's true they end up in the camps, but it's what happens afterwards which is truly worrying.'

The family had heard rumours about the atrocities, like many other Jews, but they had closed their minds to them, preferring to regard the broadcasting of such ideas as nothing more than scaremongering. They sat in silence and listened.

'I'm surprised anyone has survived to speak of their experiences.'

'You're right Papa. However, some have managed to escape and they are extremely fortunate by all accounts.' Lidia took a sip of water from her glass. 'Two days ago I bumped into Magda, in the early morning bread queue and she told me what her cousin Ola had endured.'

'On the second day of the resettlement operation, Ola, her husband and their family were hiding in a bunker when the SS, who had been systematically working their way up the street storming apartments, broke into their home. There were other parents and their children with them in the shelter, which had been constructed behind a false wall in one of the rooms. The young children had been trained, even bribed, not to utter a single sound but one little girl had become frightened by all the commotion.

'The more her mother tried to stifle the noise of her weeping, the more the child became upset until it reached the point where, as horrible as it seems, the other parents signalled for the child to be silenced by whatever means. By now, however, it was too late. A soldier heard the whimpering and within seconds he and his companions had torn the room apart, ripping down the fake partition and exposing the terrified individuals on the other side. Then these savage beasts proceeded, in cold blood and without any compunction, to snap the necks of each child like brittle twigs.

'Numb with grief and shock at the sheer barbarity they had just witnessed, Ola and her husband, Elias, were then marched out of the building to join a rapidly-increasing number of similarly stricken individuals. Soon after, the instruction was given to move northwards.

'Reaching the *Umschlagplatz,* a scene of utter chaos confronted them. A seething mass of bodies jostled for space. There was moaning, some prayed fitfully whilst others cradled their children in an attempt to shield them from the bedlam. This pandemonium endured for quite a while, until a pistol was fired. Then a deathly hush descended. Minutes later a chugging noise was heard, and creeping along the railway line were the cattle trucks, snaking the length of the platform and beyond.

'When the train had come to a standstill, the doors were pulled back by soldiers. The stench that wafted out of the compartments caused those nearest to break out into fits of coughing and to gasp in horror. Many who had handkerchiefs covered their noses, only to have them ripped from their grasp by the sadistic guards. Like animals, they were herded inside and packed together so tightly there was barely room to breathe, let alone sit down. Human excrement daubed the sides of the truck and other stains covered the floors. The desire to vomit was overwhelming and many did.'

'Did they know where they being taken?' Marek asked.

'Ola did not know where the train was headed, but soon the words "Treblinka" and "death camp" were being whispered around the carriage. This was confirmed by the north-easterly route the train was taking. Some did not want to believe what they were hearing, and instead chose to convince themselves that they were going to one of the labour camps: a lie the Germans had fobbed them off with to persuade them to board the train. The journey took four hours, and at the end of it many had perished from suffocation or had been crushed to death.'

Lidia's voice faltered as her throat became dry. She needed another drink and took several gulps.

'Ola somehow managed to wriggle her way to where a hole had been gouged out in one side of the compartment by the desperate hands of previous occupants, and for a while she was able to inhale fresh air. It was not long before others had spotted it too and roughly pushed her out of the way. After what seemed like an eternity they arrived, only to be met by a row of sinister Nazi soldiers lining the platform. Each was clutching a gun and fixing their quarry with a hard, impassive stare which could cut through you like a dagger. Getting down from the trucks was a far worse ordeal. Many who could barely move, especially the sick and elderly, were shown not a scrap of respect or compassion and were propelled along by the butt of a gun. Everyone was ordered to assemble in an open square.

'Emerging from one of the nearby huts was a fearsome-looking, high-ranking official who seemed to be in charge of running the camp. He strutted up and down the lines, determining the fates of those trembling before him. Why it was she did not know, but Ola was amongst the few selected to step away from the main group. It was then that she and her companions had to endure the sight of a humiliated and horrified group of people forced to strip naked. Their clothing and personal belongings now deposited in neat little piles on the ground, these lost souls were then told they must go to the shower house to be cleansed. Although no one could be certain what lay ahead, there was a sense of anxiety and dread. Ola told me how she watched, heartbroken, as the column wended its way to its destiny, and how amongst its number was her husband Elias.

'They entered meekly one by one, like lambs into the unknown, innocent and trusting. Those remaining behind were ordered to collect up the piles and carry them into one of the buildings. It was now their job to sift through everything, turn out each pocket and collect whatever was of value. Clothes and shoes were put to one side ready to be despatched to Germany. Jews who were already busy at their work soon explained the brutal reality. Of those who disappeared inside the shower building, not a single one would return alive. Just as the last person entered the doors would be sealed. This done, the unsuspecting victims position themselves under the shower heads, but instead of water, a poisonous gas is piped in from above, murdering all who stand below.'

Rachel had tears gathering in her eyes. Eva had let out a gasp of horror and Izak was shaking his head in disbelief; like everyone else he could find no words to express his melancholy.

'Perhaps I should stop now, Mama?' Lidia said in a low voice. Her husband placed a supportive arm about her.

'No, we need to hear everything.' Despite her distress it was Rachel who urged her sister to continue.

'The men who were spared were ordered to join a work party whose task was to dig the pits into which the bodies of the murdered Jews were then dumped. However, those who toil away are digging their own graves, for the process is cyclical and they are next for the gas chambers.'

'The Germans have the system finely tuned it seems,' Marek said, his voice heavy with irony.

'We can of course expect nothing less of them,' Izak uttered acerbically.

'Conditions in the camps are hellish and are far worse than you or I could ever imagine. Her own clothes taken off her back, Ola was issued with poorly fitting replacements which provided little protection from the elements. There are no mattresses for sleeping – merely straw-filled sacks – and sanitation for the overflowing barracks is utterly appalling. The food lacks any nutritional value and consists mainly of a thin, watery broth. The lack of nourishment and the squalid living conditions manifests itself in abscesses, irritating rashes, lice and worse. By the end of the first week, Ola was determined to escape. Some had attempted it before and failed, but a few had succeeded.

'The camp is heavily protected, like a fortress, and is completely surrounded by a barbed wire fence, with manned watchtowers positioned at strategic points. By the second week Ola had familiarised herself with the system of the sorting rooms, which included the loading of goods into freight cars for shipment to SS storehouses. Here she decided was her opportunity. She would conceal herself in one of those cars. So on a particular evening and just before a consignment was due to leave, Ola, and another woman whom she had befriended, hid themselves deep amongst the piles of clothes and were transported out of the camp to freedom.'

Her harrowing account at its end, Lidia collapsed deep into her chair, seemingly sapped of energy.

'Could the Germans, as bad as they are, really be capable of such acts of utter brutishness?'

'I fear, Mama, that their barbarity knows no end,' Lidia said taking hold of her mother's hand.

'We must be vigilant and do all we can to avoid suffering the same fate as those poor wretches,' Izak said with determination. 'It would be better to end our days here than be dragged off to the death camps.'

The horrendous news had deeply affected everyone. For several minutes the family sat in quiet reflection. The conversation had taken on a morbid direction and yet, oddly, Lidia was beaming happily.

'Ben and I have something to tell you,' Lidia said excitedly. 'I'm pregnant.'

At first nobody said anything. The look on Benjamin's face did not mirror that of his wife's. His smile was less natural and he seemed tense. The usual elated responses on hearing such news were not appropriate in the circumstances, when life expectancy was so low. Eva was the first to break the silence.

'Darling, that is wonderful news. I'm so happy for you. We both are, aren't we, Izak?'

'Yes of course, dear.'

Marek could tell that his father was doing his best to disguise his concern. He shook Benjamin's hand and offered his congratulations. In an instant the three women were embracing each other with tears of joy streaming down their faces. Suddenly, Izak, raising his glass high into the air, suggested a toast. The family shouted *Le'haim* for the unborn child, and at that moment Marek hoped with every fibre of his being that it would be given life.

Once everyone had finished eating, Eva, Rachel and Lidia cleared the table and bustled off to the kitchen where they could discuss the joys of motherhood. Ruben, Benjamin and Marek excused themselves and went out to the landing to talk. Papa took to his chair, preferring to make a start on the new reading matter his son-in-law had given him.

'What are you going to do?' Marek asked Benjamin.

'I don't think we have much of a choice, do you? Before I knew . . . before Lidia told me about the baby . . . I'd made my mind up to fight.' He tapped the ash from the end of his cigarette. 'Things are different now. We are going to have to get out to give the baby a chance.'

The Jews were abandoning the Ghetto each day now. Polish sympathisers would help pave the way, acquiring Aryan documents and arranging living quarters for them. However, it was not always easy for the Jews to adjust to life on the outside, and there were even those who had returned, preferring to be back amongst friends. For many though, with noble ideas, escape was simply not an option, for to save one's life was tantamount to wilful betrayal and selfishness. Instead their duty was to stay and fight.

'What does Lidia think?' Marek asked.

'I haven't mentioned it yet. We both wanted to be parents so much, but not now. Not here.'

They had never seen Benjamin in such an agitated state and they felt sympathy for him. What should have been wonderful news was proving to be a huge burden.

'I think getting out is a good idea. In fact it's your only option. Do you know anyone who can help you?' Ruben enquired.

'There's someone in the city who Samuel knows, who will take us in for a night or two.'

Samuel shared an apartment with the couple.

'And after that?' Marek asked.

'We'll move on. Best not to settle in one place for too long.'

'Will you break it to them tonight?' Ruben asked having lit a fresh cigarette.

'Reckon it's not the best time. I don't want to ruin their happiness by presenting them with risky schemes.'

'Speaking of which, have you heard about my latest adventure?' Ruben enquired.

Benjamin shifted his position on the window ledge so that he faced the young man.

'Which one might that be? There are so many.'

'The most daredevil and foolish so far without a doubt,' Marek declared, walking off to smoke alone. He had already heard the tale in great detail.

'And no doubt you're going to regale me with all the facts, Ruben,' Benjamin said crossing his arms and smiling.

'Indeed I shall.'

And he did, which seemed to take Benjamin's mind off his own problems. When Ruben had finished and been commended for his bravery, it was Marek's turn to pick up the conversation.

'There is something else you should know, Benjamin. Something about my work.'

'We heard what you were up to. Working at that house. Sounds pretty good to me compared with conditions in the factory workshop.'

Marek looked at Ruben. Benjamin must have noticed the change in expression on the boy's face.

'It's not quite what you think. The rest of the family don't know what I do there. It all started about two weeks ago, a Nazi officer burst in on our rehearsal.'

'And you're still alive?' Benjamin was astounded by what he heard.

'Yes, but unfortunately at a price. This man holds the rank of *Oberst-gruppenführer* and is a highly cultured intellectual. He wants me to compose a piece of music.'

'That can't be so bad, can it?' Benjamin gave a sigh of relief.

'There will be a concert in April which all the local high-ranking members of the Party will attend and the work will be performed then.'

'Wait a minute. What would the Nazis want with a work composed by a Jew? Haven't they expelled all Jewish artists from Germany?'

144

'Yes, most of them. But in my case there is to be an exception. The music must celebrate the Third Reich in all its glory.'

Benjamin chocked on cigarette smoke. A little while later he had recovered sufficiently to speak.

'That isn't possible. No Jew could ever do that.'

'I had no choice. If I had refused we would all be in our graves by now. Believe me, it was very hard.'

'What can this Nazi hope to gain from such an arrangement?'

'It is clear-cut to me. Kudos and esteem, as he perceives it, amongst his peers. Have you forgotten that these monsters thrive on the entertainment of such paradoxes as seeing a group of Jews singing their hearts out in praise of Hitler?' Izak stepped out from the shadows.

'How long have you been standing there, Papa?' Marek asked.

'Long enough.' He was clearly angered and distressed by what he had heard. 'And the composing takes place at the villa?'

Marek elaborated upon the aspects of his work which he had previously considered prudent to omit.

'How can you do this, Marek? How could you agree to it?' His father was in despair.

'How can I not, Papa? There are too many lives at stake.'

'We could have got out. We still can,' Izak said becoming more agitated.

'There wouldn't have been time, Papa. This man is manipulative and deceitful. He wouldn't have countenanced an escape. He would hunt us down. For him it would be a question of pride.'

'Izak, there is always the possibility that the situation will change. The work may never be performed,' Ruben said.

'Whether that proves to be the case or not you must go and tell your mother and sisters exactly what is going on. As a family we have always been honest with each other.'

What Izak had said was very true. They had always been honest with one another, sharing each other's troubles and often finding solutions to what seemed like insurmountable problems.

❖ ❖ ❖

'There is something I need to tell you.' The seriousness of Marek's tone caused the three women to stop what they were doing.'

'What is it?' Lidia asked, the look of joy on her face evaporating rapidly.

'The work I am composing for the German has a specific theme.'

'Is that all?' That doesn't sound too dreadful,' Rachel said.

'There's more to it than that,' Izak said. 'Tell them.' And he gave his son an encouraging pat on the shoulder.

'The music must pay tribute to the Nazis.'

An ominous silence descended over the room.

'Its purpose is to venerate Hitler and all that he stands for and the choir have to perform it in front of a hall full of Nazis.'

'That is appalling. It cannot be. No Jew should ever be forced to do such a thing,' Rachel exclaimed.

'You cannot do it, Marek. Neither can the others. It's too humiliating,' Lidia protested.

'We have no choice. It was part of the terms: the lives of our families in return for performing.'

'But what will the Nazi do with you when he no longer has a need for your skills? Do you think he'll let you go just like that?' Eva was close to tears.

'Please don't worry Mama. I haven't come to grief so far.' Marek tried to sound positive. Under the surface he was having great difficulty convincing himself.

'Ruben's right. The course of the war may change and Marek's work at the villa may come to nothing,' Benjamin said attempting to diffuse the tension. And to a degree he succeeded.

'Darling we must go. We've stayed longer than we ought,' his wife said gathering up her thick winter coat, scarf and gloves. 'Mama, Papa we will see you all soon.'

'God willing.' Eva clasped her daughter to her tightly. Her father and sister were equally reluctant to see them go.

Benjamin approached the huddle.

'I will look after her. I promise.' He thought better of mentioning his plans to leave the Ghetto. There had been enough dramatic revelations for one day.

The family's parting was an emotional one, and Marek wondered when they would see each other again.

Mrs Dabrowski was waiting for Marek when he arrived. It was a Monday, and the beginning of the third week of his new employment. They greeted each other civilly, but there was a marked change in her demeanour. She was nervous. They walked at a rattling pace and she seemed eager to reach the music room as quickly as possible. As they approached the sound of men's voices could be heard. It was not long before the source of the noise came into view and, quite unexpectedly, they found themselves within a few feet of a large group of Nazis officers. From their uniforms and insignia, Marek could tell that there was an SS *Brigadeführer* together with several other high-ranking officials. Realising they were being observed, the Germans instantly became silent. Marek remained quite still. Mrs Dabrowski – her eyes filled with fear – did not move either. The most senior of the officers walked towards them. Craning his neck, he studied Marek with cruel, piercing eyes.

'What have we here?' the officer said, beginning to circle him. 'I do believe it is a dirty Jew.'

His colleagues remained silent, clearly anticipating the prospect of what would unfold before them. The atmosphere was as tense as it could possibly be and Marek could feel his hot, stinking breath. Then, taking him off-guard, he flicked his leather glove across Marek's face. He tried not to grimace as it struck his cheek sharply.

'Do you have a name, Jew?' Now his evil face was a hair's breadth away and it was as much as Marek could do to resist wiping the supercilious smile from his lips.

'Dr Ruzanski.'

'And he is doing special work for me.' The tone was menacing.

Franz Reinecke was a formidable sight in his grey uniform. He towered several inches above his colleagues, including the *Brigadeführer*, who quickly lost his smirk, and instead stood to attention in deference to the superior officer. The master of the house uttered nothing further, but gestured to Mrs Dabrowski and Marek to continue on their way, which they did without hesitation. They covered the remaining distance in silence and then Mrs Dabrowski left, though not before Marek noticed the slight trembling of her hand as she pulled the door handle.

Anger and loathing were just some of the emotions Marek grappled with that morning, and as a result he wrote nothing of significance. At the stroke of one Angelika arrived with his lunch and he questioned her about the Nazis.

'They arrived yesterday and are staying for two or three days.'

'Do you know why they are here?'

'No. Mrs Dabrowski hasn't managed to find out anything yet. Mr Dabrowski thinks Hitler has sent them to . . .' she broke off, looking distinctly embarrassed.

'What, Angelika? What does Mr Dabrowski think?'

'He believes they're here to deal with the . . .'

'Yes?' Marek said encouragingly.

'To deal with the Jews once and for all.'

'I see.' Her words did not shock him.

'Mr Dabrowski loathes them,' she said.

'The Jews?'

'No. The Nazis. We all do. I try to keep out of their way but I have to wait on them sometimes.'

'It must be difficult for you,' Marek said sympathetically.

'Mrs Dabrowski told us what happened this morning. She said you were very brave.'

'Did she really?'

Marek was surprised to hear this.

'I think you are too.'

Her mouth creased at the corners and then she told him that she would be needed downstairs and should go. Marek reflected upon what the housekeeper had said. Maybe she admired him.

After lunch Marek took a walk. He swiftly scanned the grounds but could see no one. Until this morning he had noticed very little military presence based at the house, apart from the two guards on the gate, and the occasional German private leaning against the building, smoking. Marek often wondered how the drivers occupied themselves during the day. Perhaps after escorting him they spent the time creating havoc somewhere in the city, that is, if they weren't despatched to run errands of a questionable nature for their superior.

The ground was hard underfoot. There had been a sharp frost, and the low daytime temperatures had not precipitated a thaw. Marek strode energetically across the grass, making for the summerhouse. He was better equipped today, with two pairs of socks on his feet. The unadulterated air was almost intoxicating and with every exhalation there was a little puff of white which lingered momentarily. This time he chose to walk through the copse.

Marek stood and looked up at the tall birch trees. Each was covered in a fine layer of ice, so beautiful and yet so fragile. The scene resembled that of a magical wood one reads about in a child's fairy tale, where the snow queen and her entourage live. His imaginings were brought to an abrupt end by the squawk of a bird as it landed on a branch above his head. Soon after he reached the glade. He gazed up at the roof of the summerhouse and saw a wisp of smoke rising from the lichen-covered chimney. Curiosity got the better of him and he strained to peer through one of the windows. The tables and chairs had been pushed aside, and as he peered closer he could see someone crouched in front of the hearth, placing sticks into the flames. It was the gardener. The prospect of warming his chilled bones was too great a temptation and he went inside.

'Come in to thaw out, have you?' Mr Dabrowski laughed. He was standing with his back to the flames. 'A cold one and no mistake.' His eyes darted down to Marek's feet. 'Don't need your other boots today.'

'No, the ground is quite firm.'

The room was different to how he remembered it. The old man had been tidying up. The furniture was now stacked in one corner, and the bottles and other objects Marek had spotted during his first visit were piled up ready for removal. He offered Marek a chair by the fire. Leaning forward he warmed his hands which were white and numb.

'I come and light a fire every now and then . . . place needs drying out. Gets very damp. Walls need re-plastering,' he said pointing to a patch where the walls were peeling badly. 'Doesn't seem worth it now, of course.'

'Not when you don't know whether the building will be standing tomorrow,' Marek said cynically.

'Precarious times we live in. More so for you and your people though.'

'Certainly planning ahead is a thing of the past.'

As Marek said this he noticed his companion's forehead pucker.

'I had a Jewish friend once. Decent fellow. Went by the name of Jozef. Knew him years ago when I was in charge of the stables. He was a horse dealer. Used to meet up with him at all the horse fairs. We'd talk a lot, I recall – putting the world to rights – and drink a lot as well.' He was smiling now, and gazing at the crackling flames lost in thought.

'When did you last see him?'

'Must be over twenty years ago. One day he wasn't there. I asked around and they said he had died. Tuberculosis, I think it was.' He gave a sigh. 'Had a good sense of humour, I remember that about him. And he had family. I met them. Two sons and a daughter.' His eyes drifted back to the fire. 'I sometimes wonder what happened to them with all the present troubles. Whether they remained in the city or got away.'

'Let's hope the latter, for their sakes,' Marek said.

The gardener picked up one of the larger pieces of wood lying in the grate and buried it amongst the hot coals. There was a hissing sound caused by the moisture, followed by a thin plume of smoke.

'Do you have family Marek?'

This was the first personal question he had asked since the two men had met.

'There are my parents and I have two sisters.'

'What about a family of your own?'

'No, I'm not married.'

'I have a son, probably about your age. When his mother and I got married she was a fair bit younger than me.'

'Is he away fighting?'

'No. He lives in the city. He is a manager at one of the factories and is forced to work alongside the Germans. We don't see much of him or our grandchildren. His wife has taken them to the country where it's safer. He's a member of the Polish underground, you know.'

'Why didn't you and your wife leave? Surely it would have been better for you both?'

'It was difficult for us to abandon our employers after all these years of service, and now the Nazi's here we no longer have a choice. Will you and your family try to get out of the Ghetto? I hear that some of your people have succeeded in doing so.'

'We've decided to remain together. I'll have to stay in the city until I've completed the composition.'

'Neither of our situations is ideal, but your predicament, Marek, is far graver.'

Marek left Mr Dabrowski huddled over the fire, the spitting noises of the burning logs still reverberating in his ears as he began his bracing stroll back to the house.

By the middle of the week Marek's composition was beginning to take shape. The grandiose opening with its rich harmonies formed the backdrop to a rising motif in the bass. This theme was passed through the other voices and then heard in unison. A transition section followed, with music characterised by its short phrases and simple statements. Marek had sketched out the bass part for the next few bars, and had decided what shape the melodic line should take, when something distracted him. This time he was not alarmed by the disturbance. The Nazi had come to monitor progress and he stood, as he had done previously, a little way to one side of the piano.

'Your time here has not been entirely ill spent, Doctor. I do believe you are not as thin as you were at our first meeting. The housekeeper is a fine cook.'

'Yes, she is,' Marek responded, surprised at the German's remarks about his appearance.

He moved nearer, his tall frame blocking some of the light and casting a shadow over the pages.

'You have written a new section. I would like to hear all that you have composed so far.'

Marek arranged the pages of manuscript in order. The General walked over to the fireplace. The fire had died down and roaring flames had been supplanted by glowing embers. As Marek performed he caught sight of the officer's expression. He allowed a look of pure rapture to linger on his face. Sensing the pianist's eyes upon him, the German promptly substituted it for one of surliness.

'You have made improvements to the opening, and the linking passage is striking in its simplicity. Have you any additional ideas?'

'I have,' Marek acknowledged brusquely.

'Your rambles around the estate have not yet provided you with the necessary inspiration to write the text I see.'

Evidently he was aware of Marek's lunchtime outings. Marek wondered if the Nazi also knew that he fraternised with the staff.

'No doubt you will add them in time. For the moment I must leave you, Doctor Ruzanski. There are pressing matters which require my attention. The boy will be along shortly to see to the fire.' Just as he was about to go he stopped in his tracks. He looked perturbed. 'The incident this morning was regrettable. I give you my assurance that it will not happen again.'

The door banged shut and his footsteps echoed down the corridor.

❖　❖　❖

The news that Lidia and Benjamin were expecting a child, once absorbed, caused consternation in the Ruzanski household.

Despite Eva trying her utmost to be positive and cheerful, everyone knew the Ghetto was not the best place to raise a family and aborting the baby was dangerous and risked the onset of infection. The mortality rate of children born to Jewish mothers was distressingly high. Vulnerable babies were also prime targets for the Ukrainian sadists and many a gruesome account had reached their ears. During a round-up, and in a desperate attempt to save their children, some parents would give them a sleeping draught or chloroform before hiding them in knapsacks. If the children didn't wake during the selection process then they would have a chance of survival. However, deportation operations could take hours and inevitably some youngsters would rouse. One reported method employed for silencing this irksome, irritating noise was brutish: a Ukrainian guard was witnessed plunging his sharpened bayonet into the sack, twisting and jabbing until it had become a bloody, lifeless bundle. The distraught mother would not have to suffer long before she too was brutally murdered.

Following a heated discussion one evening, the Ruzanskis decided that, although fraught with all kinds of dangers, the only solution was for Lidia and Benjamin to leave the Ghetto. For Eva the prospect of never seeing or holding her grandchild was too distressing, and for Rachel news of her sister's pregnancy had been very unsettling. She too wanted to be a wife and mother, but Lidia's circumstances brought home the stark realisation that she might never experience this.

The final week in February began ominously. Walking to the meeting point Marek came upon a number of bodies. They looked to him to be suicide victims and were covered in nothing but newspaper. If the dead lay uncollected, the paper would bob and twitch sickeningly for huge numbers of blow flies made their home beneath.

The behaviour of the two soldiers who ferried Marek to the house had reverted to one of indifference. This particular morning, however, both were in buoyant mood and it soon became apparent that they had been out on a drinking spree the night before and each had availed himself of the city's prostitutes.

'How many women have you had, pig Jew?' Ernst asked.

'I wonder if his religion allows him to take prostitutes,' Viktor snarled.

'That slut. She was the best,' he laughed throatily. 'Spread her legs wide, and those breasts . . .'

As the soldiers continued their gloating Marek gazed out of the window. He caught sight of a mother and her young son, a satchel slung across his shoulder, some way off. Waiting to cross the road the woman looked to her right. Without any warning Viktor brought the car to a standstill inches away from the couple. Marek was thrust forward and narrowly escaped injury by stretching his arms out in front of him. Then, winding down the car window, Ernst waved his arm in the air signalling for the mother and child to cross the road. This apparent act of chivalry took Marek by surprise. The mother smiled, acknowledging their kindness, and stepped out into the road with her little boy. Just as she did so, Viktor jammed his foot on the accelerator and edged forward, closing the gap between the car and the pedestrians. Marek's stomach churned in anticipation of what was about to happen. The terrified woman sprung nimbly onto the pavement, dragged her child back, and remained there, clutching him protectively to her body.

Viktor reversed a short way and stopped. Just as before, he gestured for her to go ahead and cross the road. The woman, not certain what to do, and yet no doubt desiring above all else to safeguard the life of her son, complied and the car shunted forward again, jolting their passenger from his seat. By now the two Germans were taking great pleasure in the women's discomfort. A Polish life was regarded in a German's eyes as being only one rung up from that of a Jew. Helpless physically to prevent what was unfolding before his eyes, Marek tried to reason with them.

'Why are you doing this to a defenceless mother and her child who have done you no harm?'

So wrapped up in their depraved game were they that the men were surprised to hear Marek's voice. Ernst swung his head sharply around. Marek saw the intense hatred in those flinty eyes.

'Shut up, Jew,' he spat the words out with venom. 'Just be thankful it's not you.'

'Sit back and enjoy the spectacle,' Viktor said, casting his colleague a malicious smirk.

For a third time the woman was encouraged to cross the road, and as she stepped out from the kerb Marek screwed up his eyes. A few seconds later the vehicle rammed into them. Marek felt the bump and when he opened his eyes the car was speeding away. Marek didn't know what possessed him to look back. Maybe it was in the hope of seeing some signs of life. He saw a battered, bloody heap. The Poles were suffering too and no well meaning international conventions could guarantee them their safety. The soldiers lapsed into silence again. Not, Marek suspected, because the Germans were experiencing any feelings of guilt or remorse, rather they were probably exhausted after their night of debauchery.

The visiting Nazis had departed and there were signs that life at *Dwór nad Jeziorem* was rapidly returning to normal. Throughout their stay nerves had been strained, and Marek was certain the staff would be as relieved as he was to see the back of them. During the latter part of their visit Mrs Dubrowski had brought his meal. At the time Marek suspected that Angelika was busy elsewhere.

When there was a gentle tapping on the door at lunchtime Marek knew the maid would be waiting outside. Mrs Dabrowski's knock was louder and confident while Dominik hovered with his clanking bucket and the General, when he wanted to surprise his employee, stomped in unannounced. Marek got up from the piano expecting to see what had become her jaunty style as she carried the tray to its usual spot on the table. Instead, she kept her head bowed, and made no effort to raise it. Her initial shyness had long been usurped by a relaxed familiarity and the change in her behaviour surprised Marek.

'Are you all right, Angelika? I haven't seen you for a few days.'

She did not answer and continued to avoid his gaze. Despite her unconventional looks she was always neatly dressed, with her uniform clean and smart. Even her shoes shone from the amount of polishing they received. As Marek was inspecting her footwear he caught sight of a purple patch on her ankle, as if she had sustained a heavy blow. Still she had not uttered a single word, and then Marek noticed a slight movement of her shoulders. The girl was crying. He took her by the arm and steered her to a chair by the fireplace, kneeling next to her. Slowly she raised her chin. Then he could see the reason for her reticence. Her left eye had been blackened and was extremely painful. When she raised her hand to brush away the tears Marek noticed her wrist was also bruised.

'Who did this to you, Angelika?' He attempted to comfort her. 'If you don't want to tell me I understand.'

After a little while she quietened down and, taking a handkerchief from her dress pocket, dabbed her eyes then blew her nose. She looked straight into Marek's eyes, and there was burning

157

anger in them. Marek could not comprehend how the girl could have been injured in this way.

'Last Wednesday, after I had brought you your food, I went to help in the kitchen. One of the Nazi officers wanted his meal taken to his room. Mrs Dabrowski was busy waiting on the senior officers in the dining room, so I told her I'd take it.' She paused to dab her eyes.

'As I gave him his tray, I could feel his eyes watching me like a hawk. I wanted to get out of the room as quickly as I could, but like a sly fox he had reached the door ahead of me and dropped the latch. I stood there not knowing what to do, trying my hardest not to let him see that I was afraid.' In her agitated state, her fingers vigorously twisted her handkerchief which was now quite knotted.

'What happened next?' Marek asked.

'He could speak a little Polish, and he told me to come and sit next to him and to tell him about myself and what life was like in Warsaw. I didn't know what to do. I was so frightened. I didn't want to upset him so I did as he asked. I answered his questions and then got up to go telling him I had chores to be getting on with. I took a few steps towards the door and . . .' Her voice trailed off and her bottom lip began to tremble. 'Suddenly he gripped my wrist and pulled me towards him. I tried to stop him but then he kicked me so hard and I fell backwards onto the floor. I tried to scream, but he punched me and put his hand across my mouth. Then he lay on top of me and he . . . he . . . raped me.'

Tears were streaming down her cheeks now, dripping from the tip of her nose into her lap. Marek put his arms around her and she buried her head in his shoulder. The girl had been, he was sure, a virgin, which made what had happened to her even more traumatic, vile and despicable.

When her sobbing had eased Marek asked whether she had told anyone else what had happened. She said that she had been too ashamed to speak about it and had instead blamed it on a fall. The floors in some parts of the house were quite uneven and it was easy to trip. Mrs Dabrowski must have guessed the truth for she sent her home for a few days. The most frustrating thing was that nothing could be done about it. There would be no reparation for such a crime. Marek only hoped that despite her pain, Angelika's cheerful personality would soon return.

❖ ❖ ❖

The choir rehearsal had got off to a good start that evening and Marek had put the traumas of the day to the recesses of his mind. Amos arrived with a supply of vodka. Mendel had managed to scavenge a bundle of wood and papers. The prospect of warmth and alcohol would encourage the men to sing well. Marek guided them through the music composed to date and, although they loathed the idea of having to perform it, the performance of such a complex piece was nevertheless a stimulating challenge for them. Eli had managed to copy Marek's arrangement of a Mahler song and they moved on to that before taking a break.

About a third of the way through, and having at that exact moment turned a page, Marek noticed that the men's eyes were no longer concentrating on the music or his directions, but on something else. He swung around quickly, curious to discover the source of the distraction, and there, framed in the doorway, was General Reinecke. This time, however, the manner of his arrival had been less threatening. Despite this he was not alone. He had a heavy armed phalanx. The Germans had taken to referring to the Ghetto as 'Mexico' because the resistance seemed to be akin to groups of bandits apt to spring out from anywhere.

'Good evening, Doctor Ruzanski. I thought I would see how the choir is taking to their new project.'

For a brief moment he had the manner of a fellow music enthusiast making an informal visit, and yet his life was at great risk. Week by week the Jewish fighting force was gaining in strength and confidence and Germans who dared to visit for even the briefest amount of time were likely to be picked off. He took one of the copies from the pile. Eli shifted nervously in his seat.

'Mahler. Yes indeed, I thought so. The Jew who renounced his religion.' His remark was cutting. 'His music is quite bold and experimental. Indeed not unlike the transition passage of your new work, Doctor. I would like to hear that now, if this would be acceptable to everyone?'

The Nazi waved his arm imperiously gesturing for them to begin. His manner was infuriating, for the men had no choice but to oblige. Despite a slight nervousness perceptible in their voices, the choir began with poise and confidence. The Nazi was clearly riveted, no doubt considering the fulsome praise which would be heaped upon him in a month or two's time. When they had performed the extent of what had been composed, the clapping started. Marek felt his heart tighten.

'Well done, gentlemen. Even though your performance was marred by the lack of any words, which your director has yet to write, you are as talented as I had hoped you would be.' Despite the sarcasm and lack of any warmth in his voice, Marek knew Franz Reinecke to be sincere.

'I bid you all goodnight. Enjoy the rest of your evening.' He paused and observed wryly, 'I would wager that you have the resources with you.'

It was Amos who now looked shifty, but the German was oblivious to his discomfort because he had disappeared as swiftly as he had arrived.

❖ ❖ ❖

At sunrise the next morning, Ruben and Marek sat drinking the last of the Ersatz coffee — a not overly-delicious substitute for the real thing, composed of roasted wheat mixed in mud. With Rachel's care, Ruben had returned to his old self, and all that remained of his injuries now was a fading scare above his temple. As they drank Ruben suddenly blurted out that there was someone he wanted everyone to meet. She was a girl called Nasial. Relationships formed amongst the young could become quite intense because of their expected brevity.

Marek was interested to know what she was like. By all accounts the girl was a real beauty with a great figure — just the thing a young man would be looking for in order to sow a few wild oats — and he suggested that Ruben check with Eva about when to invite her.

Nasial was everything that Ruben had described her as being and more. Even Izak's jaw dropped when he met her. Her hair — the colour of coal — fell to her shoulders in curls and she had a pretty heart-shaped face. Her deep blue eyes sparkled and she had a delicate mouth. As a man with a healthy liking for the opposite sex Marek could not help but notice her figure. She wore a dark tight-fitting skirt — beneath which was a pair of shapely legs — and a brown cardigan. Within minutes, despite the cold, it was whipped off to reveal a blouse which was calculated to be a size too small. Her breasts, with their perky nipples could hardly be contained. Unlike other girls, who had grown thin and gaunt, she had thrived, and as the evening progressed it was obvious to see why.

Eva prepared a meal from the meagre supplies and, though by no means a feast, it was tasty. Nasial sat between Ruben and Rachel, opposite Izak and Marek. Eva sat further up the table. Nasial, it transpired, shared a crowded apartment with her elder sister, Alina, a few blocks away. Tragically their parents had not

161

survived the round-ups back in July and so the two of them were left to fend for themselves. Nasial was interested to hear about the family's lives before the war. When the attention focused on Marek and he told her his profession, she seemed impressed.

'A musician. How talented you must be,' and as she said this she leaned across the table. 'I used to have piano lessons when I was younger but with the war coming I had to stop.' Then an idea struck her and she flashed a syrupy smile. 'Would you teach me when the war ends?'

Her apparent naivety was quite touching. Marek did not have the heart to shatter the poor girl's hopes, so he said he would be happy to. Rachel was eager to know about her sister. When Nasial told her that they both got by very well in the work they did, Rachel, who, like Marek, had realised precisely what this meant, had to stifle a giggle. Ruben was nonchalantly tucking into his food. He had not gazed lovingly at the girl once and, for that matter, neither had she at him. Her interest in Marek was undisguised. After talk of piano lessons, she started to ask more probing personal questions until Eva, having given up trying to get a word in edgeways, got up from the table to fetch the pudding. Izak, like Ruben, had taken little interest in Nasial up to this point, preferring to concentrate on his meal.

With Eva's exit, followed shortly afterwards by Rachel, Nasial began to edge her chair nearer to the table until she was obliged to sit almost ramrod straight. Suddenly without any warning, Izak broke into violent spasms of spluttering and choking. He had just been taking a sip from his glass when something had upset him and his eyes darted downwards to an area beneath the table. Curious to find out what it was Marek angled his head to look.

Peering down at his father's legs, Marek caught sight of a stockinged leg being hastily withdrawn by its owner. From the angle of trajectory, it was obvious that moments earlier it had come to rest in the area of Izak's groin. Whilst patting the poor man on his back, Marek glanced across at Nasial who was behaving very sheepishly. Ruben was sniggering. Evidently the girl had made a serious miscalculation and her advances had been intended for Marek's benefit. For the rest of the meal Nasial barely said a word. Izak recovered quickly from the impropriety, but as soon as the meal was over he made his excuses and retired to his armchair. Marek struggled hard to avoid the gaze of both the girl, and more importantly Ruben, who shared his sense of humour. Nasial set out for home shortly after. That was the first and last time the Ruzanskis met her. A few weeks later a jealous SS soldier silenced her for good.

Several days had passed since Lidia and Benjamin's visit. The Ruzanski's had not received any communication from them but this was not unusual. Another Sabbath came and went – almost too peacefully – during which Izak read his papers, Eva, with Rachel's help, prepared the meals, and Ruben disappeared for a good part of the day. Marek stole away to a corner to read. Later that evening Rachel and her mother were sitting together unravelling skeins of wool. He wondered what it was they were about to make this time. Perhaps it would be something for the new baby. Marek's mother was a remarkable woman who had done her best to keep family life as normal as possible since they had come to live in the Ghetto. Seeing her now, Marek was reminded of family times together when they were children. Usually after lunch he and Lidia would play piano duets much to their parents' enjoyment and Rachel would be given the important job of page-turner.

Ruben returned home a little before eight. His jacket pockets were bulging and he made straight for the store cupboard.

'I see Lidia and Benjamin have already set off for home then. That's sensible,' he remarked, before collapsing in a chair.

'What do you mean?' Eva let the wool drop in her lap.

'Well they must be back at their apartment by now.' Ruben was puzzled by Eva's question.

Izak, who had been listening from behind his paper, leaned across to the boy.

'They haven't been to visit us.' He was grim-faced.

'That's strange. I met them earlier and they said they were on their way to see you.'

'Where did you see them?' Izak said, trying to hide his alarm.

'A few streets away from here,' Ruben said.

'And how did they seem?' Izak pressed on.

'They were fine,' Ruben answered looking perplexed.

Rachel and Marek looked at each other. The colour had drained from her face. Both of them had known too many situations like this.

'Are you certain Lidia and Benjamin were coming here?' It was almost as if Eva was pleading with the boy to tell her that he had made a mistake.

Ruben shifted uneasily in his seat. He of all people knew the gravity of the situation. There was only one thing to be done now and that was to go to their apartment to check they were there. Marek grabbed his coat and scarf.

'No, Marek, it's far too dangerous at this time of night. It will have to wait until morning,' Eva pleaded with him. There were tears in her eyes.

'No, Mama, it can't wait. I will be careful. I promise. Please don't worry,' Marek said as he wrapped his scarf high about his neck.

'I'm coming with you,' Ruben declared, jumping up.

The two men stepped out into the freezing cold. The sky was cloudy and thankfully there was no moon. Marek had only gone a few paces when Ruben tugged his sleeve. He stopped dead, assuming Ruben had spotted an approaching German.

'I couldn't say anything in front of your parents, but a couple of cunning Nazi swine have been picking people off. The bastards have been taking pot shots from over the wall. There were quite a few bodies lying around on Gesia Street.'

Marek could imagine only too easily the German marksmen performing their cowardly acts with cat-like stealth.

'Let's just hope to God that they're safe,' Marek said, thinking aloud.

Ruben and Marek crossed the street and passed by several empty buildings. The resettlement operation in January had cleared them of their occupants, and now in the darkness these lifeless structures stood like empty mausoleums. When they reached Lidia's apartment a man of about forty opened the door. Marek recognised Emil.

'Marek, what a wonderful surprise. It is good to see you, but what do you want at this time of the night?' Emil said ushering the two friends inside.

The layout of the rooms was similar to the Ruzanskis' apartment, though conditions were more cramped here. Apart from Lidia and Benjamin the apartment was also home to Emil, and his wife, his brother and sister-in-law and their teenage daughter. Emil's two children had been successfully smuggled out about a month ago. Emil's wife, Liebe, and his brother Samuel were still awake, and were surprised to discover they had visitors. Marek introduced Ruben and then explained the reason for their visit.

Apparently Lidia was keen to spend some time with her family. The fact that they had not yet returned did not worry their friends, since they had assumed that Lidia and Benjamin were spending the night. Now of course it was a different story, and the three of them became very concerned.

'And you saw them about three o'clock this afternoon Ruben?' Emil asked. 'Yes, that would be about right.'

'If they're not at yours then where are they?' Liebe said, in a whisper.

'I don't like to say this, but it doesn't look good,' Samuel said frankly.

'What are you going to do?' Emil asked.

Marek was at a loss for words. He didn't know what to do. He had hoped to find them safely at home. He sank down into the nearest chair and tried to empty his mind.

'We'll have to go and see Baumatz,' Marek said at last.

Baumatz was one of the Ghetto undertakers and it made sense to pay him a visit.

'Wait, Marek. I have another idea,' Samuel suggested. 'What if they have been taken to the collection point? Some workers were transported to the labour camp at Trawniki today. What if your sister and her husband somehow managed to get themselves caught up in that? I know a reliable source who'll be able to find out for you. The man works for Többens. He's a policeman.'

The contempt on Marek's face at the mention of a member of the Ghetto's law enforcement must have been obvious. These people had been responsible for delivering as many as five Jews each a day for transportation in the first major *Aktion*.

'I know what you're thinking, but he's not as bad as the others. However, he may need something in return for his help.'

'You mean a bribe,' Marek suggested.

'Well, yes. Unfortunately that's the way it is nowadays. The thing is, if he can't help you he'll know someone who can. Isn't it worth paying a little something to find out the truth?'

Emil was right. Not knowing was the worst part.

'Where can we find him?' Marek asked.

'He lives a few blocks away,' Samuel explained, scribbling

the address down for him. 'His name is Tadek Zuckerman. His apartment is on the third floor.'

Tadek Zuckerman, a gangling man with greying hair, was displeased at being disturbed at such a late hour and did not greet the two men with enthusiasm. He warned them of the stupidity of being out after curfew. Given the reception he gave Ruben and Marek, it seemed Samuel's opinion of the man had been misleading, and Marek was not convinced that he would help. The three men huddled in the cold on the landing.

'What do you want from me?' he asked, looking up and down the passage nervously.

'Samuel sent us. He thought you might be able to give us some information,' Marek explained.

At the mention of a familiar name his anxiety eased, and he took out some cigarettes from his pocket and offered them around.

'So, you're friends with Samuel?' Tadek said after a long drag.

'Emil and Samuel share rooms with my sister and her husband,' Marek began, explaining the reason for their visit. He listened carefully but showed no emotion.

'Samuel is a good man. The two of us go back a long way,' Tadek explained. Then, placing the cigarette between his lips, he took another heavy draw before staring into space.

Marek was not certain how to take the peculiarities of his character.

'The *Umschlagplatz*. I know it well. You wouldn't imagine that such a place could be the gateway to hell. But that is what it is. The cargo comes in all sizes. Young. Old. Good and bad, but there's no reckoning.' He took another puff. 'No reckoning at all. Just one destination. The children with their innocent expressions.

167

They haven't been bad. Don't deserve it. No one deserves it. Sure I've taken bribes. We all have. Got to think of my family. They will take them away from me if I don't do my job.' He waved his arms about and turned his head towards his apartment. 'How could I feed them if I didn't take advantage of what opportunities came my way?'

Ruben and Marek exchanged glances. They were hearing the ramblings of the unhinged mind of a man with a desperate need for atonement for what he believed were his past sins during the round-ups.

'My sister,' Marek said quietly, trying to bring Tadek back from where he was so he could help them.

'Horrified. Frightened. They huddle there like cowed animals. The terrible wailing and sobbing.' He was ranting now and beads of sweat were trickling down his neck. 'The faces. I see them everywhere. My people despise me.' His eyes were filling up with tears and his whole body seemed to sag with the weight of his burden. 'I know Lidia and Benjamin. I would recognize them but they weren't there today.'

At last he had given Marek and Ruben the information they needed and Marek did not doubt him. The image of every victim would be engrained upon his memory. Afterwards Marek wondered what would become of him, this miserable individual eaten up by so much guilt.

There was only one more thing the two friends could do that night, and that was to visit Baumatz the undertaker. Not long afterwards Ruben and Marek found themselves standing outside the home of one of the chief Ghetto undertakers. A decent burial cost money, and there was a fortune to be made transporting coffins to the Aryan side, especially when they often contained valuables which could be sold on. Not surprisingly, there was plenty of work for the man and his business was thriving. Ruben hesitated for a moment before knocking on the door of the dirty, soot-covered building. Marek needed to prepare himself for what he might discover inside those walls.

They heard a scuttling noise behind the door, and then keys jangling. It struck Marek that, of all people in the Ghetto, the undertaker would have the least to fear from the Germans. He was the person who mopped up after them and tidied away their execrable work. The man who peered out from around the half-opened door was small in stature and his face was long and angular, with a sallow complexion. His ears were large and protruded some way from his head and his eyes, perhaps his most prominent feature, were piercing and rodent-like. Tinged with grey at the temples, his oily hair was slicked back off his forehead. It was not an exaggeration to say that everything about him reeked of death.

Baumatz ushered his visitors into his office, closing the door behind them with a jerky movement of his hand which matched the spasmodic movements of his eyes. The room was dimly lit and fusty. Apart from a single wooden coffin leaning against a wall, there was little evidence of the sort of work that occurred here. All the fripperies one might have expected to see, such as choice of headstone or variety of wood, had been dispensed with: there was now one swift and easy method of despatch which suited all, unless one was especially wealthy.

He pointed to two chairs on the opposite side of his desk. Perhaps he thought they were in need of his professional services which Marek desperately hoped they were not. Clasping his hands he gave the two men a rather sickly smile.

'How can I help you, gentlemen? Whatever your business it must be urgent for you to call at this perilous hour.'

Marek explained their predicament.

'Can you describe Lidia and Benjamin to me? And where were they last seen?' He jotted down some details and agreed to take a look. 'If my memory serves me right, however, no one of that description has been delivered to us today.'

The time spent waiting for his return seemed endless. Tension was etched upon Ruben's face as he groped for a cigarette. At last Baumatz reappeared and, without saying a word, he sat down. With darting eyes he examined both of them before delivering his verdict.

'I have to say that none of my clients fit the descriptions you have given me. However,' he continued after a pause, 'that is not to say they won't be joining us shortly. You are welcome to try again tomorrow.'

'He gives me the creeps. Must be what working with the dead does to you I suppose,' Ruben said, trying to lighten the mood.

Nothing more could be done that night, and they would have to return home without answers. Despite the late hour, Izak, Eva and Rachel had not gone to bed.

'Is there any news, Marek?' Izak looked drawn.

'Nothing conclusive, Papa.'

The atmosphere in the room was tense and with these words it was as though the three of them could again draw breath.

'They were not taken to the *Umschlagplatz* and Baumatz could not help us either,' Ruben said, glancing at Eva whose cheeks were tear-stained.

They had known the mention of the undertaker would be enough to cause their hearts to miss a beat, and yet Marek was in no doubt that they would want to hear the facts, however painful.

The German soldiers had not yet arrived and this gave Marek an opportunity to consider what he needed to do next. Lidia and

Benjamin had obviously not returned home last night, for Emil would have got word to the Ruzanskis. They were still missing and the only recourse now was to go to the *Judenrat* and hope for some kind of assistance. One of the few committee members left, Dr Lukowski, had been an associate of Izak's before the war. Just then the car came into view and Marek waited as it pulled up tight to the kerb. Rather than make for the back door he approached the passenger window.

The soldier wound down the glass. 'What are you waiting for Jew? Get in,' he barked.

'I won't be coming to work today. I have important family matters to sort out. Please inform General Reinecke of this.'

There was an ominous silence. Marek had anticipated their reaction with some trepidation, thinking they might force him into the vehicle at gunpoint.

'It's your funeral, Jew,' Viktor shouted, followed by a screech of rubber tyres as he drove off.

Marek entered the tall, grey-stoned building with its maze of rooms and passages. Its activity had been considerably scaled down; in fact most of its authority had been usurped by the Jewish Combat Organisation known as the *ZOB*. At this hour, months earlier, the place would have been full of people milling about in the main hall like ants come to seek information or lodge a complaint. Now it dealt primarily in Supply. Spotting one of the clerks rushing past carrying some papers, Marek called after him. He turned and frowned, clearly annoyed at being delayed. Marek asked him politely for directions to the room of Dr Abek Lukowski and was directed to a flight of stairs.

'Come in.'

The person scribbling away was not at all as Marek remembered him, but much greyer, his face lined. Not surprisingly, the treatment of the Jews combined with the strains of his job had aged him. After completing a sentence he put his pen down and stared at his visitor inquisitively over the top of his spectacles. Moments later he smiled broadly.

'Marek Ruzanski. Izak's son. How long has it been? How is your father?'

'Papa is well, thank you.'

'And your mother?'

'She is well too.'

'I'm very glad to hear it. Now how can I help you?'

He listened, punctuating Marek's explanation with deep sighs. Abek removed his reading glasses and began to clean them.

'I'm not convinced there is a great deal I can do to help you Marek,' he said finally. 'You say you have already consulted Baumatz and spoken to a reliable source at the *Umschlagplatz*. Have you considered the possibility that Benjamin and Lidia have left under their own steam?'

'It's highly unlikely. They haven't got any papers and they would never have left without saying goodbye to my parents.'

'And they went missing late yesterday afternoon?' Abek asked, jotting down the details on a piece of paper. 'I remember your sisters. Pretty girls, both of them. Lidia is the elder, isn't she?'

'Yes, that's right.'

'It shouldn't take too long for me to make a few enquiries, but you must realise I'm unable to promise anything. I don't like to admit this, my young friend, but I would prepare your family for the worst.'

Marek took a seat downstairs in the main hall and waited patiently for Abek to return. There were regular visitors making an appearance. Those on the way out were grumbling and muttering

172

to themselves – presumably because their problems had not been resolved to their satisfaction. Marek must have sat there for nearly an hour, in which time the same clerk scampered to and fro clutching more bundles of papers. Just as he was beginning to think he had been forgotten, Marek noticed Abek descending the stairs. As he approached he prepared himself for yet more bad news.

'It is as I thought, Marek. I've consulted with my colleagues and I'm afraid we've drawn a blank. Neither name is recorded on any list. One thing that is certain, however, is that the Germans were in a bloodthirsty mood yesterday. I am reluctant to suggest this, but it may be worth paying Baumatz another visit.' Abek hesitated before continuing. 'Bodies can easily be . . . lost.'

The colour drained from Marek's face on hearing these stark words.

As they said their goodbyes, Abek asked Marek to pass on his regards to Izak and Eva. Marek understood the long-standing mutual respect Abek and his father held for each other. He was a decent and thoughtful man.

The streets were almost deserted. The work parties had passed through an hour or two earlier and only beggars who had nothing to lose were wandering along the pavements. Marek hurried on – determined to get the ordeal over – and was almost oblivious to the dangers of being out at this time. As he rounded a street corner, his stomach lurched. Two SS soldiers were kicking over the huddled bodies of a young mother and her two children. From their shrivelled condition it was apparent that malnutrition and hypothermia had killed them. Using their truncheons, they poked and prodded the corpses as if they were the carcasses of dead animals. Marek stood paralysed, wondering what to do, when he was spotted by one of them. The soldier's mouth curled into a sneer and he tapped his colleague on the shoulder. The two of them marched straight towards their Jewish prey, smiling with sinister intent. Marek tried to remain calm, even though he was certain he was moments from death. There had been near-misses in the past but this was different. Despite the Germans avoidance of the Ghetto for fear of attacks by the resistance fighters, there were some who were utterly fearless. He was up against two of the worst kind of killers.

'What have we here?' one of them said as he prodded Marek with his crop.

'A brave and fearless Jew,' the other chipped in, '. . . or a foolish one.'

'And where do you think you're off to?'

'And do you believe you will get there?' his colleague taunted, relishing the sport.

They both glowered as they waited for a reply.

'I had important business at the *Judenrat*,' was all Marek could manage to say. His heart was pumping so quickly he thought it would burst out of his chest.

'Business indeed. Important enough to risk your life for?'

'Yes, I believe so,' Marek responded defiantly, feeling remarkably bold.

Then he felt a sudden sharp pain as the crop made contact.

'On your knees, Jew.'

Marek's legs were kicked from under him by a heavy boot, followed by a blow to his stomach. Winded, he could not move. He lay there gasping and grimacing with the pain. The sudden jerking of his body had dislodged his identity card which fell onto the pavement.

'Well, Jew, you have risked your life for nothing,' said his attacker as he pressed his gun to the back of Marek's head.

'Wait!' The soldier who was watching and almost salivating at the prospect of the Jew's bloody despatch, cried out. 'Let's see who we're about to send to Hell,' he laughed.

174

He stooped down and picked the card up. After examining it thoroughly his face took on a panicked look. With a single swipe of his arm he knocked the gun out of the hand of the would-be executioner and it clattered to the ground. Then both men turned their backs and began to mutter something. A few minutes later, and much to Marek's amazement, a remarkable thing happened. The identity card was returned and he was advised to be more careful in the future.

Marek hurried along the street, expecting to hear the fatal shot ring out. It didn't come and he squatted down in a doorway breathless and dazed. His hands were shaking uncontrollably and it took several attempts to light a cigarette. It didn't take long to realise what had saved him. It was his name. On the orders of General Reinecke, Marek had been granted some kind of city wide immunity, and all SS personal he encountered must have been instructed not to harm him. This was all well and good but it was not full protection. Marek had merely survived back there on a whim. Still shaking he stubbed out the cigarette butt and, his courage restored, he made his way to Baumatz's funeral parlour.

Even in daylight the building was drab and foreboding. The door was opened by a young man in his early twenties. With his beady, wild eyes he bore a sufficient likeness to the proprietor, and was perhaps either his son or his nephew. He gestured for Marek to take a seat before slinking off somewhere. A few minutes later, a strutting Baumatz made an almost theatrical entrance. Marek knew immediately from Baumatz's manner, and the fixed smile on his lips, that he had reached the end of the search.

'I was counting upon you paying us another visit, Dr Ruzanski,' he said. 'I do have information for you today.'

Marek sat stock still.

'Last night when we spoke I was not in possession of all the facts. Earlier that evening there were two bodies . . .' he corrected himself quickly, '. . . people collected, but since we were already very crowded, my son thought it best to leave them on the cart overnight. It wasn't until early this morning that I knew of the matter, you understand, and I must apologize for any inconvenience this has caused you and your family.' He beckoned for Marek to follow him. 'If you wouldn't mind taking a look just to be sure, though from the descriptions you gave and the district where they were found . . .' his voice trailed off as he passed through a doorway.

Marek followed Baumatz along a narrow passageway which connected the front of the shop with a much larger area where all the chilling work was done. It was just as poorly-lit as the rest of the building, which was fortuitous for it made it difficult to see in detail the bodies which were stacked tidily. From what Marek had seen of this man he imagined that he had a meticulous approach to his work. They reached a corner of the room where two covered bodies had been laid side by side. A strand of hair had slipped out from under the edge of the cloth, and Marek immediately knew it was Lidia's. Baumatz had taken hold of one edge and was about to draw it back when Marek grabbed his arm.

'A much tidier set of clients than I usually see pass through my doors,' he said grimly.

Marek looked at him in astonishment. He imagined Baumatz possessed a fairly black sense of humour.

Marek's once beautiful, vivacious sister had lost all her sparkle and was just an empty vessel. Her eyes had a fixed glassy stare and her rosy complexion was now grey. There were green tinged bruises on her neck and forehead where she had fallen heavily, but the fatal wound was a single bullet to the chest. She was still wearing her favourite coat and the front of it was soaked in blood. It was bad enough having to bear the sight of Lidia's lifeless remains, but her brother now had to deal with the grisly spectacle of Benjamin. A shot to the temple had robbed him of his life, and a look of incredulity was fixed for all eternity on his face. Mercifully his death would have been instantaneous. The shock of seeing his sister and her husband deeply affected Marek. He was numb, and the tears did not come. He bent down, kissed Lidia's cheek and smoothed her hair so it was now presentable, the way she liked it to be. He stood looking for what must have seemed an age. Still he could feel nothing. The reality of it all had not yet hit him. Surprisingly, Baumatz, a busy man, did not hurry him. Instead the undertaker had taken a step backwards and was waiting patiently.

The two men returned to Baumatz's office where he now adopted a more cool and businesslike approach. He enquired whether Marek had the money to arrange for a decent burial, mentioning that if rites were required this would increase the price. The Germans had reinstated public worship some time ago; however, it would be easier if prayers were said at the funeral parlour. Marek told him that he would like to bring his family later that day when it would be safe, and that he would have the money with him then. He said that the Germans liked bodies to be disposed of straightaway, but that he might be able to make an exception. Marek said he would make it worth his while. He walked home in a state of disbelief trying to blot out the images of his dead sister and her husband in his mind.

The prospect of telling his family that their precious daughter, son-in-law and unborn grandchild had been murdered was unimaginable. By now, however, they would be fearing the worst. Climbing the stairs to the apartment, Marek hoped Ruben would be there. He could help comfort the others, especially Rachel, who would be utterly devastated. It had been dreadful enough with Mara and Ezra, but this was much, much worse. Marek was consumed with grief and could not speak. His demeanour told them everything they needed to know. Eva collapsed into her husband's arms. Her sobbing grew louder and louder with every

177

breath. Izak cradled her shuddering body. Rachel collapsed to the floor. Ruben comforted her as best he could. By now overcome with sheer exhaustion, Marek needed rest. He lay down on his bed and fell asleep. When he awoke his mother was stroking his hair.

'Thank you for what you have done.'

Her words stung like a sharp pain in Marek's heart. It had not been a dream after all. At last the tears came and mother and son clung to each other in despair.

Grief hung like a dark cloud over the apartment. Little was said, and everyone tried to keep busy. At last it was time. With all the work parties about to trudge wearily home for the night, they were able to mingle inconspicuously with the crowds.

Baumatz's funeral parlour was not as dingy as it had been on the previous evening. Candles had brightened the interior and there was a faint odour of incense. In a space at the far end of the room, two coffins were standing together and – to give him his due – the man knew how to put on a show. Before the coffins a lone figure was standing holding a book. He was vaguely familiar, and then Marek recognised him as one of the Rabbis at the Ruzanskis' old synagogue. As Eva caught sight of the boxes she let out an agonized gasp and began to cry softly. Rachel tightened her grasp on her brother's hand, sobbing.

Once the brief ceremony was over Ruben led everyone out of the building, while Marek remained behind to settle the account. Baumatz thanked him and promised to inform him of the whereabouts of the burial plot.

The evening meal was a solemn affair. No one spoke. Much later, when their parents were asleep, Rachel called her brother to her room.

'I don't think I'll ever be able to get over it.'

Her eyes were red from crying. Marek sat down next to her and cradled her reassuringly.

'The pain will ease in time. It got better with Mara and Ezra, didn't it?'

'It's not the same. We're talking about Lidia and Benjamin.'

She buried her head in her brother's chest and started to sob. Marek tried to fight back his own tears but could not.

Sleep brings relief, so they say. It is true that in an unconscious state the suspension of misery is possible; however, when consciousness is resumed so is heartbreak. That is how it was with Marek the next morning. He grabbed his case and passed through the checkpoint without any difficulty. Ever since the great cull the sight of beggar children crowding at the gate was less common. When Marek reached Gesia Street the car was already there, its exhaust fumes rising into the air like white smoke. He climbed in. As usual neither of his companions acknowledged him, nor did he receive a report about whether his absence had caused any consternation. The driver slipped into first gear and they sped along the road. Mercifully, the streets were empty.

A fire was burning in the grate and the piano lid had been raised. There was a fresh supply of manuscript paper, and the pencils had been sharpened. Everything was ready for him to pick up where he had left off, as if nothing of any significance had happened in the intervening forty-eight hours. Anger and grief bubbled over and Marek snatched up the pencils and snapped them in two, hurling the broken pieces into the fire. Next he seized the composition, screwing it up before throwing it across the room. He sat down at the piano and wildly smashed the keys. When he had eventually played out his rage and frustration, he buried his head in his hands. The grief overwhelmed him. He sat there deep in thought, the only sounds to be heard in the room coming from the ticking clock and the burning wood. It was then that an idea occurred to him. He would finish the commissioned piece, but he would write a second. He would compose the two works simultaneously, yet only one would be the true masterpiece. Yes, it was all very clear now. Marek's music would indeed praise and glorify a people, but not the Nazis. Instead it would serve as a memorial to all Jews everywhere – expiation for Lidia, Benjamin, Mara and Ezra, and those like them who were yet to die. The feelings of elation and optimism that now gripped him were exhilarating and he was oblivious to all dangers. He was set on a path from which nothing and no one would deter him.

Marek retrieved the crumpled manuscript and smoothed it out. For the moment he resolved to carry on as normal, so as not to attract suspicion. Mrs Dabrowski brought lunch, which didn't surprise him. She must have heard Marek's musical outburst and made it her business to find out the cause. At first he ignored her. He was engrossed in working out a particularly complex rhythm pattern. She smiled awkwardly when he thanked her for the food. Then, rather than leaving him to eat it, she approached the piano.

'We wondered where you were yesterday.' She spoke softly and her voice had lost its customary abruptness.

Though reluctant to speak of it, Marek felt she should know. When he had finished recounting all that had happened he felt emotionally drained. Glancing at the housekeeper, Marek saw a single tear trickle down her cheek. She wiped it away with the side of her plump little hand and then, without a word, she wrapped him in her arms. The softness and warmth of her body pressed so close to his was comforting. She was a mother who could just as easily lose her son.

The chiming of the clock signalled it was time to leave. The bleak, cheerless mood at the apartment was something Marek did not relish rushing back to, but he knew it had to be faced. When he arrived Rachel was doing some cleaning.

'How are you?' he asked as he hugged her.

'Not so good, but I'm trying to be strong for Mama and Papa.'

'They seem a little better than I thought they might be,' Marek observed.

'They're being brave for our sake I expect. The Rabbi came to see us today and I think it helped them.'

'And you?'

'I found some of what he said comforting. He explained that while it is important to grieve for our loved ones, we have to move on and that the way forward is to ensure we survive.'

'He is very wise for someone so young.'

'He was telling us that he became a Rabbi just before war broke out.'

'What a place to find yourself spending the first few years of your ministry in,' Marek observed in disbelief. 'Did he stay long?'

'Half an hour or so.'

Rachel fell silent and her brother sensed she was thinking about something.

'Marek are we going to die like Lidia and Benjamin?' she asked.

The bluntness of her question left him speechless for a moment. Marek grabbed her shoulders firmly. Her eyes were brimming with tears.

'Rachel, please don't talk like that. Ruben, Papa and I will do all we can to keep everyone safe. You must believe that.'

Marek's mind was restless that night and it was difficult to sleep.

Eventually he drifted off, but not for long: at some point during the early hours he opened his eyes. He got out of bed, pulled his jacket around his shoulders, and crept to the kitchen, taking his music case with him. He laid out a sheet of manuscript paper on the table and grabbed his writing pen, and then, by the light of one of the carbide lamps, began to scribble down the melody which was still in his head. When this was done he hummed it softly back to himself. He had composed the first and most important theme of the new work and he was pleased with it. He slipped into bed and slept peacefully until dawn.

Winter was reluctant to loosen its grip on the Jewish Ghetto in 1943. Those who eagerly anticipated the sprouting foliage and blossoms were disappointed. However, the sun was bright and went some way to raising spirits. Walter Többens, the unscrupulous German businessman, who had amassed a fortune on the backs of the subjugated Jews who he employed, made a further appeal to the remainder of his work force to transfer to the concentration labour camps of Trawniki and Poniatowa. Some had already left for Trawniki during the previous month. According to Többens, Himmler had decreed that Warsaw should be 'cleansed of Jews'. The incentive offered was that employees and their families could migrate to an area of agreeable countryside in the Lublin region where they would lead contended lives. Despite the Germans' best efforts, the majority of the Ghetto inhabitants were not fooled. It was good to see such dogged opposition.

Surreptitiously Marek had begun work on the second piece of music and in the evenings would hide himself away for considerable stretches, composing frantically. The commissioned work was nearing its conclusion. The final section had taken the form of a fugue and required modifications here and there. He had yet to add the words, but it would be finished on time. He had been sitting at the piano for most of the morning, and could feel the warmth of the sun on his shoulders. Now standing directly in front of the window, Marek surveyed the gardens. The ground was suffused with bright light, and the waters of the lake glistened and shimmered. It was then that he caught sight of someone − a woman − leaning over the bridge at the far side of the water, staring into the depths as he had done on his early forays around the estate.

'Who's that out there?' he asked Angelika, as she jostled cutlery nearby.

'I don't see anyone,' she said, peering out of the window, 'but it's probably the *Oberst-gruppenführer*'s daughter.'

'He has a daughter?' Marek asked incredulously. The thought of the man having a family was something he had never contemplated. He found it incomprehensible that Nazis could have loved ones, and yet be the perpetrators of such wickedness.

'Yes. She arrived last night,' Angelika explained.

'Have you met her?'

'Mrs Dabrowski has, and she said that for a German she's not that bad. Oh, look you need some more water. I'll fetch some.'

Marek watched Angelika pick up the jug from the dresser. There had been a noticeable change in her mood these past few days and he greatly admired her fortitude. Hard as it must have been, it struck him that Angelika had come to terms with what had happened to her and had resolved to get on with her life.

Marek ate his lunch quickly and then set out for the lake. Much of the ice had thawed now and in just a few areas a thin film remained. He had yet to see any signs of life, and had come to the conclusion that whatever fish there were must be sheltering amongst the weeds. The house looked truly magnificent with the sunshine on it, and he wondered whether it would survive the war, and what might happen to it then. His association with it was destined to be fleeting, and he felt a pang of regret that he would not witness the summer flowerbeds ablaze with colour, the trees in leaf and the vegetable garden ready for harvesting in the autumn.

Today the summerhouse was unoccupied. The two chairs were still positioned beside the hearth, but where the fire had once blazed there was now just a grey, powdery ash. Marek sat down, took off his gloves and rubbed his hands together. The bright sun was deceptive and away from its glare the temperature was bitter.

He was sitting there lost in his thoughts when, all at once, he was conscious of being observed. Standing a little way off was the young woman he had seen earlier. He jumped up. As her eyes probed his, Marek couldn't help but notice just how deep a shade of blue they were, and how long and dark her lashes were. Her nose was small and yet in perfect proportion to the rest of her face, and her mouth was very pleasing. Framing her face was an appealingly array of tumbling curls the colour of flax.

'Good afternoon. I'm Marek Ruzanski,' he said, offering her his hand.

The young woman edged a few steps nearer. He was immediately struck by the velvety warmth of her skin. His by comparison must have felt as cold as ice.

'I am pleased to meet you, Dr Ruzanski. My father has spoken of you.'

'You must be the Commander's daughter,' Marek replied. With these words her cheeks reddened a little.

'Forgive me for not introducing myself. My name is Clara. I am staying with my father for the next month.'

'Do you know why I am here?' Marek asked.

'No, not exactly, other than you are composing an important work,' she said, before adding, 'Papa says it is intended to be a surprise. Is there more that I should know?' she asked, looking at the stranger with a puzzled glance.

'Your father should be the one to tell you,' Marek responded coolly. He glanced at his watch. It was time he was getting back.

Before he left Marek snatched a fleeting glimpse of Clara. She had moved nearer to the fireplace. The deep brown colour of her coat suited her and hung elegantly on her frame, skimming the contours of her body.

The surprise encounter with the young German woman had an unsettling effect on Marek. Normally a well-mannered individual, he was somewhat bothered by the fact that he had allowed his feelings to get the better of him, even to the point of rudeness. She had treated him with respect and he had not sensed any hostility in her manner. Furthermore, she could not be held accountable for her father's actions. Later that evening, Marek began to tell his family about his meeting with Clara but the news was received with disinterest, especially after what had happened to Lidia and Benjamin.

Halfway through the evening Daniel arrived unexpectedly. His excitable state did not bode well, and it was obvious he had something important to discuss. Izak gave up his seat and the rest of the family gathered around, eager to hear what he had to say.

'I've come to say goodbye,' Daniel said abruptly.

'When are you leaving?' Rachel said, breaking the family's stunned silence.

'In a few days' time. It's all arranged. We have our papers and enough money to give us a fresh start.'

'But where will you go, Daniel?' Eva asked with maternal concern.

185

'We've found some accommodation on the Aryan side. It's in a quiet area where we should be able to blend in.'

With his fair complexion and light hair Daniel could easily pass as a Gentile, as would his wife and their young daughter, who shared his colouring.

'We've all had to learn the catechism. You'd never believe how many observances there are in the Catholic faith; all those saints' days, festivals, prayers, and of course the grace at meal times.'

'How is little Ada taking to the idea? Do you think she'll cope?' Eva asked, seeking reassurance about their preparations.

'It has been hard work but she has done very well. She is very young but it is as if she intuitively recognizes the seriousness of the situation.'

'Will you be staying in the city or moving out to the country as others have done?' Izak enquired.

'We'll go to the country as soon as something can be arranged. It may be our only chance for survival. You must all get out too. You do realise it's only a matter of time before the Germans finish the job they started in January. We shouldn't kid ourselves into thinking that we are David about to do battle with Goliath. We don't stand a chance however much of a fight we put up.'

Daniel spoke passionately and pleaded with the Ruzanskis with a heartfelt conviction and yet Marek knew, however persuasive his argument, it would be of no use. His parents had made up their minds months ago to stay and Rachel would never leave without them. Marek had no choice but to remain and in time face the consequences of his own actions. Daniel gave a half-hearted smile as if he understood his encouragement had fallen on deaf ears. Izak fetched Ruben's latest booty, a bottle of vodka. They drank a toast to Daniel, his family and their new life. When it was time for him to leave, Marek escorted him to the door and the two friends embraced each other.

'Until we meet again, my friend. May God watch over you.'
Then he was gone.

❖   ❖   ❖

Dawn broke, and with it the spectres of the night departed. Images of Lidia and Benjamin had plagued Marek's sleep and he woke in a state of exhaustion.

It was now a regular habit of his to perform a favourite piece before beginning work. To be able to play the piano freely was exhilarating, and that day Marek decided to play a Chopin Étude; despite the fact that the Nazis had banned this composer's music throughout Poland. He worked steadily all morning until, at eleven-fifteen, a visitor arrived.

'I hope I am not disturbing you, Dr Ruzanski, but I wanted to come and tell you how much I enjoyed your performance earlier. You play with such expression and sensitivity.'

It was Clara, and as Marek thanked her for her compliment he appraised her more closely. She was wearing an azure-coloured dress and the material over her undulating breasts was as taut as embroidery stretched tightly upon a frame. It was drawn in around the middle, emphasizing the narrowness of her waist.

'I have something for you,' the young woman said, digging into the left pocket of her dress and producing a small bottle of lotion. 'It's very good at softening skin. I noticed your hands when we first met.'

She glanced at him shyly.

'You're right. I'm afraid all those hours in the factory have left them in rather a state.'

Marek beckoned for Clara to sit next to him on the piano stool. He held out one of his hands, which she took in hers. Then she began to gently massage the nourishing cream into the damaged areas. She did the same with the other stroking it tenderly. Not once did Marek flinch or cry out. When she had finished Clara sensed her companion staring at her. She looked up. Their eyes met briefly. She got to her feet.

'Is Chopin a favourite of yours?' Clara asked. As she spoke Marek watched the movement of her lips.

'I greatly admire his work, but I prefer the music of Bach.'

'Do you play the church organ as well?'

'Yes, I do, although there's little opportunity at the moment . . .'

'I suppose not,' Clara said, colouring slightly.

'Do you play yourself?' Marek enquired.

'I used to have piano and singing lessons.'

'You share your father's interest in music?'

'Yes, I inherited it from him. My mother preferred to paint.' She moved towards the piano. 'Is this the work you mentioned?' she asked, leaning over Marek's shoulder. 'May I?'

Marek arranged the sheets in order. She began to play the opening section with surprising accuracy. When she had finished, she put her hands in her lap.

'It will be a great work, and yet there is something about it I can't quite put my finger on.' She wrinkled her pretty nose.

'What is that?' Marek asked.

She hesitated before answering, perhaps wishing to choose her words carefully.

'In scale it's much smaller, of course, and the style is original, but it does remind me a little of Wagner. Did my father choose the style?'

'Yes. He wanted it to be Wagnerian.'

'Does that bother you? I know one should be impartial about art,' Clara observed.

'You mean the fact that I am a Jew and Wagner was anti-Semitic and that Hitler has adopted him as the Party's composer.

Well, yes, it does bother me, very much,' Marek protested.

Her cheeks blushed to a deep red.

'I believe there is a significant date in the Nazi calendar coming up,' Marek continued.

Clara looked perplexed as if the insinuation had been lost on her.

'You surely remember the birthday of your great leader?' Marek continued.

'What does that have to do with anything?' she snapped, evidently frustrated

'Can't you see? Hitler's Birthday. A Wagnerian-style masterpiece written by a Jew. Ah! Perhaps I should have mentioned the text, which must glorify the mighty Führer and the Party. It would make a great piece of entertainment for sick minds.'

At last the truth dawned on Clara. She looked horrified.

'There . . . must . . . be . . . some . . . misunderstanding,' she spluttered in a barely audible voice. 'I cannot believe that my father would ask you to do such a thing.'

'I am surprised that my predicament should bother you,' Marek responded.

'I may be a German, but that doesn't make me callous and bereft of human decency,' she replied cuttingly with words designed to hurt.

This show of temper added more colour to her cheeks, enhancing her already considerable beauty. Neither of them spoke for a moment then Marek's conscience got the better of him.

'I must apologise for upsetting you,' he said, shaking his head. 'Lately, I find myself venting my personal frustrations all too easily.'

'Dr Ruzanski,' she began in a steady tone, 'I fully appreciate the difficulty of your situation and I intend to speak to my father about it.'

With that she was gone.

He had only encountered the woman twice and on each occasion she had brought out the worst in him and yet during both meetings he had been captivated by her. She was merely a very attractive woman, he tried to persuade himself, and what man wouldn't be interested? One thing that intrigued him – other than her appearance – was the relationship with her father. If she had not been indoctrinated by Hitler and his Party's ideology, then her father's association with Nazism must be anathema to her.

Millions of Germans had been duped by the Nazi propaganda machine; maybe she was one of the few who had not. During the previous May, film cameras swept every inch of the Ghetto. A variety of situations were staged. One such scene recorded attractive young Jewish women dressed in the finest of clothes, eating sumptuous meals with a greedy appearance at an exclusive restaurant. Knitted onto this, was the image of these satisfied diners picking their way with apparent nonchalance over dead bodies and starving individuals on the streets. In another, a cart overflowing with naked skeletons was captured. All of this was designed to propagate the idea that Jews were morally corrupt and indifferent to the misery and suffering of their kinsmen.

The morning had been dull, wet and misty, but now as lunchtime approached the sky had begun to clear. Marek had not seen much of Mr Dabrowski for about a week and decided to seek him out. His first stop was the vegetable patch, where Marek found him bent over a spade. He was shovelling something, working it into the patch of earth he had recently turned over.

'Hello,' Marek called out.

'Dr Ruzanski. How are you? I haven't seen you out and about lately,' he said, straightening up from what he was doing.

'My composition is taking up a lot of my time.'

'I was saddened to hear about your sister and her husband. A monstrous thing.'

'Thank you for your kind words.' There was a moment of silence. 'What are you doing?' Marek asked, pointing to the patch of ground.

'Good stuff this. Makes the soil fertile for when it's time for planting.'

To one side of the plot was a barrow, full to the brim with a pungent steaming mass.

'How are your flowers coming along?'

'See for yourself, if you like.'

Marek slid the door open, and was almost knocked insensible by the potency of the sweet perfume. Almost all of the irises had now blossomed and he could see other exotic looking plants that he didn't recognize. He complimented Mr Dabrowski on his magnificent display, especially the new specimens, and the gardener beamed. Raising his fork slightly in the air, he brought it down smartly, lodging it firmly in the ground, and beckoned him to follow. Soon Marek discovered the source of his good mood. Popping its head over the top of a stall in the stable block and seeming very pleased to see them was a horse – not just any horse but a majestic creature.

'Whose is it?' Marek asked as he stretched out his hand to stroke it.

'He belongs to Clara. Her father had the stallion transported from Germany especially for her,' the old man replied, gazing up at the animal with admiration written all over his face.

Marek patted its nose gently and it nuzzled up against his hand. It really was a magnificent beast, strong and powerful, with a brown body and black mane and tail.

'Give him these, if you like?' Mr Dabrowski suggested, holding out some cubes of sugar.

Marek presented his flat palm to the horse's mouth and with a slight tickling sensation it swept them up with its lips.

'He won't bite. The breed has a gentle temperament.'

'What type is he?'

'Oldenburg. First bred in the sixteenth century. Good at dressage.'

Mr Dabrowski's knowledge was impressive and it was obvious he was in his element.

'Have you ridden him?'

'Too old for that. My riding days are over. Feeding and watering him is enough for me.'

The horse shifted his front hoof and whinnied softly.

'He knows I've got more sugar in my pocket.' Mr Dabrowski laughed.

Marek fed him another helping of the little white cubes and this time it snorted with appreciation.

'Have you met Clara yet?' Marek asked.

'Yes. She comes to the stable every day. A fine horsewoman. And you've met her too, I believe. You both have an interest in the summerhouse.'

Marek smiled. The gardener must have seen them. He was cannier than he appeared.

'And what do you think of her?' he asked. There was a glint in his eye.

'She's different.'

'For a German, you mean. Yes, you're right. It's strange to think that she's *his* daughter. Follows him in good looks but not in other ways, perhaps? So you have noticed then,' and a crafty smile crossed his lips. 'Remember, we have to make the most of what little pleasures come our way these days. None of us knows how long we'll be around to enjoy them.'

'Where's Rachel?' Marek asked his mother.

'She's gone to see Miriam,' came Eva's reply.

Miriam was an old childhood friend of Rachel's, who lived a few streets away with her mother and younger brother.

'Has she gone by herself?' he asked, starting to feel a little uneasy.

'No. Ruben said he'd take her on the way to one of his meetings and then collect her when he returned.'

Since Lidia and Benjamin's murders, every precaution possible was taken to safeguard the family.

'We'll be able to have some coffee tonight. Come and see what else Ruben's been able to get hold of.'

Eva put down the half peeled potato and pointed to some packages and tins stacked to one side of the draining board. Next to the coffee was an equally prized food item, a honey substitute and some butter which had been obtained on the black market. Marek brought whatever he could from the mansion, and ate less of the family evening meal, passing some of his share to the others. The weeks of extra nourishment had begun to make a difference. Marek was still lean but there was a little more meat on his bones and he was no longer as gaunt as he had been.

He went to talk with his father while his mother prepared dinner. Izak had become noticeably frailer over the past few months and was no longer the robust man his son had once known. The strains and stresses of the Ruzanskis' existence, especially the tragic loss of Lidia and Benjamin, had taken their toll, and was reflected in Izak's weary eyes. Marek thought about the future, in the event that the Germans were defeated, and whether the Jews could merely pick up where they had left off. Could his father reclaim what had once been a thriving business, or would he be able to enjoy an early retirement? It would be impossible to slip back effortlessly into their former lives as if nothing had happened. There would have to be a period of readjustment. Maybe the consequences of such a mighty upheaval would be a reordering of society, but where would the Jews fit in?

'Everything all right?' Izak asked, peering over the top of his paper.

'As well as it can be, Papa,' Marek explained as he pulled up the other chair.

'I took a walk in the grounds today and chatted with the gardener. He has a passion for exotic flowers.'

'Perhaps you could persuade him to let you bring some home. We need something to brighten up this dreary place,' Izak said wistfully.

Marek must have dozed off for a while, for he was woken by Rachel gently pulling at his shirt sleeve.

'How is Miriam?' he enquired sleepily, conjuring up an image of the girl in his mind. As a child she had been gawky and plain. Growing up, she had not, as some ugly ducklings had done, blossomed into a swan, but she had a pleasant nature and was a loyal companion

'She's a little under the weather at the moment,' Rachel said.

'She's not ill, is she?'

Another major priority regarding life in the Ghetto was never to fall seriously ill if it could be helped. Survival rates, especially with a lack of adequate medication, were appalling.

'No. It's not that. I think she's just out of sorts. It's her birthday soon, marking, I suppose, yet another year of our miserable confinement.'

'Perhaps you could make her something, Rachel,' Eva suggested.

'I could bake a cake if I could get hold of some eggs,' Rachel suggested, flashing Ruben a winning smile.

'I'll see what I can do,' Ruben responded, but Marek could tell the boy's mind was elsewhere. Much later that night he revealed the source of his preoccupation.

'I thought I was going to die today,' he blurted out suddenly taking Marek to one side.

'I saw the dog again.'

Marek broke into a sweat.

'Where was it?'

'Outside the Ghetto. In one of the markets. It materialised from nowhere with that leering Nazi bastard. It's just a game to him, mere entertainment seeing another human writhing in terrible agony. Suddenly the beast stopped dead as if it could sense we were around. I don't know why but I stared it straight in the eye. It had a wild, devilish look and it was foaming at the mouth and straining on the leash, impatient to get on with its work.'

Ruben's mouth tightened. Marek said nothing, aware that he would need to get the rest off his chest.

'Micah and I stared at one another with eyes like saucers. Who would it be? Who would the beast go for? Its eyes were locked on mine and I was sure he would come for me. My heart was racing and I was drenched in sweat. There was a deathly hush. Then one of the crowd, a middle-aged Polish woman, caught hold of my arm and pulled me to her side as if I were her son. The German let him go and he lunged forward. I was preparing to take the pain and then I heard a thud. He had gone for Micah. His fear had given him away and the dog sensed it. The wind was knocked out of him and that evil creature locked his jaw around his leg. He bared his head, tried his best to smile, just as you were supposed to do back in the Ghetto, but he couldn't keep it up and his face was twisted from the excruciating pain. I willed him to be strong – to endure it and not flinch. I stood there unable to move, powerless to do anything but watch the animal gnawing into the bone blood collecting in pools in the dirt. He truly did the best he could, but when the teeth tore off a long strip of his skin it was just too much. His screams echoed around the market place. He pulled away and attempted to run. He had lost the game and the Nazi shot him.'

Marek leaned across and put an arm around the boy's shoulders. Because of his tough exterior it was easy to forget Ruben was only a boy, without a mother or father to comfort him.

Not since Marek's first day at the mansion had he been escorted to the music room by the *Oberst-gruppenführer*, and he wondered whether this gesture was significant. His behaviour where Marek was concerned was always punctilious, and Marek knew that his toleration was merely for his own ends. With a broad sweep of his arm, he signalled for Marek to take a seat. Glancing up at him Marek could see what the gardener had meant. Clara did have a look of her father.

'It is time to discuss the arrangements for the concert with you, Doctor Ruzanski.' He began to pace the perimeters of the room.

'Yesterday I received news that I am to be recalled to Berlin for two – perhaps three – weeks so everything must be agreed now. There will be no time later.'

'And the date?'

'Ah! Of course, Doctor. The concert will mark the start of a weekend's celebrations in honour of our great Führer. On the evening of April 16th my colleagues and I shall look forward to hearing your great music.'

'Where will the event be held? In the city?' Marek asked nonchalantly.

'In the main hall. The piano will be moved the day before, and then retuned of course.' In his fastidious way he had thought of everything. 'And your men. They will need to rehearse. I will have them brought here. My daughter will sing for us. She will open the programme and then your contribution will follow.'

So his daughter had not managed – or perhaps had not attempted – to persuade her father to alter his plans, and would now be participating herself. Her apparent outrage had all been a sham.

'You have already made the acquaintance of my daughter, I gather.' He fixed the man with his eyes, which Marek found unnerving. 'She possesses the voice of an angel and has performed for the Führer, at his request, on several occasions.'

Marek said nothing, the anger rising in him at the mention of such a monster.

'She is impressed with your work, as am I. We are both very similar in the way we respect talent. Naturally, of course, there are differences between us and like a headstrong, unschooled filly she has to be reined in from time to time.'

His pointed remarks confirmed that Clara's appeal had fallen upon deaf ears. Maybe Marek had judged her too harshly.

'Should you require anything else – if there has been any detail I have overlooked – you must let me know before I leave.' He had almost reached the door.

'There is one thing. During our first encounter you said that the men's lives would be guaranteed. Do you still stand by what you said then?'

'I recall our exchange quite clearly, Doctor.' His tone had changed.

'Would you agree that I alone am responsible for the composition of the work and that the choir merely do what I instruct them?'

'It is indeed the case that you are culpable, Doctor.'

Marek could tell from his expression that the questions had annoyed him.

'I want your word that after the concert, whatever happens, the men will be unharmed and returned safely to their homes.'

'You are not in a position, Dr Ruzanski, to negotiate. You surprise me with your pessimism. I have every faith in your ability to provide a polished and inspiring performance, so no punishments will be required.'

Whether or not he would keep his word time would tell, but his assurances had helped to salve Marek's conscience. For a while he remained in the chair. Despite no longer fearing the man as he once did, their conversations exhausted him.

Marek decided not to take a walk that day. There was no time to waste. The second composition had to be completed as soon as possible, so there would be sufficient time for the choir to learn both pieces. Minutes before the hands of the clock struck six he put the finishing touches to the work, and then, without any warning, he began to weep. So much emotional energy had been expended in creating the music and now he felt drained. This was the most important and meaningful work he had ever created in his entire life.

Izak Ruzanski was preparing to say the *Kiddush* when there was a loud, heavy rap at the door. Shortly after, and having first checked the spy hole, Izak quickly let the person waiting patiently on the other side in. What business would Mendel want here with them at this time he wondered? Surely he should be at home celebrating the Sabbath with the rest of his family, not risking his life out on the streets. The forlorn looking figure hovered on the threshold of the room, and tried to compose himself.

'Please forgive me for disturbing your meal, but I had to come and see Marek.'

'Take a seat,' Izak urged him. 'Get him a glass of vodka, will you, Ruben.'

The boy obliged and handed it to Mendel, who put it to his lips and took a swig of the clear fluid. Now revived, he lifted his head and Marek saw there were tears in his eyes.

'Edek is dying and he has been asking for you. He won't last the night. Adam sent me to see if you'll come.'

His words struck Marek like a blow and he felt a pang of deep regret. Since leaving the workshop he had not seen Edek but Adam had provided regular reports of his brother's condition at the rehearsals, and Marek had assumed he was bearing up well. News of his dramatic decline came as a shock. He grabbed his coat, stuffing bread into his pockets at his mother's insistence, even though he no longer had much of an appetite and hurried out of the apartment with Mendel.

'It is tuberculosis?' Marek asked as they crossed the street.

'Yes. It's worsened these past few days. He hasn't been able to work. Far too dangerous.'

'Is he lucid?'

'He drifts in and out of consciousness and he calls out your name. He may not recognise you. You should be prepared for that. He doesn't know his own brother at times. But it is good that you will be there. It will be a comfort for Adam,' Mendel assured him

'Of course. I shall do what I can.'

In truth, as much as he cared for Edek, Marek didn't relish the prospect of watching him die. All the other deaths he had witnessed – and there had been many – were swift and brutal. Edek would suffer a slow and painful end. The two men were met by Adam. His face appeared strained and pale in the weak light and his eyes were moist with tears.

'Thank you for coming, Marek. He's been calling your name constantly throughout the day.'

Adam led his guest to one of the smaller rooms away from the main living area. Mendel had left for his own lodgings. There was nothing more he could do at the present time, but he said he would return in the morning.

'The Rabbi has been with him for hours now,' Adam explained.

Marek could hear a hushed voice chanting what sounded like a prayer. A number of candles were grouped on a small table by the bedside, their flickering flames creating dancing shadows on the wall above but they did little to relieve the oppressive atmosphere which was suffused with the smell of death. To one side of the bed stood the Rabbi. Marek took a few steps nearer. At first he didn't recognize Edek: there had been such a marked transformation. To see his friend struck down in this pitiful manner shocked him greatly. The eyes had no discernible flicker of life in them. His once noble head with its strong features had become pinched, the healthy complexion now ashen. His breathing was extremely laboured, and he could hear a whining sound as Edek exhaled.

'Edek, it's me, Marek,' he whispered. 'I'm here. I've come to see you.'

There was no response and Marek assumed his friend had arrived at a point where he could no longer be reached. Then he noticed a slight twitch of Edek's lips and bent nearer.

'Marek, you have come.' The voice was so small and weak it was hard to imagine Edek's once dynamic and forceful personality. Before he could say anything else, he started to cough, a hacking abrasive sound. Adam rushed to his side with an already heavily stained cloth.

'Don't try to speak, Edek. You must rest,' his brother said, his voice cracking.

'Sit me up will you, please,' he croaked.

It was as though Marek's presence had restored a little physical strength. Then clutching at his brother's wrist, he gestured for some water. Adam took hold of Edek's shoulder and, with

Marek's assistance, they gently hoisted him up into a sitting position, propping him up with two pillows. His body was light and it was like lifting the weight of a young child. Eventually the convulsions eased and Adam now gently pressed the glass of fresh water close to his brother's mouth. Edek sipped. Some of the liquid dribbled down his chin and fell in droplets onto his chest. In Marek's jacket pocket was a handkerchief which Mara had made and he took it out and dabbed his friend's night shirt. Marek assumed he would drift off into a coma-like-state, but he did not.

'I wish to talk with Marek alone,' Edek said, having mustered all of his reserves of energy and willpower. 'Sit next to me.'

Marek took hold of a nearby chair and shifted it beside the bed.

'What is it you wish to talk about, my old friend?'

'Do you recall our lunchtime discussions?' He started to splutter again and Marek gently patted his bloody mouth.

'I do, Edek. We were always putting the world to rights were we not?' A flicker of a smile passed over his lips and he nodded. 'And you were always right. However gloomy your predictions, they invariably came to pass.'

'I am like my father. Always the pessimist. Adam takes after our mother. He's more hopeful.'

There was something Marek needed to say that had been troubling him.

'Edek. Please forgive me for not coming to see you sooner. I should have, and I am sorry.'

'You are here now and that is all that matters,' and he took hold of his hand. 'I am a dying man, Marek, and there is little time. When one is on the threshold of death, remarkable things can happen. During these past few days, my friend, I have witnessed the future.'

'The future!' Marek exclaimed, and Edek must have registered his friend's surprise.

'Please indulge me. What I have to tell you are not the ramblings of a decaying mind.'

He had overexerted himself and each breath was now accompanied by harsh rasping sounds. Marek passed him the glass of water and he took a sip.

'I had a dream and in it I witnessed the obliteration of our people on a scale which has never been seen before. Buildings were reduced to rubble and there was a fire destroying everything in its path, even the Torah was engulfed in flames. Bodies lay broken and bleeding and there was the terrible sound of moaning.' His eyes flickered like two near-spent coals in their sockets.

'Don't distress yourself, Edek. You need to save your strength.'

'You were there too,' he said, squeezing his friend's hand as hard as his weakened state would allow.

'Me.' The words took Marek by surprise. 'What was I doing there?'

'You were feverishly conducting music as if oblivious to all the turmoil happening about you and there was a woman standing watching all the while with a deep sadness in her eyes.'

'What sort of music?' Marek asked solemnly.

'A mighty work. A testimony to our people.'

Marek could feel his heart pounding and, unnerved, he loosened his grip on Edek's hand. He went across to the window and stared out unseeing into the blackness. No one knew of his plans to compose a second work.

Edek's husky voice called out in the eerie stillness.

'So, there is truth in what I say?'

Marek returned to the bedside. Edek's fragile torso had sunk into the pillows.

'Whatever happens, Marek, remember it is your destiny.'

Exhaustion overwhelmed him and his eyelids had become heavy. Marek pulled the blanket higher to keep his shoulders warm and then left the room.

'How is he, Marek? Does he need anything?' Adam asked anxiously.

'Edek is resting.'

Adam did not press for details of their conversation. Perhaps it was not an appropriate time to mention the apocalyptic dream.

'Has the Rabbi gone?' Marek enquired, sensing that they were alone.

'Yes. He had others to see.'

'How are you coping, Adam?'

'I've never really imagined what it would be like without him. It's been just the two of us since our parents died. We ran the family business together until the war started, and Edek was always the dominant and capable one. I had always assumed we would die together – at one of the death camps or in a raid – but I never thought he would leave me behind.'

'Perhaps it's a good thing if he isn't here to endure what might happen in the coming months.'

'Yes, Marek, you're right. He's one of the lucky ones.' Adam's voice was stronger. 'Would you like something to drink before you go?'

'I'll stay if you would like me to. We can watch him together.'

Adam appeared relieved at Marek's suggestion.

The night passed slowly and the two men took it in turns to keep their vigil. Edek remained in a state of delirium. Then, at about four o'clock in the morning, his eyelids fluttered open. His lips moved as if he were trying to say something. Marek could barely make out the words.

'*Shalom aleichem.*'

Marek took his dying friend's hand and noticed his breathing was very shallow. Within seconds it had ceased and he was gone.

'*Shalom* my friend until we meet again,' he whispered and kissed Edek's forehead.

Adam had dropped off to sleep. Marek shook him gently and he sprang up quickly as if instinctively knowing that something had happened. He took the news stoically, and a little while later Marek left him alone to grieve.

❖   ❖   ❖

General Reinecke had departed for Berlin at last, and the mood throughout the mansion was noticeably lighter.

Over the past few weeks Marek had become accustomed to the scent of the flowers which brightened up the music room. However, the fragrance that morning was different. He inspected the vase in the centre of the table and saw it was full of fresh irises. In a glazed pot, strategically positioned on the piano lid for greater impact, was a wonderful specimen. From the brilliant pink of its petals, Marek remembered it as being one of the mysterious varieties growing in Mr Dabrowski's glasshouse. His recent complimentary remarks to the gardener must have prompted its delivery and this brought a smile to his lips.

Spending the night with Adam and Edek had left Marek weary and affected his concentration. By late morning he was in need of a diversion. Clara had not been in the forefront of his mind for several days. Now, however, he began to wonder if he might see her again, or whether she had accompanied her father to Germany. He decided to take a walk over to the summerhouse.

Marek noticed a streak of smoke in the distance. It was coming from the little building. The gardener must have lit a fire. Through a crack in the door he caught sight of a woman crouching at the edge of the hearth with a piece of wood in her hand. It was Clara. She placed it carefully in the grate before selecting a thinner stick to use as a poker. Then she began to stoke the embers, encouraging the flames to take hold. Once this was done she rubbed her hands on the hem of her skirt to clean them. At first Clara did not know she was being observed until, that is, his boot landed on a small pine cone and the noise of it snapping startled her.

'I'm sorry if I frightened you,' Marek said apologetically. 'I thought I might find Mr Dabrowski here.'

'Well, I've not seen him,' she said, in an offhand manner.

They were both self-conscious and uncomfortable around each other, probably because of their last encounter.

'I was hoping to see him. He left one of his exquisite plants for me in the music room.'

With this somewhat trivial piece of information Marek hoped to clear the air.

'He certainly cherishes his flowers doesn't he? I notice the house is adorned with them. Have you seen his greenhouse?'

'Yes he showed me around. What an experience. It is so very hot and humid in there. It's like stepping into the jungle.'

She laughed shyly as if she had found Marek's comments amusing. When she smiled the dimples in her cheeks were more noticeable, and he liked the way she had styled her hair. Just then a log slipped in the grate. They gazed into the glowing hearth — the balletic flames weaved their hypnotic spell upon them. Clara's milky, fair skin glowed in the amber light, and Marek's gaze was drawn towards her.

'What are you thinking about?'

'The futility of this war,' she replied in a resigned tone.

'I would have thought that since your father is such a committed member of the Party . . .'

'Not all Germans support Hitler,' she said quietly. 'I do not condone my father's allegiance to the Party. He, like so many others, has been swept along with the tide.'

'Surely your father can listen to his own conscience?' Marek suggested.

'You don't know what it is like to defy Hitler. Papa is such a proud man.'

'That doesn't excuse his actions.'

'I did what I said I would do. I spoke to him, but I could not change his mind.'

She grew silent again and stared into the fire.

'Your father tells me you are like your mother.'

'Yes, I am more like her I suppose,' Clara said thoughtfully.

'Where is she now?' he asked curiously.

'Mama died when I was ten years old,' she replied. Her voice was tinged with sadness.

'I'm sorry.'

'Papa has never recovered, just as I have not, but it was a long time ago.'

'What was she like?'

'Beautiful and loving, and she was so kind to everyone,' Clara said smiling.

'Where is your home?'

'I come from Freiburg in south-west Germany.'

'Is it a pretty place?'

'It has charm and character because of its old buildings and cobbled streets, and it has an ancient university founded in the fifteenth century.'

'Is that where you studied?'

'Yes. History. I studied under Gerhard Ritter, who is a distinguished professor.'

'Have you a job, yet?'

'When I go home I'm taking up a teaching position. Do you have family?'

Marek told her about his parents and Rachel and Ruben, and then she asked about the living conditions in the Ghetto. He satisfied her curiosity but decided against providing some of the more unsavoury details. By now the fire was beginning to die down and he added more wood.

'You remind me very much of someone I once knew. His name was Michael.'

'Was he Jewish?'

'Yes. Our two families were neighbours for many years. We used to play together all the time. I remember how upset I was when one day he went away.'

'And your father permitted your friendship?' Marek asked in astonishment.

'Oh yes. He didn't have a say in the matter, for my mother and Michael's were like sisters. Besides, I don't think it bothered him. Papa was dispassionate about it all then. In those days there was greater tolerance. The insidious corruption of people's minds had not yet taken hold. I often wonder what happened to Michael. I hope he and his family are safe.'

The sticks of wood had burnt rapidly and the room was beginning to feel cold.

'Shall we put another log on?' Clara asked.

The block of wood she pointed to was rather large and needed splitting in half. Marek remembered seeing an axe resting beside a wall of the building, so he picked up the log and carried it outside. The sharp tool bit deep into the timber, splintering it in two, but as it did so it nicked the side of his hand. The pain was severe, causing him to cry out. Apprehensively he examined the wound. He cursed aloud, angry at his own stupidity, and wiped away the blood. He felt for Mara's handkerchief in his jacket pocket but could not find it. Then he remembered he had used it on the night of Edek's death. Instead, he cleaned the wound as best he could by rubbing it on the wet grass, and went back inside to find Clara. She was sitting gazing into the flames. As Marek leaned towards the grate with one of the pieces of wood, a few drops of blood spattered onto the hearth.

'What's happened?' Clara exclaimed in horror.

'It's not as bad as it seems. I caught it with the axe.'

'Let me help,' she said taking hold of his left hand and cradling it in her lap. The blood oozed from the cut, staining her dress.

'It is quite deep and might need proper attention. Is there a doctor where you live?'

'Yes.'

She looked about the room as if searching for something.

'There doesn't appear to be any water here to bathe it.'

She reached into her coat pocket and took out a white hand-kerchief. It had a deep pink rosebud sown onto it. When she had finished binding the injury Marek thanked her for her kindness.

'I will come and see how it is tomorrow, but you really should let a doctor see it.'

He assured her he would and she seemed content with that.

By the time Marek came to unwrap the bandage later that evening, the cut had already begun to heal and a visit from the doctor was considered unnecessary. His parents were surprised to hear how he had managed to injure himself, although Marek omitted Clara's role in patching up the wound, which was a good thing as there followed an angry outburst against the Germans and the lack of firewood in the Ghetto. Assuming that Mrs Dabrowski had given her son the handkerchief, Eva set about washing the cloth so it could be returned freshly laundered the next morning.

Painful as the wound was, other things dominated Marek's

thoughts. It was the night when the choir met, and he knew he could no longer keep the truth from them. Amos was setting out the benches in rows when Marek reached the warehouse.

'How are you this evening?' Then he noticed the bandage. 'What have you been doing to yourself?'

Marek explained he had cut it at work. He was never more in need of a drink than now, and the two men toasted their dead comrades. As the others started to arrive, Marek laid out the manuscript and started to sing the tenor solo which would soar above the body of the choir. He had set it to verses from one of the Psalms.

'What is that?' several of the men asked.

'I need to show you something,' Marek said, nervously holding out the work to them.

Jacob and Adam were first to take it and the scrutiny commenced. Soon all the men were huddled together, humming phrases, muttering in low voices, and from time to time throwing glances in Marek's direction. He had retreated to a corner of the room. After an interval of several minutes Enoch called for silence.

'What you have created, Marek, is something that transcends greatness. A work of genius which honours our people.'

'Are we going to perform it?' Mendel asked boldly, having guessed its true purpose.

'My friends, I cannot insist upon it. The decision must be yours alone. I wanted to show you what I have felt compelled to do, even though it is the act of a madman. I have fought long and hard with my conscience and I now know that I cannot do what the Nazi requires of me.'

'As I see it there are three options available to us,' Enoch said. 'The first is that we comply with what the German wants, and in so doing glorify Hitler and his henchmen. The second is to run away before the night of the concert. The downside to this, of course, is that the Nazi will come after us. The third and only alternative . . .' he hesitated before finishing his sentence, 'is to sing the new work and if we die for it, we die with dignity.'

❖ ❖ ❖

Marek had set out his things at the piano and was about to begin the daily stint when he heard what sounded like the chink of glass. It was Clara who had come to check on his hand, and she had brought a bottle of antiseptic with her. He watched as she tenderly untied the new dressing

'You would make a good nurse,' he told her as she unravelled the last strand of what had once been part of a cotton sheet.

'I'm far too squeamish to cope with anything more serious than this,' she laughed. You didn't need stitches, I see. It's healing very well.' She dabbed on a little of the solution and the smarting made Marek wince.

'I'm sorry. I know it's probably a bit late now, but I thought it might help prevent any infection setting in. I came across these things in the kitchen and the housekeeper said I could have them.'

'What do you think of the Dabrowskis?' he asked.

'They're good people. Mrs Dabrowski was on her guard at first, then, since she's discovered that I'm not this demanding monster of a German Fraulein, she's been quite amiable. Her husband is a sweet old man who absolutely dotes on my horse. Apparently, at one time the stables here were full of horses and he was in charge of them all.'

'Yes, he told me. We've reminisced about the old days.'

'What surprised me most when I first arrived is how few staff there are.'

'The previous owners had fallen on bad times and they were forced to sell all the livestock.'

She listened whilst applying a fresh bandage, neatly tucking in all the edges to prevent it from coming unfastened.

'Does it feel comfortable? Please tell me if it is too tight.'

'It's perfect.'

'How is your work coming along? Can I take a look?'

'Of course. Go ahead.'

Marek watched as she walked to the piano and leant over to examine the music. Suddenly her brow furrowed.

'This isn't the manuscript you've been working on. It's a different piece.'

A feeling of panic swept over Marek as he realised what must have happened. He had taken the wrong pages out of his case.

'It is another composition of mine,' he said, trying to sound casual and hoping that she wouldn't have guessed the truth.

'This is what you want to look at,' he said rapidly switching the scripts.

From her demeanour she appeared not to have suspected anything, and after all, why should she? There in front of her, borne out of sweat and toil and in all its glory was the commissioned 'masterpiece'. It did not take her long to discover the fugue almost near completion, forming the finale. She was eager to learn all the intricacies of the complex form.

When it was time for Clara to go, he remembered he had something of hers. Digging into his pocket he brought out the freshly laundered handkerchief she had wrapped around his wound the day before. She would not take it, insisting he keep it.

'Will you be out walking later?' she asked, before adding, 'There's something I'd like to show you if you come as far as the summerhouse.'

'Yes, I'll meet you there.'

When Angelika appeared Marek asked her how she was feeling.

She replied that every member of the household was relieved to be rid of the Nazi even though, it was true to say, they never really saw a great deal of him when he was there. His ominous presence was unsettling.

'The Fraulein is not at all like her father is she?'

'No, she's not. The other day when I was cleaning her room she gave me one of her scarves as a gift. Even Mrs Dabrowski says that she is too charming to be his child.'

As Marek took the tray from her, Angelika caught sight of the bandage.

'You hurt your hand yesterday, didn't you? The Fraulein asked Mrs Dabrowski for a dressing and some antiseptic. She has a soft spot for you.' The young girl was teasing him, a sign she was back to her old self.

On the menu today was a steaming hot plate of meat, potatoes and cabbage, and as he tucked in, Marek reflected upon what Angelika had said. He could well imagine the gossip amongst the staff about the two outsiders. With the *Oberst-gruppenführer* away, and most of his entourage gone, there would be little else to interest them were it not for Clara and Marek.

In the space of a day the temperature had risen a degree or two, and this was perceptible as he stepped out into the spring sunshine. Approaching the summerhouse, something struck him as odd. At first he could not make out what had changed. There was no smoke escaping from its chimney, but this was not surprising given the improvement in the weather. He stood there for several minutes trying to fathom it and then it hit him. The windows were adorned with floral drapes. So this was what Clara had meant: she was making it more homely – her special retreat, perhaps.

'Well, what do you think?' the young woman asked impatiently.

'It's very impressive,' he replied taking a few steps further inside.

All the old clutter of broken chairs and other rubbish had vanished and had been substituted with new items of furniture. There were two armchairs on either side of the fireplace covered in brightly coloured fabric, and a collection of china objects on the mantelpiece. Hanging on the walls, disguising the worst patches of flaking plaster, were paintings.

Clara plumped up the seat cushions. Marek inspected the ornaments on the ledge and there was one that caught his eye. Next to a porcelain lady was a delicate bone china bell. The pretty little thing, with its mauve hand-painted flowers, was very familiar, and he tried to remember where he had seen it before. Then it came to him: Lidia had one just like it on her dresser in the days when they were all living at home. Shortly after their grandmother had died they had each been given a gift to remember her by, and his sister had cherished hers. As Marek held it now in the palm of his hand, all the sorrow and wretchedness of his sister's death came flooding back. In the Ghetto the hardening of one's heart was a form of defence mechanism. Here, it was very different and he could allow some feelings to resurface.

'It is such a pretty thing, Marek, but why do you seem so sad?' Clara asked.

He could say nothing at first as he wrestled with his emotions.

'My sister, Lidia, died recently. She had one just like this. It reminds me of her and our family in happier times.'

'I am so sorry,' Clara cried out. 'I shouldn't have done this. I feel so ashamed. You and your people endure such suffering and loss, and here I am meddling with pieces of furniture. You must think me so shallow and heartless.'

Her shoulders heaved and she started to cry. Marek took hold of her hand.

'You are none of those things, Clara. You are compassionate, thoughtful and caring, just like your mother was.'

He took her handkerchief from his pocket and gently began to wipe the glistening drops which had formed about her eyes. For a moment they held each other's gaze. He let the cloth fall to the ground and instead brushed her cheeks with his lips. The taste of her salt tears was as sweet as honey. He kissed her nose, her forehead, her chin and the little cleft in her throat. Her skin was like satin. The smell of narcissi drifted towards them.

Marek drew her down and sensing his desire Clara removed her cardigan. One by one he undid the buttons on her blouse, his fingers trembling with the anticipation of what he would find beneath. Her breasts were round and full and their ruby nipples had stiffened. She let out a little moan. A log slipped in the hearth as he parted her legs and her body gave a slight shudder. Slowly at first their bodies moved as one and then he quickened his pace. Clara's eyes were no longer open and Marek kissed their lids. Her breathing had become shallow and he could feel the warmth of her breath upon his neck. Soon there was a heightening of sensation and at its most intense point Clara cried out.

They rested on the rug. Neither spoke, not because they felt shame at what they had done, but because they dared not express in words their feelings for one another. Marek was a Jew and Clara a German and, in the eyes of the world, his enemy. And yet, as he beheld her now, he knew that he loved this woman so very deeply. While she was dressing he got up and walked to the window. Outside a squirrel darted across the expanse of grass. How he wished that they could have been somewhere else, far away, where there was tolerance and no war. He felt her near him.

'I love you, Clara,' he uttered softly.

'I love you, Marek.'

Marek longed to tell his family about his deep affection for Clara, and yet he knew he could not – just as it was not possible to discuss the second composition. As it was to turn out, they would soon be challenged with more serious concerns. One evening, having climbed the stairs leading to the apartment, he found Izak waiting on the landing. He looked extremely worried, and his heart sank in anticipation of what he might be about to hear.

'I'm relieved you're home. It's Rachel. She's not well.'

'What's the matter with her, Papa?' he asked, although he already knew.

'It's typhus,' Izak said quietly, as if he could hardly bring himself to articulate the word aloud.

'Are you sure? Has Dr Bilinski seen her?'

'Yes, I fetched him myself. When she awoke this morning she complained of a bad head and aches all over her body.'

'And he's confirmed the disease?'

'Yes, Marek. The symptoms are consistent with the early stages of the illness.'

'Has Dr Bilinski given her something?'

'His supplies are running low, but she has had pyramidon and a glucose injection, and he's going to call again tomorrow.'

There was no known cure for the illness and if you contracted it you prayed to be one of the lucky ones to survive. It had rampaged through the Ghetto and everyone lived in constant fear of experiencing those early signs; the headache and muscular pains. There had been an anti-typhus injection available back in 1941, for the few who could afford it on the black market. As a family the Ruzanskis had been extremely fortunate in avoiding this plague . . . until now.

Marek followed his father into the apartment and to the room which Rachel shared with her parents. It was in near-total darkness so as not to strain Rachel's aching eyes. Her mother was sitting with a basin of cold water on her lap, into which she dipped a cloth and then tenderly dabbed her daughter's feverish brow.

'Marek. I'm so glad you're home.' Eva sounded strained.

'How is she, Mama?'

'Not very well, darling. The doctor has been and he's going to come each day until Rachel's better.'

'Would you fetch me some fresh water please?'

His mother held out the metal container. Marek carried it to the kitchen, where his father was preparing some food.

'How bad a case do you think it is, Papa?' he asked, refilling the basin with icy cold water from the tap.

'Dr Bilinski feels it's too early to tell. We'll have to be patient and let it run its course.'

Marek carried the bowl back to the room.

'Where would Rachel have caught it Mama?' Marek asked as he perched at the foot of the bed.

Though there were admittedly no foolproof preventative measures which could be taken to guard against such a disease, they had all been so careful.

'Miriam has it,' she said ominously.

Miriam. Of course. Rachel had visited her friend a couple of weeks ago — precisely the period of incubation — and she had commented that the girl had been out of sorts.

'How is Miriam now?'

'She is very weak indeed. All those in her apartment have it, including Miriam's sister. Don't say anything to Rachel.'

'No, of course I won't.'

'According to Dr Bilinski, she'll wake up from time to time, but she may not recognize any of us because of the high fever.'

When Ruben arrived home Marek took him aside and broke the news about Rachel's condition. He was appalled. The evening meal was a depressing affair and no one did more than pick at their food. The remaining hours before bedtime ticked away slowly and they occupied themselves in various pursuits. Flipping over a page of the book he was reading, Marek thought he heard a whimpering noise. Izak did not seem to have heard it, but Eva did and quickly rose to her feet.

'I'll see to it, Mama. You must rest.'

Marek knew it was going to be a long haul and he wanted to do his bit. It was vital that they all took a share, as the more tired and worn-out any one of them became, the more susceptible they would be to catching the illness. He took hold of Rachel's hand. It felt clammy and warm. The skin on her face had a sheen to it and little beads of perspiration had formed upon her forehead and temples. The thick lustrous hair now fell lank and damp about her shoulders and as she lay there, her brother thought how much he would miss her if she did not get better. Marek picked up the cloth and patted it lightly over Rachel's skin, gently brushing away a few strands of hair which had strayed over one of her eyes.

'Marek,' she said her voice barely a whisper.

'Hello Rachel. How are you feeling?'

He felt her fingers tighten, and the half-smile she had given him a moment ago was now twisted into a grimace.

'My head hurts.'

Marek wondered if the pain relief had worn off. He picked up one of the bottles of medication the doctor had left next to the bedside lamp. He stroked his sister's head and called for his mother. Within seconds she was there, enveloping Rachel in her arms whilst Marek, under her instruction, fetched a glass of drinking water and emptied out some pills onto the palm of his hand. A little later Rachel sank back into the pillow and then slipped into unconsciousness. Eva and her son swapped worried looks, both aware that this had been a rare instance of lucidity and that soon the delirium would take hold.

On the way to Gesia Street early the next morning, Marek met Dr Bilinski.

'How is your sister today? Has there been any change?' he asked.

'She had a relatively peaceful night,' Marek explained.

'The disease has its stages. She'll get worse before she gets better. That is if she survives. We must wait and hope.'

'Is there anything else we can do?' Marek asked anxiously.

'If I could get hold of more supplies it might help. Do you think Ruben could come by some?

'I'll ask. I'm sure he'll try his best.'

Because of the latest developments, trying to focus on his composition was proving a struggle. By mid-morning, Marek had written nothing of significance and when Clara breezed in he was grateful for the distraction. She was as lovely as ever, but just as he was about to take her in his arms he suddenly drew away. What if he were carrying the disease?

'What's wrong Marek?' Clara asked, taken aback by his reaction.

'Rachel has typhus.'

She did not recoil on hearing this. On the contrary there was real concern in her eyes.

'Are you certain of the diagnosis?' Clara asked.

'Unfortunately so. She caught it from a friend of hers who is now gravely ill.'

'Is there a doctor who can treat her?'

'Yes. His methods are sound and he's very thorough. He's hampered because of the limited supply of medicines. It's not easy to get hold of them in the Ghetto,' Marek explained

'I'd like to help if I can,' she said, taking both his hands in hers.

218

She thought for a moment. 'Maybe I can find some medicine for her. It shouldn't be too difficult.'

As much as the idea appealed to him, Marek didn't want Clara to compromise herself, especially since she was the daughter of a high-ranking officer. The Nazis were not averse to turning on their own.

'It might prove too much of a risk for you, Clara. If your father found out . . .' He stroked her cheek without thinking, then, realising what he had done, snatched his hand away. Before he could stop her she was kissing him.

'You must never be afraid to touch me, Marek. I could not bear that.'

Rachel had now been ill for four days, and keeping to the pattern, she had developed the rash – a multitude of flat, red spots which soon darkened to resemble little bruises. Life for the rest of the family continued as normal except for the nursing. On one particular evening during Marek's watch, he had begun to feel drowsy and was about to nod off when he heard the repeated calling of a name. Rachel had opened her eyes and appeared to be focussing on a point beyond the end of the bed.

'Lidia Lidia! Wait for me, Lidia. Wait!'

He cradled his sister in his arms and soon her eyelids drooped shut again. Had the dead come back to claim the living? If so, Marek was grateful that their beloved sister had not taken her.

Clara did not visit the following day, nor did he see her on the next. By lunchtime of the third Marek's curiosity was getting the better of him, and he decided to mention her absence to Angelika.

'The Fraulein has gone to the hospital today.'

'Is she ill?' he asked, trying not to sound anxious.

The young girl didn't think Clara was sick, although she did not know the reason for her visit either. At about mid-afternoon the music room door burst open and, standing there with a bundle in her arms, was Clara.

'I have all the medicines you need Marek. Take them and give them to your sister.'

'How did you get them?' he asked stuffing the package into his case.

'I told them one of my father's aides was exhibiting symptoms of the illness and that Papa had sent me, on his behalf, to fetch some medicine. At first they weren't at all eager to give up some of their precious supplies and so, as much as I hated doing it, I had to become the arrogant Nazi's daughter.' Clara's eyes sparkled. 'The Polish doctors and nurses loathe us so very much. I could see it in their faces.'

During the journey back to the Ghetto that night, Marek imagined the look on the doctor's face when he saw what he had to give him. Dr Bilinski clasped the package in his fingers, and whilst the two men both understood that nothing could bring about a miraculous cure, Rachel's chances of recovery might be improved.

The concert was now less than two weeks away, and as each day passed Ruben's words of reassurance – that the war might end – seemed sadly hollow. There was, nonetheless, a suspicion amongst the Jews, and especially the leaders of the *ZZW* and the *ZOB*, the latter whose headquarters were on Mila Street, that the Germans were about to perpetrate the final act of their sinister drama. As regards Marek's own intentions, it struck him that now was the time to put things in order. He would need to speak with Ruben and there was one other person, so dear to him, in whom he needed to confide.

'How is your sister?' Clara asked, entering the music room.

'She's showing signs of improvement,' Marek said, glancing up from his work. 'Dr Bilinski was most grateful for the medicine and says it will help make her more comfortable.'

The sun was streaming in through the window, and dazzling her eyes, but at that very moment it was as if Clara had metamorphosed into a beautiful, heavenly vision.

'I am glad that I was able to help,' she said warmly.

She took a seat at the table and Marek joined her.

'Did you know I am expected to perform at the concert?'

'Yes, your father told me.' Marek took hold of her hands. 'Clara, there's something that I have to . . .'

Before he was able to finish the sentence Dominik arrived, weighed down with a bucket of coal and an armful of kindling. Clara quickly slipped away and Marek helped the boy fill the coal scuttle and the wood basket.

'Do you enjoy your work here, Dominik?' Marek asked.

'It does for now. After the war though, I want to have a proper training.'

'What profession do you have in mind?'

'Agriculture I think,' the young man replied.

'A very good choice and one which will suit you well,' Marek said encouragingly.

'That's what Mr Dabrowski says too.'

'Well, let's hope the war will be over soon.'

'I've joined up with the Polish resistance, you know. I want to fight the Germans.'

His immature face had flushed pink with excitement though Marek could not suppress a feeling of foreboding. As Dominik was leaving Marek warned him to be careful.

The fact that Marek had been interrupted while attempting to speak to Clara preyed on his mind for the rest of the morning. He ate his lunch hurriedly. He hoped that if he went to the summerhouse he might find her there. On the other side of the lake he spied Mr Dabrowski, and, as their paths almost converged, he shouted something across to him.

'Off to the summerhouse, are you? The Fraulein is there. She's done a good job of tidying it up.' He waved and, giving a wry smile, carried on his way. The man and his wife were indeed an astute pair, Marek thought to himself as he plodded along.

He found Clara sitting close to the fire reading a book, her legs curled up under her.

'Hello Marek. What a lovely surprise. I thought you might have been the housekeeper's husband coming back,' she said giving him one of her captivating smiles.

'Yes, I saw him on the way here. No doubt he's heading to his glasshouse and his beloved plants by now.'

'I was hoping you would come,' she said quietly. 'You started to tell me something.'

Marek pulled up a chair next to her. It was more difficult now to say what needed to be said, and he took a deep breath.

'When your father proposed that I should compose the work, the very idea was abhorrent to me, yet I knew that if I did not agree the precious lives of those I cared for deeply would be at risk. I began the task knowing full well that I had been manipulated into doing it, but even though this was the case, in the end I could not reconcile what I was doing with my conscience. I'm a proud man, Clara, and maybe this weakness will be my undoing, but I have decided upon another way and I cannot turn back now.'

'What other way, Marek?' she asked as tears began to form in her eyes.

222

'I have composed a second work. One which my principles, and those of the choir, will allow us to perform.'

Tears had begun to trickle now. Crouching beside her, Marek took hold of both her hands.

'And do your consciences condone your deaths too?' She pulled away from his grasp, angry and frustrated. 'I know the work. I saw it the other morning and you lied to me about it. How can you be so selfish, and so irresponsible, Marek? You obviously care little for me, but what about your family?'

She made for the door. Marek took hold of her and spun her around. Clutched tightly in his arms, she struggled to break free, but he would not let go.

'Do you really believe I don't care about you, Clara? I love you so much.'

All the tension drained from her body, and she sank her head against his shoulder. Eventually she looked up at him with her blotched and reddened face.

'If I cannot persuade you to change your mind, Marek, then there is something I must do to help me understand the sacrifice you are making. I have to witness your people's suffering for myself.'

Her words struck him like a thunderbolt.

'What you are asking is impossible. The risks are too great.'

'Please, Marek. Will you do this for me?'

'Clara, do you have any idea how foolish an idea that is? Do you think you can simply walk into the Ghetto, wander around and then leave unnoticed? Your father has spies everywhere. He would discover what you had done and then what? You might be killed and I couldn't protect you. You would be so vulnerable.'

'We have a few days before my father returns, and if we're careful he'll never know.'

'*Careful.* Careful is not a word that comes to mind when contemplating a visit to the Ghetto.'

'You could smuggle me in.' She was determined. 'What about Ruben? The boy you told me about. Isn't he the smuggler?'

Marek's mind was racing. Ruben was indeed the expert in concealment, a resourceful importer and exporter of prohibited goods, but not, however, of humans.

'I will talk to him, but you have to understand that it could only be done if he says that it is possible.'

She nodded her head. 'Papa told me he would be returning at the earliest in the middle of next week, so we should have enough time.'

Marek leaned towards her and their lips touched. Soon the two lovers had given in to their passions.

'Hello, Dr Ruzanski. Have you had a good day at work?'

Marek was about to mount the stairs when he caught sight of a little figure off to the right.

'Yes, thank you.' Squatting before him, his eyes burning with excitement, was the boy who Ruben and Marek had encountered on that fateful day in January. 'What are you doing here Moshe?'

'Papa says that I can take a turn with the alarm for an hour or so,' he replied proudly.

'Good for you, but mind you don't fall asleep on duty,' Marek teased him.

'I won't. I promise.'

Marek was certain he would not, for children were as responsible and as dependable as adults. They had to be in order to survive in this highly unstable environment.

According to Eva's report, Rachel had reached the comatose stage of the illness. Sitting beside her now, Marek noticed how sunken her cheeks and how hollow her eyes had become; and yet, ironically, if she recovered Rachel would experience the ravenous appetite of the typhus convalescent. Some time had passed since the illness had taken hold, and Dr Bilinski believed it was unlikely the rest of the family would catch it now.

The conversation at meal times had become more perfunctory. None of them had anything pleasant or uplifting to talk about. Ruben's news, courtesy of the Polish underground, was that the Germans had devised a plan to liquidate the Ghetto. The fact it could begin any day now was deeply disturbing. After he had helped with the dirty plates, Marek motioned for Ruben to follow him out to the landing.

'Have you got a match? I've run out.'

Marek held out a cigarette for him to light.

'Your hand's shaking. Are you all right?' Ruben asked.

He hadn't noticed before, but as Marek held his hand up before his eyes, there was a definite tremor.

'Yes, I'm fine.' He inhaled deeply on the cigarette. It felt good and he needed it.

'What's on your mind?' The boy was athletic and he pulled himself onto the ledge effortlessly.

'There are some important things I need to discuss with you,' Marek said as the smoke rose in a trail, curling in the cool air. 'My work at the mansion . . .'

'Ah yes. The piece praising the mighty Führer,' he cut in.

'Indeed. Well it won't be on the programme.'

'The Nazi has changed his mind after all?' His jaw dropped.

'No. He has not.'

'I don't understand,' Ruben said shaking his head.

'It will be finished. In fact the music is almost complete, but it will not be performed.'

'Then you'd better explain what you mean.' Ruben was becoming increasingly perplexed at his friend's vagueness.

'Wait here. I want to show you something.'

A few minutes later Marek thrust the new composition into Ruben's hand. The young man shifted his position slightly. With the aid of the moonlight he could see the score more clearly. Marek retreated to the shadows and lit another cigarette. Ruben pored over page after page of the manuscript. When at last he had seen enough, he let it drop to his side.

'What you are intending to do is suicidal. Tell me I'm wrong, Marek, because this is pure madness. You do know that you won't get past the first few bars. And what about the others? Have they lost their minds?'

'No, everyone in the choir has agreed to perform it.'

'Then they are as crazy as you are.'

There was a moment of awkwardness before Ruben continued.

'And what do you think this wretched Nazi is going to do when he discovers that you have defied him? Well I can tell you what he'll do. He'll shoot you.'

'We all take gambles in life,' Marek said defiantly.

'There is a fundamental difference between the risks I take and the one you are taking. Mine are calculated and have a reasonable chance of success. I would say yours has none.'

Just then Izak stuck his head out from the apartment. As soon as he saw them having a quiet smoke together, he went back inside.

'Tell me what you would have done in my position, Ruben?' Marek said angrily when he was certain his father was out of earshot.

'You're right. You know me too well. I would have done the same.' He paused. 'Is there anything I can do?'

'I want you to get my family out.'

'Are you going to tell them?' Ruben asked.

'It will be better if they don't know for the moment. You must tell them afterwards if I . . . if I'm not able to. Will you do that for me?'

Ruben nodded his head solemnly.

'There is one more thing I have to tell you. Something you might find surprising.'

'I can't imagine it could be any more startling than what you've just said.'

'I think it might be.' Marek sat down beside him. 'Do you remember me telling you about Clara?'

'The attractive one?'

'Yes.'

'Well, what about her?'

'She knows the truth about what we are planning.'

'What!' The shock caused him to choke on some smoke and break into a paroxysm of coughing. 'You *told* her,' he exclaimed in between splutters. 'What possessed you, Marek? She's bound to tell her father. Ah, wait a moment, maybe she won't.' A smile spread across his lips. 'Jews do not fall in love with the daughters of high-ranking Nazi officers. It's against all the rules.' The boy was shrewd.

'Believe me, I didn't want it to happen, but it has and I can't change how I feel about her.'

'Are you certain she won't tell anyone?' Ruben asked.

'Yes, I'm sure. But there is something she wants to do.'

'What's that?'

'Come to the Ghetto.'

'Here?' This time he managed not to choke. 'Why here? I hope you told her it's impossible?'

'She wants to see how we live. Experience all the suffering at first hand. I said it would be your decision.'

'My decision? Why? You know it's as crazy an idea as I do. Too risky.'

'She knows you're an expert at getting in and out of the Ghetto.'

The young man slid from his seat and began to pace the length of the passage.

'It will need a lot of careful planning. When does her father get back?'

'Middle of next week.'

'Well, if she is half as nice as you say she is then I will have to meet her.'

The challenge, as Marek had anticipated, proved too great for him to resist. They agreed to discuss it again the next day.

Marek was awoken by Rachel's cries, and soon after, he could hear his mother's soothing tones attempting to calm her. It had been a rough night for Rachel. The hallucinations had returned but this time, however, it was not Lidia who her fevered mind had conjured up, but Miriam. Though she did not know it, Rachel's dear friend had passed away just two days earlier. The disease had claimed yet another victim. When he next awoke, Ruben had risen early. Marek assumed he had gone out on business connected with Clara's request.

Ruben stayed away for most of the day, reappearing late in the afternoon with a rather curious-looking bundle tucked under his arm. Making straight for his room he gestured for Marek to follow.

'I've been thinking about Clara and how we could bring her in and out. The best and safest method, by far, is for her to join the work parties. She would be too conspicuous at any other time.'

'I'd come to the same conclusion.'

'The best chance she'd have is to join the tailors. Coming in with them in the evening and joining the eight o'clock column out the next day. There's a group of women and children she could easily mingle with. What do you think?'

'She'd have to spend the night here,' Marek suggested.

'Yes. I don't see an alternative,' Ruben explained. 'It would be too risky otherwise. The advantages of the tailoring workshop are that, according to my source, the guards are easy going and don't notice too much. They also take bribes.'

'She'll have to disguise herself as one of us, I suppose.'

'Earlier today I made contact with some friends of mine – an old girlfriend and a Pole – who work in the office at the tailoring factory and put our plan to them. I've found some clothes which should fit Clara, assuming she's not too well-fed.'

Marek told him she was quite slender.

'What about papers?'

'I'll sort something out. Clara must turn up as the Polish customer a few minutes before closing time and then once inside the office she can change into these clothes,' and he pointed to the bundle on the bed. 'She must wear them underneath her other garments and be ready just in time to join the column. I'll be waiting for her nearby.'

'And the following day?' Marek enquired.

'The next morning she'll have to tag on to the work party, and when she arrives at the workshop she'll make an excuse to go to the office. Quickly changing into her normal clothes, she is the client from the day before, come to check on her order.'

'There's one thing I'm curious about. How did you manage to persuade this Pole to help us?'

'I've known him since I was young. He's older than me but our mothers were at school together. He detests the Germans as much as we do. The opportunity to get one over on them appeals to him greatly.'

'Does he know who Clara is?'

'Of course not. By the way, does she speak any Polish?'

'Yes, enough.'

'I've explained she's a girlfriend of mine wanting to pay me an overnight visit. Well, you understand with my charisma and handsome looks, the women go to any lengths to be with me,' Ruben said mischievously.

'When have you arranged for Clara to come?'

'Monday,' he replied without hesitation. 'She'll need to change her hair colour. With her German appearance she'll stand out too much.'

The two men spent about half an hour discussing the finer details of the plan, all of which Marek would relay to Clara, before they were called for supper.

Clara arrived clutching a large brown book in her hands. It was a collection of songs by Schubert and she wanted Marek's advice on which she should choose. He had not yet heard her voice, but as soon as she began to sing he was enchanted. The rehearsal was intense and when it was over Clara sat down beside him.

'Now, Marek, do you have any news?'

He had hoped she had forgotten about her dangerous scheme but evidently not. He explained what Ruben had devised and she listened avidly.

'I'll go and buy something for my hair in the city today, and if I'm to be away for the night I'll have to think up an excuse for Mrs Dabrowski. She's bound to notice my absence.'

Before they parted, Marek gave her the parcel of clothes which he had concealed under his jacket. She grabbed them eagerly. The next time they would see each other would be in the Ghetto.

Despite his cluttered mind it was crucial for Marek to remain focused on the work still to be done. There was only time for three more choir rehearsals and then it would be the night of the performance. He was later than usual arriving at the warehouse and could hear the men's vociferous exchanges. When they saw him the conversation stopped dead and he was met by a sea of anxious faces.

'Have you heard the news, Marek?' Eli said.

'What news?'

'Daniel has been killed.'

What he had said took a while to sink in, and Marek slumped down on one of the benches. His oldest and dearest of friends was dead and the news had shaken him badly.

'How? What happened?' His emotions were threatening to get the better of him.

'Everything was going very well for them,' Enoch explained. 'Then yesterday two Germans turned up at the house where they were staying. Before anything could be done they had barged their way inside and threatened to shoot dead on the spot the man and his family if they didn't give up the Jews. Apparently Daniel could hear what was happening where he was hiding.'

'And so he did the noble thing,' Marek said, his voice wavering.

'Vera and the child were bundled into a truck and driven away, but not before they had been forced to see Daniel dragged outside and his body riddled with bullets.'

Marek channelled all his anguish and pain into the rehearsal that evening. For his friends, singing acted as a form of catharsis.

A little before five, Clara arrived at the tailoring shop, one of the many of its kind permitted to trade by the Germans once war had broken out. Several made uniforms for the German army. Ruben's contact treated Clara as a customer, but then, just before closing time, he ushered her into his office. Once inside, and aided by the two willing accomplices, her convincing transformation into a Jewish worker was complete. Clara waited for a few moments until the hooter sounded, and then emerging she mingled with the multitude preparing to make its way back to the Ghetto. On reaching the northern end of Zamenhofa Street, where the workers normally congregated after work for a few minutes chat, Ruben was already in place, waiting to take Clara to a pre-arranged meeting point to await Marek's arrival.

The tailors' work party had begun their procession home several minutes ago, and Marek knew he needed to move quickly if he was to have any chance of catching them up. Leaving Gesia Street and stepping onto Zamenhofa, Marek caught sight of them a little way ahead. Soon he was parallel with the snaking line on the opposite side of the street. One of the guards attached to them caught Marek's eye, but quickly looked away, uninterested. Ruben had been correct about their slack approach.

Ahead of the long procession of men was a horse-drawn wagon packed with women and children. Marek scrutinized the faces of those huddled together inside as best he could, but could not see Clara anywhere. He scanned the faces a second time, a feeling of panic rising within him. Suppose Ruben's plan had failed? Marek feared what might happen to her once her father discovered what she'd done. Then he saw them: those enchanting blue eyes. She was perched in the left-hand corner of the vehicle and Marek wanted to wave or shout to her, but knew he could not. By this time he had reached the junction with Wolynska Street and decided it might be sensible to take a slight detour, catching up with them, as planned, on Muranowska. He rounded a corner just in time to see Clara disembark with a group of women wearing her white and blue armband. She continued to walk with them for a short distance. When she had broken free of them, Marek watched as

232

Ruben stepped out from the front of a nearby house to join her. Then Marek caught up with them and took hold of her arm. The three of them walked swiftly on.

'Did everything go smoothly?' Marek asked her.

'Yes. Everything happened just as it was supposed to, though I'm not certain your tailor friend really believed I was Ruben's lover,' Clara said quietly.

'He was probably amazed that someone like you should bother with someone like him,' Marek laughed.

The hour of homecoming had been, for some while now, hazard free. There had always been exceptions to the rule, however, and today was one of those instances. Quite by surprise the three of them came upon a Nazi soldier. They had just passed by the entrance to one of the many residential buildings when two young children spilled out onto the street. Seconds later they were joined by their screaming mother, who was being dragged along by her hair. It was too late to try and make a run for it. All the three friends could do was stand and watch the horror unfold.

'Ah! Jews. I am very pleased to see you. You will be the audience for my little show,' he said, gesturing with his hand like a master of ceremonies.

His voice was indistinct, the words slurred, and he was rocking unsteadily on his feet. Ruben and Marek glanced apprehensively at one another. They both knew what was about to happen, and they feared for Clara who did not. Marek clasped her hand tightly and Ruben shifted closer to her side.

'At my feet is a Jewish whore,' the inebriated German struck up again.

The woman looked up at him imploringly, but to no avail. He struck her in the face with the full force of his boot. She whimpered like a wounded animal and blood started to flow from her nose and mouth. Clara flinched. Her bewildered children,

233

daughters of about four and two, were calling out for their mother with looks of abject terror on their little faces.

'I pay her a visit and she gives me vodka. Tried to get me drunk, didn't you, whore?'

He raised his boot for a second time and it landing squarely in her stomach. She slumped to the ground, winded and doubled up in agony. At this fresh assault Clara lunged forward, intending perhaps to go to the woman's aid, but the two men restrained her.

'And what about these two, eh? If their mother is a whore then they will grow up to be whores too.'

In a split second, and despite his drunken state, he had blasted the little figures dead where they cowered – a single bullet passing through both their skulls. Ruben, having foreseen this outcome, clapped his hand across Clara's mouth before she had a chance to cry out. The German, who was a tall, heavily-built man, lurched at them and ended up sneering at Clara.

'Upset are you?' His body swayed and then he staggered as if he had lost his footing.

'Perhaps you are a whore like her?' As he spoke he took hold of Clara's chin, lifting it with his blood stained hand. 'You'll have to wait your turn, bitch,' he hissed at Clara, turning his head to spit at the woman who was cradling her children in her lap and making the most pitiful sound.

The soldier staggered precariously towards the little huddle and stood behind the woman. She did not afford him the satisfaction of looking up at him, for she knew and accepted her fate. A second shot rang out and she slumped forwards. The colour had ebbed from Clara's cheeks and she was shaking uncontrollably. Ruben and Marek stepped in front of her as a barrier, ready for the worst, but the alcohol had, at last, rendered the German insensible. This hulk of a man sank heavily to the ground with his body sprawling. He made no attempt to stop the three of them as they crept past him. His eyes did not see them with their unfocused stare. This man's chances of leaving the Ghetto that night alive would be slim, especially if members of the fighting organisations came across him. They broke out into a frantic run until they reached the bottom of the street. Pausing for breath, Marek noticed Clara was swallowing back her tears.

'Are you all right?' he asked, drawing her closer.

'Why did he do it? I don't understand. Those poor innocent children. What could they possibly have done to deserve that?' She spoke through her tears and there was bitterness in her voice.

'Their only crime was his weakness,' Marek told her. 'A Nazi soldier does not admit his mistakes. The mother and her children suffered for his indiscretions.'

Clara walked a few paces ahead of them. Marek knew she was finding it hard to come to terms with the fact that the perpetrator of such a heinous crime could have been her compatriot. They had stopped for long enough and needed to push on. If there was one Nazi – albeit an intoxicated one – lurking about the streets, there would probably be others, and they would be sober. Much to Marek's relief, they reached the Ruzanski's apartment building without further incident. Ruben led the way inside. As Clara followed behind him, Marek suddenly felt a yanking of his arm.

'Do your family know who I am, Marek?' she asked anxiously.

'There's no need to be worried, Clara, they will welcome you.'

'But surely they will resent me because I am German?'

'You must trust me, Clara. Everything will be all right.' He bent forward and kissed her.

She smiled with relief, and then, moments before entering the living room, he felt another tug.

'Marek, my hair. What should I do?'

He took the wig from her and hurriedly stuffed it into his coat pocket.

Izak, taken by surprise at the stranger's entrance, rose from his chair to welcome her. Seconds later Eva appeared wiping her hands on a towel, and, from her expression, it was obvious that she too was astonished at seeing the young woman standing there.

'Mama, Papa – this is Clara. Clara my mother Eva and father Izak.'

Nobody said anything at first, and Marek watched as his mother cast a suspicious eye over the pretty young woman.

'I'm pleased to meet you,' she said at last, offering her hand.

Clara took it nervously.

'Do sit down,' Eva said pointing to one of the armchairs, 'I believe my son has mentioned you.' She had remembered after all, Marek thought to himself, but there had been little warmth in her voice. 'If you'll excuse me, I have to finish the meal preparations. You'll share some food with us?'

Clara accepted politely.

Marek remained for a while listening with interest to the conversation that the young woman and his father had struck up. Then he excused himself and crossed the room. Eva was standing at the sink filling a saucepan with water when her son entered the kitchen.

'Mama?'

'Why have you brought her here, Marek?' She turned to face .....There was hurt and disappointment in her eyes. 'She's a Nazi's daughter, isn't she?'

'Yes, Mama.'

'What does she want with us here in this godforsaken prison of ours?'

'She pleaded with me, Mama, to bring her here. She needed to come and see all we have to endure.'

Marek could tell that his mother did not understand.

'She is not like them, Mama. She is different. Do you remember when you, and Papa and I talked about there having to be some goodness amongst all this evil, even though we thought it would be impossible to find?'

She nodded.

'Well she is that goodness. Did you not wonder where the medicine for Rachel came from?'

'Your father and I assumed it came from Dr Bilinski's supplies.'

'It was Clara who obtained it for her. She wanted so much to help us that she went to the hospital.'

'I see.' Eva leant over the sink, perhaps needing a little time to absorb everything she had been told. 'You had better go and talk to our guest, Marek, otherwise we will seem unsociable. Send your father in here please. I need his help.'

Ruben was entertaining Clara with stories about some of his most daring exploits, and she was apparently enjoying it all. She smiled up at Marek as he passed her on his way to find his father. He was sitting beside Rachel's bed.

'How is she today?'

'A lot better Marek. The fever has subsided and Dr Bilinski thinks she may have turned a corner. The coughing has begun.'

'That's excellent news, Papa.' Coughing was a sign that the illness was in its final stages. 'Mama needs you. I'll sit with Rachel.'

'Yes, I'd better go and help her.'

'She seems a pleasant person, your friend,' Izak observed.

Rachel appeared far more comfortable than she had been in recent weeks. She had stopped perspiring and her cheeks were less florid. Her mother had washed and combed her hair. As her brother squeezed her hand gently it felt cool, having lost its clamminess. Marek had missed his sister more than he had ever imagined. The bond between them since childhood had been strong – they were each other's confidante – but they had not been able to talk since the sickness had taken hold. He leaned over and blew on her eyelids. Her lashes fluttered like the wings of a butterfly.

'How are you feeling?'

'I . . . I think the pain in my head has gone.' She stretched out her arms in an attempt to raise herself, but couldn't quite manage it. 'I feel so weak.' Speaking caused her to cough a little.

'Here, let me help you,' Marek offered, puffing up the pillows and then gently lifting her up into a sitting position. Her body was much lighter and she would need nourishment when her appetite returned.

'It is so long since we talked, Marek.'

'We will soon. When you're stronger.' He felt her grip on his hand tighten.

'I saw Lidia. She came for me and I wanted to be with her so much, but she wouldn't let me join her.'

'She probably felt it was best that you stay with us, Rachel,' and he wiped her tears away. 'There is someone here who has come to visit us. When she heard you were sick she wanted to help and went to the hospital to get you some medicine. Would you like to meet her?'

She nodded and Marek went to fetch Clara. Ruben had come to the end of one of his lengthier tales, and his audience of one was doing her best to maintain a show of interest. Marek took hold of her arm and guided her to the bedroom. His sister examined the young woman through wary eyes, just as her mother had done.

'Marek tells me that I have you to thank for my recovery.'

'I'm so glad I was able to help,' Clara responded graciously.

'I am grateful,' Rachel said. She started to cough again. She pointed to a jug of water and a half empty glass on the bedside table.

Marek held the glass to her lips and she sipped some of the liquid. All her energy had been spent, and despite her attempts to stay awake, her eyelids had started to droop. Clara noticed this, touched his shoulder, and discreetly left. Marek bent low to kiss Rachel goodnight and, as he did so, she whispered something in his ear.

'Clara is very beautiful.'

Then she sank into a deep slumber.

❖   ❖   ❖

Halfway through the meal Clara pushed her knife and fork to one side of her plate. The conversation had flowed well, and as he had hoped, Marek's family warmed to her. Now, however, Clara had something of a more serious nature she wanted to say.

'You must be wondering why I have come to this place? I needed to see for myself what it was really like. What I had been told is beyond the bounds of comprehension, but now I know it to be true. Today I have witnessed something which has seriously shaken my faith in humanity.' Recollecting the incident her eyes began to moisten. 'On the way here a young mother and her two children were savagely and callously murdered by a Nazi soldier. Since then I have tried hard to understand why such a dreadful thing as that should have happened. For what conceivable purpose? The only conclusion I have come to is that their murders were carried out purely to satiate an overwhelming lust for evil. The fact that I am German and the daughter of a Nazi officer cannot be changed, but I wish you to know that if it was in my power to put an end to all of this senseless persecution then I surely would.' Clara had said what she had needed to, and now sat there with downcast eyes.

'You have helped our precious Rachel and for that Eva and I are eternally indebted to you. Ruben, fetch the bottle from the store cupboard, would you, please?' Izak said.

The family talked late into the evening. Ruben went over the arrangements for the following day, regardless of the fact that they were already engrained upon each of their memories, and then peace descended over the household. Marek must have lain there for at least an hour or two, unable to rest. He decided to get up. The curtains were drawn, but chinks of light had penetrated the fraying cloth, falling on the spot where Eva had made up a bed for their guest. Marek had not seen Clara sleeping before and as he gazed at her, he was overwhelmed by her loveliness. He knelt down beside her, not wanting to wake her, but he could not stop himself from tenderly stroking her glistening hair, for the light had given it the characteristics of white, spun gold.

'Marek?' she mumbled sleepily.

'I didn't mean to wake you. Are you warm enough?'

'Yes, I'm fine thank you,' Clara said.

'You should rest. I'll leave you now.'

'Where do you go when you can't sleep Marek?'

'Usually out onto the landing.'

'I'll come with you.'

'Here, you'll need your coat,' he said balancing it over her shoulders.

Marek sat on the ledge, and drew Clara down beside him.

'It's so dark and sinister out there,' she said nervously as she peered through the glass at the street below and the buildings opposite.

He embraced her whilst telling her about the empty apartments and the fates of their occupants. She listened but seemed preoccupied.

'I saw them in my dreams. The terrified looks upon those children's faces, and their mother knowing that they were going to be murdered. Such courage and all I did was stand there and watch.' She shuddered.

240

'There was nothing you could have done, Clara.'

'I was very angry when you and Ruben prevented me from doing anything. Angry with you, Marek, for not doing something yourself. Then when I saw the hatred in that evil brute's eyes, I knew he would have killed us as well if we'd retaliated, wouldn't he?'

'With the SS there is rarely any mercy. If he had not been so drunk we wouldn't be here now. It was better to do nothing in the circumstances, especially with the other one close by.'

'What other one?' She did not understand what he meant.

'The SS rove in packs and there would almost certainly have been another soldier with him,' Marek explained. 'He was probably in a worse state than his companion. All of us here are prepared to die, but it is better to leave this world having in some way thwarted the enemy rather than not.'

'How can you talk about death in such a detached way, Marek?' Clara was astonished.

'Perhaps because it no longer holds the fear or mystery it once did. What you saw today was something you would never have envisaged seeing during the whole of your lifetime. For my family events like that are part of our daily existence. I cannot recall how many brutal deaths I have witnessed, or how many bodies I have seen strewn across the streets. All I know is that there have been too many. In time, you become immune to it in order to bear it.'

'Your family. They are so . . .' She hesitated.

'Normal? Yes, you're right, I suppose. To the outsider looking in, normalcy prevails, but it is superficial. Dig deeper and there is frailty, heartache, unrelenting grief and tribulation.'

A shiver ran through her body.

'We'd better get back inside. You need to sleep, Clara. We've got to be up early tomorrow.'

He pulled the blanket and his coat over her for extra warmth, and as they embraced she twisted his hair through her fingers.

'I understand so much now,' were her last words before drifting into sleep.

A little after seven o'clock the next morning, the three of them were out on the street. Marek's parents saw them off, wishing their guest a safe journey. Neither party expressed the hope of a reunion, perhaps not wishing to tempt fate. Their progress was unimpeded, and, at Muranowska Street, Marek watched Clara climb into the wagon with the same group of women she had travelled with the day before. None of them seemed to notice her, nor were they the slightest bit interested in their regular travelling companions for that matter. Their faces were drawn and tired and reflected the tedium of their daily routine. Marek waited until the wagon had disappeared from sight. Ruben would shadow the workers for as long as he could, but the two men knew he would be helpless should anything go wrong.

❖   ❖   ❖

Several hours later, Marek was sitting in the summerhouse. He had arranged to meet Clara there, but she had not arrived yet. A feeling of anxiety took hold and his overactive imagination began to conjure up images of what might have befallen her, when something startled him.

'So this is where you find inspiration Dr Ruzanski.'

Marek clenched his teeth.

'A pleasant haven, is it not? My daughter has made it most comfortable. Ah, but I am here to talk of more serious things.'

So he must know, Marek concluded, especially given his premature return. Perhaps he had already interrogated Clara and she had been forced to tell him all that had happened. Marek prepared himself for the worst.

'Do sit down, Doctor. We have an important matter to discuss. The concert will soon be upon us.'

The relief was overwhelming. Marek hoped it did not show in his demeanour.

'I expect to complete the composition imminently,' Marek told him.

'That is good news. Ahead of schedule.'

He walked to the fireplace and rested his hand upon the mantelpiece. There was no fire burning today, but he gazed, unseeing, into the empty grate regardless.

'You and your men will have ample time to rehearse,' he continued, unaware of the figure who had silently slipped into the building. From her expression, it was clear Clara was as surprised to see her father as Marek had been.

'Ah, Papa, I thought I might find you here. Oh, I'm sorry to interrupt your meeting with Dr Ruzanski.'

She smiled at Marek in the same way she might a stranger.

'We have discussed all we need to for the time being. I will check on your progress in a day or so. Come, Clara, we should leave Dr Ruzanski to his thoughts.'

Like a dutiful daughter, Clara took her father's arm and together they left. Marek did not see her for the rest of that day.

Izak and Eva did not discuss the events of the previous evening at great length. Eva enquired about Clara's safe return, and Izak remarked on her charm and attractiveness. With regard to the precise nature of their son's relationship with the woman there would be no scrutiny, and Marek knew his parents would have dismissed any kind of intimacy between them as doomed. Rachel's appetite had improved; Eva prepared a dish of clear soup and there was bread. Marek offered to take it to her to relieve his mother who was looking tired. The death of her eldest daughter, followed rapidly by the strain of seeing her youngest struggling with a life-threatening disease, had exhausted her emotionally and physically. Rachel was sitting up when he entered her room

'You're home,' she smiled, pleased to see her brother.

'You're looking much better today,' he said putting the tray down.

'I feel better, except for this cough. Dr Bilinski says it's part of the sickness.'

'Yes. Shouldn't last too much longer though. Now, are you going to eat some soup? Mama's made it specially.'

'I had better try some then,' Rachel laughed slightly.

She was beginning to sound like the sister he knew and loved. He was glad.

'Would you like me to help?'

'Thank you. I still feel so weak.'

Gently Marek brought the spoon to her lips and she swallowed. Then he dipped pieces of bread in the soup. After a few spoonfuls she started to giggle.

'I feel like a child again.'

'Did I feed you when we were young? I don't remember.'

'Yes, I think Mama let you do it sometimes.'

'I do recall the day you were born as if it were yesterday – coming home from school and Grandma giving us the news. I rushed up the stairs and there you were, looking so sweet with your big eyes, only a few hours old. Lidia and I went to stay with Grandma for a few days, but I couldn't wait to come home and see you again. We were both so proud of our little sister.'

'Those were happier times.' She let out a sigh.

When Rachel had eaten as much as she could, she shifted her position in the bed so she was now able to look her brother full in the face. Her eyes were still ringed with dark circles but they had regained some of their former impish sparkle.

'Now then you must tell me about our visitor yesterday. I expect you thought I'd forgotten about her. Papa told me she'd come to see what Ghetto life was like and that, unfortunately, she did. You're very fond of her, Marek. I can tell.'

'Was it that obvious?'

'It was to me,' Rachel said laughing.

'Do you think Mama knows?'

'She didn't say anything. Anyway what would be the point? With the way things are there could be no future for her son and a Nazi officer's daughter.'

'I cannot help myself Rachel. I have feelings for her which I have never had for any other woman.'

'And what about Clara? Does she care for you?'

'She does. Very much.'

Neither of them said anything for a while. Rachel was pondering the implications of what her brother had said.

'Presumably her father is oblivious to all of this?'

'He knows nothing of it. He's been away in Berlin for almost three weeks.'

'Planning the next murderous acts I shouldn't wonder?' Her comment was barbed.

'If it weren't for this war and our circumstances I am sure that in time I would grow to like her very much. Sadly I doubt I will have the opportunity.'

Marek could not offer her any reassurances.

'When is the concert?' she said changing the subject.

He told her and she expressed surprise and concern at how close it was.

'No one will blame you for what you are being made to do. You do know that, don't you?'

'Yes, I know.' The desire to blurt out the truth at that moment was overwhelming but he did not. Instead he gathered up the food things, and was about to take them to the kitchen.

'Miriam. How is Miriam? I asked Papa earlier, but I don't think he heard me properly. I think he must be going deaf.'

Marek did not want to be the one to tell Rachel the sad news, and it was blatantly obvious that others didn't want to be the harbingers of misery either. In the end, words were unnecessary – his lack of response was enough – and her eyes began to fill with tears. He put down the tray.

'I'm sorry, Rachel. Don't be sad. The doctor said she was really very sick.' She started to sob. 'I will send Ruben to see you when he comes home. That should cheer you up.'

She gave a mock groan at his suggestion. Laid up in bed as she was, Rachel was a captive audience to Ruben's ribbing, something she pretended not to enjoy. Sure enough, a little later that evening, her tears of sorrow had vanished and were followed by those precipitated by laughter.

It occurred to Marek the next morning – as he grappled with the heavy front door and took the now familiar passage to the music room – that this ritual would soon be at an end. The days at the house were drawing to a close and he wondered how he would feel when it was all over. He was contemplating the many kindnesses he had experienced and had begun to take for granted – the warmth, good food and friendship – when Clara popped her head around the door. Marek made space for her on the piano stool and she snuggled up to him. He kissed her.

'How are you?'

'Better now I'm with you. Yesterday I wanted to come and see you desperately, but my father needed me.'

'You're devoted to him?' Marek suggested. 'In the summerhouse before you turned up I was beginning to think things had gone wrong. I was worried about you.'

'You need not have been. Ruben's friend at the shop was very kind. If only my father could meet your family, Marek, and discuss things properly, I'm sure he would see how futile this is.'

'You must not say anything to him, Clara. Your father has made his choice. If he has any feelings of sympathy for us he has chosen to suppress them. Maybe he has done this because of self-preservation, for it would take a very brave person, or a foolish one, to stand against the might of the Party.'

She turned away. His words had upset her.

'I'm sorry, Clara. I didn't mean to hurt you.'

'What you have said is true, Marek. I wish it wasn't.' She rummaged in her skirt pocket and a moment or two later pulled out a crumpled piece of paper. 'I have something for you.'

Reading the words written in her own hand he knew instantly what she had done. Clara had spared him a great ignominy.

'Thank you,' Marek said, embracing her.

Without warning there was a rap on the door. They sprang apart, both anticipating the worst. Much to their relief it was just Dominik hovering outside. He had been sent to fetch the water jug. The young man gave Clara a curious, almost comical, sideways glance as he made his way to the dresser.

Marek and Clara did not arrange to meet again that day. She would come when it was safe.

❖   ❖   ❖

The end of the week arrived all too quickly, and by the time General Reinecke put in an appearance Marek had, reluctantly and with increasing resentment, adapted several lines of Clara's words to fit his music. General Reinecke stood to one side of the composer, near enough to view the score, but never allowing himself to get too close. Perhaps Marek repulsed him or he feared contamination, as many of his countrymen did. Marek thought about his daughter and the intimacy they had shared.

'May I take a closer look, Doctor?'

Marek stepped aside and the German swept the manuscript up in both hands and took it to the window. He was analysing Marek's efforts. He gave a satisfied smirk which vanished as quickly as it had come. He had at last complied with the instructions and written the text. Ironically, and unbeknownst to him, his own flesh and blood had been responsible for its conception, and at that moment a smile passed over Marek's lips. Without a word Franz Reinecke sat down at the piano, and for the first time began to play. His sight reading was impressive.

'Very good, Doctor, very good. The use of Wagnerian harmony, texture and not least the leitmotif, is executed with the greatest of skill. Your audience will be most impressed. It is a pity . . .' he continued but suddenly checked himself, realising he had spoken aloud.

'. . . that I am a Jew,' Marek added, finishing his sentence. 'Such talent is wasted on someone like me.'

'I have business to attend to and you have work to complete,' he retorted heading towards the door.

'Does the business you speak of involve the murder of my friends?'

He stopped in his tracks and swung his body around.

'Daniel Jankowski. Does his name sound familiar to you?' Marek asked.

General Reinecke's expression remained impassive.

'Ah! A member of your choir, no doubt?' he snapped.

'Someone who was murdered in cold blood in front of his wife and child.' The anger was boiling up.

'Unfortunately when your friend reneged on our agreement and decided to leave the Ghetto, he was no longer under my protection.' His delivery was matter of fact.

'What agreement? There was never any agreement. None of us had a choice. It was blackmail and you know it.' Marek was furious at his glibness.

'Your emotional outbursts are unbecoming, Doctor. Perhaps it is a sign that you have been working too hard. It is rather fortuitous that your assignment is nearing a resolution. We will meet again when the work is finally completed.'

He slammed the door with considerable force.

Marek's eighth and final week at the house began like any other with the exception that the sun shone more brilliantly than it had done all season. As they travelled through Warsaw, it was as though all the drabness had been replaced by vibrancy. The damaged edifices and piles of rubble did not evoke the same poignancy which they usually did, and an air of tranquillity had descended over the city. Such moments as these were rare, and frequently preceded a period of turbulence and calamity.

The composition was almost complete, and yet Marek delayed its conclusion. Each additional day gave him an opportunity to spend time with his beloved Clara.

Letting himself into the music room, he was met by the sight of at least a dozen blooms of yellow and red standing upright in their container. They cheered his mood.

When Angelika called in at her usual hour, they chatted for a little while. She informed Marek that they had celebrated Mrs Dabrowski's birthday at the weekend, and that she herself had made a special cake for the occasion. Dominik, being artistic, had carved a figurine out of wood, and Mr Dabrowski had presented his wife with one of his finest potted flowers. The *Oberst-gruppenführer* had been out all evening, which meant they had been able to enjoy a little party. When Clara learnt of their plans, she had daringly taken a bottle of her father's wine to help the celebrations along.

Earlier in the day Marek had found one of Clara's notes poking out between the leaves of a book. He had pounced on it thirsty to learn whatever news of her it might contain. He was not disappointed. She was intending to take her horse out for a ride and a time was specified. As there was no longer any urgency in resuming his task, and, coupled with the fact that his desire to see Clara was beginning to get the better of him, Marek packed away his things and set off. He followed the path which ran parallel with the house, towards the stables. He passed the track leading off towards the vegetable garden and glasshouse, and made for the stone outbuildings where Clara's horse was stabled.

'Hello, Marek,' Mr Dabrowski said.

'Doctor Ruzanski.' Clara's greeting was friendly but deliberately formal.

'Are you taking a break from your work to enjoy the sunshine?' Mr Dabrowski asked.

'It is indeed a lovely day,' Marek replied, snatching a brief look at Clara.

'The Fraulein is going for a ride. It's a pity there are not more horses otherwise we could have joined her.'

Marek watched as Clara mounted the magnificent-looking animal. Then she pulled on the reins, dug her boots into the horse's side, and the creature set off at a steady canter, heading for the parkland.

'Such a splendid beast and so powerful,' Mr Dabrowski observed, and he followed its progress with a wistful eye until both horse and rider were merely tiny outlines.

Marek could not deny that it was indeed a fine animal, but his attention had been drawn as ever to its rider. He waited while Mr Dabrowski returned a few items to the tack room.

'This is your last week with us then?'

'Yes, that's right. The next time I am here will be on the night of the concert.'

'All the local Nazi bigwigs will be here as well. It's just an excuse to get drunk, and my poor wife will have to wait on them. If I had my way I'd have the lot of them strangled in their beds.'

The angry tirade continued for some time. Marek had not seen such a show of enmity from the man before.

'Do you know why the Nazi was recalled to Berlin at such short notice?' he said to Marek. The two men had by now started to walk.

'To organise something unspeakable, no doubt,' Marek replied sardonically.

'I'm afraid you may be right. Your people are likely to come to grief soon. My son tells me the resistance are pretty certain that the Nazi's are going to clean out the Ghetto. It's only a matter of time.'

What he said did not come as a surprise since the Ruzanskis had heard similar rumours.

'You and your family should think about getting out, if you can, before it's too late. Do your people have anything to fight with?'

Marek explained the situation as he understood it from his discussions with Ruben. The Ghetto inhabitants were as well-equipped as they could expect to be given the circumstances and there was a willingness to resist. What they possessed was woefully inadequate against such a powerful adversary. Mr Dabrowski shook his head in despair. The two men walked on in silence.

Reaching the walled garden, Marek congratulated him on the magnificence of his spring flowers. The remark seemed to lighten his mood and when his companion left him he was whistling merrily. While making his way back to the house, Marek's thoughts were dominated by what Mr Dabrowski had said. What if, when the big fight came, he wasn't there to protect his family? Ruben had been entrusted with their safety if his friend was no longer able to protect them, but was he being selfish, indulging his obsession for revenge? Marek tried hard to put these maudlin thoughts out of his mind.

The remaining days of the week slipped by, and Clara and Marek saw relatively little of each other. Her father had remained at the house for most of that time, which meant extended meetings were not possible. They had abandoned the summerhouse following the unwelcome invasion by the *Oberst-gruppenführer*, but on Marek's final day they decided to chance it. Clara had got there first. Marek lingered on the threshold, taking in the room's interior with all its pretty features, since this would almost certainly be the last time he would see it. Perhaps sensing his thoughts, Clara came to him and took hold of his hand. She led him to where the soft rug was spread. They sank down upon it and kissed each other feverishly. She surrendered to him willingly. The softness of her skin was even more pleasurable now to the touch of his lips. They lay together curled up in each other's arms.

'I hate the thought of not being able to see you, Marek.'

'It won't be for long, darling. Only a week,' he said reassuringly, stroking her hair gently.

'But we can never be like we are now.'

He watched her as she dressed, and the misery of their impending separation began to take hold of him.

'What are the arrangements for the concert?' Clara's tremulous voice revealed her unhappiness.

'We will be picked up from the Ghetto at five o'clock and we'll rehearse here beforehand.'

'My father has planned everything so meticulously. He will expect the performance to be no less than perfect.'

For the first time Clara spoke of him contemptuously.

'What do you think he'll do if he finds out about us?' Marek asked.

'He'd send me away – perhaps to some convent in the mountains – as a punishment.' A wan smile crossed Clara's lips.

'And I would be taken somewhere and shot no doubt.'

'He wouldn't admit it, but I'm sure you remind him of Michael in many ways.'

'Your Jewish friend?'

'Yes. It wasn't only my mother who was fond of him. He was too.'

'Well, your father does not spare him much thought now, otherwise he couldn't possibly do what he does without having a severely troubled conscience.'

'Perhaps my father is no longer capable of remorse or feelings of self-reproach. He has changed. He refuses to listen to me or anyone else.' Clara paused and looked towards him intently. 'Please Marek, will you reconsider and do what my father has requested? It is only a piece of music. What about your family? I'm petrified about what will happen to you and what Papa will do if you defy him. Don't you love me enough to do this one thing?'

Marek turned his back on her. Nothing could ever fracture the affection they held for one another, but at this moment in time both of them knew they were standing on the brink of the unknown. Before leaving for the night Marek placed the completed manuscript on the piano. Some time later the Nazi would arrange for it to be collected and duplicated. The following morning Marek was to be at Gesia Street at the usual hour, when he would be handed copies.

❖ ❖ ❖

The men had agreed to meet earlier on their way home from the workshop. Although the majority of their practice time to date had been devoted to perfecting the second composition, it was crucial for them to perform a competent rendition of the original piece. The *Oberst-gruppenführer* was not the sort of man to leave anything to chance. Marek felt sure he would make an appearance during their rehearsals. Since they were all keen to be securely in their homes for the start of the Sabbath the meeting was brief. The next rehearsal would take place on Sunday.

Rachel was fast asleep when her brother had checked on her first thing that morning. Now Marek found her sitting on the couch chatting animatedly with her mother. This was the first time in over three weeks that she had felt well enough to leave her room. Still dressed in her nightclothes, she looked frail and thin, and her eyes were disproportionately large, but this did not matter now she was out of danger and on the road to recovery.

'You'll be with Mama in the kitchen again soon,' her brother teased her.

'As soon as I'm a bit stronger,' she said gesturing for him to sit beside her.

The clatter of dinner plates signalled that the meal was ready.

A little while later the five of them were sitting around the table, eating and laughing just like old times. Marek was determined to savour every precious moment that they spent together during the next week.

By Thursday evening the choir was ready. Marek was astounded at the men's professionalism and the quality of their singing. This was to be their last rehearsal in familiar settings and the mood was strained. Fear had firmly gripped them all. Only Amos could improve their morale and this he did, surpassing his usual generosity by producing four bottles of his most potent concoction. They drank like condemned men, and, for that brief period, were happy and carefree.

At some point during the night Marek awoke stone cold sober, and it was not long before his mind began to speculate about what might happen. Although he had often contemplated his fate, it was only now, in the early hours of the morning of the concert, that the full implications of his actions hit home. The thought of never seeing Clara or his family again was distressing and painful, and the desire to go and wake them and reveal everything was difficult to resist. Perhaps he wanted to give them the opportunity to talk him out of it, which he knew they would try their best to do. The emotional torment he endured in those moments of bleak reflection was not something he would wish on anyone.

Ruben was already up and out when Marek woke again, and he found his mother and father preparing breakfast. Both of them looked up when he entered the kitchen.

'Ruben said he'll be back before you leave,' Izak informed him. Inwardly Marek was relieved to hear that. He needed to speak with him.

'I've washed your shirt, Marek.'

He thanked his mother, knowing she had done it so that her son would look clean and smart.

'What time do you and the others need to leave?' she asked.

'We have to be waiting on the other side of the wall at five.'

'There's plenty of time then.'

She looked anxious and so Marek thought it best to change the conversation.

'Hopefully, when tonight is over, I can get my old job back. It shouldn't be a problem. They must be missing my exceptional skills at the factory,' he laughed wryly.

His mother managed to smile.

Rachel woke early, and weary of her nightclothes, announced that she was going to get dressed. Mama helped her, and soon Rachel was smiling cheerfully and parading her old – and now baggy – dress like a model. It was still the 'safe' period of the day when people could be out and about, and the family received a visit from Dr Bilinski. Regardless of Rachel's steady improvement, he made it his business to check on her every day. He enjoyed his visits. Eva would give him coffee or whatever concoction she might have in her stores, and he would engage in heated debates with Izak.

The day passed slowly, and initially Marek found he was able to block out all thoughts of the night's event. However, by early afternoon his anxiety had returned with a vengeance, and he had to fight hard to disguise his feelings. On several occasions during the morning he had noticed Rachel studying him surreptitiously from her vantage-point on the couch, but she remained silent. Then, about an hour before Marek was due to leave, she asked if he would accompany her across the landing, saying that she felt like stretching her legs. Marek obliged and, as she leant heavily on his arm for support, they covered the short distance along the passage. The sun was sinking fast but it warmed her skin.

'Is there something you would like to tell me, Marek? You've been incredibly agitated all afternoon.'

'Is it that obvious?' he asked. His sister's perceptiveness made him chuckle.

'You forget I know you better than you know yourself. You can't keep anything from me.'

It was true. She had always known his mind from an early age. Marek knew that he could not keep the truth from her any longer.

'Will you promise me that regardless of what I tell you now you will not say anything to Mama and Papa — at least not today? When I am gone then I want you to be the one to explain what I've done.'

'Done what, Marek?'

From her expression and the tone of her voice Marek could tell that he had unnerved her. She listened just as Clara had done, and only when she had heard it all did the tears flow. They clung to each other.

'I have no choice, Rachel,' Marek said defiantly, pulling away from her embrace.

'You don't suppose this German is going to forgive you for disobeying him in front of his superiors?' Rachel shouted angrily.

'How can I possibly do what he asks after what happened to Lidia and Benjamin, Ezra and Mara and now Daniel?'

'You don't have to die for them. They wouldn't expect it of you.'

'It won't come to that, Rachel. Please say you understand. I must go soon and I don't want to leave you like this.'

She blew her nose and tried to compose herself.

'I cannot condone what you are doing, Marek, you must understand that. But I love you and I shall always be proud of you.'

The two siblings hugged each other and then, wiping her eyes with the sleeve of her cardigan, Rachel smiled at her brother weakly and they walked back to join the others. The unburdening, though harrowing, had been a great release for Marek. It was now late afternoon and soon the choir would be gathering at the designated pick-up point. Marek kissed his parents goodbye, telling his mother that he would probably be back late that night. Rachel had remained in her room and did not see her brother off. They had said their farewells, and she felt she wouldn't be able to trust her emotions in front of her unsuspecting parents. Ruben followed Marek out of the apartment.

'It's not too late to change your mind you know,' he said, as they shook hands. He did not seem to want to loosen his firm grip on his friend's hand. 'But you won't, will you?'

'If . . .' Marek's voice began to falter. 'If I don't come home you will do as we discussed?'

'Of course I will.'

They shook hands again. Marek looked back before reaching the staircase and thought he caught the young man wiping his eye quickly. He had never known Ruben to weep before.

❖   ❖   ❖

The friends were huddled together in small groups. Marek nervously checked his watch again. It was a little before five. Suddenly Amos, who was keeping an eye out for any sign of transport, pointed at a fast-approaching vehicle.

'Here it is,' he shouted to the rest of the choir.

Still some way off, but making its way towards them, was a large truck. It came to a stop a yard or two away from where the men had formed a neat line. Their lives over the past few years had become so regimented that they did this automatically, without any thought. The doors of the vehicle opened and out bounced two soldiers.

'More musical Jews,' Ernst said sarcastically.

258

His comrade, Viktor, who had gone to open up the back of the truck, now reappeared.

'Get in,' he ordered gruffly.

One by one they clambered inside and sat down on the benches lining either side and began the journey to the house. Marek had forgotten that the men had not seen vast areas of Warsaw for many months, and being reminded of the destruction proved to be disquieting for them.

'So much has changed since before the war. It is hardly recognizable from the city I remember,' Jakub remarked, as he took his turn to peer through the slits of the truck's canvas.

'There was a lot of damage from the raids,' Adam said over the droning sound of the engine.

'Thankfully, there's a lot still standing including some of the older buildings,' added Enoch.

The truck continued to make its way along the city's roads, and then eventually it began to slow down. Further peeking revealed a sentry at his post who waved them through, and the vehicle trundled up the long drive and parked in front of the steps to the house. The men waited patiently until the cords securing the canvas cover were untied, and then jumped down onto the gravel path. Marek watched as the men took in the magnificent splendour of their surroundings and filled their lungs with the sweet, clean air and recalled his first experiences there. Within a few minutes of disembarking, Marek sensed they were being observed. Turning he saw the imposing figure of the *Oberst-gruppenführer* at the top of the steps. Marek's throat went dry at the thought of openly defying this man.

Marek beckoned to the others and they ascended the steps. Their host turned on his heels and the choir followed him to a part of the house Marek had not seen before. Eventually they came to a stop in front of an ornate set of wooden doors, elegantly carved and decorated with gold, which opened onto a grand hall. Unlike other areas of the house, this room was well-preserved. The opulence of previous centuries was conspicuous in the paintings, furnishings and ornaments. There were several objects Marek estimated to be of significant value: the two golden urns resting on each side of the marble fireplace, and the glittering chandeliers immediately caught his eye. At the far end of the hall stood a piano, which Marek recognized as the one from the music room. Its removal must have been achieved with some degree of difficulty, given the width of the corridors through which they had walked. Facing it were several rows of chairs, arranged in an arc, and beyond them were a number of trestle tables draped with crisp linen cloths.

'My guests will be arriving from seven o'clock onwards and I expect your rehearsal to be finished well before then. I have arranged for some refreshments to be available in the adjoining room. The housekeeper will collect you and take you there.' His strong voice resonated about the large space. 'Now you must excuse me.'

The sound of his boots striking the polished wooden floor reverberated in the stillness. The overwhelming relief at his departure was like the exhalation of a long held breath.

'Well, he's in for a shock,' Enoch said in an attempt to lighten the mood, despite the discernible anxiety in his voice.

'Indeed he is.' Jakub's delivery was steadier. 'We are at the point of no return. Let's get on with it. It will be worth it just to wipe the arrogant looks from their faces.'

The choir warmed up with some vocal exercises, following them with the first of the carefully pre-selected passages. An hour must have passed when, unexpectedly, Clara walked in. Marek's heart skipped a beat when he saw her. He had missed her so much and it was all he could do to stop himself from running over to her.

260

'My friends, I would like you to meet Clara Reinecke.'

'I am very pleased to make your acquaintance. You were all singing beautifully,' Clara said warmly, putting them at their ease.

'Fraulein Reinecke herself is an accomplished singer and will be performing tonight,' Marek explained.

Clara blushed with embarrassment at his words. There were some strange looks from the men, and Marek imagined his apparent consorting with an attractive German woman would be a cause of consternation. Not many minutes later Mrs Dabrowski entered the hall. She had come to escort the members of the choir to the area which had been set aside.

It was quite small and functional. Any fine furniture or elaborate furnishings had been removed, and instead plain wooden chairs lined the walls. In the centre was a table generously stacked with plates of food including meats, bread, real butter and a variety of different cheeses. There was no alcohol, but jugs of water and several bottles of a fruit-based drink. Marek thanked Mrs Dabrowski for her efforts and she smiled appreciatively.

'The Last Supper,' Jakub said caustically as he surveyed the food. 'Well, we might as well enjoy it.'

The men began to tuck in heartily. Marek struggled to force down every mouthful. Fear had not left him, and it now robbed him of his appetite.

'Who is that woman?' Enoch asked, reaching across the table for another slice of ham.

The chattering stopped and everyone focused on Marek, eagerly anticipating his response. Marek explained who Clara was and described how their friendship had grown when they discovered a shared interest in music.

'And her father allows his daughter to fraternise with a Jew?' Eli asked in disbelief.

Without revealing the true nature of their attachment, Marek explained they had become friends while her father had been away in Berlin and that he was unaware of it. This satisfied their curiosity, and they quickly resumed what was, to them, the more crucial matter of eating. By now Marek had consumed as much as he could, and crossed the room to the window with its view of the lake. It was not yet dark and the light from the electric lanterns on the fairy tale bridge was shining onto the water, making it glisten. He looked at his watch; it was now after seven.

'How do you feel, Marek?' Amos' voice came from behind.

'Not too good. It's the waiting that is so hard. How are you?'

'We all feel the same. Like you we're trying hard not to give in to our fear,' Amos said.

'Am I doing the right thing? I have questioned my actions over and over, and now at this very moment I am beginning to doubt myself.'

'My friend, you have nothing to worry yourself about. Our faith in you is implicit. You have forgotten, perhaps, that this was our decision too.'

'My dread is not for me but for you and the men. I do not know what will happen. I cannot guarantee your safety.'

'I know this, Marek, just as I know that there has never been another choice,' Amos said.

He held out his hand and Marek shook it. Then he went to join the others, who were still drinking and eating. Marek felt in his pockets in the hope of finding a cigarette, but realised he had forgotten to ask Ruben for some of his before he left. Soon the concert would begin and Marek asked Eli to lead them in prayer. This he did, and then they waited. Through the thickness of the wall it was just possible to distinguish what was taking place in the hall. At precisely half past seven the general hubbub ceased, and they could hear a man speaking. It was General Reinecke. It was not possible to make out every word, but he welcomed his guests, promising an evening of entertainment the Führer himself would approve of. There was a loud scraping of chairs as the audience rose to its feet, followed by the shouting of their leader's name in chorus. A hush descended over the room. Clara began to sing.

So pure and beautiful was the sound that it could not fail to touch and melt even the wickedest of hearts. The choir listened spellbound until the very last note had faded away, and then a solitary clap sparked off such tumultuous applause Marek thought it would never end. But it did, and they waited with trepidation in their hearts. The door opened and a young, bespectacled German entered the room. He was wearing a military uniform, and yet his appearance was more reminiscent of a secretary or clerk. Politely he asked if the men would follow him.

The atmosphere was hazy, full of cigarette and cigar smoke. Having gathered just inside the doorway Marek could see each row was filled with formidable looking individuals drinking from glasses which Angelika and Mrs Dabrowski had handed out. Loud conversation was punctuated by raucous laughter. The Nazi was standing near to the piano and before they advanced the clerk sought a signal from him. It came with a distinct wave of the hand, and they began their orderly procession. Heads swivelled and soon it felt as if every pair of eyes was boring into them with curiosity, but also with hatred and repulsion. Marek stared straight ahead, as did his friends, and although he couldn't see the source of the cutting remarks, Marek could hear what they were saying.

'Why on earth is a group of filthy Jews here?' asked one.

'Ah, ah!' uttered another, craning his neck to speak to his colleague sitting behind him, 'this must be the "novel" item.'

'I wonder what it is they do? Perhaps they will perform a circus act like the animals they are.'

'I could make them dance all right,' another laughed sinisterly. Out of the corner of his eye Marek saw him brandish a gun.

As they neared the front row Marek's eyes skimmed each occupant as he tried to locate Clara. Perhaps she had chosen to leave rather than stay and witness what was to come. He did not blame her. When he had almost given up Marek spotted her sitting three chairs from the end of the first row beside her father. Unlike the others who had stared with mouths gaping wide, Clara had her head bowed. Marek wondered what she was feeling at this precise moment. His throat had become so parched that swallowing was difficult and a wave of panic threatened to engulf him. He wished he could feel strong and courageous but he was, after all, merely mortal.

The men had formed two lines and the lights were dimmed. Marek spread his fingers over the keys. His hands started to tremble and he had difficulty in steadying them. When he had sounded the notes he moved to the spot from where he would conduct. As he found Clara in the semi-darkness their eyes met. In hers there was unimaginable sorrow but Marek's heart leapt as she smiled. The sight of her was enough to boost his resolve. Marek held his arms poised in the air before allowing them to fall. The arresting opening rang out, followed by Jakub's tenor solo rising from the depths. His voice was as clear as a bell, almost ethereal. His eyelids were closed and he seemed totally immersed in what he was doing. It was as if all the terror had been expunged from his being and in its place was an inner serenity. By the time they reached the twelfth bar Marek suddenly heard someone rise abruptly. He knew instinctively who it would be. He carried on conducting and the men sang, but he could now see a look of dread in their eyes. The Nazi was standing right behind Marek. The force of his anger was conveyed in a single word.

'Stop!'

Marek stayed his hand and the men grew silent. Slowly, he

turned around and the two men faced one another. His eyes were bloodshot and Marek saw wild rage in them. Marek steeled himself against being struck dead on the spot. This man had suffered the greatest indignity in front of a hall full of Nazis, many of high rank, and he was barely in control of himself.

The two adversaries continued to stare at each other. What Marek had thought would inevitably happen did not, and he received no physical injury or mortal blow. Maybe the German wished to maintain his dignity and yet where Jews were concerned the Nazis rarely considered propriety. His features still contorted with the intensity of his wrath, he began to move his lips as if to speak. What he said was meant for Marek's ears only.

'You have deceived me and for that you must pay,' he whispered viciously.

The venomous tone of his delivery made Marek shudder. With a wave of his left arm, the Nazi signalled to the two soldiers standing to attention not far away. As they emerged from the darkness Marek recognized the familiar figures of Ernst and Viktor. He glanced at the choir, who were no doubt contemplating their own fates, and forced a smile. Marek wanted to give them hope, although in reality the alarm imprinted on his face must have had the opposite effect.

'Lock him in the cellar!'

Now, Marek thought to himself, these two men had become his gaolers. As he was being marched away they passed Clara. Her eyes were red from weeping. He wanted so much to reach out and comfort her.

Marek was frogmarched some distance from the hall and then down several flights of stairs. They were making their way to the bowels of the house, and as the three men neared the bottom of the staircase, one of the guards uttered something.

'I don't fancy your chances now, Jew,' Ernst said.

'Brave though,' Viktor acknowledged with almost a hint of admiration, 'especially when you know you're going to die.'

They had reached the entrance to a cellar. One of the guards took hold of the black metal handle in the centre of a heavy, dark, panelled door and turned the key. The door was pushed open and Marek peered into the gloom.

'I suppose, given the present circumstances, you're not as valuable as you once were.'

Without any warning the soldier rammed his pistol down hard onto Marek's head, catapulting him forward into the darkness.

When Marek regained consciousness, his whole body was wracked with pain and he could taste blood. Gradually, and with most of his faculties restored, the reality of his situation struck home. He was lying in total darkness on the floor of an underground room. It was damp and utterly miserable. As something brushed past his ear, he cringed with revulsion. Fearing the worst, Marek moved each of his limbs gingerly to see if they were broken. Thankfully, none appeared to be, despite the heavy fall. He had a bloody nose and cut lip which was now smarting badly. He slowly got to his knees, but the process of moving made his head spin. He tried to stand, but there was nothing to hold on to for support. It was then he remembered the stairs, and so he fumbled in the darkness on his hands and knees, until he located a rail. He hauled himself upright and tried to find a light switch.

Marek began the agonising business of climbing the stairs, dragging his bruised and throbbing body slowly up each step. With a downward flick, the blackness was replaced by an amber glow. He slumped down on the top step, all his energy spent, and reviewed the scene below. The dungeon, for that was what it was, resembled a stone cavern. At one time, deep, round cavities had been scooped out of the walls and now housed the Nazi's store of wine. At least, he thought, he could spend his last hours in drunken oblivion. There was little else in this gloomy place, apart from some large wooden boxes, and, of course the rats. It was then, resting his sore head in his hands, he thought of his friends. His own fate concerned him far less than what might happen to them. He could only hope that, somewhere in his being, the Nazi possessed a shred of decency. The dizziness had returned and Marek needed somewhere to lie down other than the floor. The packing cases would have to do. If he positioned them side by side they would form an area big enough to lie on. Mustering all his physical strength he dragged the boxes next to one of the walls and lined them up. This done, he hoisted himself up, as best he could, on top.

Marek must have slept for hours, though for how long he could not tell. The glass of his watch had smashed when he fell and it had stopped working. His head now ached less, but the rest of his body felt stiff and painful. To while away a little time he decided to explore the prison. The neatly stacked bottles of wine did look tempting, and he slid out one or two. They were of an impressive vintage. Evidently his captor's refined tastes were not limited to music and the arts. He could quite easily have opened a bottle there and then. He was hungry, and now regretted the paltry amount he had eaten prior to the concert. In the end he resisted. Now was perhaps not the time. Marek completed a circuit of the cellar and then a second, a little faster. The stiffness gradually eased and he decided to keep mobile. As he limped about images of the *Oberst-gruppenführer* and his habitual pacing formed in his mind. No doubt he would be doing it at this very moment in some other part of the house, whilst considering how to dispense with his prisoner. Just then he became distracted by the sound of the heavy door being shoved open. Marek stepped back into the semi-darkness, expecting to encounter the man himself. He could make out someone hovering at the top of the stairs, but it was not General Reinecke. It was Mrs Dabrowski. She was carrying a tray piled high with what Marek recognised were leftovers from the evening's entertainment. He thanked her for her kindness and placed the food down on the narrow landing.

'Please, wait,' he called out as she closed the door.

'I must get back,' she said fretfully.

Again she made to go and this time Marek grabbed her arm.

'Please, there are things that I must know.'

She paused.

'You've been hurt. Your cheek is badly bruised and your lip must be sore.'

'I fell,' he said.

'I see.'

Marek could never fool Mrs Dabrowski. She would know the truth.

'You should have something for it.'

'No. You have done enough. You must not involve yourself further.'

Marek caught hold of her hand and looked into her kindly face.

'Do you know what has happened to my friends?'

'They were locked in a room and detained for several hours.' Her words surprised him. He imagined their punishment would have been meted out swiftly. 'Then quite suddenly they were herded into a truck and driven off.'

'Where to?' he asked anxiously.

'Back to the Ghetto,' Mrs Dabrowski explained.

'Are you sure? How do you know?'

'Dominik was outside at the time and overheard the General's orders.'

Then she explained how the officer had attempted to placate his fellow Nazis by suggesting his daughter sing again. Unfortunately, Clara had fled from the room in a distraught state, and so Mrs Dabrowski and Angelika were called upon to serve endless supplies of food and drink to the disgruntled guests for the remainder of the evening. Many of them had become very intoxicated and riotous by the time they departed for the night.

'I have to go now otherwise he'll become suspicious.'

'Please. There's something I need you to do.'

The woman turned to face him.

'Will you tell Clara that I am all right and that I . . . I . . . love her?'

'I will tell her,' she agreed nervously.

Marek thanked her. She fastened the door shut and he was alone once more.

So the Nazi had released his friends. He ate some of the food and sipped the water. It had slipped his mind to ask Mrs Dabrowski what time it was, but he estimated it was around midnight. Suddenly an idea came to him that old buildings like this often had a network of passages. He set about exploring. Carefully Marek examined every stone of the walls and floors he could reach. Much to his disappointment he had to concede defeat. Feeling dejected he returned to his makeshift bed. Lying there deep in thought his mind drifted, for the first time since his imprisonment, to his family. By now his parents would be aware of what he had done. Marek hoped they could find it in their hearts to forgive him.

Not surprisingly his dreams were unpleasant, taking the form of nightmares. In them he was standing on a battlefield that had been laid waste. There were no trees and no buildings, but large amounts of debris and pools of blood. Lying strewn amongst this desolation were the bodies of Amos and Eli and other members of the choir. Then he caught sight of the distraught figures of his mother, Rachel and Clara weeping over his body, united in their grief. His calls to them went unnoticed. Flitting in and out of the dream was a dark, cloaked character who Marek knew to be that of the Nazi. His face was hidden from view and he resembled the awful figure of Don Juan who dragged his victims off to hell.

Despite the dank and cold atmosphere, Marek was sweating when he woke. The remains of the food were consumed quickly, and then he examined his bruises. He had not seen such a livid assortment since being obliged to view Ruben's injuries following one of his reckless adventures. There were shades of deepest blue, violet, various tinges of red, green and yellow, and each was extremely painful. As there was no mirror or reflective surface to hand, Marek could not determine the full extent of his wounds, though there was a tender area high up on his cheekbone and he could feel the cut on his lip beginning to close up. He sat on one of the boxes and then moved to foot of the stairs and stayed there for what must have been hours. Still no one came. The waiting was wearisome and soon became intolerable. Maybe this was part of the punishment. If so, Marek resolved to retaliate in kind, enduring this solitary imprisonment without weakening.

Much later, and, in the middle of counting how many wine bottles there were, Marek heard a noise. Peering upwards he saw Viktor in the doorway. He was taken aback to hear the soldier announce that he had a visitor. As the man disappeared from view he caught sight of someone he never thought he would see again. Clara threw her arms around his neck and they clung to each other, neither one wanting to let go. Then noticing Marek's battered face she held it lovingly in her hands.

'You poor darling.'

She kissed him so delicately he felt no pain.

'I've wanted to come and see you so much, but Papa's been watching me all day.'

'Where is he now?' Marek asked her.

'He had to go out. There was an important meeting in the city.'

'What about the guards?'

'They don't care as long as they have their regular supply of vodka and cigarettes, and Mrs Dabrowski sees to that.'

So that is why they had left him alone, Marek realised. Clara's face looked pale and drawn in the dim light.

'Have the men really been sent back to the Ghetto?' he asked.

'I believed my father when he told me that they had,' Clara replied.

'But why did he let them go? I don't understand.'

'He wouldn't give me a reason.'

'And what about me? Do you know my fate?'

'No, my darling, I don't. He won't discuss you. You have made him very angry. He feels humiliated and cheated.'

'Your father is a very proud man, but could he really have been that surprised at what I did?'

'Marek, I believe that, deep down, my father respects you for what you have done, though he would never admit it. I do not think he knows what to do and that is why you have been kept down here.'

'Clara,' he said in a low voice, 'we both know the man your father is and what he has to do.'

The apparent hopelessness and misery of it all engulfed the two of them as they held each other in the murkiness. She began to weep, all her fortitude having evaporated with his stark words. He held her tightly in his arms.

'Marek,' she said, trying to control her sobs. 'The pain of losing you would be unbearable.'

'Don't say such things.'

'No, you don't understand. Whatever happens to you I want to share it, but . . .' her voice trailed off.

'What is it, Clara?'

'Something has happened, Marek. At first I decided not to tell you. I thought it would be better that way. But the sadness of you never knowing . . .'

'Tell me, Clara, please.'

'I am going to have a child, Marek. Our child.'

Her words echoed in his ears and he felt a sharp pain in his heart as if a shard of glass had pierced it. He was to be a father – something he had always hoped for – but it was a cruel trick life had played on him.

'Marek?' Clara's voice was distant. 'Marek?' She stroked his face and wiped away the tears coursing down his cheeks. 'You must escape, and together we will leave this dreadful place.'

He tried to remain positive but in reality he was far less optimistic. The prospect of fleeing was impossible. Even if they managed to sneak past the guards what chance did they have? Clara's father would not rest until he had hunted them down and Marek might not be able to defend both of them.

'I will think of something, my darling. There's got to be a way. We must not give up,' Clara said with desperation in her voice.

'You must be strong for both of us, Clara. Will you promise me that you will do that, whatever happens? I will never stop loving you. You will always be here.' Marek placed her hand upon his heart.

A dull clinking sound of metal hitting metal abruptly shattered those few moments of peace and Clara started. The door opened to reveal the intimidating shape of the *Oberst-gruppenführer*. When she saw her father, Clara crept nearer to Marek's side. For a moment he eyed them with disdain. His rage had abated, but the atmosphere was ice-cold.

'I suspected I would find you here, Clara. Go to your room. My business is with Dr Ruzanski alone.'

'Papa . . .' she pleaded.

'Do as I say, Clara. Now.'

She glanced at Marek. He could see fear in her eyes.

'Go now, Clara. Everything will be all right,' he said reassuringly.

'Do take a seat, Doctor,' he said after his daughter had done his bidding. He looked across at one of the boxes. 'I see you have made yourself as comfortable as it is possible to do so in such inhospitable conditions.'

Marek declined his offer, preferring to stand.

'My daughter has obviously retained her weakness for Jews. I had hoped this predilection had gone away, but clearly I was wrong. Have you eaten?' He caught sight of the tray. 'Ah, I see you have. Mrs Dabrowski is a good woman, duty-bound to help mankind, and she will not rest until she has. There are no empty bottles, Doctor. Such temptation and you have not yet succumbed. Perhaps you should. It will lighten your mood.'

'I'd rather be lucid,' Marek retorted, following him as he began his inevitable striding.

'Quite so,' he said dryly.

'What has become of my friends?'

General Reinecke stopped moving.

'I thought you might want to know.'

'Well, are they safe?' Marek asked impatiently, the irritation in his voice barely disguised.

'Safe is not the most appropriate word to use at this juncture, but if you mean did I send them back to the Ghetto, then yes, I did.'

'Thank you,' Marek said without thinking, such was his relief upon hearing these words.

'As you once said all responsibility should lie with you. And so it does, Doctor.' The pitch of his voice had noticeably risen. He had resumed his marching. 'I must say that it was an ingenious plan of yours to compose not one, but two masterpieces. And there is the question of my daughter.'

'Clara had nothing to do with it,' Marek said defiantly.

A small bead of sweat trickled down over one of his eyes. He wiped it away with a trembling hand.

'It was a brave thing to do in the face of such dangerous consequences and I should like to know why you did it?'

'I would have thought a man like you would not need to ask.'

'Such a noble race. A people so eager to die for their convictions.'

'Many of us are given no choice.'

'You and I, Marek, are not so very different. We're proud men. Both principled and with a shared appreciation of the finer things in life. You, however, are also blessed with a rare God-given talent, and it is in my power to preserve or destroy it.' He cast him one of his imperious stares.

'I should like to know what it is that you intend to do with me and when?'

The question was direct and it demanded an unequivocal response.

'You will have realised by now that I cannot permit you to leave,' he said in an emotionless voice.

'If you intend to kill me then I would prefer it to be done now. I see little point in delaying the inevitable,' Marek reasoned.

General Reinecke's mouth curled into a half-smile at the suggestion.

'You seem eager to leave this world, Doctor. However, there will be a little time for you to consider your choices.'

274

He climbed the cellar steps and, with a heavy bang, slammed the door fast. Marek slid to the floor with his back against a crate. Peering through open fingers, his eyes fixed on one of the bottles in the wall. He grabbed it. Prising out the cork screw with the prongs of a fork was a much harder job than he had bargained for, but out it popped and he took a substantial gulp. He started to feel better immediately, and his thoughts returned to the conversations he had had with Clara and her father. The revelation about her pregnancy had not yet fully sunk in and the General's words had greatly confused him. Surely it was inevitable he would die, and at his hand? He must, after all, be seething from the crushing embarrassment he had endured. What did he mean by giving him time to consider his choices? Surely his destiny lay in the German's hands alone? Marek then realised he had used his first name, something he had never done before.

Marek put down the half-consumed bottle. Then it clicked and he knew the answer. He didn't want to do it; he did not want to kill him. Instead, he wanted him to provide him with an excuse to spare him. His love and passion for music was so all-consuming that it really troubled him to extinguish what he regarded as a great talent. His conscience was bothering him – this powerful, ruthless man – and he would give him time to save himself. But how? Marek would never perform the work and he must know that. Then, as if out of the darkness, the final piece of the jigsaw slotted into place. He wanted Marek to apologise, ask for his forgiveness and plead for his life. He picked up the brandy bottle and poured the remainder of its contents down his throat. Sometime later Marek slipped into oblivion.

❖ ❖ ❖

When Marek awoke, his head was pulsating with pain, due mainly to the effects of drinking such a large amount of alcohol. He felt disorientated, the lack of distinction between night and day adding to his confused state. His throat was dry and the taste in his mouth was unpleasant. He managed to prop himself up, and in doing so kicked the empty bottle. In his delicate condition the sound of the glass as it hit the hard stone floor was magnified a hundred times. It came to rest at the side of a flattish object upon which were mounds and shapes of various sizes. His vision was still blurred and he rubbed his eyes and tried to focus. When he looked at the mysterious item again, Marek could make out a tray of fresh food and drink. He would have consumed it greedily, but he did not have much of an appetite. Despite this, he drank and ate what he could to improve his stamina and then, feeling light-headed, dozed off.

This time when the key turned Marek heard it. His head still ached, but the after-effects of his excesses were less intense and he felt more alert. At first he did not recognize the youthful-looking soldier who hesitated on the landing before making his way down. Then Marek noticed his spectacles and remembered the quiet, almost nervous, clerk who had led the choir into the hall prior to the performance. Marek wondered what errand his superior had entrusted him with this time. He stopped a little way off. He was decidedly ill-at-ease, as if wishing he could be anywhere else rather than in this depressing place. The two men stared at one another for a little while and then the soldier realised that he should speak first.

'The *Oberst-gruppenführer* has sent me to enquire whether you have come to a decision regarding the matter that was discussed between you. He also would like you to know that time is nearly up.'

Having said his piece, the young German reached for the flat briefcase resting under his right arm. He looked around and alighted on the packing cases. Marek watched as he extracted a single sheet of white writing paper, which he set down on top of the middle of the three boxes together with a dark-coloured fountain pen.

'He would prefer your response in writing. I am to return in an hour to collect it.'

The soldier clicked his heels, probably more out of habit than as a conscious act, and began to retrace his steps. As his hand gripped the door handle Marek called out to him.

'Captain. I should be grateful if you would give me the correct time.'

'It's a quarter past six.'

It was much later than Marek had thought. Another whole day had passed. He wondered if he would see Clara again. She would have come if she had been able to, but no doubt her father had prevented her from doing so. Marek snatched the paper and pen. Shifting the boxes towards the dim light he arranged them so that they would serve as a writing desk and chair.

Sunday April 18th 1943
My Dearest Clara,

When you read these words I shall have gone away. I want you to know that I accept my fate, and that, when the moment, comes it will be the strength of your love which will make it easier to bear.

Do not be sad at my loss, for remember you will not be alone. Soon you will have our precious child to comfort you and if he or she possesses just one of your fine qualities it will have been truly blessed. It saddens me to think I will not be there to share its life with you, but perhaps one day you will tell our child about its father. Please forgive me,

Clara, for the choice I have made. I love you, my darling, and I will for all eternity.

Marek

When he had finished writing, he folded the paper and tucked it inside his jacket pocket and waited for the messenger's return. The time passed slowly. His thoughts did not dwell on the future – there was little point – but rather the past. Working backwards Marek had reached his childhood by the time the clerk appeared.

'Will you please tell your superior that I thank him for the opportunity he has given me. However I made my decision long ago and it cannot be altered?'

The soldier fidgeted, as if waiting for something, which Marek quickly realised was the paper.

'Tell him, please, that I did not regard it necessary to communicate my words in writing.'

He nodded, as if respectful of Marek's wishes, and ascended the stairs. As he did so, Marek noticed a slight bulge in the breast pocket of his uniform.

'Captain, a moment please?' He halted in mid-step. 'I was wondering if by any chance, you had a cigarette. I would be most glad of one.'

Without saying a word he reached into his pocket and drew out a handful.

Now the real waiting game had begun. Marek succumbed to nervous pacing. Hour after hour passed in his lonely confinement. The lack of any sound at all was unnerving, and as much as he wanted it, sleep would not come. The cigarettes were soon whittled down to stubs and the calming effect upon his nerves was unfortunately short-lived. When the long night had passed and morning finally came, Marek heard the door unfasten.

'Will you please follow me, Dr Ruzanski?' the youthful captain asked in his courteous manner.

Marek climbed the stairs and was soon out in the passage. He had expected to encounter the guards, but they were nowhere to be seen. Then it occurred to him that their job was now done. The two men retraced the route Marek had been obliged to take on that fateful evening until they reached the entrance of the mansion. The large wooden doors were pushed open and for the first time in two days and three nights, Marek could see daylight. It was glorious spring weather, and they walked across the grass and past the lake. Marek stopped for a moment to look back at the house and then at the little bridge where he had first seen Clara.

'If you wouldn't mind, Doctor. The *Oberst-gruppenführer* said . . .'

'Don't worry, I will not delay you further,' Marek interrupted him. 'What is your name?'

'Hans.'

'And what were you doing before the war?'

'I was studying mathematics.'

At that moment Marek thought of Ezra scrawling at his desk.

'I hope you will be able to resume your studies when the war is over.'

'So do I sir.'

They made their way over the expanse of land. Marek thought of the boots that the gardener had given him and what would become of them. Marek stopped walking and called to the inexperienced youth some short distance ahead.

'Hans, you don't need to come any further. I can make my own way now. You have done your job admirably.'

From his reaction Marek could tell that Hans was torn between fulfilling his obligations and doing as he had suggested.

'You really don't have to be there. I will speak to the *Oberst-*

gruppenführer. There is one thing I would like you to do for me, however, if you will.'

Marek reached into his jacket pocket and took out the folded letter. A smile crossed his lips.

'I would be very grateful if you could give this to Fraulein Clara.'

Hans looked around nervously, and then quickly took it and put it away out of sight. The young soldier held out his hand and Marek shook it.

'Goodbye, Doctor Ruzanski.'

Marek entered the clearing. Standing a short way ahead was a solitary, dark figure. He had seen Marek, and was observing him keenly as he walked towards him. Marek could sense his piercing eyes staring at him.

'You have come by yourself, Doctor?'

'Only the last part. I thought it best I continue alone.'

'Quite so. The boy is young. Very conscientious at his job. A mathematician, you know.'

'Yes he told me. A talented individual.'

'Like yourself.'

Marek heard the noise of gunfire in the distance, somewhere in the city. He too listened. The final liquidation had begun.

'You will be in good company today, Doctor.' He reached inside his pocket.

New York
2008

I dropped the letter to my side and gazed out of the window. I sat for some moments in silence after my grandmother had finished her story. Life on the sidewalk went on. A small child and its mother passed by – the infant kicking up dry autumn leaves with his feet – and for a brief moment I was distracted. The sunlight was fading fast. Clara switched her bedside lamp on.

'This man. Marek. My grandfather. He was a Jew?'

My grandmother's silence was confirmation enough.

'Then I . . . we . . . that is . . . this means Mom and I are part Jewish . . .'

This time she nodded.

'Does Mom know? Have you told her and kept it a secret from me all these years?'

'Your mother doesn't know anything yet,' Clara said in a quivering voice.

For a moment I stood there motionless trying to come to terms with my feelings.

'Why, Grandma? I don't understand. Why didn't you tell her? Surely she needed to know the truth? Was it because you were ashamed?'

'*Ashamed*. How could you possibly accuse me of such a thing?' she said angrily. 'You don't understand. You don't see what I'm trying to tell you. I betrayed him. I could do nothing to save him.' She caught hold of my hand and squeezed it tightly.

'Papa kept me prisoner in my room because he knew I wanted to be with Marek. Then when I heard it, that terrible sound, early in the morning, I knew he was dead and I was too late.'

Talking had made her cough so I fetched her some water. She took a few small sips before handing the glass back to me.

'What did you do afterwards?' I asked.

'I ran away. I hated my father so much for what he had done.'

'Where to? Germany?'

'Yes. I went to a village in the mountains where nobody knew me, and I stayed there until the war ended.'

'Then you came here with Mom.'

'Yes.'

'Did your father ever find out?'

'I was very careful. I could not find it in my heart to forgive him. It was my way of punishing him – never allowing him to see me again or his grandchild ever.'

'What happened to him?'

'Although he could never know where we were, I needed to know whether he had suffered. Then I was bitter and angry and I wanted him to get what he deserved. I discovered he was tried and found guilty of crimes against humanity, and was given a prison sentence. But he did not live to complete it.'

'I see.'

'It was as though he willed himself to die. At least that was what they said. He spent the last days of his life ranting about a man who had composed a magnificent piece of music. I think my father never came to terms with what he had done to Marek and was tormented by guilt and remorse.'

284

'And have you forgiven him?' I asked.

There was a long silence, and just as I had begun to wonder whether my question had been too impertinent, she spoke.

'He took something precious away from me. How could I ever forgive him for that? But now, as I am nearing the end of my life, I have tried to understand.'

'Wait a minute. The music you gave me – the masterpiece – it's Marek's composition isn't it? He's willing me to perform it isn't he? That's it. His work as it should be heard. A complete performance. I've been struggling to write for weeks – months – but I wasn't meant to.'

Bemused, Clara watched me as I paced the length of the room, not comprehending any of my ramblings. I told her about the evening I had spent with David and his family, and their unexpected request. Then she understood.

'Yes, you must do it Jonathan?'

'Yes, Grandma, I will and you must be there to hear it. Marek would have wanted that.'

I bent down and kissed her cheek.

'He was a very brave man and I am proud to be his grandson.'

'Marek would have been so very proud of you as well.'

She raised her hand and stroked my face.

'Grandma. I would like to take a copy of the photograph, if you would let me?'

I noticed a flicker of concern in Clara's eyes as if she was reluctant to let the precious object out of her sight.

'I promise I'll look after it. It will only take a few minutes.'

'Of course darling,' she said, sounding relieved.

I made my way down to my father's office. I lifted up the lid of the copier and with the greatest of care positioned the delicate object face down upon the glass. The machine came to life and in seconds the job was done. I returned the original to my grandmother. She smiled as she placed it safely back in the box.

'I need to get going. I'll send Mom up to see you.'

Before hitting the sidewalk I paused for a moment and glanced up at Clara's bedroom window. By now she would have started to explain Elizabeth's true heritage, and I tried to imagine my mother's reaction. Both women were very much alike – not only physically, but emotionally – and were never prone to open displays of strong feeling. My mother coped with situations – good or bad – with equal restraint. I had seldom witnessed either woman weep, and when one of them did it was all the more distressing.

It was late and although New York was pulsating with life the cacophony of voices, horns and sirens were nothing more than a faint murmur in my disordered mind. I must have walked for several hours criss-crossing the city. Times Square with its flashing neon signs and explosions of light had been little more than a blur of colour. From time to time a noisy yellow cab streaking past would break my trance-like state. I recalled gazing up at St. Patrick's Cathedral and the Empire State both buildings having assumed a majestic quality at night. Eventually, I found myself staring into the dark waters of the harbour. Lifting my eyes I focused on the horizon, trying to picture the land where generations of my family had lived. A current of air passed over me, ruffling my hair, and I thought of the freedoms which my generation was privileged to enjoy and took for granted. I had not realised I had been weeping until I felt the warm tears sliding down my cheeks. It was nearing midnight when I looked at my watch. I had lost all awareness of time.

The red light of the answer machine winked at me as I returned to the apartment, and I knew instinctively who would have called.

'Hello, Jon. It's Mom. Just calling to see if you got home safely and that you're all right.' There was a short pause. 'I love you, darling.'

It was too late to call back. My parents would have retired for the night. I slipped off my shoes and sat down on the edge of my bed and, as I did so, I was sure I could hear the faint sound of music in the distance. I strained to hear it again but there was nothing. I undressed and climbed into bed. Exhaustion overwhelmed me and I needed to sleep.

❖   ❖   ❖

'David!' I shouted, as I spotted my friend ahead of me, being carried along in a sea of students making their way to the first lectures of the day.

He turned and, seeing me, waited for me to catch up.

'Hi, Jon,' he bellowed above the noise.

'Can we meet me up over lunch?' I asked him.

'Sure. We usually do, don't we? Why?'

'There's something I need to tell you.'

'OK. I'll be there.'

'Thanks,' I said as we forged our way through the seething mass of bodies. 'How come you're so early today?'

'Thought I ought to turn over a new leaf,' David replied before being swept away.

That particular morning was comprised of back-to-back lectures, and normally the time would have passed quickly but because on this occasion I had particularly wanted it to, it did not, and my constant observation of the clock hanging on the wall at the far end of the lecture hall must have been obvious. At last the hands struck one o'clock, and I hastily packed my things away.

I waited for David at our regular meeting place. It was a bright, sunny day but – with winter just around the corner – not too warm. I was just wishing I had brought a scarf with me when I caught sight of him. Uncharacteristically he was jogging.

'Sorry I'm late,' he said, panting. 'Had to go over something with one of my students.'

David was still puffing as we approached our trusty hot dog vendor.

'You're not very fit, old man,' I said jokingly. 'What's with all the jogging?'

'Thought I could do with some exercise. Now what was it you wanted to tell me? Sounds pretty important.'

'It can wait until we get to the park.'

By the time we reached the cart the line had shrunk to a handful of people and we were served quickly.

'I went to visit Clara yesterday. She's not been too well.'

'I'm sorry to hear that,' David said with concern.

'It's just a bad cold, maybe a touch of flu. She'll be fine in a day or two,' I reassured him. 'At first we talked for a while about nothing in particular, and then she asked me to fetch something from her closet.'

'What was it?'

'An old box. You know the sort of thing. The antique variety made of polished wood.'

'What was in it?' David asked impatiently.

'Documents from the war. You know – identity card, ration book – the usual sort of stuff. She also gave me this.'

I reached into my pocket and brought out the copy of the faded, sepia-tinted photograph. David examined it, glanced up at me and then looked back at the image.

'I know what you're thinking.'

'The likeness is uncanny. Who is he?' David asked.

'My grandfather,' I blurted out.

'I don't understand. This was taken during the war, wasn't it, Jon? But where? It looks like . . .'

'It's Poland. The Warsaw Ghetto. My mother and I are part Jewish.'

I started to tell him the story and he listened, engrossed.

'Your grandfather must have been an extraordinarily courageous man,' David said when I'd finished. He smiled and held the faded image next to my face. 'It's quite eerie. The resemblance is striking.'

'Clara has always said I remind her of my grandfather but when I saw the picture for the first time it was quite a shock.'

'How's your father taking it?' David asked.

'I haven't discussed it with him yet, but in his usual level-headed way no doubt.'

'Such a long time to keep a secret. Why didn't she tell you sooner?'

'I think it was just too painful for her.'

'She must have truly loved him. You must have been a constant reminder of him all these years, not least your choice of career.'

'I know. And there's something else. Do you remember the manuscript that Clara gave me?'

'Yes.'

'It's Marek's composition. I've decided to perform it at the Holocaust Remembrance Day ceremony. It's perfect for the occasion and it's what my grandfather would have wanted. I'm sure of that.'

'It's a great idea,' David said enthusiastically. 'Who's going to perform it? Have you given it any thought?'

'Not yet. But I . . .'

'Hey! I've got a lecture at two. What about you?' David blurted out.

'Tutorials,' I cried.

We were a good few minutes away from the Conservatory and we would have to hurry to make it. We broke into a fast jog.

'How does it feel to be Jewish, my friend?' David said breathlessly.

'No different to how I felt before.'

The two colleagues rushed on in silence.

'How's your budding romance coming along by the way?' David suddenly asked mischievously.

'What do you mean?'

'Abigail,' David reminded me.

'What?' I slowed down. We were now only a short distance away from the entrance. 'What's that supposed to mean?'

'I saw you staring at her the other night. There's more than a bit of innocent music-making going on there.'

'You would think that, wouldn't you?' I said, gasping for air. 'Was it really that obvious?'

'Who's out of breath now, old man?' David laughed, patting me on the shoulder and heading for the steps. 'I'll tell my father to expect you this evening, if that's OK? He'll want to see the music and so do I.'

'I'll be there.'

A few hours later I was standing on the porch of my parents' house and, for the first time in my life, I felt apprehensive about going inside. I hadn't talked to my mother since my last visit, and wondered how she would react when she saw me. As much as it had affected me to learn the truth, it must have had a far deeper impact upon her. I let myself in. I hung my coat on the wooden, art deco cloak stand and made my way into the living room. It was empty. It wasn't long before I heard footsteps on the wooden stairs, and low, yet audible, women's voices.

'Jonathan, is that you? We'll be down in a moment.'

Clara was looking much better and her cheeks had a little more colour in them but as I helped her into the living room it was evident she was still rather frail. I spotted my mother casting her eyes over me as if I were a stranger she was meeting for the first time. It was an odd, almost disturbing experience.

'You are so like my father, Jonathan.'

'I know, Mom.'

Seeing me had upset her. I enveloped her in my arms. Recovering her composure, she wiped her eyes.

'Clara felt well enough to get up today so she's come down for tea. Do you think you could get the fire started, darling? It's a bit chillier and I don't want Mama catching any more colds.'

'That's a good idea. Jonathan and I will sit next to the fire and chat,' Clara said.

'Would you like to be a bit closer, Grandma?' I asked as I picked up a shovel full of coal.

'Yes please. I like to see the flames with all their different colours.'

I pushed her chair nearer, and positioned another close by for myself. She sighed, as if my simple actions had rekindled some distant memory.

'How did Mama take the news?'

'Just like you did darling. Your mother is as strong as her father, and very forgiving.'

'Forgiving?' I was surprised at her choice of word.

'I feared she would despise me for keeping it from her all this time, but she didn't.'

'Of course she wouldn't. She loves you too much.'

I patted her hand affectionately. She drew a handkerchief from her sleeve, but her unsteady fingers lost their grip and it fell to the ground. I passed it back to her. For as long as I could recall it had been her favourite, with its hand-embroidered flower in one of the corners. There was the clatter of cups, and my mother returned carrying a tray of dainty things. She had evidently been baking during the day, and had arranged slices of lemon cake and fresh muffins on a pretty china plate. As she approached I moved the small coffee table next to the couch.

'A fire makes all the difference, don't you think?' said my mother.

I agreed, and watched as she poured each of us a cup of coffee.

'Have you brought Marek's composition with you Jonathan?'

'Yes. Hang on I'll go and fetch it,' I said.

'Tell me about the music?' she asked, almost imploringly.

'It is, in my opinion, a true masterpiece in its craftsmanship. My grandfather was a highly gifted musician and your father's assessment of his talent was right on the button,' I said addressing my last comments to Clara.

I said no more. Others would soon be able to judge for themselves. The old clock on the mantel struck the half hour, and moments later the latch on the front door clicked. It was my father. His homecoming greeting for the two women in his life had never altered, and consisted of a kiss for both of them. As for me, I received a firm hug and a ruffling of my hair.

'I'll make you some fresh coffee, darling. Help yourself to cake.'

'I'll come and help Elizabeth,' my grandmother offered.

'You stay here and keep warm Mama?'

'I need to stretch my legs,' Clara said getting up from her chair. 'Take my arm, please dear.'

'Does Clara's story change anything, Pop?' I asked as the two women disappeared into the kitchen.

He had settled himself down in one of the chairs and was staring into the fire.

'I love you and your mother very much and nothing will ever

change that? Your grandmother has shown great bravery, just as your grandfather did, and it makes me immensely proud.'

'You know I love you too Pop. I don't think I've told you this before but I couldn't have a better father. I'm blessed to be your son.'

He turned his head in my direction as I approached his chair and smiled. Stooping down I kissed his forehead.

There was nothing else that needed to be said.

'Come in, Jonathan. It is good to see you again,' Ira Rosen said, ushering me in.

'I hope it's convenient. You don't have guests?'

'No, no.' Ira steered me in the direction of the living room. 'Have you eaten?'

Rebecca was in the kitchen, but suddenly popped her head around the door when she heard my voice. Elaborate food preparations were underway, for she was wearing a colourful apron.

'Hello, Jon. Have you eaten? Let me get you something. A sandwich perhaps?' Rebecca asked.

I thanked her and reassured her that I had eaten before setting off and that a cup of coffee would suffice. She bristled with excitement at my request.

'I have the perfect thing to go with your coffee.'

I glanced at Ira who was chuckling and shaking his head.

'You know how Rebecca loves to bake. It's her passion. She'll bring you a plate of cookies I expect.'

'I'm sure they'll be delicious,' I replied, fervently hoping that his wife's cookies would not be of such gargantuan proportions as some of her past offerings.

Whilst we both waited for Rebecca's return, I took the

opportunity to look about the room. I had spent many a happy evening here before but I now examined the surroundings with a renewed interest, especially those objects associated with the Jewish faith. It wasn't long before I sensed Ira watching me.

'Has David mentioned the reason for my visit?' I asked him.

'No. Only that you had something important you wanted to discuss about the ceremony. Is everything all right, Jonathan? You seem a little tense. Let me go see where that coffee has got to.'

Ira wandered out to the kitchen and soon reappeared, clutching a tray piled high with three large cups and an assortment of the most substantial cookies I had ever seen. I took hold of a cup of aromatic, black coffee and chose one of the smaller cookies. It was mouth-wateringly scrumptious, and I complimented Rebecca on her culinary skills. She was thrilled.

'We need more light, I think. It's getting quite gloomy in here.' Ira switched on the lamp next to the piano.

'Is it too hot, Jon? Would you like a little more milk or cream? Help yourself to sugar.'

'I think Jon has something important to tell us, my dear,' Ira explained gently, adding, 'I'm right, aren't I, my friend?'

They listened to the story Clara had told me and, it was only when I had finished that the full effect of it upon them became apparent. Rebecca had tears in her eyes when she took hold of my hand and clung on to it for some time. Ira's reaction was one of anger.

'A waste of an exceptional talent.'

He stood up, and took a few paces forwards then a few backwards before bringing his hand down heavily on the arm of his chair.

'Your poor grandmother,' Rebecca said, still visibly upset. 'And what happened to the choir?'

'We don't know. They were allowed to return to their homes,

but General Franz Reinecke, my great-grandfather . . .' I stumbled for a moment as my emotions got the better of me, '. . . must have known the Ghetto was about to be liquidated. Three days after the concert the liquidation of the Ghetto began.'

'And what about your great-grandfather? Did he pay for his crimes?'

'He died in prison shortly after the war, tormented by his own demons.'

'Do you know of any other relatives?' Rebecca asked.

'My grandmother told me she only met Marek's family once. And there was a young boy who lived with them, but she can't remember his name,' I explained.

'Tragically, they probably perished. Packed off to the camps alongside thousands of others after the Ghetto had been razed,' Ira said with vitriol. 'If we can help in any way you know you only have to ask Jonathan.'

I acknowledged their kind offer and took another sip of coffee.

'Ira my dear,' Rebecca said, smiling at her husband, 'perhaps Jonathan might enjoy something stronger. I know I would.'

Rebecca gathered up the crockery and headed for the kitchen. Ira fixed us all a drink while I reached over for my case and started rummaging through my papers.

'Ah! Do you have your grandfather's composition with you?' Ira handed me a glass.

'Would you like to see it?'

'I'd be honoured,' Ira replied.

Ira reached in his jacket pocket for his reading glasses and took the music from me. He was quietly studying the piece and did not hear the front door open. I looked up as I heard someone hurrying along the hallway and saw David enter. When he realised what his father was reading he sat down and began perusing every page with him.

'Your grandfather was very talented. In fact, he was probably one of the finest musicians of his generation,' Ira observed.

'What did you say his name was, Jonathan?' David asked.

'Dr Marek Ruzanski,' I said.

'And were any of his other works published?'

'Sadly, the war cut short his career,' Ira pointed out.

'I wanted you all to see the composition because I would like to perform it at the memorial service. I could never create the emotional intensity you see there. This music was born out of genuine suffering and unimaginable tragedy.'

'It would be an honour and a privilege for us to hear Dr Ruzanski's music. And how fitting that his grandson should conduct the performance,' Ira said.

'And how fitting that I am a Jew.'

'Yes, Jonathan,' Ira smiled warmly, 'how fitting that you are a Jew.'

❖   ❖   ❖

Christmas came and went and was, on the whole, a quiet family affair. Gradually routines re-established themselves, and I made a New Year's resolution not to eat so much of Stefano's delicious food. Not surprisingly I was soon lured back down to the restaurant by Maria. Clara had recovered well from her illness, and copies of the manuscript had been made in preparation for rehearsals which were scheduled to begin next month. Then one evening in the middle of January the phone rang, just as I was climbing the last few steps to my apartment.

'Hello. Is that you, Jonathan?'

It was a woman's voice.

'Yes,' I said apologizing for sounding breathless. 'Can I help you?' I did not recognize the caller.

'It's Abigail. We met at the Rosens' a few weeks ago.'

'Oh yes, of course, I remember. How are you?'

'Very well, thank you. And you?'

'I'm well thank you.'

'I was wondering if you are still interested in accompanying me. I know the service is some way off, but I would really appreciate it,' Abigail explained and then paused. 'If you're too busy, I understand.'

'No, not at all. I'm sure I can fit it in,' I reassured her. Life was always hectic, but I would make time for Abigail.

'Thank you, Jonathan. When would you like to meet?'

'Maybe next week?' I thought for a moment. 'How about Thursday?'

'Thursday's good for me. Where would you like to rehearse?

Her voice had a sweetness I found most attractive.

'I could call by on my way home after work, if you like? What's your address?' I enquired reaching for a pen.

' Lafayette Avenue . . .' she began.

I scribbled down her address on the back of an envelope, noting that she lived in a fashionable area of Brooklyn.

The days flew by with unusual rapidity, and before I knew it I was standing outside Abigail's apartment. It was a little after seven. The mental image of the women I had retained in my mind did not do her justice. She was much more attractive than I remembered.

Walking behind her as she led me to the room where we would work, I noticed how tastefully furnished and ordered everything was. The living room was spacious, with an oval table in its centre, and there were several pictures on the wall. We walked along a hallway, off which radiated a number of other rooms. She pushed open the door to one and entered what had originally been designed as a second bedroom, but which now served as a study. Bookshelves lined one of the walls, and along another stood the piano. There was a small window and from where I was standing,

297

I could just see the tops of trees in the park on the opposite side of the street.

'Is this all right? It's not as large a room as the others, but I don't disturb the neighbours when I'm in here.'

'It will be perfect,' I said, smiling at her.

'Can I get you anything? A drink or something to eat perhaps?' Abigail asked, clearly relieved.

'I'm fine for the moment thanks. A coffee later would be good.'

She arranged her music and I sat down at the piano and started to play.

'That's beautiful,' she said, drawing up a chair next to me. 'I didn't volunteer to sing, you know,' she carried on. 'It was Ira. He's so persuasive. I'm not at all sure my voice is good enough for such an important event. You must tell me if it isn't. I won't mind.'

I remembered a confident and self-assured woman from our first meeting but the person sitting beside me now seemed somewhat reserved and diffident.

'What have you got, there?' I asked, pointing to the musical scores she was clutching.

She handed the collection to me, and amongst them I found some works by the composer, Ben-Haim.

'Shall we begin with these then?' I suggested. As Abigail handed me a copy I caught a whiff of scent.

I began to play the introduction, wondering what quality of sound would emanate from such a delicate mouth. When it came, I had not envisaged such clarity of tone.

We rehearsed for a good hour or so, and then she glanced up at the clock above the piano.

'Gosh I didn't realise it was so late. I mustn't keep you. I've taken up enough of your time.'

I waited for her in the living room while she made us some coffee.

'How do you take your coffee? Cream and sugar?' she called to me from the kitchen.

'Just cream thanks.'

Sitting there, I caught sight of some framed photographs on the small wooden dresser and went over to take a look. One was of Abigail with her parents and the other was a portrait of a young man, which I examined more closely. I was just about to replace it when she appeared carrying the drinks.

'That's Aaron, my younger brother,' Abigail said as she handed me my coffee. 'How's work?'

'Fine.' I said. 'How about you?'

'Busy as usual. There are quite a few new cases.'

Abigail raised the cup to her lips and took a sip of the honey-coloured liquid.

'Is the piano your main instrument?'

'I've played it for as long as I have the cello, but I am a better cellist.'

'It's my favourite of the string family. Could you play for me? I'd really like it if you would.'

'Yes, of course. I'll bring it along next time.'

She thanked me, patting my arm lightly.

'Tell me about the piece you are going to write for the service. Have you begun it yet?' Before I could explain what had happened the doorbell rang and she excused herself. I heard voices and then moments later Abigail walked in with a stranger by her side.

'This is, Robert, my neighbour, who lives on the floor above.'

Belatedly remembering my manners, I stood up and offered him my hand. He gripped it firmly and as he did so looked me straight in the eye, almost as if he were weighing me up. Maybe, I thought to myself, this person was a prospective suitor and regarded me as an interloper.

'I'm really sorry to interrupt. Look, I can come back another time,' Robert said.

'I promised to lend Robert a novel,' Abigail said, pointing to the bookshelf in the corner of the room.

'I've got to get going anyway,' I said, reaching for my coat.

'Oh! So soon?' she asked with an air of disappointment.

Robert shifted to let me pass through to the hallway.

'It was a pleasure to meet you,' I said politely.

'And you too,' he replied.

'Thank you for coming. I really enjoyed our rehearsal,' Abigail said as she followed me into the hall.

'Me too,' I replied, smiling.

'May I call you?' Abigail asked.

'Please do.'

Just over a week later, I found myself waiting outside Abigail's apartment. The door opened, and the young woman gasped with delight when she spotted what I was carrying.

'How lovely. You've remembered your cello. I was hoping you would.' She ushered me inside excitedly.

We concentrated our efforts on improving the songs, and, almost an hour and a half later, had finally selected the pieces Abigail would perform. Whilst she made some coffee I took my cello out of its case and started to tighten my bow.

'What will you play?'

'Do you have a preference?'

'Some Bach, please.'

As I played I sensed her eyes upon me and, as the last note melted away and my bow had left the string, I saw tears in her eyes.

'I didn't mean to upset you Abigail,' I said, suddenly feeling awkward.

'It was so moving I couldn't help myself. You play with such passion.'

'I think I'd better choose something more cheerful next time.'

'Will you tell me about the piece you are composing for the ceremony? What form will it take? Choral I know, but I was wondering about the style?'

'Actually, we've decided to perform a different piece.'

I began to explain a little about what had happened since we had first met. As I did so my voice took on a more solemn tone.

'So is David going to write the composition after all?' Abigail asked, slightly taken aback.

'No. My grandmother gave me a piece of music which was written by a Jewish composer during the war.'

'Oh, is he a survivor of the Holocaust. Is he well known? What's his name?'

'Marek Ruzanski. He was my grandfather.'

'Your grandfather?' She appeared baffled.

I started to tell her the story about the Nazi, Marek's love for Clara, and the performance of the music for which my grandfather paid with his life.

'You must be very proud of your grandfather but it must have been a shock for you and your mother after all this time. Does he have any surviving relatives?'

'My mother, Elizabeth, has been trying to trace them but she's not had much success so far.'

'I suppose these things take time,' she said thoughtfully. 'I would really like to help if I can. Will you show me your grandfather's music?'

'Yes. I'd be delighted. I'd value your opinion.'

'You will need a skilful choir to perform it. Have you been to the synagogue?'

'Not yet but I've arranged to meet the choir there next week.'

'I'm sure they won't let you down.'

We said goodnight, but I sensed a reluctance on her part to end the evening. Sitting there in an almost deserted subway carriage, I thought of everything that had happened these past few months, and wondered if the future held any more surprises for me.

❖ ❖ ❖

The following Monday evening, at eight o'clock precisely, I reached the synagogue. I had never set foot inside a religious building like this before. There had been no reason to, and besides, I'd been raised a Protestant. I stared up at its rather impressive façade and went inside. As I passed through the large and somewhat imposing entrance, I was struck by the irony of it all. Here was a place where, up until a relatively short time ago, I might have passed by mildly curious about what went on within its walls. Now I had been welcomed as a new member of its congregation. The air was cloying and I could smell the pungent aroma of incense. The interior of the synagogue was dramatic. It had two deep, narrow aisles and a high, brightly-painted ceiling from which were suspended ornate chandeliers. The stained glass windows, with geometrical designs in blue, gold and red were just as spectacular.

I had arranged to meet Ira Rosen here half an hour before the choir was due to arrive, but I couldn't see anyone. Just as I had begun to think I had muddled up my days, I heard the sound of a door opening somewhere at the back of the synagogue.

'Hello Jonathan. How are you? It's good to see you. What do you think of the building?' Ira asked.

'It's very interesting and not at all what I had expected. Excellent acoustics as well.'

'Indeed. It makes a perfect venue. Now what do you think about this as a suitable position for you and the choir?' Ira asked as he walked over to the area directly in front of the raised altar.

'Sure. That will be perfect. Plenty of space. Is there a piano?' I asked looking around.

'Over there,' Ira said, pointing to the corner where a beautifully polished piano stood.

'Make?' I enquired.

'It's a Bluthner.'

I nodded approvingly. Will anyone object if I try it?'

'Go ahead.'

I sat down and lifted the lid. Its tone was mellow and the keys responded easily to the touch of my fingers.

'It ought to be moved a little nearer. Maybe there?' I pointed.

'The work — your grandfather's composition — is unaccompanied, isn't it, Jonathan?'

Yes it is, but I'm playing for Abigail, remember?'

'Of course, so you are. I'd forgotten. Have you two met up yet?' Ira asked.

'As a matter of fact we have.'

'No doubt she led you to believe that her voice was mediocre, but when she opened her mouth, you heard the voice of an angel.'

'Spot on,' I said smiling.

'Abigail's a lovely girl. Highly capable and intelligent, and yet at the same time modest to the point of diffidence. What has she chosen to sing?'

'A couple of songs by Ben-Haim.'

'Ah. Twentieth century. That should be interesting. Would you play something on your cello as well?'

'Sure, if you'd like me to.'

I sat down on one of the wooden chairs and Ira joined me.

'You haven't told me much about the choir yet,' I said.

'They are all good singers. You won't be disappointed. I believe they've prepared something to give you an idea of their range,' Ira explained.

'That's a sensible idea.'

'How's your grandmother these days?'

'Physically much better but emotionally not so robust.'

'To harbour such a secret for so many years must have taken its toll,' Ira said.

Before I could agree with him, another man entered the synagogue. He was grey-haired and bearded and had a wiry stature. He looked as though he was probably in his early sixties.

'Good to see you Nathan,' Ira shouted. Turning to me he said quietly, 'Always the first to arrive for any occasion. Good singer as well. A high tenor.'

I held out my hand. He took it and as he did so my eyes were drawn to the clothes he was wearing. Despite looking smart in his grey pants and matching jacket, something about his outfit was uncoordinated. I couldn't quite put my finger on it and then I spotted the hand-knitted sweater peeping out from under the coat with its clashing red and orange stripes. The three of us swung our heads in the direction of the front of the building to observe the arrival of two very similar-looking men.

'These are the Franks brothers, Gabriel and Barnaby. Our best basses,' Ira informed me, evidently finding the whole experience exhilarating.

I welcomed them.

'The other basses are Joseph, Matthew and Walter. Then there are the tenors Joshua, Noah, James and one more . . .' Ira paused for a moment to think. 'Of course, Tobias. How could I forget his fine voice?'

Once the remaining seven men had arrived – there were ten members of the choir – it was time for Ira to leave.

Tonight, I had decided to keep things fairly informal for our first meeting. I handed around copies of my grandfather's composition. A collective appraisal of the music commenced, with some of the men reaching into their pockets for their glasses. Several minutes passed in near-total silence, but for the muffled sound of pages being turned. I watched them, fascinated. The first to speak was a member of the bass line called Joseph.

'Warsaw April 1943. That would be the time of the liquidation.'

'So many of our people lost,' Gabriel, the elder of the two Franks brothers joined in.

'Who is the composer?' Joseph chirped up.

'Dr Marek Ruzanski. A pupil, then later a teacher, at the Warsaw Conservatoire. He and his family were interned in the Ghetto. Before his death he wrote this music as a testament to all Jews who had suffered. He was my grandfather.'

Excited chatter broke out amongst the group and then Walter, a baritone, cleared his throat.

'We have prepared a piece to sing, if you would like to hear it, Jonathan?'

'Yes, that would be a good idea,' I agreed.

I was pleased. It would give me an opportunity to determine the general quality and blending of their voices. They gave a fine performance, which I found greatly encouraging. Nathan agreed to tackle the solo tenor line and I then proceeded to guide them through my grandfather's work, hoping that they would not be put off by its more testing elements. When almost an hour had passed I sought their decision. Their response was enthusiastic.

'The music is indeed demanding,' Joseph Biram said as he rose to his feet 'but it is also a great work and on behalf of all of us, I wish to say we would regard it as an honour to perform it.'

'I am the one who is honoured, directing such an accomplished group of singers,' I told them grateful for their encouraging words.

'Shall we meet in a week's time?' Noah enquired, looking around at his companions.

'That's a good idea,' Matthew agreed, and the rest of the group nodded their heads in approval. 'And we all promise to study the score in the meantime.'

Reaching for my case, I had the feeling I was being observed.

'Your grandfather was a gifted musician and a brave one too,' Joseph observed.

'Yes, he was,' I said thoughtfully.

'And you, his grandson, have inherited his talent and will conduct his work on such an important occasion. That is as it should be. I am very pleased to be able to help you.'

'Thank you. May I enquire who normally organises and trains the choir for services?'

'I do. I am the *Chazan*,' Joseph explained.

'Ah! The cantor. I have heard of this role.'

'It is my task to lead the congregation in prayer.'

'And you don't object to me directing your choir,' I asked.

'Certainly not. You must do it,' Joseph said emphatically.

I knew he was sincere. Perhaps, intuitively, he had some understanding of the tragedy that had unfolded when the composition had first been performed. Leaving the synagogue, I felt both relieved and optimistic. The responsibility for performing my grandfather's work had lain heavily on my shoulders but I knew now it was achievable.

'Hello, Jon. I was just calling to see how your practice went. Is that music I can hear?'

'Well, I wouldn't exactly call it that.'

Abigail had phoned during the middle of a lesson with Henry. Tonight I was introducing him to third position, and as usual he was finding it a mighty struggle to keep pitch.

'You poor thing,' she said sympathetically.

'Henry, a little softer please, and will you take it from the top?' I instructed the boy. 'Can I ring you back later?' I said, lowering my voice and pressing the handset to my mouth.

'Yes, of course. You can tell me all about it then.'

Much to my relief and to the relief of those working in the kitchens below the noise eventually came to an end. Henry packed his cello and book of studies away, and a few minutes later I bundled him into a taxi. Returning to my apartment, I collapsed into a chair, receiver in hand, and dialled Abigail's number. It rang for several seconds and, just as I thought she must have decided to go out for the evening, I heard her at the other end of the line.

'Hello.'

'Hello Abigail. It's me. Jonathan Gray. I wasn't sure you were there.'

'I was just seeing Robert out. He'd brought the book back I lent him. You met him the night you were here. Do you remember?'

'Sure I remember,' I said trying not to sound in any way put out at learning of her friend's visit.

'Well. How did it go? Did everyone sing as wonderfully as I said they would?'

I told her how impressed I had been with the choir.

'I expect Joseph, our *Chazan*, introduced himself to you, and did you meet Nathan as well? He's my favourite. He always wears . . .'

'. . . bright sweaters . . .' I interjected.

'. . . which clash.' She giggled mischievously. 'Did they enjoy your grandfather's music?' She sounded more serious now.

'Yes, they seemed to like it, and said they would do their best to perform it as well as they could.'

'I'm pleased for you, Jon,' Abigail said.

Just talking to her lifted my spirits and I was eager to arrange another meeting.

'Thursday would be good and, if you like, I'll cook us something to eat afterwards,' she offered.

We hung up. Soon, I thought, I would introduce her to my family, and of course to Stefano and Maria, though not just yet.

The weeks passed and Monday evenings at the synagogue – or temple as I learnt to call it – became a high point of them. Not only were the men proving to be the most capable band of singers I had ever worked with but they were also most charming and likeable too. Despite having grown equally fond of all of them my favourite was Nathan. Whatever time I turned up for rehearsals, and I was always early, there he would be, score in one hand and a bag of candy in the other. Each time, without fail, he would proffer the latter, and every time I would obligingly dip my hand into the bag and pull out three or four candies from the mixture of toffees, mints, lemon drops and butterscotch. For several minutes we would sit and talk. I often wondered what state his teeth were in and whether, in fact, they were all original. On more than one occasion I feared for the stability of my own.

My relationship with Joseph was developing well, and we had a healthy respect for each other, and never once was my directorship challenged or questioned. As the date of the service grew nearer, I began to think more and more about my grandfather and the feelings of apprehension he must have experienced. It was on the nights I was unable to sleep that I felt closest to him.

At last the evening of the final rehearsal arrived. Abigail came along to listen. Our usual break, during which we all received our ration of sweets, had ended and practice was about to resume, when I suddenly felt rather warm. Reaching out to hang my jacket over a nearby chair, I caught sight of a figure standing in the aisle. Thinking him to be merely an interested observer, I returned to the main focus of my attention, which was the choir, now assembled in a small semi-circle.

'Is it you, my friend?' a voice called out in the silence before their singing resumed.

I turned around and found myself staring into the eyes of the stranger. The expression on the face of this deathly pale, frail old man was one of disbelief. His tired eyes penetrated mine and he mouthed something which I could not understand. Then he began to stumble as if he were about to fall and, being nearest to him, I reached out to steady him. Placing an arm about his shoulders, I helped him to a chair. Abigail and the choir members quickly gathered around.

'Are you all right *Gabbai*?' Abigail asked, taking hold of his hand.

I retreated slightly, not wishing to upset him further. He must have sensed this, for his eyelids twitched and then opened wide.

'I am sorry,' he said in a weak, hoarse voice. 'I thought for a moment you were someone I knew a long time ago. You look so much like . . .' His voice petered out and then, drawing strength, he added, 'Forgive me. I have not been well.'

Joseph, who had gone to fetch some water, held it out to the elderly man who grasped it in trembling fingers. After several sips he brightened.

'Who did you think I was?' I asked, kneeling down in front of him.

He did not respond, and his eyes had a glazed expression as though he were far away. Just as I had come to the conclusion that he was incapable of telling us anything further he came to, pulling himself up in his seat.

'There was a man I used to know. A man I called my brother.' His voice was shaking with emotion.

'What was his name, *Gabbai*?' Abigail asked, still clutching his hand and stroking it affectionately.

'Ruzanski. Dr Marek Ruzanski.'

'You knew my grandfather?' I asked in disbelief.

'Yes. I am Ruben.'

❖   ❖   ❖

Ruben Kenigsberg had worshipped at the Synagogue for over six decades. He had emigrated to America shortly after the war had ended. He was well-known and liked by everyone in the community, and had for a number of years enjoyed the important position of *Gabbai*. Those who held this privileged post were chiefly responsible for the smooth running of services, and assisting with readings from the Torah. He lived nearby in Brooklyn with his wife, and according to Abigail, had recently returned home after a spell in hospital. This man was the missing link in the chain, the one person who could complete the story.

My mother and grandmother sat together on the couch, and, given how they were holding themselves, both seemed extremely nervous. It was not an exaggeration to say that an air of tension had hung over the whole house for most of the day. When I opened the front door I was met by not one visitor, as I had expected, but two.

'Hello, Ruben. It's good to see you. Please come in.'

I helped him into the hallway. The woman at his side, who I suspected was his wife, followed. She was of the right age and, like my grandmother, the years had not robbed her of her beauty. Her eyes, in particular, had an intensity about them but it was the manner in which she now looked at me that I found disquieting.

Without uttering a single word she held out her hand and I shook it.

'Ruben.'

Clara held out her arms and the two embraced one other. The other woman stood to one side and her eyes were brimming with tears. Then my grandmother let out a gasp and she started to cry.

'Rachel? Rachel, is that you?' Clara's voice cracked with emotion.

'Yes, Clara, it's me.' Tears began to trickle down Rachel's cheeks.

'And who is this? Can you really be Marek's child?'

'Yes, I'm Elizabeth,' my mother said warmly, hugging her aunt.

'When Ruben told me I did not believe him at first. To learn, after all this time, that there had been a child. My brother's child,' Rachel said, her smile tinged with sadness.

Rachel glanced at my mother and then back to me. She had not taken her eyes off me for more than a few minutes since arriving at the house.

'The resemblance between your son and . . .' it was almost too difficult for her to speak the words, 'is uncanny. It is like seeing my beloved Marek again.'

Some while later, and after a reviving cup of coffee, Rachel began to tell us her story. She described her parents and her brother and sister and what their lives had been like before the war. She recalled her parents' immense pride when their son – my grandfather – had won the much-coveted music scholarship to study at the prestigious Warsaw Conservatoire. Then the German occupation began, and with it many hopes and dreams were dashed. She spoke of the enforced move to the Ghetto.

'Dear Clara helped my recovery from typhus. In fact she probably saved my life,' Rachel explained.

'Did you, Mama?'

Clara said nothing, happy to let Rachel tell the tale.

'Your grandmother even came to see us in the Ghetto.'

'But how was that possible? Surely it must have been very dangerous?' I interrupted. Clara had never mentioned this during any of our recent conversations.

'Marek tried his best to persuade me against the idea because of the risks, but I was determined to do it. I had to see what life was like for him and his family and friends. So Ruben devised a clever plan,' she explained, smiling at Ruben who was nodding at the memory. My grandmother recounted how she had been smuggled in and out of the Ghetto, and we all listened in amazement.

'Did my father tell you what he planned to do on the night of the performance?' my mother asked Rachel.

'Yes, Marek told me everything. He told me about the music and his love for Clara, though I had worked that out already. We never kept secrets from each other. He asked me to tell our parents the truth if he didn't come back.'

At this point Rachel's grief resurfaced. She gestured to Ruben and he began to speak.

'I tried my best to stop him. Marek was a proud man and for him it was the only solution. As much as I hoped he'd come home that night, I knew in my heart I would never see him again. The last time I saw him alive he reminded me of the promise I'd made to him, to keep his family safe. We all knew the liquidation was imminent; word had come to us via the Polish underground. What those of us left behind didn't know was that the end would come quite as spectacularly as it did.' Ruben took a sip of his coffee.

'Late on a Sunday night – April 18th, 1943 – the Ghetto was surrounded by Polish police backed up later by Latvian, Ukrainian and German forces. They were complying with Himmler's orders for the destruction of the Ghetto. Those who possessed arms prepared to do battle whilst others, who knew what lay ahead, made alternative arrangements in the form of cyanide pills. When Marek did not return I feared the worst. Then Jakub, one of the choir members, came to tell us what had happened, and how he and the others had miraculously escaped unpunished. Marek's father, Izak, took it especially hard. The frustration of not being able to do anything for his son was agonizing. We could only hope and pray, but no news came.

'Early the next morning on the eve of Passover a mass of Waffen SS surged into the Ghetto. I had made a decision, once, to fight alongside my comrades to the death, but I had also made a promise to Marek to protect his family. How could I let him down? I watched the battles on Nalewki and Gesia Street and Muranow Square. Although the odds were heavily stacked against us, we successfully did away with so many Germans with our rifles and Molotov cocktails that the enemy was forced to withdraw. However, we could not match the firepower of our enemy nor could we equal their ruthlessness.'

'Do you know the most shocking and inhumane act the Nazis carried out that day?' Rachel interjected, needing perhaps to vent some of her pent-up emotion. 'The cowardly, pitiless killing of the vulnerable people in the Ghetto hospital and then afterwards, just to ensure that no one within remained alive, they shelled and incinerated the building. That night the air was smoke-filled and the glowing sky reflected the flames devouring the forlorn tenements of the Ghetto.'

Rachel glanced in Ruben's direction as if signalling for him to continue.

'I knew we would have to try and get away,' Ruben said, his eyes widening with excitement. 'The Germans were mustering reinforcements and planning new attacks which we could no longer effectively counter. At first Izak and Eva could not be persuaded to leave, preferring to stay and accept their fate, but

Rachel was not willing to give in. I told them of the preparations I had made – new identity papers for us all and a safe house on the Aryan side – and they finally agreed.'

'I have heard before that it was difficult to escape once the Germans had moved in,' William said.

'Our only route, providing the Nazis hadn't got there before us, was through the sewers. I knew them like the back of my hand.'

'When the odds in favour of your survival are non-existent, things that are normally sickening and repugnant can seem bearable,' Rachel said, with contempt in her voice.

'Eventually we reached a manhole in a quiet street well beyond the Ghetto boundary,' Ruben explained. 'We had been fortunate. Shortly afterwards the Germans had realised how people were evading capture, and many were caught and executed.'

Ruben was beginning to tire.

'Can I get you something?' William asked.

'A glass of water, please?'

'Of course. I'll fetch you one,' and he headed off in the direction of the kitchen.

'We stayed in the safe house on the Aryan side for as long as possible but it became too risky to remain,' Rachel told us. 'Mama and I lightened our hair and swapped our clothes, and Ruben, who has naturally fair skin and light hair, fetched additional supplies for us. From where our building was situated it was possible to witness the final scenes of the liquidation played out in all its horror. Two days later, SS General Jurgen Stroop, the man appointed to the job of destroying the Ghetto, put his callous and sadistic plan into practice. Realising survivors had holed themselves up in bunkers, this monster came to the decision that, if he couldn't prise them out, he would burn everyone out who would not surrender to go to the camps. No building was spared and soon the flamethrowers were put to work. On our last night in the city we watched the raging furnace, our hearts full of sorrow.' Rachel paused. 'The next morning we set off for the forests near Hrubieszow some way out in the country. We travelled for days across difficult terrain, tired and hungry.'

'Did you see anyone else?' I was eager to know.

'We came across Jews, who had fled the round-ups hiding out in a chalk cave near Chelm. They were very generous and gave us some of their food. Later we narrowly missed capture by a patrol of Nazis. Fortunately, there was plenty of thick vegetation about and we managed to hide just in time. We discovered a derelict woodman's cottage, and we stayed there until the war ended. We rarely went very far and we were careful not to draw attention to ourselves. Except for dear Papa,' Rachel said in a whisper. A tear rolled down her cheek. 'During the first winter we had very little fuel and Papa became sick. Without proper medicine, a simple cold developed into pneumonia and he did not have the strength to fight it. He never came to terms with the deaths of Marek and Lidia. It destroyed Papa's spirit.'

'I'm so sorry Rachel. Even though it was for such a brief time, I was very privileged to have met him,' Clara said.

'I wish I could have met him too,' Elizabeth said with regret in her voice.

'And then you decided to come to America and make a new life here?' William asked, having returned with the water.

'Like so many others we decided to leave the past behind and start afresh.'

'Do you have any children, Rachel?' Clara asked.

'Two sons and a daughter a little younger than Elizabeth. I have some pictures of them with their own children.'

Smiling to herself she dug into her purse and drew out some well-thumbed photographs.

'And your husband?' my mother asked.

'He passed away a few years ago, not long after Mama died,' Rachel told us.

My father and I smiled at each other as we watched Clara, Elizabeth and Rachel huddle together to view the snapshots. Then there was a change in my grandmother.

'Do you know what happened to Marek after that night?' Clara asked.

'Only that he must have died. Jakub told us he'd been led away by guards and that the Nazi . . .' Rachel checked herself, realising the delicateness of the situation.

'. . . was responsible for his death,' Clara completed the sentence for her.

'Yes. That is what we believed happened,' Rachel said, nodding her head. There was no hint of malice or acrimony in Rachel's tone.

'He told me what he had done to Marek after . . . afterwards,' Clara told them.

'Mama?' Elizabeth uttered in almost a whisper. She was visibly moved.

'When the Ghetto had finally been destroyed, my father arranged for his body to be taken to the Jewish cemetery for a proper burial. Forgive me, but I could not talk of it. The guilt was too much.' Clara turned her head away.

'What do you mean Grandma?' I asked.

'I should have gone to see his grave. I braced myself to do it so many times − to go back − but I could not. I was not strong enough. All those memories, and the terrible grief.' Clara was close to anguish.

No one spoke. Each of us needed a moment or two to take in this new revelation.

Clara's voice, small but determined, broke the silence.

'I know where he is buried and now I should like to go there.'

There were only a few days left before the evening of the Holocaust ceremony and I felt confident, as did the members of the choir, that everything would go well. As regards my family, we all hoped that soon the ghosts of the past would finally be laid to rest.

I awoke early on the morning of the Day of Remembrance to glorious spring weather. A little after half past six my mother rang, the suspense of the occasion no doubt responsible for her rising early. She wanted to know whether I had managed to get any rest – which, surprisingly, I had – and asked about our arrangements for later in the day.

My journey to work followed its usual pattern, with the exception of one slight deviation. I decided to cover the last bit on foot across Brooklyn Bridge. As I did so, I thought of my grandfather on that fateful morning all those years ago. The ceremony was scheduled to begin at seven-thirty, and at five forty-five, after getting washed and changed, I let myself into my parents' home. Clara was ready, and tonight she exuded sheer elegance. The dress she was wearing was of pale pink, which complemented her complexion and silver hair, and around her neck hung a double row of pearls.

'Hello, Grandma.' I greeted her with a kiss.

'Let me look at you. Very handsome, darling.'

I had chosen to wear a dark suit with a white shirt and a maroon tie which Clara had given me as a birthday present.

We allowed good time for the subway. It was crowded with people making their way home after a hard day at work. The final stretch to the synagogue in the evening sunshine was pleasant, and helped to dispel some of my anxieties. The choir had arranged to meet in one of the smaller rooms, and after seeing my family to their seats in the main hall, I joined them.

'Ah, Jonathan, come and have a drink with us,' Joseph said when he saw me.

Laid out on a table were plates of food and a collection of bottles.

'Don't look so worried. We're saving most of it for later,' Nathan whispered in my ear.

I poured myself some wine, and was about to put the glass to my lips when Abigail walked in. She was welcomed warmly by the cheery band of men as she made her way towards me.

'How beautiful you are.'

I kissed her on both cheeks and she smiled shyly.

'How are you feeling?'

'Like I usually feel at this time. Pretty nervous.'

'You've no reason to be,' Abigail said.

'It's a force of habit, I'm afraid. How about you?'

'The same. This is nice.' She pointed at the food. 'I hope your little choir aren't over-indulging before the performance.'

'They promised me they wouldn't.'

'I'm going to slip out and see if my parents have arrived. It's nearly time,' Abigail said looking at her watch.

She turned to go, but I caught her wrist.

'There's something I wanted to say to you . . . ?'

'I know,' she smiled stroking my face with her other hand. 'Later,' and she pulled gently away from me.

I drained my glass and called for the men's attention, since there was a little time before the start. We wished each other luck and I thanked them for all their efforts over the past weeks. Then they filed out to take up their positions and I followed.

The atmosphere was charged with excitement and every seat was full. There was a sea of unfamiliar faces and everywhere people were engaged in animated discussions with their neighbours. Occasionally, individuals would catch my eye as if curious to know who I might be. Clara and my parents sat in the seats reserved for them in the front row.

'Do you think Stefano and Maria will be able to make it?' my grandmother asked.

'They said they would,' William replied.

I had mentioned the event to them a few weeks ago, and they said they would try to be there. However, I was aware that tonight would be a particularly busy time for them in the restaurant and I wondered whether they would find it difficult to get away. Glancing again towards the rear of the synagogue, where a group had huddled to wash their hands, I caught sight of a hand waving. From its size it had to belong to a child and, moments later, a little face with a beaming smile came into view. It was Henry and beside him, much to my astonishment, were his mother and father. I waved back. Someone pulled on the sleeve of my jacket. It was Abigail.

'Stefano and Maria are here.'

'How long do we have before the service starts?' I leapt up.

'A couple of minutes, if you're quick.'

Their eyes lit up when they saw me approaching.

'How are you, my boy? Not too nervous,' Stefano enquired, placing a hand across my shoulder.

'I'm trying not to be, but there are so many people here.'

'Interesting place. I've never seen the inside of a synagogue before.'

'Thank you for coming.'

'We wouldn't have missed it,' Stefano said.

'Who have you left in charge?'

' Lena,' Maria informed me.

'Yes. And Marco.' Stefano winked at me.

'The restaurant's in good hands, then,' I said.

Promising to find them after the service I hurried back to my seat. David and other members of his family had arrived during my absence, and squeezed in next to my parents.

'I reckon they've come from all over the city to hear your grandfather's music.'

'You really think so?'

'News travels fast in this community,' David laughed.

'But why would so many people be interested in a forgotten work by an obscure composer?' I was genuinely surprised.

'You forget that an occasion such as this is very significant. It is part of our heritage and your grandfather played an important role in that. He is as brave and heroic a figure to us as he is to you and your family, and it is fitting to honour him.'

Movement caught my eye and I glanced up to see the Rabbi, Ruben and the *Kohein* and another elderly gentleman, making their entrance. I glanced down at the programme. There would be prayers, blessings and a reading from the Torah. Abigail's song and my cello piece had been slotted in between these more formal sections, and the choral item would form the grand finale. When it was time for Abigail to perform I took my seat at the piano. I looked across at Clara. Her face had a pensive expression. I wondered if she was recalling her own performance, before a very different audience, all those years ago in 1943.

The service continued, with an extract from the Torah, the lighting of *Yahrzeit* memorial candles and the *Kaddish* (prayer for the departed). Then the Rabbi introduced the elderly gentleman, who had up until now occupied a chair on the other side of the arc, and he stood up to speak. It soon became apparent that Rudek Koffler was a victim of the Holocaust who had been interned with his entire family in one of the camps and was the only survivor. His account was moving, and he spoke with dignity and grace.

Then at last it was the choir's turn. I gave the signal to move, and without any fuss the men arranged themselves in the grouping we had discussed. The heavy, elaborately-carved wooden stand had already been moved into position and resting on it was my grandfather's score. The choir had learned their parts by rote. I unbuttoned my jacket so I could move my arms freely. Then I spread my fingers over the piano keys to sound the notes of the chord. The lights dimmed and an expectant hush fell over the synagogue.

The sustained opening passage was beautifully executed. I glanced at Nathan, poised to enter with his solo. At first his voice was indistinct, barely perceptible and then gradually, phrase by phrase, bar by bar, its volume increased until finally the warm impassioned tones rang out, resonating in every corner of the auditorium. It was then that I felt him at my side. My face was damp, but not from the trickle of sweat that had made its way unchecked from my brow. The all-consuming feelings of pride and joy, mingled with sadness, had caused me to cry. We had reached that sublime moment when the tenor soars above the other voices and the spirit is finally released . . . and then it was over. I half-heard the tumultuous applause from the audience which had risen to its feet in recognition of true greatness. By then I had abandoned the platform and had dashed to Clara's side.

'He was with me, Grandma,' I said breathlessly holding her hands.

'Yes, darling, I know,' Clara said shaking with emotion.

Warsaw
2009

'Any progress?' my mother asked as our paths crossed.

'No, not yet. How about you?'

'Nothing at all.'

I could see the others some way off in the distance. Rachel was crouched down on her hands and knees, whilst Ruben was stooping slightly to examine yet another inscription. Abigail had paused to take a rest and was leaning against one of the larger tombs.

We had arrived yesterday, the five of us, and this morning had begun our search in earnest. All that Clara could remember of her father's instructions was that my grandfather's body had been buried in a corner of the cemetery near to a large tree, and that orders had been given for a headstone to be erected. However, the burial site – the Jewish Cemetery of Warsaw on Okopowa Street – contained a vast number of graves and had sustained decades of vandalism and neglect. As to there being any inscription – if one had been engraved – whatever it said had manifestly not been recorded. It was like searching for a needle in a haystack. Despite this, it was a beautiful early summer's morning and the birds were chirruping merrily.

We had been searching for over an hour, and the eldest amongst us were becoming weary, when something caught my eye. A ray of light had struck the metal part of an empty flower-container on a grave a little way off, causing it to glint. The light had worked its way through the dense foliage of a lofty old tree and although Rachel and Ruben had already scoured this area, I decided to take a look for myself. Saying nothing, I picked my way through the densely packed resting places of the dead, then looked around. To my right was a rather grand tomb and next to it a more modest one. I squatted down to read the words on the magnificent-looking sepulchre, but they were in Polish, a language I was not familiar with. However, as I did this, my level of vision was now much lower and suddenly I saw a grey flat slab, tucked in between two other stones. Roughly a third of its original height had sunk into the earth.

I did not know why, but my heart began to beat faster as I clambered rather irreverently over the surrounding graves to reach it. Some kindly person had cut the grass around it by hand, but it was in a poor state of repair. The headstone was dirty, having never been cleaned it seemed, and moss was spreading around its edges. Most of its surface was mottled with that green powdery substance often to be found on ageing masonry. Placing my hands over it I felt for signs of indentation. There did seem to be some. With increasing excitement, I rubbed the stone frantically with the sleeves of my shirt as hard as I could. Almost magically the words revealed themselves. I got to my feet. I had a strange sense that I was not alone. I turned around slowly. Abigail took hold of my hand.

'We have found him at last.' Her voice was full of emotion.

I looked again at the inscription. It read '*Kapellmeister*'.

For a long moment I fancied that on the breeze, gusting through the churchyard elms, I could hear a familiar strain. Was it my imagination? Perhaps, but I knew that my grandfather Marek would now find peace at last.